Waiting for Grandfather

Michael De Stefano

Night to Dawn Magazine & Books LLC
P. O. Box 643
Abington, PA 19001

www.bloodredshadow.com

Copyright © 2019 by Michael De Stefano
Paperback ISBN: 978-1-937769-57-4
Ebook ISBN: 978-1-937769-58-1

Cover Artist: Snehitdesign
Editor: Barbara Custer
Published in the United States of America

For Dina and Richard

Table of Contents

Prologue...1

Chapter One: Sunday Mornings..3

Chapter Two: Pig Stench 16

Chapter Three: A Coal Miner's Christmas......................... 39

Chapter Four: Mothballs and Cicoria 58

Chapter Five: Love at First Reach 66

Chapter Six: Life is But a Dream 97

Chapter Seven: The Magnificent Number One 144

Chapter Eight: The Best Laid Plans.................................... 222

About the Author.. 239

Prologue

Uncle Al was a moron. I'm sorry to have to say it, but it's true. But don't take me at my word if you're not inclined; ask around. There's still plenty of folks floating around from the old crowd that would be more than willing to back me on the matter of this unflattering assertion. Yet, when you get right down to it, a moron is hardly an anomaly; I'm told nowadays they're plentiful and that many of us have known their share—present company included. But Uncle Al's time wasn't *nowadays;* it was *the good old days;* and unlike the justifications for war in Afghanistan and Iraq, and the legality of the Iran/Contra affair—all highly debatable issues of their respective times—that Uncle Al was a moron was never a question. And yes, I can guess what you must be thinking: this brutally candid assessment is too harsh, never mind a palpable attack on a man's acumen. You would be right. Nevertheless, the abovementioned has little if any wiggle room; *and,* regardless to whom you defer on the matter, you will come to learn it hardly lacks precision.

Whenever faced with a decision or placed at a crossroad, when left to his own devices, Uncle Al either made the wrong choice or went the wrong way. He was a model of consistency—an unwavering force of nature with the innate ability to confound any situation no matter how promising the situation first appeared. But while we are on the subject of moronic uncles, so too was Uncle Nunzio a moron. Uncle Nunzio was your classic pull-my-finger uncle; every family has at least one. Nothing like a flatulent relative able to perform on cue, take his show on the road, and owns the facility to amuse himself—while adhering to the notion that he is also amusing others—with the variety of noises his body can readily produce. Yep, he was a real life of the party our Uncle Nunzio.

But before we travel any further into our narrative, it should be duly noted that Uncle Al and Uncle Nunzio were my grandfather's brothers, and therefore my *great*-uncles. However, that we were separated by two generations made *me* no less related nor *them,* unfortunately, and

1

often with catastrophic results, no less moronic. And applying the word "great" when referring to Uncle Al or Uncle Nunzio would be an egregious misuse of a word to a degree that makes it an obscenity. Joe Montana was a *great* quarterback. Pete Rose was a *great* hitter. Uncle Al and Uncle Nunzio weren't *great* at anything that anyone would wish to be great at. Run-of-the-mill would be exceedingly generous.

I became well aware of my "great" uncles' numerous shortcomings by age ten. Ricky and Munchk knew them as well, and they were my younger siblings. (Munchk was what Ricky and I affectionately and, at times, antagonistically, called Lizzy, our half-pint sister.) We avoided sharpening our tongues whenever our uncles came up in conversation, as we didn't wish for our parents, who were odd in their own right, to hear us disparaging our elders. Mostly, we went on pretending that our ragtag family, with all its dubious characters—in our family dubious characters were hardly in short supply—was just as normal as any other American family. Yep, that was my two younger siblings and yours truly: pretenders. Surviving in our family required that one pretend. Nevertheless, we loved Uncle Al and Uncle Nunzio. They were our grandfather's brothers. And as we came to learn, quite categorically, there were those whom we love freely through the application of free will influenced by merit, while others gain our affection through means of default.

Moving right along to our grandfather: he was a wonderful human being—big, strong, and with the gentlest nature—a truly caring man he was, and in many ways like no other. Antonio Corelli looked like a bear and laughed like you would imagine a bear might laugh had nature been kinder and blessed it with the capability. Among ourselves, we referred to our grandfather as Marilyn Munster, for he was the only *normal* member of the Corelli clan. Of course, *normal*, in most cases, is subjective, a matter of opinion that's up for debate. And by *we,* I'm referring to Ricky, Munchk, and yours truly. Incidentally, my name is Frank. Frank Corelli. And this is the story of the life and times of my highly oddball and often disorderly family leading up to our grandfather's surprise sixtieth birthday party.

Chapter One
Sunday Mornings

Early, and without fail, every Sunday morning—for when least appreciated, he was as reliable as a heatwave in July—Uncle Al would appear at our front door. We need not guess his arrival, as the awful clanking sound that his pickup truck made, when it turned onto our street, was sufficient warning that Uncle Al was near. Others on the block knew it as well and would interrupt their breakfasts or less wholesome Sunday morning rituals and dash from their tables or beds to the window or front door, to either peek through blinds or sneer with contempt at the monstrous contraption that clanked its way into their otherwise peaceful mornings. Some would use Uncle Al's clamorous arrival as a signal that it was time to ready themselves for church or fetch the morning newspaper.

Regarding the latter, Mr. Profacci was one such individual. In fact, some of my scariest childhood moments were Mr. Profacci's doorstep cameos, which saw him fetch his newspaper attired in only a bathrobe. His few strands of hair, which before marching off to church would find themselves skillfully combed into a swirl for optimum coverage, always managed to hang to the wrong side, thus exposing his bald head which sopped with the grease that had accumulated since his last showering. Then, for it became part of the Sunday morning routine, Mr. Profacci would turn his weathered, bulbous old face toward Uncle Al's pickup truck—that woeful looking vehicle that appeared as if slapped together with the spare parts of vehicles of equal woefulness—and sneer as though it had no right to take up space on our street. For this, I do not blame Mr. Profacci. But then comes the worst part of all: Mr. Profacci bends over to pick up his newspaper. I know that it's coming, as it is Sunday morning and Uncle Al's pickup truck is in plain view. But like a train wreck or horrible deformity, I cannot bring myself to look away or resist sneaking a peek. Mr. Profacci's bathrobe, which is two sizes too small (What the hell was Mrs. Profacci thinking?), did not cover nearly enough of his rotund figure; therefore, when he bends over, his chest, which hangs like a cow's udders, becomes frighteningly exposed. On those udders is more hair than was ever seen gathered in any one place, Uncle Nunzio excluded. *EEK!* Not even the stoutest plumber's malfunctioning pants can be considered as disturbing a sight as Mr. Profacci's hairy udders. When he thankfully straightens up, he always takes a moment to sneer yet again at Uncle Al's pickup truck.

It is said that everyone is endowed with a gift and Mr. Profacci excelled at sneering. He was so exceptional that he once caused a young boy standing inside the confines of his own house to duck below a windowsill. When he finishes sneering, with all his stoutness, he pirouettes back toward the door through which he will thankfully disappear. It is remarkable how many steps it takes Mr. Profacci to accomplish what for most would be a simple maneuver. Ricky and I joked that Mr. Profacci had the agility of a tree stump as he was the most cumbersome looking man we would ever come to know. And seldom if ever did we get close enough to Mr. Profacci to learn the effects that a man of such abundance, and generous secretions, might have on our nostrils. We played it safe while imagining the level of Mrs. Profacci's heroism.

Back to Uncle Al: Uncle Al spent most Saturdays tinkering away under the hood of Mr. Profacci's pet peeve. It was anyone's guess what his goals were for the dismal looking contraption as it never looked or sounded any better; yet he was always boasting about some vast improvement he just made. According to Uncle Al, the truck either "purred like a kitten" or was "ready for NASCAR." Uncle Al was what folks used to call "a grease monkey," the sort who every weekend had a vehicle half-dismantled in the driveway, a look of consternation on his face, and a multitude of tools spewed about the ground.

"What's the old man up to?" Uncle Al would growl once I made my reluctant march to the door.

That was how Uncle Al would begin, by growling the same question and in the same tone; although it required not a shred of capacity for the prophetic to predict a question that Uncle Al might pose, nor information that he thought pertinent enough to relay. He was the type to show up at your front door in the middle of a monsoon and announce: "Ya know, it's really raining out there!"

On those Sunday mornings of yesteryear, he never began with *good morning* or *how was breakfast* or *did you see the ballgame last night.* "What's the old man up to?" came the growl, and instantly I was enveloped in an

4

atmosphere overwhelmed by the ten Lucky Strikes Uncle Al had already smoked. And there was hardly a trace of inquisitiveness in his tone, for Uncle Al was perfectly aware that my "old man" was still in bed. Moreover, my "old man's" whereabouts was Uncle Al's way of patting himself on the back, thus intimating that while the rest of the adult world on Sunday morning was enjoying its time of slumber and relaxation, he had already been up for hours and was a man of superhuman stamina. Then again, two packs of cigarettes and twenty cups of coffee a day was enough to keep a rhinoceros awake. I had always wanted to say to Uncle Al, *the "old man," just like you fuck up your truck, is in the basement fucking up the plumbing.* Oh yeah, dear old Dad was a *real* crackerjack plumber. He was to pipes what Uncle Al was to engine parts and bodywork. On my honor, we shall later visit the family plumbing catastrophes.

"Dad is still sleeping," I told Uncle Al.

Readily I had divulged this tidbit, while attempting to hold down two bowls of some artificially flavored and sugar-infused cereal, after having caught a glimpse of Mr. Profacci's hairy udders, and also taking into my nostrils a stench that would have given the CEO of Philip Morris an erection and an oncologist a heart attack. And with so many Sundays already come and gone with me having sampled both men in this manner, you might wonder why, unless I was a masochist, would I once again get close enough to Uncle Al to peer over his shoulder at Mr. Profacci? I couldn't help myself. The morbid curiosity of Mr. Profacci's hairy udders was worth enduring the Lucky Strike residue that hung so copiously about Uncle Al. Sometimes I wouldn't even hear myself tell Uncle Al that my "old man" was still sleeping. But Uncle Al already knew it. Not that Mr. Profacci had hairy udders mind you, but that my "old man" was still asleep.

"Still sleeping, is he!" shrieked Uncle Al, as if no offense was more unpardonable than a sexually viable man spending Sunday morning in bed with his still sexually viable wife. Afterward, Uncle Al would make his customary gestures, which was an exaggerated deflation of his chest and slumping of the shoulders, before letting loose the contemptuous grunt he reserved for those whose ambitions for the a.m. portion of Sunday didn't travel beyond the comfort of a mattress. Then he would scowl and mutter, *"That* figures."

Once all the predictable and idiotic preamble was put to rest, Uncle Al would lean through the doorway and holler out, "Who wants to go for a ride?" There was a time when, not without a fair amount of enthusiasm, Ricky, Munchk, and I would all leap to our feet and let out a collective shout of, "I do!"

"What's that?" Uncle Al would bellow. "I can't *hearrrr* you!"

As younger children, we didn't realize it was Uncle Al's intention to provoke a clamorous response to stir our "old man." Once, Uncle Al even showed up armed with one of those clown horns; you know, the ones with the rubber bulb on the end that you squeeze. God bless him, he truly believed he had the makings of a vaudeville comic. Once we caught onto the game, our responses to whether or not we wanted to go for a ride became more tempered. Besides, riding around the neighborhood in the bed of Uncle Al's pickup truck has long since lost its luster. The Sunday morning ride has become one of those things a child does to appease an aging relative. In all fairness to Uncle Al, from his perspective of two generations removed, he could not see how quickly our childhood was slipping away.

"Yeah, sure, Uncle Al, we'll go," was my tempered reply. "What do you say, guys; are youse up for a ride?"

"Sure," said Munchk, as she shoveled another spoonful of soggy Fruit Loops into her mouth, then used the lapel of her bathrobe to wipe the milk from her chin.

"Okay," said Ricky, though it was painfully evident that my middle sibling preferred to remain behind and watch the condensed replay of Saturday's Penn State football game, despite already knowing the result, as yesterday he coughed up most of the afternoon to watch the game in real time.

Like always, with one swift maneuver, I hurdled my way up and onto the truck's bed. With only the benefit of my hands positioned on the ledge, I was able to make it cleanly—a real athletic exercise if I don't say so myself. Ricky followed by placing his foot on the tire, his hands on the ledge, and then with some effort, he hoisted himself up and onto the bed. Then came Munchk. Poor Munchk was too tiny to gain the truck's bed without someone assisting her. But it sure didn't stop her from trying. Over and over again she would leap with all the might she possessed—with every ounce of strength available in those slender little legs of hers, she would leap—and with each attempt, she would let out one of her little munchkin grunts. Ricky and I would stand, arms folded, and watch, amused by her tenacity and the cute grunting sounds she would let loose.

"Careful, Munchk, you don't shit yourself," I called down to her.

She hollered back, "Come on, Frank, you prick; gimme a hand!"

Prick that I was, I reached down and just as Munchk was about to grab hold of my hand, I pulled it back. Then Ricky and I let loose with a chorus of antagonistic laughter as Munchk, in all her frustration, repeatedly kicked the tire, while letting loose a barrage of her favorite expletives. And allow me to state for the record, our baby sister had no shortage of favorites. This I knew better than anyone; for often I had been the recipient of those preferred expletives and the fury with which they were delivered.

"What's the matter, Munchk?" I teased. "Too short, are you?"

Often, we would tell Munchk that she wasn't a *real* person, but a woodland pixie our folks found wandering about, felt sorry for, and was kind enough to bring home.

"One day soon, Munchk, they're gonna return you to the woods and you'll be reunited with all the elves and trolls!" Other times we would tease, "Next week, your real parents are getting released from prison and coming for you, Munchk; so you better start packing!"

Poor Munchk. Ricky and I tortured her. We would have treated a dog better if we had one. The minute Munchk was about to enter a room, one of us would quickly grab the phone and pretend to be talking to the police concerning one of her minor infractions that we exaggerated into an incarceration-worthy crime, or her *real* parents, who just learned of her whereabouts.

"They're on their way, Munchk," we would threaten. "It was nice knowing you."

Then, finally, it happened. Munchk decided that she had enough of our bullying and shenanigans and slipped a note under our door. It read:

Dear Fuckers,
I hate both you bastards! Frank, I hope while you're sleeping bugs eat your puny dick. And Ricky, I hope something crawls up your ass and you die from it.
Signed, the munchkin bitch in the next room

Naturally, "fuckers" that we were, and after laughing until our sides nearly split and we were in tears, Ricky and I took the letter and went straightaway to our parents. We thought it best to make them well aware of what an evil little munchkin they were raising; that way they could look back over their mistakes and correct them before it was too late. After all, Munchk was still so young and could be saved before going too far to the bad. How lucky was Munchk to have such thoughtful older brothers, and our parents for having sons willing to act as their eyes and ears when they were too busy doing whatever it was they did when they were not paying attention?

Munchk's punishment was a week of bedroom confinement with bathroom privileges. Unfortunately, her punishment—which for a while gave her tormentors cause to celebrate—ended up working against us, as hour after hour, day after day, Munchk had nothing to do but lie about and devise schemes of vengeance. Ricky and I were in for a world of hurt. We had no idea of the level of Munchk's creativity. For instance, once paroled, she waited around for the neighbor's bulldog, Tank, to drop two ripe and rather impressive specimens, one which she planted in my league baseball cap and the other she positioned between the three and the two of Ricky's brand-new Steve Carlton jersey. This far surpassed the old salt-in-the-underwear prank. Munchk meant business and, as we would discover, when it came to pranking, her mind was not merely diabolical but limitless. Every day we were introduced to a new depth of her vengefulness. She was highly proficient, equally secretive, and bound only by the limit of her imagination. It reached the point where the house was so damned rigged, we were afraid to venture inside and once opted to remain outside in the rain. "We stand outside in the rain all the time," I hollered over to Mrs. Profacci, as I saw her forehead furrow and eyes narrow in confusion, while high and dry inside her front door. "I'm surprised you never noticed."

There was a well-wooded park in our neighborhood with many hiking trails. Kids did that sort of thing back in the 70s; they hiked when hiking was available. Every path had a spur that led to another path, and all paths led to a bridge that spanned a creek, and across the creek were stables where, on Saturday afternoons, horses could be rented by the hour. Horses were seen trotting around the neighborhood, and by late Saturday afternoon, there was a liberal amount of manure lying about the streets. This manure could easily be collected, if one was so inclined, and the evil little munchkin, with bucket and trowel, scooped up a generous amount of these equine endowments for the express purpose of liberally smearing and placing it in unsuspecting areas. I can say firsthand that placing a foot inside a sneaker in which horse manure was planted, and then feeling its sickening squish, is a life-altering experience from which one never fully recovers. Whether early in life in the high school locker room or nowadays at the fitness center, I could sense the curiosity of others who witnessed my comprehensive examination of a shoe before I dared to place it on my foot. Nothing like leaving others with the impression that sniffing your own gym shoes is what gets you off. That's some helluva negative residual to a prank. A nervous tic would have been kinder; instead of a lunatic, the probing eyes in the locker room would have dismissed me as some poor bastard with Tourette's. No one at the fitness center has ever asked ol' Frank Corelli to go for a post-workout beer.

Once paranoia sets in, nothing in life is easy. Every move made was executed with extreme caution. This is what's otherwise known as having been defeated. The clincher, though, came one morning when Munchk came strolling into the bathroom just as I was brushing my teeth.

"I guess you didn't bother sniffing that toothbrush before you started using it, ay, Frank?" she said.

"No, why?" My face twisted in anguish.

"You just can't imagine where that thing has been," came her smirky reply.

To Munchk's amusement, I began spitting and gagging in the sink. "Oh God, Munchk!" I pleaded. "Please don't tell me you stuck my toothbrush up your ass! Fucking lie to me, but don't tell me you did *that!*"

"Fine, Frank," Munchk said. I even detected a note of compassion. Then she added, "I shoved it up Tank's ass. *Now,* do you feel better?"

From our knees, after displaying genuine regret for showing our parents the letter that led to Munchk's punishment, we begged her to cease the pranks.

We had it coming, Ricky and I. Not just for ratting out Munchk for the letter she slipped under our door but for all the years of torment that led to it. It all started back in late summer of '71 when Munchk was only four years old. School was going to resume in less than a week, and it had been raining for two straight days. "Bored to death" were the words we repeatedly moaned to ourselves and to our mother, who had long since stopped listening. We had already exhausted every available means of inside entertainment and were bleeding out of our eyes to get outside. That's when Ricky and I went brainstorming and convinced Munchk that if she danced naked like a wild Indian on the front steps under the awning, the rain would stop and we could all go out and play.

"You'll save the whole summer, Munchk!" we told her. "You'll be a hero! Everyone will love you!"

It worked. No, the rain didn't stop, but Munchk was out there on the front step, naked as a jaybird and dancing up a storm. And all the while she danced, she waved to passing cars with her hands held high above her head. Ricky and I banged on the window and urged, "Dance faster, Munchk! Dance faster!" It didn't take long for the phone to ring, and the ringing was followed by Mom rumbling up the cellar stairs. The urgency in her rumbling sent Ricky and I scampering to our bedroom, where we pretended to be well engrossed in our baseball cards. We heard Mom say to herself in the currently empty living room: "I just got the strangest phone call from Mrs. Profacci..." A second later, we heard her hollering hysterically, "Lizzy, what the hell do you think you're doing!"

Looking back on it, those were the best days of my life. There are days when I laugh myself silly imagining our little Munchk, combing the streets of the neighborhood with a bucket and trowel, looking for horse manure. God, how I miss her.

****

"For cryin' out loud, Lizzy," cried Uncle Al, "you're gonna bust your foot kickin' that tire."

Uncle Al scooped up Munchk from behind and eased her onto the bed of the truck.

As was the case with Uncle Nunzio and our grandfather, Uncle Al favored Munchk. All three of them saw her as the spark that lit the family fire. Unlike Ricky and I, who derived great pleasure in torturing Munchk, they ate out of her hand like three obedient puppies. In their eyes, Munchk could do no wrong.

"Ready or not," called Uncle Al from the driver's seat, or captain's chair as he liked to think of it on Sunday mornings. Then off we rode, knocking and pinging are way around the neighborhood in an unsightly contraption.

In the past, whenever Uncle Al applied the brakes, all three of us would go lurching forward, crashing into the back window, greatly exaggerating the effect of this otherwise simple driving maneuver. When he hit the gas, and *did* he ever hit it, as Uncle Al was no stranger to speed, we would all go flying backward, pretending that we were on a ship on the high seas getting tossed about in an epic storm and that there existed the possibility of being thrown overboard and lost forever at the depths of some foreign ocean. Munchk would then jump up and down, her little feet pounding on the truck's bed, yelling, "Faster, Uncle Al! Go faster!" We could hear Uncle Al behind the wheel laughing like a hyena, while our bodies shifted back and forth. After a mile or so on the high seas, we would settle down and lean over the sides of the truck bed to enjoy the sensation of the wind in our faces and blowing through our hair. We frothed with enthusiasm, waving and hollering hello to all those walking to church and going for their morning newspaper, and did this as though way up in some lofty place, and while in that lofty place we were the envy of the world. But then the years went by, and we found ourselves cowering in the truck's bed, praying that no one we knew would discover that it was *us* riding around the neighborhood like "a bunch of fucking hillbillies" in what we came to refer to as "Uncle Al's dumpster-on-wheels."

In its infancy, which, incidentally, was before my time, I believe Uncle Al's truck was sky blue. Possibly it was light gray. No matter, during the days of the Sunday morning road trips, its primary color could only be described as rust to go along with numerous patches of home-made primer yet to be painted. Uncle Al had made several trips to the local Pep Boys, where he purchased more than his share of those do-it-yourself dent repair kits. He was always grumbling that his truck was a magnet for those whose capacity for navigating a vehicle was suspect.

"Damn those old bats at the Food Fair, they keep ramming into me!" *Old bats* was the unflattering term that Uncle Al assigned to women over the age of fifty. Nowadays, that would sound ridiculous. "They can't see where the hell they're goin'! Not one time have I drove outa that damn lot without picking up a ding or dent." I'm not disputing Uncle Al's claim, but the insurance adjuster able to make sense of Uncle Al's truck has yet to be born.

"And as for the 'old goats?'" our mother asked with a raised eyebrow and flaring with indignation at what Uncle Al had implied.

One of our mother's pet peeves—and lord knows she had accumulated a bunch—was the disparaging of women drivers, especially when it was clear that her driving skills were superior to that of dear old Dad's.

It would be more than fair to describe our mother as *combat ready*; Mary Corelli lived for confrontation. It was a good day when she was presented with an opportunity to *rip someone a new one* or *get in someone's grill*. She was a hammer in search of a nail—a rumble fiendishly scouring the landscape for a place to occur. Conversely, and at all costs, dear old Dad was an excellent evader of confrontations. Whenever Mom would go off on someone—say, for instance, Uncle Al or Uncle Nunzio—Dad would usually involve himself with such mundane matters as the nutritional value on the back of a milk carton, or the key ingredients on the side of a cereal box. He would use whatever means handy to divert his attention from the fray. Once, with the concentration of a scientist testing a cure for an infectious disease, I watched him study an imaginary stain on his shirt-sleeve, while Mom lambasted some poor bastard over the right to a parking space to which she believed she was entitled and eventually, through means of unyielding persistence, procured. (She hollered at the man until he finally concluded, *this woman is out of her fucking mind*, then went in search of another spot.)

Whenever our mother gave Uncle Al or Uncle Nunzio a piece of her mind, dear old Dad would morph into a mental patient or imbecile. Searching his sweater for lint that had the audacity to cling to its fibers was a favorite—an old reliable. If Dad was fortunate enough to find a piece of pesky fuzz, he would hold it up to his eyes and examine at it as if to say, *"How dare you turn up on my sweater."* Or, *"Who invited you?"* To observe Dad with a piece of fuzz would leave one with the impression that he expected it to interact with him, or that it was an extraordinary substance worthy of turning over to a scientist for evaluation. Uncommon diligence was how he would approach these imbecilic tasks; but the minute Mary Corelli was through grinding someone up, the lint that had come under inspection or the information on the back of the milk carton would lose all its significance. Afterward, Freddy Corelli would go back to being dear old Dad.

Freddy Corelli couldn't fool his children, though. He may have fooled Uncle Al, Uncle Nunzio, and our mother, who was busy at war, that he preferred the high road and saw himself an isolationist existing above the fray—that none of Mary Corelli's disputes were consequential enough to elicit his involvement—but often we saw him cringing inside, his guts turning as he shrank in his seat. Dad was especially sensitive to Mom's lambasting of Uncle Al and Uncle Nunzio. When he was growing up, Uncle Al and Uncle Nunzio treated Dad like a baby brother, and when he got older, one of the guys. So it was only natural for Dad to have looked up to his uncles. By no means were they role models, but it thrilled a youthful Freddy Corelli to play the part of the mascot to two guys who were well-known in the old neighborhood. In later years, Uncle Al and Uncle Nunzio would be all that stood between dear old Dad and being labeled the family's most prolific screwup. In the "screw-up" department, Freddy Corelli was merely accomplished. Uncle Al and Uncle Nunzio were inexhaustible legends.

Despite our mother's raised eyebrow and hard glare, Uncle Al was an excellent driver—it was the one thing at which he truly excelled, and he seemed to know every street in a city (Philadelphia) many complained was difficult to get around because it was built around several parks.

Though in every other aspect of life, Uncle Al was the type that exhausted every shortcut. He was forever looking to play the angles, and as a result, he became your classic one-step-forward-two-steps-backward kind of guy. Yet, this didn't prevent him from boasting of having all the answers and was often heard touting some ridiculous scheme he would soon launch that was sure to put him over the top. In listening to Uncle Al, one might come away with the impression that they were in the company of a man who had his finger on the pulse of the world—a real mover and shaker who was holding all the strings. But whenever matters didn't turn out the way he planned, which was always, he was handy with an excuse. Yessiree, when it came to making up excuses, Uncle Al was quicker than an old western gunslinger. He would usually cite that the circumstances we stacked against him, or that his partner in the venture (he always had a conveniently inept partner) backed out at the last minute, leaving him to "hold the bag." When the wind was at his back, no one was more pompous than Uncle Al, but let it shift and blow in his face and a sulkier man one would be hard pressed to find.

I was left holding the bag, he often moaned. It is written that the good Lord gave us two hands; one for giving, the other for taking. Uncle Al held bags.

Poor Uncle Al; he never could take responsibility when things went kerflooey, but the man, despite the condition of his vehicle, could drive. And while we're on the subject, his radio only got AM stations, most of which played static, and the only amenity was the beanbag ashtray that he kept on the dashboard, which was never seen empty. (The pulldown ashtray below the staticky radio was accidentally glued shut.) Lying beside the ashtray was the ever-handy soft pack of Lucky Strikes. But the real trick when riding with Uncle Al was trying to find a spot on the passenger seat where a spring wasn't poking up your ass. We had a running joke: You may enter Uncle Al's truck a virgin, but that's not necessarily how you'll leave.

****

Uncle Al was born Alfonzo Corelli and was the middle child of immigrant parents, who, after crossing the Atlantic, settled in Scranton, Pennsylvania. Scranton is an old coal-mining town in Northeastern Pennsylvania, and those coal mines were precisely where immigrants, many of Italian descent, were channeled. Like cattle, many of the woebegotten coming from overseas were herded into the mines.

After school, Uncle Al and Uncle Nunzio would sit outside the house, awaiting the return of their big brother, Antonio (our grandfather), who was taken from school in the sixth grade and shoved into a coal mine. *Here's your life, kiddo, get used to it.* Depriving their firstborn of an education wasn't what our great grandparents had in mind when into view came the thorny crown of the Statue of Liberty before being dropped at Ellis Island. But the need for additional wages was too great, leaving them no choice but to look beyond the *American Dream* in favor of merely surviving. Alfonzo and Nunzio idolized their big brother and every day, in a celebratory manner, they ran wildly to his side when they saw him emerge from the hill over yonder. They thought their big brother was brave for allowing himself—not that he had any choice in the matter—to be lowered into a mineshaft and were anxious to hear all about it.

"How dark was it? Were you scared? Were there any vampire bats flying around!" they wanted to know when Antonio returned home from his first day.

In the beginning, Antonio was terrified. And it was a while before his terror subsided to where he was able to work alongside grown men and act like a grown man, though he never revealed any misgivings he had about the mines to his young brothers. His lack of disclosure wasn't born out of fear of compromising the heroic status he enjoyed with his brothers. Instead, he did not wish for their days to be consumed with worry on his account.

For the Italian immigrants, who came from a poor country ruled unsafe—its weak government was all but overtaken by the Cosa Nostra—the Scranton coal mines seemed a reasonable alternative. Our grandfather never spoke much to Uncle Al and Uncle Nunzio about the dreaded mines, other than to say that it was "swell" or "fine" and that he would much rather hear about what they learned at school. Then he would take the younger Nunzio and place him high atop his adult-like shoulders and with a long, powerful arm draped around Alfonzo, the three brothers walked home together happily.

It wasn't long before Antonio started driving and quickly gained a reputation as someone capable of operating trucks and other utility vehicles. This led to him being offered a job delivering coal instead of mining it. It came with no additional pay, which came as no surprise; nevertheless, he was thrilled to be free of the mines, moving about, and breathing *real* air! Naturally, Alfonzo and Nunzio wanted to forget all about school and ride along in the truck, while their big brother delivered coal all over the Northeastern region of Pennsylvania, but Antonio wouldn't hear of it. Neither would Mama or Poppa Corelli, who already had to manage the guilt over cheating their oldest and most capable son out of an education.

A few years passed when Antonio was offered a job with a trucking outfit based in Philadelphia. It took not a single twist of the arm for him to pack up what few possessions he had accumulated and bid farewell to Scranton, Pennsylvania. However, against his better judgment but to unburden his parents, he took along with him *one* Uncle Al and *one* Uncle Nunzio. From that day forward, our poor grandfather spent the remainder of his natural life bailing those two morons out of one jam after another.

Chapter Two
Pig Stench

Nowadays I live in the great State of New Jersey. It is with tongue-in-cheek that I say this. I'd like to claim that one morning I woke up and discovered my body in New Jersey, either by way of kidnapping or exile, but I truly did elect to move there; although, of the two of us, my wife was the more heavy-handed in the decision. I live there with my wife of seventeen years, our currently soon-to-be teenage son, and two Maltese puppies, who spend the day sitting in the bay window and listening to girls wail, "Aww, how cuuuute!" These self-appointed sentinels awarded themselves the task of patrolling the street and Heaven help us should an unfamiliar face appear. No breed of dog can claim a shriller bark than the Maltese; they're akin to being locked in a cell with a colicky infant ... for fifteen years! Along with moving to New Jersey, the pups were also my wife's idea. Really, what testicle-bearing creature would decide: *I know what I'm gonna do today: I'm going to acquire a Maltese puppy ... or two!* Had it been up to me, I would have bought some sort of Retriever, or at least a Jack Russell—some breed willing to chase a stick or roughhouse. I'm forever threatening dog soup with these two, but Buddy and Rocky, despite all the yapping, have managed to win my heart. They look up at me, tilting their heads as if owning the inclination to say, "We know we're annoying, but we're pups, we can't help ourselves. You'll forgive us, though, won't you, Frank?" This is not a look that humans are capable of conveying, and this is why we desire to *cuddle* with our pets but hold in reserve the proclivity to *kill* one another.

For decades I was known only as *Frank*—it's what everyone called me. Not one person called me anything *but*, except childhood friends from the old neighborhood, who took to hollering, "Hey, Yo, Corelli!" followed by something even more colorful. For some odd reason, following our first date, which went swimmingly (Sorry, no details; this is a novel for the whole family), my soon-to-be bride decided that I was Francis. I still can't get used to it; *Francis* sounds foreign to me and terribly formal. But now that I'm a suburbanite, or had suburbanization thrust upon me, I suppose that I shouldn't buck protocol and subscribe to all the pretentious bullshit that accompanies life beyond the city limits.

When neighbors wave and call "Hello Francis," my first reaction is one of confusion. Once my confusion settles, I stop and look over my shoulder. When I notice no one in the vicinity, it occurs to me that I am the recipient of the friendly greeting, which I return with an initial show of surprise, followed by a delayed and feeble wave. I enter the house knowing full well that everyone on the block is convinced that I'm dim-witted. Fuck 'em!

Before my wife, the last person to call me Francis—although I have no recollection and furthermore, it's based on an assumption—was the priest who performed my baptism. Teachers, friends, and later my ex-wife called me Frank, among other things that weren't necessarily related to my birth name. My ex had some beauties: Assholenstein was a favorite.

Yes, I have an ex-wife. Us Corellis, especially the men, require a second bite of the apple before getting it right. Be it engines, plumbing, *wives*, we're a family that's forever practicing, hoping that the day will arrive when finally, we can look back and utter the magic words *well done*—or, as a former president regrettably once said, *mission accomplished.* Down through the generations, our results have been meager but, every so often, we manage to mix in a rare triumph. Flukes, aberrations, call them what you wish, they are nevertheless cherished. As for the catastrophes? It's the curse of Uncle Al and Uncle Nunzio, whose jackassery is believed to be transcendent and has affected those born years after their deaths. In fact, posthumously, Uncle Al and Uncle Nunzio have attained a status worthy of symbolism and are often times referred to with allegory. For instance, my current wife once remarked at the end of a long and laborious day, "I see we did a *real* Uncle Al job laying those kitchen tiles, Francis."

The last thing that I wanted to hear—especially after groping around on all fours for more hours than I thought the job would take—achy and in need of medication, preferably the recreational variety, was to hear my name mentioned with Uncle Al.

"Who is Uncle Al?" So innocent, so delightfully inquisitive was my son, and at an age when he had yet to learn the family folklore and legend.

"Never mind who Uncle Al is!" I snapped, before childishly storming off.

The truth is, I was angrier with myself than I was with my wife, whose criticism was hardly inaccurate. I *had* done an *Uncle Al* job laying those blasted tiles but was in no mood to have someone inform me of the obvious. What really got me all hot and bothered, though, was her use of the word "we." Two measly letters, *w* and *e*, and yet she managed to put those measly letters together in a manner that served as a pretentious suburban dagger that if not used as a tool to emasculate me, it was being inserted up my ass. "Boy, did *we* ever fuck that up," she was fond of saying. "*We* surely fucked things up this time, ay, Francis?" was another favorite. I went from an effectively combative mother to a slyly critical wife and have reached the conclusion there's a secret society that teaches methodology only to women. Probably on Sundays, when men, like ravenous animals, are busy devouring ten hours of the NFL. *Honey, I'm going to the mall, enjoy the game.* Next thing I know, I am getting mind-fucked by two letter words.

Later that night in a quiet moment, I explained to my boy the unfortunate legacy of Uncle Al. "Fear not," I told him. "You're far from doomed. You have your whole life ahead of you, and I'm confident you'll be the one to buck the trend." That's when he confessed that just the other day, he heard his mother muttering in anger, "Your father really Nunzi-oed my Acer this time; probably looking up porn!" Naturally, this made my son curious about porn. When I finished explaining, not about porn but about Uncle Nunzio, he cried, "But Dad, that's not fair; that makes it two against one." I could only smile, remembering our poor grandfather and all he went through all those years ago.

****

When the three brothers reached Philadelphia, Antonio saw the vast city with all its diversity, as a unique and expansive cityscape with a multitude of opportunities for a young man in need of a buck. And best of all, no coal mines!

Conversely, Uncle Al and Uncle Nunzio didn't see anything that resembled an honest pathway to a buck. What they saw was a vast playground—square block after square block of endless circus and carnival awaiting their participation. The Scrantonians became fascinated with the many streets and narrow alleyways—one after another—they seemed to go on forever, or for longer than anyone could walk in a given day. The storefronts on the avenues, the porches, stoops, and alcoves, along with the many other ways in which a big city forms its nooks and crannies, became a great source of fascination for Antonio Corelli's young brothers. For them, the city was a maze of adventure and one which they quickly learned to navigate. They discovered that the town was subdivided into neighborhoods and parishes, although no discernible boundaries seemed to exist. And while Antonio was away most of the day driving an eighteen-wheeler all over the tri-state area to make a living for himself and to support his young brothers in their new home and environs, Al and Nunzio would skip school in favor of partaking in a disorderly pastime known as *rolling drunks* for pocket change. They would play hooky from school in favor of casually standing guard outside any one of the many neighborhood taverns. They would bide their time, appearing to mind their own business—just a couple of guys hanging out shootin' the breeze or whatever doing nothing was called back in 1938. Then, when noticing a patron of the tavern emerging without putting one foot in front of the other with the same agility as they had earlier upon entering, they would shadow the poor bastard until they were close enough to dip their hands in his pockets, and then, off they'd run. Once, though, a fellow emerged so drunk he began tossing coins into the air and shouting, "Who needs Roosevelt when it's raining nickels!" Whenever the duo looted enough coins, they'd run straightaway to Shibe Park to watch the Philadelphia A's make a plausible attempt at playing baseball.

Unfortunately, or perhaps fittingly, Uncle Al and Uncle Nunzio's drunk-rolling days coincided with one of the many transitional periods in Philadelphia A's baseball history. These transitional periods saw manager/owner Connie Mack sell off all his higher priced and otherwise more talented players, essentially dooming his ballclub to several consecutive last-place finishes. Although the team's abysmal play mattered not to Uncle Al and Uncle Nunzio, as they only went to cheer for the Italian ballplayers of the day, or as they dubbed them: *dugout Degos*; therefore, with names like DiMaggio, Crosetti, and Lazzeri penciled into Joe McCarthy's lineup, our uncles became devoted fans of the New York Yankees. Whenever the *Lords of the Diamond* or *Titans of America's Pastime* made their southern migration from the Bronx, the drunk-rollers made sure they had enough coin for admittance into the park. If for whatever reason business was slow—rascals that they were—they would find a way to sneak into the park.

Uncle Al and Uncle Nunzio's misguided devotion to The Bombers was later reinforced when, in 1941, the Yankees added Phil Rizzuto to play shortstop. A few years later, the colorful, talented, and remarkably baseball-savvy Yogi Berra was added to squat behind the plate. Uncle Al and Uncle Nunzio may have been losers in life, but they had little trouble latching onto a winning ballclub, never mind that their initial rationale for having done so had absolutely nothing to do with the game itself. Sometimes it's better to have luck than brains, especially when brains are in short supply.

Then came 1950, the year the Yankees and Phillies met in the World Series. Uncle Al and Uncle Nunzio had to be careful not to tout their allegiance too loudly but then afterward jibed: "*Whiz Kids?* That's a perfect nickname for them bums, the Phillies. The Yankees *whizzed* right on by them! Four games to none!" I was born in 1962, twelve years after the baseball world had turned its attention to that ill-fated New York/Philadelphia match, and yet my entire childhood was relentlessly bludgeoned by the constant recounting of the 1950 Series. Those two old birds could recite the sequence of every damn inning; just mention the word *baseball,* and they'd go on, like a couple of merciless vaudevillians. Regarding the '50 Series, their memory was long, longer, and longest, and they would turn it on me with the force of a firehose! *Great* uncles, my ass!

On Sundays, our grandfather and great-uncles made a habit of hiking on over to Fairmount Park with a picnic lunch in tow. They would sit perched atop Lemon Hill and, with an excellent view of the East River Drive and Schuylkill River, watch motorists in their luxurious vehicles out for a Sunday drive, rowers canoeing on the Schuylkill, and couples strolling the river walk. With the shadow of Lemon Hill Mansion at their backs, they would laze about and ponder the acquisition of such fanciful items as fine automobiles and canoes. Once, they arrived at Lemon Hill still in their church clothes because they found out that the mansion, for a modest fee, was available to tour. They learned that its original owner, Robert Morris, was one of the signers of the Declaration of Independence and Constitution, and was also our nation's superintendent of finance. Their jaws dropped when learning that one man could be so wealthy that he could use his own funds to help finance the Revolutionary War, particularly Washington's troops before entering into the battles of Trenton and Princeton. This level of generosity was difficult for three Italian men from the coal-mining region of northeastern Pennsylvania to grasp. It saddened them to learn that years later, Robert Morris died in debtors' prison.

"How do ya like that?" started Uncle Al. "Of all the lowdown dirty tricks I heard played on a fella, I ain't never heard none worse than that!"

"You ain't ever heard worse because no worser than that was ever done," added Uncle Nunzio. "What kind of city lets a fella like Robert Morris, with all he done for this lousy country, die in debtors' prison?"

"I say screw this town!" said Uncle Al.

"Screw it is right!" added Uncle Nunzio.

"First off," our grandfather said, "it was likely the Feds that jailed 'im, not the city. But it was ages ago; they don't even have debtors' prisons anymore."

"You mean we could run up a bunch of debt and get away without payin'?" Uncle Nunzio gleamed over the prospect. Then, by their arms, Antonio Corelli took firm hold of his brothers. "Look," he said, before pointing to the scenic Schuylkill River, East River Drive, and budding Philadelphia skyline that had long featured a statue of William Penn. "If we play our cards right, we could do well here. *If* we play them right."

It was our grandfather's hope that his pep talk would continue ringing in the ears of his brothers, especially when he wasn't available to look after them, which was most of the time. But, the very next day, he received the sort of phone call one dreads.

During his earliest days in Philadelphia, our grandfather had yet to scrape together enough dough for an automobile. Besides, when taking into account his lifestyle, he considered it more a luxury than a necessity. Traveling to and from work required two units of public transportation, followed by a four-block walk; not a big deal for a young man at his peak. At the end of what had been a typically long day, which saw many miles of road, he barely had his feet planted on the porch and key inserted in the door, when from inside the house he heard the telephone ringing. Assuming it was Mama or Poppa Corelli calling from Scranton, he went bursting through the door and lunged for the receiver. At the other end, he was quick to learn, was not the most courteous of voices, as he was rather brusquely informed that his "wayward kin" was at the precinct "waiting to be collected." Our grandfather wasn't scholarly enough to know the meaning of *wayward*, but correctly assumed it wasn't grounds for receiving a gold star. He was, however, well aware of what *collected* meant. *Trash* was collected, he thought, and therefore, he had little appreciation for what the unfriendly voice was insinuating. Nevertheless, starving and exhausted, he trekked to the precinct to collect his *wayward kin*.

By the looks that appeared on the faces of the policemen manning the precinct, it was clear that Antonio Corelli was hardly what they were expecting. Uncle Al had the physique of a fly rod, not too tall but wiry. If he

21

was the pinky finger, then Uncle Nunzio was the thumb, short and squat. Everyone stopped whatever it was they were doing to glance up admiringly at this Italianized version of Jack Dempsey, with his imposing shoulders, long arms, and huge, powerful-looking hands.

"Christ, he could choke a rhinoceros with those meat hooks," he overheard one of the policemen say.

"I'm here to *collect* my brothers," he told an officer.

"Come again?" the officer said with a note of incredulity. "You mean to tell me that those two bunglers belong to *you*?" The second half of the officer's question was added as if he had subscribed to the notion that our grandfather must be mistaken. Then he shrugged as if to say, *Of course, they belong to you. Who would admit to two such knuckleheads unless bound by an unholy obligation?*

"Yes sir," came our grandfather's painful reply. "They belong to me."

"I caught them rolling a drunk coming out of Nicastro's at Twenty-second and Lehigh," the officer told our grandfather. "I saw 'em last week, too, but couldn't catch 'em. So that makes it's twice that I know of. One more time, and I won't have any choice but to lock 'em up. Then they'll have to go before a judge. By the way, shouldn't they be in school?" the officer asked, as if it were more an afterthought, not a genuine concern.

"I see," said our grandfather, alluding to the consequences of a third infraction, not his brothers' habitual truancy from school. He stood posed with downcast eyes, his massive shoulders slumping as if apologizing for thirty years of Italian immigration. Then he looked the policeman square in the eye and told him, "There won't be a third time. That I can promise."

Our grandfather was quiet when they hiked home from the precinct. Along the way, Uncle Al and Uncle Nunzio repeatedly apologized with the hope their efforts would spark conversation, as their big brother's silence made them uneasy. Finally, Uncle Nunzio said with pride, "You really had that puny cop shaking in his boots, Antonio!"

"Yeah, Antonio," boasted Uncle Al. "They were all scared stiff of *you*!"

It was then that our grandfather decided to speak. Before he did, he stopped dead in the middle of the intersection of Twenty-fourth and Cambria. With his huge, powerful hands, he took firm hold of his quivering brothers. He didn't shout; his imposing size made shouting unnecessary. He quietly and calmly told them, "If I ever receive another phone call from that precinct, I'll ship both of you back to Scranton, and you can spend the rest of your days working the coal mines. You embarrassed me today."

The remainder of the way home was spent walking in silence. By the time they reached Twenty-sixth and Indiana, Antonio was walking with his arms gently draped around his *wayward kin*. Despite the confidence of knowing all along that their big brother would never ship them back to Scranton, where they would be doomed for the coal mines, Uncle Al and Uncle Nunzio were breathing easier. Nevertheless, it did bother them that they embarrassed their big brother. In a small, close-knit community that was comprised mainly of folks of a common ethnicity, the majority of whom assembled at the same church, it would not be long before everyone learned that Antonio Corelli had to go and collect his two dopey brothers from the local precinct. The following day, our grandfather announced: "If you two are gonna go on skipping school, you're gonna have to find full-time work. No more slummin' around the neighborhood. Understood?"

Antonio didn't begrudge taking care of his brothers as long as they were in school, but he wasn't about to stand for them getting into mischief and leading a life that would likely lead to them becoming a couple of hoodlum freeloaders. So, he walked with them up to the corner of Twenty-sixth and Lehigh and told them: "Al, you go this way. Nunz, you go that way. And don't either of you come home until someone has hired you."

That was Tuesday morning. By Friday, Antonio heard all the excuses he would listen to and took matters into his own hands. Whenever he reached that point, matters had a way of getting done and done swiftly. That was our grandfather; when the ineptness of others forced him to take action, it ended up a swift and methodical affair. It just so happened that Antonio had a friend who knew someone, and this third party was able to line up Uncle Al and Uncle Nunzio with jobs at one of the Aramingo Avenue slaughterhouses.

****

Growing up, I had three wishes: to get naked with Farah Fawcett, see the Phillies win the World Series, and to somehow, despite it occurring more than two decades before I was born, have been standing beside my grandfather when he informed Uncle Al and Uncle Nunzio where they would be gainfully employed. He never let on as much, nor at the time did he let it show—for he truly was not a vengeful person—but breaking the news to Uncle Al and Uncle Nunzio that they were soon to be grunts at a slaughterhouse must have tickled the pleasure center of his brain, if not have sent it careening like a pinball.

"But, Antonio, that's *worse* than a coal mine!" wailed Uncle Al.

"We'll have to clean up cow guts and pig shit!" cried Uncle Nunzio. "And be in that stink all day!"

Antonio refused to stick around and listen to any moaning and protesting. Leaving Uncle Al and Uncle Nunzio alone to grumble among themselves, he went to the kitchen and started dinner.

To go along with his kind and gentle nature, our grandfather had an exceptional mind. Unfortunately, with only the benefit of a sixth-grade education, he wasn't able to cite Upton Sinclair's novel *The Jungle* as a work that, for the better, sparked change in the country's working conditions, especially within such places as slaughterhouses. Many years later, after agonizing through Mr. Sinclair's highly effective classic, I took it upon myself to illustrate that very point, when once again having to endure Uncle Al and Uncle Nunzio's unrelenting drone that my generation "is too soft" and "a bunch of creampuffs," and that "slaughterhouses weren't fit for man or beast." It wasn't as satisfying as the Phillies, had they made it, meeting and defeating the Yankees in the '77 Series, but I had to take what I could get.

"I told you we shoulda took that lumber yard job," whispered Uncle Al. While his ear was pressed to the wall, a most satisfying grin formed on our grandfather's face.

"Yeah, well, what about the pool room?" moaned Uncle Nunzio. "That wouldn't a been so bad. Now we gotta shovel pig shit and cow guts! Slop lackeys; that's what we're gonna be. I rather die in debtors' prison like Robert Morris, the poor sonofabitch."

Back in 1938, there was no way to effectively go from Twenty-sixth and Indiana to where stood the Aramingo Avenue slaughterhouses without the benefit of an automobile. But like always, Antonio Corelli was prepared. To the delight of Uncle Al and Uncle Nunzio, and sometimes to their dismay, he usually was prepared. Antonio had a friend who knew someone that was selling a 1934 Dodge Sedan. He woke early Saturday morning, and with cash in hand, he walked all the way to the Girard Avenue Bridge to meet this convenient friend of a friend. Later that day, he came rolling down Twenty-sixth Street with the very first automobile ever owned by a Corelli in America. He beeped the horn until Uncle Al and Uncle Nunzio came running out onto the porch. They sauntered forward as if unable to believe their eyes. Their big brother, of whom they were so proud, was grinning beautifully from behind the wheel of an actual automobile! The thrill took all the sting out of the potential misery they were sure a slaughterhouse would provide. With much deliberation, they walked around the car, peered through the windows, ran their fingers along the hood, rapped gently on the roof, then stooped to see their reflections in the car's chrome accessories.

"Look Nunz," said Uncle Al, "you're just as ugly a bastard in the front bumper as you were in the back."

"Yeah," said Uncle Nunzio, "well it ain't exactly making you look like Errol Flynn neither, you ratty old beanpole."

While still in the afterglow of what was a life-altering acquisition, Antonio handed them each a rag and polish, and the three of them took to task. They spent the remainder of the day getting a four-year-old car to look as if it just rolled out of a showroom. By the time the sun was hanging low over the Schuylkill River, three brothers from a cold, Northeastern Pennsylvania coal-mining town were feeling pleased with the way the new addition was shaping up. After a mild dispute over who would sit beside Antonio when it came time to take her for a spin, Uncle Al and Uncle Nunzio were each introduced to the back seat.

"Just enjoy the ride," Antonio called to them from the envious position of the driver's seat. "And keep a sharp eye out for those girls youse been eyeballing. If they see you wavin' to 'em from a car, they might take you serious."

"You're the best, Antonio," said Uncle Al.

"Yeah, Antonio," added Uncle Nunzio. "We're lucky to have you as our big brother. And things are gonna work out just fine at the slaughterhouse; you just wait and see."

Our great-uncles were right; our grandfather *was* the best and they were *damn* lucky. Antonio Corelli was the best brother, father, uncle, husband, and most certainly, as Ricky, Munchk, and I would decades later attest, the best grandfather.

The following day, three Corellis proudly joined the parade of Sunday drivers on the East River Drive, which skirted along the Schuylkill River. They also wound their way along the many roads of Fairmount Park and the streets of Strawberry Mansion, before crossing the Falls Bridge—a 556-foot span that links the East and West River Drives. They headed toward the art museum and looped around the magnificent structure before making their way to their favorite spot: Lemon Hill. They rolled out a blanket and enjoyed what had become their customary

Sunday. They ate, lazed about, and talked about life going forward and the freedom their new acquisition would provide. Before they ran out of words, the day had all but disappeared. The early evening sun was setting ablaze the art museum's magnificent stone walls and, too, the statue of William Penn that was sitting high atop the tower that carries the famous Quaker's name. The setting sun would soon give way to the stars, and one by one, the rowers on the Schuylkill River and the Sunday drivers on both side of the river would disappear and leave alone the three occupiers of a hill that once served as the front yard of a man who financed a war then died in debtors' prison. For a while, three brothers from a dismal Northeastern Pennsylvania coal-mining town let loose in a big city puffed up with pride that anchoring a place in society was not so fanciful a notion as once believed. They stood tall atop their lofty plateau. As they gazed across the way at the darkening skyline, they felt taller than they were and more entitled to the familiar ground upon which they stood. Not even Antonio informing Uncle Al and Uncle Nunzio that it was their car "only to travel back and forth to work," and that otherwise, "the car belongs to me," could dampen their spirits. Uncle Al and Uncle Nunzio figured the time traveling to and from work would be their fun time— the adventurous part of the day. They would speed to work as though operating a fine-tuned racecar, then mosey on home like a couple of tomcats on the prowl. Gawking at pretty girls whenever the opportunity presented and grinning as though they were the envy of all would highlight their days. As for the time spent in between? That, as we are about to find out, would be another story.

****

The Aramingo Avenue slaughterhouses stood in a section of town called Port Richmond—a typical inner-city Philadelphia neighborhood jampacked with row homes occupied by folks of a given ethnicity who worshipped in the same fashion. Within Philly's old neighborhoods, as was the case in many big cities of yesteryear, there existed ethnic boundaries. They may have been loose, these boundaries; therefore, one might find the occasional stray, but they did exist.

Port Richmond was a riverward neighborhood, where once upon a time nestled within its bosom was a darling little section called Smearsville. Smearsville wasn't the sort of place one bragged about. Never seen was a bumper sticker that read: *Honk if you're from Smearsville.* In fact, this charming section of town was named for the industrial waste material produced by the glue factories, fertilizer companies, and, of course, slaughterhouses. The Reading Railroad, which serviced much of the area's industries and employed thousands from Port Richmond, came rolling in with boxcars filled with livestock so that *we* who sit high atop the food chain could enjoy our share of beef, pork, and poultry. The unfortunate animals were herded, or in the case of the chickens, carried to their proper compartment, where they awaited their turn for the ax. Uncle Al and Uncle Nunzio did none of the slaughtering. Slaughtering takes a degree of skill, which supposedly keeps the poor animals from enduring unnecessary suffering—or so it is written. To the best of my knowledge, no animal has gotten back to us regarding the manner in which they are slaughtered and any suffering that might occur as a result.

Nevertheless, we take comfort believing *that* which we consume is slaughtered properly before moving on to be butchered, packaged, and sold. Incidentally, I am not a vegetarian. No Corelli is or ever was.

It was Uncle Al and Uncle Nunzio's job to clean up the *pig shit*, as they begrudgingly called swine feces, *cow puckies*, as my grandmother was fond of referring to bovine waste, and whatever it's called that chickens leave behind—dung, doo, turds, take your pick. It was also their unenviable task to clean up the remains of the slaughtering: blood and various animal entrails—as Uncle Nunzio so eloquently stated, they were slop lackies—save for the stomach lining of the cows, which they learned was harvested and packaged as a mystery meat known as tripe.

"That tripe crap," said Uncle Al, "ain't that what Ma puts in minestrone?"

"From here on, I ain't eatin' nothin' but spaghetti," said Uncle Nunzio.

To break up the monotony, they were hoping for an opportunity to hang and hose down the insides of the carcasses.

"Maybe next week," their boss told them. Although, from what Uncle Al and Uncle Nunzio could gather, their boss didn't sound too encouraging. To them, *maybe next week* meant *deal with the slop and be grateful to have a job.*

The stench of the slaughterhouse was as expected, perhaps even worse and it was punctuated by the ever-present swine.

"What's with these bastards," moaned Uncle Nunzio. "I bet I could breathe better if I stuck my head up one of them cow's asses! And how can the shit of one animal smell so much worse than another?"

"Must be what they feed 'em," said Uncle Al.

"They'd do us all a favor if they ate each other," Uncle Nunzio griped.

As the hours passed, the humdrum classroom, which they ditched in favor of becoming a couple of neighborhood agitators, and the dreaded Scranton coal mines, which they had feared since childhood, seemed friendlier and friendlier. To get through the day, Uncle Al and Uncle Nunzio kept reminding themselves of the shiny Dodge Sedan that awaited them and all the excitement that they would have driving home.

After arriving home, Uncle Al and Uncle Nunzio—feeling a twinge of guilt that they were awarded the luxury of driving home when Antonio's trek required two units of public transportation and a hike—waited at the kitchen table for Antonio to return. They were seized with a sudden mixture of excitement and trepidation when they heard his boots climbing the stairs to the porch. Antonio had a similar mix of feelings when wondering about Uncle Al and Uncle Nunzio's first day on the job. Admittedly, he spent a good deal of the day distracted when he considered all that could go wrong. At the very least, he was certain that they drove off to someplace; he smirked upon noticing how crookedly the Dodge Sedan was parked at the curb. What he couldn't explain, when at first, he opened the door, was the awful smell that accosted him, but he quickly came to his senses and figured that it must be the remnants of the slaughterhouse come home on his brothers' clothing. He didn't take into account having *that* to look forward to every night.

"I can smell that you two actually made it to work today," he called to Uncle Al and Uncle Nunzio from the parlor.

"We wouldn't let you down, Antonio," Uncle Al called back.

"Yeah, Antonio," Uncle Nunzio followed. "We want you to be proud of us; especially after buying us that nice car."

"What the hell it that!" Uncle Al and Uncle Nunzio were not used to hearing Antonio shriek or appear astonished, but that's precisely how he appeared and sounded once he reached the entry way to the kitchen.

"It's a pig," said Uncle Al, gesturing to the beast's unmistakable snout.

"I can see it's a pig, Al!" First, Antonio's eyes widened, then his nostrils flared. Lastly, the veins in his neck became visible "Trust me, I know a pig when I see one. But why is one on top of our kitchen table?"

"His name is Frank," said Uncle Nunzio. "We named 'im after Frank Crosetti. You know, the shortstop for the Yankees? Only instead of scooping up grounders and tossin' 'em to Gehrig, he's gonna give us pork chops for the next year!" Proudly, Uncle Nunzio patted the swine's rump.

"Is that so? Ol' Frank, here, is gonna give us pork chops, is he? Well, what about *this*?" Antonio pointed to the coat of fur that was still blanketing the swine. "And look," he added, "the sonofabitch still has hoofs!"

"We thought *you* could take care of that, Antonio," said Uncle Al.

"*I* could take care of it?" Antonio's hard glare made Uncle Al and Uncle Nunzio shrink in their seats.

"Yeah, Antonio," Uncle Nunzio shakily began. "Like always, we thought you'd know what to do."

"Nunz, be thankful we don't own a meat cleaver," said Antonio. "Be very thankful; 'cause once I got the hang of it, I wouldn't stop with the pig."

Antonio collapsed in a chair, buried his head in his huge, powerful hands, and tried to figure out what one does when presented with, of all matters, contraband swine. "Pig smuggling," he mumbled under his breath. "I coulda guessed." Already, a week passed since Antonio went to *collect* his *wayward kin;* yet somehow it seemed like only yesterday if not hours ago. He should have left Uncle Al and Uncle Nunzio in holding instead of racing to the precinct; they needed to be taught a lesson. He pondered how peaceful life would be had he left them in Scranton. He also considered that Philadelphia was a place that presented too many opportunities to get into mischief, especially for those so easily tempted.

****

The twelve o'clock whistle blew, signaling lunchtime. That's when Uncle Al and Uncle Nunzio went brainstorming. If only they made off with a pig that was already dehaired, split open, and cleaned of all its entrails. Instead, they helped themselves to the pig most recently slaughtered. They smuggled the fat, smelly, not to mention still oozing beast out the back door of the slaughterhouse and into the back seat of their recently cleaned and polished Dodge Sedan. All my life, I have had this idiotic image of my two moronic great-uncles in white aprons stained and smudged with the blood and guts of slaughtered animals, urging each other to hurry along as they went running sideways through the back ally of a slaughterhouse carrying a dead pig. It's right up near the top of the list of Corelli folklore, besides being a favorite anecdote at parties. For years, friends, coworkers, and in-laws have all enjoyed the pig smuggling story or *The Corelli Pig Caper.* Even for those never having had the opportunity *or* misfortune to meet our great-uncles, they have become lasting and endearing figures. The pig smuggling story has become sort of like a chain letter that I expect one day will come back to me. It's fascinating how, posthumously, some manage to increase in charm, even when charm was clearly lacking in their lifetime. I suppose haphazard behavior has a unique brand of appeal. This is difficult to dispute; for over the years, Uncle Al and Uncle Nunzio have lent so much to our holiday dinners.

****

"That settles it," Antonio declared. "You can't return a stolen pig; not after only a day on the job. We're gonna have to bury the sonofabitch."

"Bury 'im?" Uncle Nunzio began to protest. "Frank?" Antonio's raised eyebrow thwarted Uncle Nunzio from going any further. Then he sent Uncle Al and Uncle Nunzio to the cellar for two coal shovels. Next, he hoisted up the poor beast named after the Yankees' shortstop, Frank Crosetti, slung him over his shoulder, and ordered a march to the car. Before depositing the pig into the recently polished Dodge Sedan, he took a moment to lament over the condition of the back seat.

"Well, don't just stand there," Antonio hollered. "We got work to do!"

Uncle Al and Uncle Nunzio stood staring at a slaughtered pig that was laid out such, it covered the length of the back seat. They eyeballed the one remaining seat up front, then one another as they tried to determine who had the inside track.

"What are youse waitin' for," Antonio bellowed. "We don't have all night."

Uncle Al and Uncle Nunzio hesitated, then each made an abrupt move for the front seat.

"Oh no youse don't," Antonio warned them. "If ol' Frank here was good enough to steal and eat, then he's good enough to ride with. Now in youse go!"

Uncle Al and Uncle Nunzio did not make a fuss. They knew Antonio meant business and so they did as they were told; they held their noses while the weighty, smelly, and oozing Frank sank into their laps. Once Antonio started the engine, not a single word was exchanged on the way to Frank's final resting place.

Antonio drove down Hunting Park Avenue until it dead-ended on East River Drive. Uncle Al and Uncle Nunzio looked curiously at one another when Antonio turned off East River Drive onto Sedgely; they couldn't imagine that Antonio would choose Lemon Hill, their favorite spot, as a place to entomb a stolen pig. Antonio slowed and veered onto Thirty-third Street before reentering Fairmount Park by way of Reservoir Drive. He wound his way around to Fountain Green Drive, and that was where he brought the smelly Dodge Sedan to a stop. The headlights illuminated Mount Pleasant—a mansion built in 1761, and later owned by the infamous traitor, Benedict Arnold. They were as far from the East River Drive as that were from Thirty-third Street, and therefore well enveloped in the park.

"Each of you grab a shovel," Antonio told them.

Uncle Al and Uncle Nunzio did as they were told. Antonio picked up Frank, slung him over his shoulder, grabbed his lantern, and marched toward the perimeter of the mansion's front lawn. He figured the middle, where the ground was likely to be softest, would have been too conspicuous never mind disrespectful. Uncle Al and Uncle Nunzio followed a few paces behind.

"This is as good a spot as any," said Antonio. Respectfully, as though Frank was still able to feel pain, he settled the swine onto the cool grass. "Start digging," he ordered. While Uncle Al and Uncle Nunzio labored, Antonio held the lantern and supervised.

Coal shovels are fine for shoveling coal; that's why they're called coal shovels. They are not particularly conducive when what's required is penetrating far enough into the earth to bury a full-grown hog. Not only wasn't Antonio feeling particularly sympathetic; he took pleasure in the effort it took to produce a subterranean hollow large enough to accommodate an adult-sized animal. More than once I heard it said during the many retellings of *The Corelli Pig Caper*, that Antonio mocked Uncle Al and Uncle Nunzio by whistling while they labored long past the point of their hands blistering.

****

"Yeah, that's right," Uncle Al and Uncle Nunzio each complained, when on Thanksgiving the entire Corelli clan was assembled. "He stood there with his arms folded and whistled 'Nice Work If You Can Get It' and 'Whistle While You Work!'" Pointing to our father, that notorious evader of confrontation, Uncle Nunzio added, "That's your father we're talkin' about. He was some helluva guy, ya know." Then Uncle Nunzio winked at me, Ricky, and Munchk to let us know that it was all in jest and that our grandfather was as fine a man as there ever was.

Meanwhile, our Grandfather sat quietly, pretending to remember very little of the *Frank the Pig* episode. "After all these years, who can remember such things," he said. Then he gave a wry shrug of his massive shoulders as if to say, *maybe I remember, and then again maybe I don't.*

That was our grandfather—the strong and silent type. He spoke when it mattered and was the glue that held together the entire Corelli Clan.

****

"All right, that's good enough," Antonio told Uncle Al and Uncle Nunzio. "Throw the bastard in the ditch."

"I guess this is it, ol' Frankie boy," said Uncle Nunzio. "It was sure nice knowin' ya."

"Yeah, Frank," added Uncle Al, "you were some helluva pig. You'd a made us some fine suppers if only things worked out better."

"Enough with the last rites," grumbled Antonio. "Bury the sonofabitch so we can scram before someone sees us and wonders what the hell we're doin'."

As Antonio held the lantern over the two unlikely sextons, he wondered to himself how accurate of a headcount a slaughterhouse took on incoming animals. Should it turn out that this was the only instance an animal went missing, and with today having been Uncle Al and Uncle Nunzio's first day on the job, it wouldn't be too difficult to determine who among the workers were the culprits. He wasn't worried so much about restitution for the pig as much as how the incident would reflect on *the friend of a friend* who was kind enough to line up his reckless brothers with stable employment.

"Well," said Antonio, once Uncle Al and Uncle Nunzio threw the final shovelfuls of dirt on Frank, "it's not everyone that can claim to have snuck into a park to bury a stolen pig by moonlight. Not that we should brag." Shining the lantern on the faces of the two sextons, he wondered, "What's the matter with you two? You buried a pig, not your senses of humor." Antonio expected his remark to draw a light chuckle. Instead, Uncle Al and Uncle Nunzio appeared more anxious than ever.

"There's just one more thing, Antonio," said Uncle Al. He squeezed out the words before swallowing nervously.

"Yeah," said Uncle Nunzio. He was clutching his coal shovel as one would a life preserver in the ocean. His head was pointed toward the ground. "Well, go on, Al," he urged. "*You* tell 'im."

"Tell me what?" Antonio demanded. Although, because the evening had already been an eventful one, he wasn't so eager to become enlightened as to why Uncle Al and Uncle Nunzio were swaying nervously.

"Why do *I* have to be the one to tell him?" moaned Uncle Al.

"Because it was you who was driving," Uncle Nunzio was alert to point out.

"Out with it, already," barked Antonio. "It can't be any worse than *this*." He pointed emphatically to the spot on the ground where a pig named for Yankee shortstop Frank Crosetti lay buried.

****

By the time Uncle Al and Uncle Nunzio returned to the Dodge Sedan, at the end of their work day, Frank the pig had gotten quite ripe and had done a fair share of oozing.

"Jesus *Christ*, it stinks in here!" cried Uncle Al.

"Hurry up and roll down your damn window!" implored Uncle Nunzio.

The two brothers cruised south along Aramingo Avenue with all four windows rolled down, but the stench emanating from Frank was stubborn and refused to dissipate as they had hoped.

"Drive faster, Al!" urged Uncle Nunzio. "It still stinks in here!" Uncle Al hit the gas.

"Jesus *Christ*, Frank!" Then Uncle Al turned and began unloading a slew of profanity at the dead pig, blaming the poor swine for the inconvenience. The result of Uncle Al's diatribe was a smelly Dodge Sedan swerving all over the road and horns blaring in both directions. This led to Uncle Nunzio crying, "Stop hollering at the goddamn pig, Al, and drive faster!" Uncle Al steadied the car and hit the gas. This time he accelerated to 50 mph in the 25-mph zone. Instead of several blaring horns, what they heard was a single police siren.

"Antonio is gonna wring our necks!" cried Uncle Al.

"Ya better pull over," warned Uncle Nunzio, "or we're gonna end up in jail; and this time he'll leave us there to rot."

"Jail? That's the least of our worries," cried Uncle Al. "We're gonna end up in them goddamn coal mines! That's where we're headed!"

"Just pull over," said Uncle Nunzio. "Let me do the talking."

"Why should *you* do the talking? I'm the one who's driving."

"Trust me," Uncle Nunzio insisted, "it'll go better if I do the talking."

The two morons held their collective breaths in a smelly Dodge Sedan and waited for a police officer to exit his patrol car and approach.

"So, ahh, who's your friend there in the back seat?" the policeman wryly asked.

"Friend? Oh, that's just Frank," Uncle Nunzio told the policeman. "He's our pet pig. He's usually much friendlier, but right now he's taking a nap."

"Taking a nap, is he?" For the moment, the policeman doesn't seem to mind playing along.

"Sure," replied Uncle Nunzio. "You see officer, Frank here usually sleeps in till eight, but this morning, he was up at the crack of dawn. Probably had gas. You know pigs with all they eat. Anyway, he shoulda been napping hours ago. Go figure."

"You boys always take your pig out for a drive?"

"Ya see, officer, sometimes ol' Frankie here suffers what they call insomnia," explained Uncle Nunzio. "The motion of the car helps him to sleep. Otherwise, he's up all day. Then come the nighttime he gets cranky, and when he's cranky you can't do a damn thing with him!"

"Is that right?" said the policeman, whose raised brow was an indication that he was losing appreciation for Uncle Nunzio's humor. "Well, I sure hope the owner of that pig has a damn good sense of humor. Meanwhile, you boys can take this with you." The policeman handed Uncle Al a ticket.

"Trust *you*? It'll go better if *you* do the talking? Well, lookie-fucking-here at what I'm holding," cried Uncle Al. Then he slumped down in his seat when he looked over a ticket that cited him for speeding and reckless endangerment.

"Holy shit!" cried Uncle Nunzio, when he saw the size of the fine.

"Christ, are we in big trouble now," said Uncle Al.

"Maybe after we're finished explaining to Antonio how much money we're gonna save on pork chops, he won't mind so much," said Uncle Nunzio.

"Yeah, sure thing, Nunz," said Uncle Al. "I'll let *you* try and explain it to him. I'm sure he'll see the upside."

"At least this time Antonio won't have to bail us out of jail," said Uncle Nunzio. "That's something, ain't it?"

"Thank God for small favors," muttered Uncle Al.

****

Antonio folded up the hefty violation and shoved it into his pocket. Thoughtfully, he looked over Uncle Al and Uncle Nunzio, then very matter-of-factly told them, "Since we're already here, maybe youse wouldn't mind digging two more holes?"

"For a minute there, we thought he was serious," Uncle Al told the crowd that had thus far assembled at my parents' house for our grandfather's surprise sixtieth birthday party. Our grandfather had yet to arrive.

"It's true!" added Uncle Nunzio. "We *did* think that he was serious. And then he told us that after we were all through digging, that we should beat each other to death with the coal shovels and that afterward, he would take the time and trouble to bury us."

"Imagine," said Uncle Al. "Taking the time and trouble to bury us? What a guy!"

"He had us shaking in our shoes that night," said Uncle Nunzio. "You see, the one thing about our Antonio, you *wanted* him to holler and act angry. It was when he got all calm and quiet that you knew you were in *real* trouble."

The pig smuggling story was a true gem. It was told and retold at every family gathering. It didn't grow appendages as stories tend to do in the course of retelling, nor was there any need for embellishment. It wasn't one of those family legends that down through the ages develops into something else entirely. It is today just as it was back then in the late 1930s—a classic anecdote. Uncle Al would usually begin the story. Often, he would begin before we took our places at the table, figuring it would put everyone in a festive mood before the food was served. Other times, he would wait until after dinner, figuring we would laugh off our full bellies before it was time for dessert. I have to admit, laughter as a means of digestion was pretty smart on Uncle Al's part. Uncle Nunzio would chime in from time to time before taking over. Uncle Nunzio was exceedingly gregarious; when he spoke, he waved his arms about like a conductor guiding an orchestra through a vigorous passage. Once he got a little momentum, there was no stopping him. He was a short, squat, fireball of a comic, whereas Uncle Al was more the tall, slender, straight man type. You might say they were the Corelli version of Abbott and Costello; they even bore a resemblance to the famous comic duo. And whether as an hors d`oeuvre or later on as a palate cleanser between courses, their anecdotes never failed to bring laughter.

All family gatherings were held at our house. There wasn't anything special about the house except the woman who presided over it; Mary Corelli was the undisputed champion cook of the Corelli clan. Our mother did two things exceedingly well: find confrontation and make a pot of gravy. Her gravy surpassed cuisine along the way to a rarefied and lofty combination of art and science; and when she was at work on this *oth-*

enworldly combination, she could not be spoken to. Well, you could *speak* to her—there was no written rule to prohibit one from doing so—just don't expect a reply or any sort of gesture that whatever it was you were attempting to convey had registered. Naturally, Ricky, Munchk, and I did all we could to distract our mother with all sorts of shenanigans.

"Mom, the house is on fire!" Munchk would yell as she went dashing into the kitchen, apparently winded from all the excitement.

"Mom, you better come quick!" Ricky would urge. "Dad did another *Uncle Al job* on the plumbing!"

We each had our favorites when attempting to distract our mother when she was engaged in her *second claim to fame,* but no matter how clever or impromptu the gag, the result was always the same. On a positive note, the Corelli children were never disciplined via the business end of a wooden spoon, as it was always submerged in a pot of gravy.

****

An unnervingly quiet Antonio, along with an anxious Uncle Al and Uncle Nunzio, marched from a dark meadow in front of Mount Pleasant mansion to a Dodge Sedan that was still quite redolent with the remains of Frank the pig. Once again, Antonio made the hog burglars ride in the back seat. Moreover, he denied them the benefit of riding home with the windows rolled down. Without a single utterance, it was clearly understood that the rolling down of windows was an indulgence to which they dared not propose entitlement. The stealers and buriers of a substantial swine rode from Thirty-third Street and Reservoir Drive to Twenty-sixth and Indiana, wilting and gasping in pig stench and with nary a word of conversation to distract them. When they arrived home, Antonio, despite the hour, somewhat unceremoniously handed Uncle Al and Uncle Nunzio buckets, rags, and detergent. It wasn't necessary for him to tell them to *make it look showroom new.* There was no need for catchphrases such as *shipshape, spic and span,* or *shine like a baby's bottom.* Without the benefit of language, he issued the necessary implements and material for cleaning the ooze of a slaughtered animal. And you can best believe that Uncle Al and Uncle Nunzio went at that Dodge Sedan as if their very lives depended on it.

Luckily for the two bunglers, ol' Frank went undetected; therefore, no restitution was due to the slaughterhouse. I suppose back in those days, particularly in places such as slaughterhouses, inventory was accounted for by some roustabout with a number-two pencil and tablet. The end result: Uncle Al and Uncle Nunzio kept their jobs … at least for the time being. But poor ol' Frank the pig's carcass was committed to the ground without ever yielding a single chop or roast—not even a measly slice of bacon! The poor swine never fetched a single penny of profit. However, luckily, no one aside from the stealers and buriers of ol' Frank was ever the wiser. Unloved, unheralded, unnoticed, and, tragically, of no value. Very sad commentary for what was once a sturdy animal a rancher was proud of and had raised for a much loftier purpose than to end up buried in a park in front of a home once owned by America's most infamous traitor.

Once the Dodge Sedan was cleaned to Antonio's satisfaction and the hefty violation paid, the pig smuggling episode, with all the worry of financial setback and possibly job loss, was laid to rest. However, at our grandfather's surprise sixtieth birthday party, Uncle Nunzio admitted to an old scheme:

"If the slaughterhouse didn't notice when pigs went AWOL, we thought that maybe next time we'd help ourselves to a live pig! 'We could keep it in the backyard,' I told Antonio. The way Al and me figured, every so often we'd make off with another one, and by the end of the year, we'd have our very own pig farm. 'We could make a fortune!' we told Antonio."

"He never even looked up at us when we explained to him our plan," said Uncle Al. "He just went right on sipping his coffee and reading his evening paper, like we weren't even there. We thought maybe he was laughing inside, but with Antonio, you couldn't always tell."

"Sometimes he'd laugh like a big ol' bear, and other times he'd just stare at us like we were imbeciles," said Uncle Nunzio. "He must've hated the pig farm idea, 'cause he didn't do neither. Like Al said, he just sipped his coffee and read the paper. We walked away hoping his silence meant that he was considering it, but no such luck. Anyway, here's to Antonio Corelli, the world's greatest big brother!"

Uncle Nunzio was right; our grandfather *was* the world's greatest big brother, along with being the greatest father, husband, uncle and, of course, grandfather. He was as fine a human being as everyone in the room had known, and they all raised a glass to Uncle Nunzio's fine sentiments— the lone exception being our mother, who was held captive at the stove by a pot of gravy that needed constant attention, or so she believed. Everyone hoped that perfection would be achieved soon or before our grandfather's arrival. Unfortunately, the process could not be rushed. Uncle Nunzio, who knew a thing or two about ponies, declared that our grandfather's arrival and the completion of the gravy would be a photo finish.

Ricky and I would often jibe, "She would prefer her children to turn out poorly than her gravy."

Our grandfather took his role of big brother seriously. He figured being the only adult to preside over two restless young men turned loose in a big city required that he remain serious, always on his game. By no means was he a rigid disciplinarian—rigidness was not in his nature—but with their parents situated a hundred miles to the north, there could not be any mistake over who was in charge. Despite their antics, most often Antonio would drape his huge powerful arms around Uncle Al and Nunzio and calmly explain matters. Always did they listen. Seldom did it sink in.

Nevertheless, they respected their big brother like no other. Since the day Uncle Al and Uncle Nunzio saw Antonio coming over the hill after his first day in the coal mine, they looked up to him as a hero. In that respect, they were not alone.

Chapter Three
A Coal Miner's Christmas

Iron ore, coal, and freight trains: those are the three things that first come to mind when I think of Scranton or for that matter, all of Northern Pennsylvania. My great-grandfather would have been an iron ore worker if not for the dwindling iron ore supply, which ultimately chased the Lackawanna Steel Company over the border into New York. Enter the Scranton coal mining industry.

Sometime back in the late 1980s, I watched a John Sayles movie called *Matewan* starring Chris Cooper and James Earl Jones. It was based on the Matewan Massacre, which took place after the initial attempt to unionize the West Virginia coal mines. Afterward, I wondered whether my great-grandfather had the opportunity to stand up against the establishment, or "the company," as the power brokers were known in the coal industry. In the course of my research, though, I discovered that the Matewan Massacre took place in 1920, a time when my great-grandfather was just arriving in America, along with my great-grandmother and their two-year-old son, Antonio. In 1920, my great-grandfather had but a few rudimentary words of English resting on his lips. By the time that he was able to express himself in a language that would make anyone pay attention, the dreaded days of "the company store" were over. So, as it turned out, my great-grandfather was just a simple immigrant coal miner, along with many other immigrant coal miners in Northeastern Pennsylvania who worked hard and had little to say regarding their welfare. They were the mules, the grunts of society, but they felt fortunate to be working and able to feed their families and no longer part of the desperate poor who remained overseas with no chance of improving their station. *Did anyone really believe the streets were paved with gold?*

When I first began to translate this so-called family tapestry into words on a page, to my dismay, I discovered that no one alive knew for sure my great-grandmother's first name. So, going forward, I shall refer to both great-grandparents using only their hierarchy names: Mama and Poppa Corelli.

Scranton's Pre-World War II demographics being what it was, many of its hills were, and to this day still are, dotted with Catholic Churches. *Where there were coal mines, there were Italians, and where there were Italians ... you get the picture?* They are still a few Corellis lingering in Scranton—mostly second cousins a generation removed and an aunt or two through marriage. We're not close, but every so often we force ourselves to trek up the Northeast extension of the Pennsylvania Turnpike. We usually reserve this once-every-third-year trip for the autumn, when the leaves are changing. Once through the Lehigh Tunnel, presto! Slopes, rambling hills, and mountains magically appear. Northern Pennsylvania is a real treat for the eye and gives travelers plenty of cause to reach for the camera. But in 1938, a decade before the Northeast extension of the turnpike was even thought of, Philadelphia to Scranton was an all-day affair. Moreover, for a man making the journey with two brothers whose behavior cannot always be predicted, the drive was anything *but* uneventful.

Antonio had promised Mama and Poppa Corelli that they would return home for the Christmas holidays. But before they set out on their journey, Antonio made sure that his brothers had their hair cut along with clean and freshly pressed shirts to wear. He wanted them looking presentable for the home folks, especially Mama Corelli, or he could expect to receive an earful.

Bright and early on the morning of Saturday, December 24, with flurries of snow falling from the sky, which lent nicely to the Christmas spirit, Antonio Corelli placed his well-dressed and groomed dependents in the Dodge Sedan; and along with a brand-new radio purchased at Strawbridge's, a Christmas gift for Poppa Corelli, and a handmade silk sweater from Wannamaker's, a gift for Mama Corelli, he began the long, winding trek up into Lackawanna County and Scranton, Pennsylvania.

Antonio was proud of their selections; he knew Poppa Corelli would be thrilled with the radio, that it would bring him hours of enjoyment. Meanwhile, Mama Corelli, despite how she might feel about the garment itself, would express joy over her sons' thoughtfulness and wear it proudly. The gifts were also a means of making the statement that, despite any misgivings Mama and Poppa Corelli might have, matters were going swimmingly down in Philadelphia and that there was no need to waste any worry. That was the general perception that Antonio was hoping to inspire.

Occasionally, Antonio glided his fingertips over the radio's sleek, elegant walnut cabinetry, then smiled as if he couldn't wait another minute to present Poppa Corelli with his gift. No sooner had he spotted it, when lumbering with Uncle Al and Uncle Nunzio through Strawbridge's—a grand department store positioned between Seventh and Eighth Street on Market Street in downtown Philadelphia—he knew he had to have it. However, selecting Mama Corelli's gift didn't come nearly as easy.

A few blocks away at Thirteenth and Market, where stood Wannamaker's, the grandest of all the Philadelphia department stores, the three brothers held up thousands of garments before settling on the handmade silk sweater. They had reached the point of exhaustion and frustration, and everything began to look alike. That's when Uncle Al proposed, "Why don't we give Ma the radio and buy Pop a necktie?"

"Sure thing," said Uncle Nunzio. "Just what every coal miner needs—a necktie! That way if he ever runs outa rope, he can still hang himself."

"He can wear the tie to church!" protested Uncle Al. "Ma'll be happy that he looks real spiffy in the pew, and then they can listen to *Abbott and Costello* and *Dick Tracy* on the radio."

"Ma'll complain she wants to hear *The Guiding Light* instead, and Pop'll end up throwin' the goddamn radio out the window," said Uncle Nunzio.

The goal was simple; to find something that would make Mama Corelli *ooh and ahh* with delight but that they could also afford. It didn't take them long to figure this was a merger not easily achievable. As Uncle Al and Uncle Nunzio were bickering, it was Antonio, naturally, whose eye caught the handmade silk sweater. When on their journey back to Scranton, occasionally he peeked in the box. With each peek, he gained confidence that Mama Corelli would cherish the sweater.

While agonizing over the perfect gift, they were occasionally serenaded with Christmas Carols from the famous Wannamaker pipe organ. The organ was believed to be the world's largest, though a half-dozen others have claimed that distinction, including the pipe organ in Atlantic City's Convention Hall. And despite spending more money than what they planned to, they managed lunch at Wannamaker's Crystal Tea Room. The famous ninth floor restaurant was known as the city's largest and was quite elegant. As they were finding out, there was much to Wanamaker's, its elegance notwithstanding, that was impressive, including a five-story cathedral ceiling. From the position of the main floor, they stood and gaped upward until their necks ached. By the day's end, they also learned a phrase unique to Philadelphia: *Meet me at the eagle.*

The Wannamaker eagle is a 2,500-pound bronze statue, which stands in the main floor below the five-story cathedral ceiling and is said to have 5,000 feathers. Uncle Al began to count the feathers but didn't reach ten before strongly discouraged by our grandfather and Uncle Nunzio.

"Just trust it, Al. Okay? Just trust it," pleaded Antonio.

"Besides," said Uncle Nunzio, "you can't count past your own age; so, unless you're five thousand years old, forget about it!"

Those entering the grand thirteen-story structure afraid of becoming separated from those with whom they came would instruct: *at such and such a time, meet me at the eagle.*

Afterward, the three bothers strolled along Market Street, looking in all the store windows decorated with the expected holiday tradition and finery. It was only days before Christmas, and everywhere they looked, there was hustle and bustle mixed with good cheer and festivity. One would find it difficult to imagine, as I once heard our grandfather lamenting, that America was still in the throes of a depression and that overseas, a war was brewing that would change human history. In retrospect, the juxtaposition to the latter seems eerie.

Whenever our grandfather spoke about the days of old, Ricky, Munchk, and I would stop whatever we were doing and pick up our ears. Even if what he was saying wasn't necessarily for our benefit, we would drop our respective activities and inch to within earshot. When Munchk was very young, she would climb onto his lap. Ricky and I would watch our baby sister all but disappear behind our grandfather's massive, powerful hands. He would sometimes pause at the end of a thought and kiss Munchk on top of her head, as if to ask, "*Well, now, what do you think about that?*" Looking back, that huge, powerful man seeking the opinion of one so young has become one of my more endearing childhood memories. How our grandfather adored our little Munchk.

The "good old days," as those of our grandfather's generation referred to their youth, seemed so trying, yet he managed to lend to them charm and romance. It was for that reason everyone sat quietly and listened with delight. When he was through, you were left wishing somehow you could have been part of the past—*his* past—to get close enough to brush up against it so that it would always be with you. He would end by turning to his grandchildren and reminding us how fortunate we were to be growing up in present times, but that our *today* would also become *the good old days*. Nevertheless, we always walked away feeling a bit nostalgic for a time that we never had the chance to experience firsthand.

Continuing their stroll on Market Street, the three brothers wondered how they would ever begin to explain to the home folks in Scranton all the opulence and festivity that surrounded them; how would they ever find the words? The Christmas hustle and bustle of a big city made the coal mines of Northeastern Pennsylvania seem worlds away. Busy sidewalks, silver bells, the anticipatory air that elevated everyone's spirit; this surely couldn't be the same Jack Frost that used to nip their noses in Scranton. It was difficult to imagine that the Market Street Christmas rush and the coal mines were separated by mere hours by car.

Once they had their fill of Market Street, its grand department stores, elegantly attired patronage, and Salvation Army Santa Clauses, they turned south onto Ninth Street and headed toward the famous Italian Market. They had just recently learned of its existence and were thrilled that an entire marketplace was based strictly on their ethnicity. The prospect was unimaginable, and they walked with pride. They knew they were getting close when they heard a familiar language barked out by street vendors attempting to entice passersby.

I can recall as children our grandfather taking us to the Italian Market. I don't remember my precise age, but Munchk was young enough to have wanted to be picked up and carried. She wasn't tired of walking; it was the view of the backs of people's legs and rear ends while strolling hand-in-hand with our grandfather through a densely crowded marketplace that made her disgruntled. As usual, she was readily accommodated; Munchk was rarely if ever refused. Aside from Ricky and me, Munchk knew the heartstrings of everyone in our family and could manipulate them like a master puppeteer.

My memory of the Italian market was wooden carts with big wooden wheels lining the street, baskets of every shape and size scattered about, and men in aprons barking out using a language I failed to comprehend. The place seemed random and haphazard and comported itself as if in a great big hurry. Moreover, it was difficult to determine *what* belonged to *who* and *who* was selling *what*. And what would happen, God forbid, if someone accidentally sold a tomato from someone else's basket?

The marketplace was a century old, and its appearance was well in accordance with its age: the sidewalks were worn and dingy, the tar on the street was well stained, the wood was warped, and the canvas awnings were long since discolored—from beginning to end, the place looked and reeked of age. The same could not be said, though, of the constant buzz and energy that rang throughout—the Italian Market was as alive and bustling as any place in the city—it had a brand of excitement unique unto itself. We stood and watched with fascination our grandfather engaging in a conversation that seemed to us excessively animated, with a cheese vendor. They began in English, before lapsing into Italian, only to return to English. The cheese vendor swung his hands about vigorously as if flinging the words through the air. Our grandfather didn't quite match the cheese vendor's animation, but his eyes smiled when he spoke. I didn't think it was possible to converse so long and excitedly about chunks of dairy—I never figured cheese as a compelling subject—but who knows what they were saying in Italian. Whatever it was, they sure made it seem exciting.

"His name is Vito," our grandfather, anticipating the question, told us. "He's my cousin from Toscana and a very good man. I've been buying cheese from him since Christmas of 1938."

Christmas of 1938? Suddenly, cheese and the Italian Market had history, charm, and romance, and it belonged to that golden era our grandfather called *the good old days*. I was old enough to have been aware that Richard Nixon was currently president. I also knew that back in 1938, Franklin Roosevelt sat in the oval office. Holding to those well-known facts, I spent the remainder of the afternoon trying to put a relationship built on cheese, which thus far had spanned the presidencies of Roosevelt, Truman, Eisenhower, Kennedy, Johnson, and Nixon, into some sort of perspective. It boggled the mind to think that a simple chunk of dairy could keep two men linked together for so long. I also began to calculate how many places our grandfather passed along the way to the Italian Market, where a similar hunk of cheese could have been purchased. But it was a time when loyalty and quality mattered more than the few pennies one might have saved elsewhere. No supermarkets for Antonio Corelli!

As we continued on our stroll through the marketplace, the exchange of pleasantries was a constant affair, and many of these pleasantries resulted in brief conversations—few in English, most in Italian, all demonstrative. We couldn't imagine that our grandfather knew so many people or that he had so many friends. That afternoon, as we were leaving the marketplace, it occurred to me that our grandfather's relationship with Vito the cheese man had almost nothing to do with cheese.

"Hey, tre, venite sopra e provate un certo formaggio!" ("Hey, you three, come over and try some cheese!") calls Vito to the three unfamiliar faces

that appear lost and overwhelmed in the bustling holiday crowd within the Italian Market.

"Antonio, is he talking to us?" asks Uncle Al. Uncle Al's Italian was too limited to comprehend the high-spirited cheese vendor.

By the time Uncle Al was brought into the world, and then shortly afterward, Uncle Nunzio, Mama and Poppa Corelli were able to muddle through conversing in English. The same could not be said when Antonio was a child. Until he went off to school, Antonio spoke only Italian.

"Nessuna nona via dei fogli senza provare alcuno del formaggio del Vito!" ("No one leaves Ninth Street without trying some of Vito's cheese!") the cheese vendor shouts to the three unfamiliar faces.

Antonio gives a shrug of a burly shoulder, then turns to Uncle Al and Uncle Nunzio and says, "I guess we better go and try some cheese."

"Sono Vito, da Toscana." ("I'm Vito, from Toscana,") said the cheese vendor.

"Antonio, da Umbria." ("Antonio, from Umbria,") was Antonio's reply.

"Amperora, siamo praticamente vicini; e chi sa, potremmo persino essere cugini." ("Ah, we're practically neighbors; and who knows, we might even be cousins,") said Vito. A warm smile forms on his mouth and a twinkle in his eye. Antonio smiles in return, despite the unlikelihood of what the cheese vendor has suggested.

"Cosi da dove sono i vostri amici?" ("So where are your friends from?") Vito asks Antonio, as immediately he is able to establish that Italian is not Uncle Al's and Uncle Nunzio's first language. He also assumes they are not relations. Uncle Nunzio was short, dark, and hairy. Uncle Al was slender and pale by comparison. Neither of them bore much resemblance to Antonio.

"Sono i miei fratello e provengono da Scranton." ("They're my brothers, and they're from Scranton, Pennsylvania,") Antonio tells the affable cheese vendor.

"Coal miners?" said Vito. The word flies from his lips with surprising fluidity. Also, his face contorts when enunciating the word; it is as though he finds it distasteful even to utter, or perhaps the mere notion of mining coal gives him a case of the willies. Whatever, he assumes anyone from Scranton, particularly if they are Italian, is a coal miner.

Antonio looks at his brothers as if momentarily stumped at what to say on their behalf. Drunk-rollers, pig thieves, and all-around menaces to society all would fit nicely. After a moment of deliberation, he shrugs and tells Vito, *"Vivono con me di destra qui a Filadelfia."* ("They live with me right here in Philadelphia.")

"Amperora, bene, in quell caso, nel benvenuto alla nona via!" ("Ah, well, in that case, welcome to Ninth Street!") said Vito, in a celebratory manner. Next, the cheese vendor extends a tray of his finest cheese, which all along he was slicing during his and Antonio's exchange.

"Amperora, che cosa gli ho ditto? Il la cosa migliore!" ("Ah, what did I tell you? The best!") Vito exultantly declares. What follows are three nods of agreement, and when all is said and done, Vito sells two pounds of his finest cheese.

"Hey, il mio cugino dal'Umbria; Li vedro` ancora, destra?" ("Hey, my cousin from Umbria,") Vito calls out to Antonio, as he and Uncle Al and Uncle Nunzio turn to leave. ("I'll see you again, right?")

Antonio turns, nods, and smiles warmly at a man approximately his own age, who came all the way from the Toscana region of Italy to peddle cheese in America.

"Antonio, let's not forget to buy some grapefruit," said Uncle Al. "You know how Pop loves grapefruit."

After the purchase of grapefruit, they combed the marketplace in search of items unique to their ethnicity and which were hard to come by in Scranton if not impossible.

****

"Maybe it's my imagination," said Uncle Nunzio, from his position in the back seat as they were motoring their way through Lehigh County, "but sometimes I can still smell our old friend, Frank."

"You know, Nunz, I saved 'ol Frank's tail," teased Antonio. "In fact, I have it right here in the glove box if you want it. You can tie it around your neck and use it as a good luck charm!"

"Very funny, Antonio." Uncle Nunzio sulked. "Besides, Al's the one who believes in all that superstitious nonsense."

"Hey, why drag me into it?" complained Uncle Al. "I don't smell a thing."

"Really, Nunz," Antonio continued to taunt. "I was gonna wait 'til tomorrow and give it to you for Christmas, but now that I spoiled the surprise, you might as well have it today." He feigned reaching for the glove box. That's when Uncle Al got in on the act. "Here, Nunz, this'll take away the imaginary pig smell," and he grabbed the two-pound chunk of cheese and held it under Uncle Nunzio's nose.

"Nothing like a hunk of aged Italian cheese to kill off another smell," said Antonio.

Uncle Nunzio waved a hand in exasperation; he wished he never mentioned Frank or the imaginary smell.

"Maybe this'll work," said Uncle Al. He unveiled a head of kale and began waving it near Uncle Nunzio's nose.

"Kale doesn't smell unless you cook it, you dumb bastard!" snapped Uncle Nunzio.

Antonio raised a hand to signal that it was time for the banter to end. More often than not, a raised hand was all that was needed.

Along their journey, they stopped at Oriole Hill in Carbon County for a scenic view of the town of Mahoning, the surrounding landscape with its rambling hills and the Lehigh River. Next, they stopped at a gas station to top off the tank and also for a map. Antonio wanted to make sure of the roads. He had done his share of highway driving in Pennsylvania, but didn't want to run the risk of being late for Christmas Eve dinner. Tardiness for a meal, especially one so important, would not have sat well with Mama Corelli. No sooner he pulled alongside the pump, he asked with a note of suspicion, "Where do you two think you're going?" Before the Dodge came to a complete stop, an antsy Uncle Al and Uncle Nunzio were reaching for door handles. Antonio suffered misgivings whenever his brothers were preparing to wander off in tandem. Who wouldn't?

"For a little walk, Antonio," said Uncle Al.

"Yeah, Antonio, we just wanna stretch our legs," said Uncle Nunzio.

"Fine, stretch your legs," said Antonio "But I won't need more than a few minutes to look over the map; then I wanna get right back on the road."

"Don't worry, Antonio," they called back as they headed toward a vast expanse of rural landscape that appeared to present nary a prospect for trouble. Nevertheless, Antonio was wary.

Not getting into trouble was a concept that should have rung true, as there were no drunks to roll, pigs to steal, people to hustle, or movie houses or ballparks into which to sneak. However, it wasn't long after settling up with the gas station attendant and having turned his attention to the map that Antonio and the attendant heard a loud bang. Both men tried to determine whether it was some sort of an explosion and what might have caused it, or if it was rifle fire coming from over the hill when again the booming sound ricocheted through the air and reached their ears.

"Oh, that's rifle fire, all right," the attendant decided. "And I got me a fairly good idea to whom the rifle belongs." Then the attendant and Antonio turned to face north, where they determined the shots to have come from. A moment later, Uncle Al and Uncle Nunzio were emerging from over a hill, running for their lives, their faces white as ghosts.

"Jesus Christ, Antonio!" Uncle Al managed through his huffs and puffs. "Some crazy old bastard tried to kill us!"

"Why would someone try and kill you if all you were doing was stretching your legs?" Antonio turned to the attendant and asked, "There's no law against that, is there?"

"We were just doin' some harmless cow tipping!" Uncle Al admitted.

"Honest, Antonio, that's all," Uncle Nunzio readily confirmed, as though cow tipping was the equivalent of skimming stones.

"Stu Larsen don't like no one tippin' his cows," the deadpan attendant made clear. "'Specially if it's troublemakers he suspects ain't from around here. Good thing he wasn't really aimin' for youse, 'cause he's a helluva shot. Won the shootin' contest at the county fair last spring, he did. If he were aimin' for youse, youse 'id be layin' back yonder and full of holes."

"Antonio, where are you going?" Uncle Al and Uncle Nunzio nervously asked.

"Both of you, get back in the car," he ordered.

Antonio's quiet, dispassionate tone caused Uncle Al and Uncle Nunzio to shudder. Turning to the attendant, he added sternly but without raising his voice, "If they as much as blink, I wanna know about it." He then turned back to Uncle Al and Uncle Nunzio, and with ominous severity, he said, "I'm gonna go and pay that farmer a visit. First, I'm gonna apologize. Then I'm gonna plead with him to shoot me. If he doesn't do as I ask, I'm gonna ask to borrow his rifle so I can do what he failed to do but should have."

That's the way it was for our poor grandfather, always pulling his brothers out of hot water, always having to go behind them and clean up their messes. There was a time in his life when he had to be responsible for three generations of Corellis, and if ever he begrudged it, he never let it show. Whenever I think of the letters *MVP*, it's never Mike Schmidt or Ryan Howard that first come to mind, but our grandfather, who, according to any Corelli and many folks from the old neighborhood, was the world's most valuable person.

"I'll bet Ma's working hard on them seven fishes," said Uncle Al, as they were entering Lackawanna County. Uncle Al wasn't necessarily concerned about how hard Mama Corelli was working to put together Christmas Eve dinner, nor was he anticipating the traditional seven fishes with any measure of delight. Instead, and rather transparently, he was attempting to break the silence that hung so heavily in the Dodge Sedan by drawing Antonio into a conversation that had nothing to do with rolling drunks, smuggling pigs from slaughterhouses, or the latest fiasco—cow tipping.

"I can't stand them sonofabitchin' smelts," complained Uncle Nunzio. "They should leave 'em in the ocean, where they belong." Uncle Nunzio may have a point; not everything in the sea was meant to be consumed by humans. And although smelts aren't nearly as awful as Uncle Nunzio makes them out to be, when have they ever appeared on a menu? I'm no stranger to dining out; between Philadelphia and New Jersey, I have dined in my share of gems. With that the case, I can state unequivocally that the one word that I have never heard uttered by a waiter or waitress rattling off the chef's specials was the word *smelts*. Pan-seared, almond-encrusted, Florentine with a white wine reduction or Fra Diavolo—no smelts of any kind!

"And what about baccala?" teased Uncle Al. Baccala was another of Uncle Nunzio's "favorites," not to mention a "favorite" of Uncle Al's.

"What's with all these goddamn fishes, anyway?" Uncle Nunzio threw a hand in the air, his face all twisted as if the fish and those who catch them were out to get him ... a conspiracy! "Why can't we have a nice lasagna and forget all these fish? *Everybody* likes lasagna: Krauts, Poles, Micks, Hebes; it ain't just us Degos, ya know. But not everybody likes *fish!*"

"The way I learned it," Antonio attempted to explain to his disgruntled youngest brother, "the seven fishes are supposed to be part of a vigil leading up to the midnight birth of Jesus."

"Yeah, well, whudda ya think Christ would rather eat, *smelts* or *lasagna?*" Our grandfather and Uncle Al had to admit, Uncle Nunzio's rather droll question gave them pause. And to add to his point, if given the choice between the two, who in their right mind would opt for smelts? Had Christ the opportunity to taste *our* mother's lasagna, He might have had a reservation or two about what ultimately took place at Calvary. "If He had any sense," Uncle Nunzio further protested, "He'd throw them goddamn smelts to the seagulls and ask for some lasagna with sausage and meatballs! Besides, what if Christ was born at noon instead of midnight? We'd be just like the Hebes, eatin' fish for breakfast! 'Yeah, sure, Ma, I'd love another cup of coffee with my *baccala*.' Can you just imagine!'"

When Uncle Nunzio finished with his diatribe, Uncle Al watched Antonio's mouth crease into a smile. He looked at his comical brother and covertly winked as if to say *mission accomplished*. But a moment later, a thoughtful Antonio raised a hand and spoke.

"It takes a lot of courage to come to another country, especially when you don't know the language or customs. But it makes it a little easier when you can hold on to some of your own traditions. I think the seven fishes have more to do with comfort and ... *femminile* than it does with Jesus's birth." (Antonio struggled to say the word *familiarity* in English.) He slowed the Dodge Sedan, then cast sincere eyes upon Uncle Al and Uncle Nunzio. "We could be back in Italy hiding out from the Cosa Nostra. Instead, we're in this nice car, driving home to see our parents. It's really not so terrible to have to eat smelts *or* baccala."

Our grandfather always raised a hand before delivering such monologues; it was his polite way of letting others know that he had something to add. Whenever he did this, the room would fall silent. He didn't demand this level of respect, though it was nevertheless granted—graciously handed over—and not just by us Corellis but by everyone. Antonio Corelli brought out the best in people. He was that kind of guy.

****

Mama Corelli oohed and ahhed when Antonio gave her the handmade silk sweater. Poppa Corelli was thrilled with the radio. But afterward, each took a turn scolding their sons for "spending *so* much money."

"Look, Mama," mocked Poppa Corelli in his heavily broken English, "we had no idea that all along, we were raising millionaires!"

"How lucky for us," added Mama Corelli.

"It's not a big deal, Pop," said Antonio. "Besides, you work hard and deserve some nice things."

At first, Poppa Corelli responded with an indecisive shrug. He didn't necessarily want to agree nor disagree with his son's assessment of how hard he worked and what he might deserve as a result. Afterward, he muttered something to the effect that, more often than not, life doesn't give us what we deserve but instead spits in our eye. Then in typical Italian fashion, he threw his hands in the air and rather jovially stated, "It's Christmas! Not a time to complain!"

"Come outside, Pop," urged Antonio. "There's something I wanna show you." Antonio led Poppa Corelli outside and showed off a recently cleaned and polished Dodge Sedan. Twice, he rapped his bare knuckles on the hood, a gesture to let Poppa Corelli know that life did more than lurk around corners with a mouthful of saliva intended for our eye.

"This is *some* machine, Antonio," said Poppa Corelli. "It must've cost a fortune!"

"Pop, don't worry so much about money," said Antonio. "You should start enjoying yourself. In case you hadn't noticed, you're hardly a kid anymore."

"You know, Antonio," Poppa Corelli began. His tone grew somewhat solemn; perhaps he became distracted by his age. "Mama—she misses you boys terribly. I never seen her work so hard to get ready for Christmas Eve dinner."

"I know, Pop," said Antonio. "I know how much Ma misses us. And believe me, not one crumb of her hard work will go to waste. We've been on the road all day, and we're hungry as bears." Antonio gave Poppa Corelli an affectionate pat on the shoulder followed by a wink and a smile. They were simple gestures but gave the message clearly: *it's all right, Pop, you and I don't have to get all sentimental. We can talk through Ma about how much we miss each other.*

"Look at the time!" said Poppa Corelli. "We better go and wash up for dinner."

"I'm right behind you, Pop," said Antonio.

Before they disappeared into the house, Poppa Corelli turned and glanced back at the shiny Dodge Sedan. The smile that formed on his face was a proud one. For an immigrant coal-mining family, ownership of an automobile was a true milestone.

"Hey, Ma, the smelts are delicious!" Antonio lauded, once everyone was assembled at the table and prayers were said. "It's the best they've ever come. What do you say, Nunz? Aren't they the best darn smelts you ever had?"

"Yeah, sure, Antonio." Uncle Nunzio concurred through clenched teeth as he set his narrowing eyes upon Antonio. "They're the best."

"And what about the baccala? I don't remember it tasting so good. What do you say, Al? Delicious, isn't it?"

"Sure thing, Antonio." Uncle Al's tall, slender form was shrinking in his seat. His shoulders became rounded, his face sallow while grudgingly he squeezed out the words, "It's … delicious." Both Uncle Al and Uncle Nunzio gingerly held their forks and prepared themselves for the revolting ick they were about to take into their mouths.

51

"Glad to hear it," said Antonio. Grinning victoriously, he reached for a serving spoon. "Before Pop and I finish it all up, I wanna make sure you two get second helpings. Don't wanna cheat youse none." He dumped a heaping serving spoonful of smelts onto Uncle Nunzio's plate, then shoveled the largest remaining piece of baccala onto Uncle Al's plate.

"Looks like our boys missed our home cooking," chirped Mama Corelli, before delivering a satisfied wink to Poppa Corelli, who was seated at the opposite end of the table.

"We sure did, Ma," said Antonio. "Isn't that right?" He gestured to Uncle Al and Uncle Nunzio, who were busy cringing and twisting in agony, to remind them of their manners. They snapped to attention and offered their agreement. Then Antonio winked at his drunk-rolling, pig-smuggling, cow-tipping brothers, and, with a smirk that was less appetizing than smelts and baccala, he wished them each a Merry Christmas. "As a matter of fact, Ma," Antonio went on to add, "just the other day, Al and Nunz were bragging to the whole block about your seven fishes. They couldn't stop talking about it; I thought we were gonna have to invite the whole neighborhood back to Scranton. Al, Nunz; what about it?" Poor Uncle Al and Uncle Nunzio. But you can't say they didn't have it coming to them.

"Antonio, where did you ever get such good tasting cheese?" asked Poppa Corelli. "I haven't tasted cheese like this in years!"

"I brought it off our cousin from Toscana," said Antonio.

"Our cousin? From Toscana?" Poppa Corelli, who was ordinarily soft of voice and doleful of expression, brightened and grew animated. "This is news to me. I didn't know we *had* any cousins from Toscana. I didn't realize we even *knew* anyone from Toscana."

Mama and Poppa Corelli looked quizzically, their eyes roving from son to son to son, who couldn't hold back any longer, having broken into a chorus of laughter. Afterward, Antonio told the story of their day in downtown Philadelphia, starting with all the splendor of the Market Street department stores, not forgetting to mention The Crystal Tea Room, the Wanamaker organ, and all five-thousand feathers of the Wanamaker eagle. Uncle Al chimed in, before giving way to the much more gregarious Uncle Nunzio. When Uncle Nunzio took the stage, he turned the story into a vaudeville act that encored with a comical mimic of Vito, the cheese vendor. And as the story goes, he really nailed it!

After all seven fishes were finally and, in some cases, regrettably consumed, Antonio took everyone for a ride in what Poppa Corelli called, "The machine."

"Here, Ma," said Uncle Al, "you can sit back here between Nunz and me. "It's where poor ol' Frank used to sit." Antonio swallowed nervously.

"Who's poor ol' Frank?" asked Poppa Corelli.

"Oh, he was just a friend from the neighborhood," Antonio alertly replied, before glaring at his idiot brother. "He died only a few weeks ago. It was very sad. Everyone from the neighborhood went to the funeral."

"How did he die?" asked Mama Corelli, who promptly made the sign of the cross on her head and chest on behalf of a poor soul whom she assumed her sons knew well and kindly befriended them upon their arrival in Philadelphia. After all, as Uncle Al had mentioned, they went for rides together in the Dodge Sedan. Meanwhile, the words *He was slaughtered, he was killed, he had a heart attack* reached Mama Corelli's ears all at once and in an indecipherable jumble. It was Antonio, naturally, who had called out *He had a heart attack* before glaring back at both his idiot brothers, in an effort to implore: *Could youse just keep your mouths shut and look out the damn windows!* Then, hurriedly, he repeated, "Or friend Frank had a heart attack."

In a much more composed manner, he added, "It was a massive heart attack. They said it was sudden and that he didn't feel any pain— thank God for that." One last time, Antonio glared back at his idiot brothers, then said, "Not all of us, when we leave this world, will be so fortunate."

After the ride, Poppa Corelli signaled for Uncle Al and Uncle Nunzio to go inside and help Mama Corelli set the table for dessert. Poppa Corelli and Antonio remained in the car. Poppa Corelli took hold of one of his oldest son's massive hands. "So, tell me, Antonio, how are things going for you down in Philadelphia?"

"Everything's fine, Pop," said Antonio. "Couldn't be better. So far city life has been treating me good."

"And your brothers?" asked Poppa Corelli. "They've been behaving themselves? You're able to manage all right with them?"

"Sure, Pop," Antonio lied. "They're no trouble. They're practically adults now. I've been managing just fine."

"Good to hear it, Antonio. I'm proud of you. It's not easy to leave your home and all the things that you're used to, even if those things weren't always so good. If I could teach you one thing, it would be to never get too used to things, because they're bound to change."

Antonio's senses were playing tricks on him. For a second, he thought he caught a whiff of Frank the pig emanating from the back seat. He began to wonder whether Poppa Corelli had caught it as well; but then it occurred to him that it might not be Frank at all, that lying on behalf of his dimwitted brothers was what summoned the imaginary smell. Nevertheless, he rolled down the window and deeply inhaled the freezing cold night air.

"You're warm, Antonio?" Poppa Corelli was curious how anyone could feel anything resembling warmth on such a frigid northern Pennsylvania night.

"Just a little," lied Antonio.

"Well, we should go inside, Antonio. Dessert is waiting for us."

"I'm right behind you, Pop." Antonio couldn't get out of the car fast enough.

Following dessert, and coffee so strong that it wouldn't permit a yawn, never mind sleep or a momentary nod, it was off to Midnight Mass. Along with smelts, Midnight Mass was another of Uncle Nunzio's favorites.

Mama Corelli was a devout Roman Catholic; she followed this most stringent of Christian doctrines the way Uncle Al and Uncle Nunzio followed the Yankees. She willingly and gladly surrendered to all the totalitarian rules put in place by theists who for centuries have managed to con the herd regarding God's intentions for man. With every fiber of her being, she believed in an Almighty Master of the Universe and that He (Whudda dad!) sent us His son to be bludgeoned to death for our sins. Therefore, attending Midnight Mass on Christmas Eve was *not* optional.

Following dessert, the Corelli men continued to drink coffee until supremely confident that they wouldn't nod off in church. Poppa Corelli wasn't nearly as devout as Mama Corelli, but he was a good sport in matters of the church. He figured, whoever was smart enough to compile all that went into the scriptures, gospels, and doctrines must have been right about a *few* things. However, his true religious convictions could be summed up with the simple phrase: *whatever makes Mama happy.* Poppa Corelli was one smart dude!

Our grandfather didn't waste time pondering such matters. If God existed, fine. If not, that was fine, too. He was a kind, caring man no matter, and adhering to a set of beliefs, whether religious based or the rudiments of quantum physics, would not have added or subtracted from the man he was. Conversely, Uncle Al ate fish on Fridays, or whatever else that the Vatican decided wasn't a sacrilege, and he wouldn't dare miss a Saturday afternoon Mass. Uncle Al touched on most of the basics, along with whatever else was expected of a twentieth-century man living in everyday American society, which has been known to distract those attempting any level of observation. However, as is often the case, Uncle Al's faith was born not out of love but for fear of the consequences should he not adhere or conform. In other words, it was perfectly acceptable to roll a drunk, make off with a slaughtered pig, and tip an occasional cow, but don't dare sneak a sliver of lunchmeat into Friday's sandwich. Rules are rules.

Then there was Uncle Nunzio, an atheist through and through, or so he proclaimed. Uncle Nunzio was a gambler; he liked to lay wagers: horse races, boxing matches, ballgames—it made no difference. His religion was *"the odds,"* and he was betting that there was no Almighty Master of the Universe, that instead, the world was one big free-for-all that paid you when you won and shat on you when you lost. On Fridays, he made a habit of devouring meat right in front of Uncle Al, then tease that when his time was up, Saint Peter would be waiting for him at the pearly gates dressed as a drill sergeant, equipped with a whistle and poised to make him hit the deck and complete ten thousand push-ups before granting his passage into heaven—boot camp purgatory for mockers and unbelievers. "And just to be a wise guy, I bet ol' Pete'll mock me by chompin' down on a goddamn ham sandwich while he's countin'; and just for spite, I bet he'll be eatin' that processed tavern ham, not the good stuff from Ninth Street, and it'll cause 'im to lose count." Uncle Nunzio may have had his fun with Uncle Al, but he didn't dare scoff or sneer at the obligatory Midnight Mass, which, incidentally, he continued attending years after Mama Corelli's death. Uncle Nunzio may not have had faith in an Almighty Master of the Universe, nor believed in anything as fanciful as Heaven, but he wholeheartedly believed in the posthumous wrath of Mama Corelli. Go figure.

After Mass, Mama Corelli changed into her night clothes and neatly folded her handmade silk sweater so that it could be worn the following day again at Christmas dinner.

"How beautiful is this sweater?" she beamed to Poppa Corelli. "And what thoughtful sons we raised."

"We should be very proud," said Poppa Corelli, as he watched Mama Corelli's hands busily tugging and smoothing over the fine fabric until it rested without a single wrinkle or lump. Antonio, who was standing just outside the doorway and was preparing to wish them a good night's sleep, smiled.

On the night of Christmas, in a private moment after dinner, Antonio made an offer: "Pop, why don't you take the day off tomorrow. I'll go in and work for you. You deserve a break."

"Nonsense, Antonio," said Poppa Corelli. "Mama's waited all these months to see you. You need to spend the day with *her*, not in a coal mine. I'll be home before you know it. Besides, Botticelli is coming to visit tomorrow. He's been asking me all week, 'Are you sure Antonio's coming for Christmas?' He'll be so disappointed if you're not here."

Nico Botticelli was one of the town elders and the man who taught our grandfather the game of chess. He would complain to Poppa Corelli that no one else in town was capable of giving him a decent game. "Only Antonio was a worthy opponent," he would say to Poppa. Our grandfather tried to teach Uncle Al and Uncle Nunzio the game, but both were too rambunctious to concentrate on the game's intricacies. Later he tried to teach his son, Freddy (our father), but he had no head for the game. Finally, he was able to teach chess to his eager-to-learn grandchildren. We all took to the game quickly. As for myself, I played competitively all through school; from third grade on up, I was in the chess club and always held a high rank. Ricky enjoyed a good game of chess but wasn't so serious-minded about the result. If he lost, he shrugged it off as easily as one would losing a hand of penny poker or a round of rock paper scissors. Then there was Munchk. Perhaps it was to compensate for her diminutive size, but no one competed more fiercely than Munchk, and chess, more than any other game, brought forth her ferocity. She would prefer to lose a tooth than her queen! I can tell you firsthand, when sitting across the table from Munchk, if ever you have the opportunity to utter the word *checkmate,* you had better utter it as though you were apologizing; otherwise she'll get that look—the one where her eyes narrow and her nose crinkles, and she appears as if poised to tear off your scrotum. That last thing you wanted to see was Munchk narrowing her eyes and crinkling her nose. Ricky and I called it the "scrotum look," and if you saw it, it was time to make yourself scarce. *Uh oh, Munchk has the scrotum look, better beat it!*

Antonio did as Poppa Corelli wished; he spent the day with Mama Corelli and managed two games of chess with Nico Botticelli. He and Mama Corelli were up bright and early to see off the old coal miner.

"When you get home, Pop, we'll go for another ride in the car," Antonio promised him.

"And what a fine machine it is!" Poppa Corelli lauded with pride.

Antonio would spend the remainder of his life wondering the outcome had he been more insistent that day and entered the mineshaft instead of Poppa Corelli. It is interesting how without the benefit of experience, we can know certain happenings when they occur. This innate sense is particularly true when coming face-to-face with such matters as falling in love, earthquakes, heart attacks ... mineshaft explosions? Immediately following the boom, the underground rumbled. The rumbling trailed toward the humble Corelli abode. A moment later, the house shook as did hundreds of other homes. This was followed by a moment of ominous quiet. Nico Botticelli's eyes, after he removed his glasses, traveled disquietingly from the chess board to the floor. Uncle Al and Uncle Nunzio made for the door and then outside; if the world was coming to an end, they wanted to see it for themselves. Slowly, but not so steadily, Mama Corelli sank into her chair. She made the sign of the cross on her head and chest. Grimly, she looked over at Antonio and whispered solemnly, "Poppa is with God."

The journey back to Philadelphia was long and quiet. Whatever lamenting that was done—and there was plenty—was done in silence. Antonio tried to imagine the world and how it might have changed had Poppa Corelli not overruled him. There was nothing to gain from pondering such matters, but he did arrive at an understanding. He would work his heart out and do everything in his power to hold together the family, not just for the sake of the present-day Corellis but for their future generations.

Chapter Four
Mothballs and Cicoria

Long before *The Eagle Has Landed*, Nixon visited China, and the Ayatollah took hostages, Mama Corelli came to Philadelphia ... to stay! I never met Mama; she died long before I was born. I know her only from the colorful stories told at holiday dinners and by the many photographs that were taken during her years in Philadelphia.

During her earliest days in Philly, Mama Corelli was paraded around to every tourist attraction the city had to offer, as well as to all of her sons' favorite places, including Lemon Hill, where she was photographed numerous times on different occasions. And whether in front of all five-thousand feathers of the Wannamaker Eagle or the Liberty Bell, Mama Corelli wore the same grim expression. In the earliest days upon her arriving in town, Mama was only forty-something, but she looked ancient. The black and white film used in the late 1930s, unless in the hands of Cecil B. DeMille and a Hollywood camera crew, wasn't particularly kind and was good for adding a few years ... or decades. Besides the film, other detractions dulled Mama Corelli's appearance. Most notably her stout shoes and shapeless housedress, which managed to turn up in every photo, along with a brown paper bag complexion that was dotted with lifeless features. She might as well have been holding up a sign that read: *Old immigrant woman in mourning.* Mama Corelli was more somber and tragic looking than a late Rembrandt.

Uncle Nunzio did every silly thing imaginable to provoke a smile from Mama Corelli but to no avail. When flipping through old photo albums, I find it hard to imagine that a smile ever creased from those thin and tightly frowning lips. At first, I wondered why my grandfather and great-uncles didn't leave Mama Corelli at home to grieve in solitude, which, judging from the photographs, was what she would have preferred. However, their generation, perhaps more than most, understood a thing or two of posterity.

Wherever the Corelli brothers went, so too went Mama. And wherever they happened to turn up, she was photographed a total of eight times: once with each son, in combinations of two, in the all-important group shot taken by an accommodating bystander, and lastly alone. In each photo, Mama Corelli appears so utterly dissimilar that, in effect but unwittingly, she lends a rather odd sense of drollness to the scene. Long before Flat Stanley and all the imitations that followed, there was the stout and grim looking Mama Corelli.

During Mama Corelli's years in Philly, our grandfather and great-uncles would often bicker over whose turn it was to take her to Fairmount Park. She was always demanding that one of her sons take there for the purpose of harvesting dandelion greens. Antonio tolerated dandelion greens. Uncle Al and Uncle Nunzio considered them a notch below dog food; dandelion greens stood alone, above smelts and baccala, on their list of most hated foods. Whenever it was one of their turns to drive Mama Corelli to the park, they would wait for her in the car; they didn't wish to be seen accompanying a crazy woman on her quest for what Uncle Nunzio called, "a bunch of friggin' weeds." Mama would set off into the park with her trusty pair of scissors and a bag, scouring the ground in search of a good harvest. *Cicoria* was what Mama called dandelion greens. I'm guessing, in Italian, *cicoria* means chicory—a word used to describe a variety of edible and in most instances bitter greens. Uncle Al and Uncle Nunzio didn't care for the way cicoria smelled when it was cooking. As soon as the aroma began filling the house, off they'd go.

"I'd rather run behind a bus than smell that garbage cooking," Uncle Nunzio complained while all were gathered for our grandfather's surprise sixtieth birthday party. "And then to add insult to injury, we had to look at it on our plates, and it touched our other food, and then we'd have to eat it so Ma wouldn't get her feelings hurt."

"It was too damn bitter," said Uncle Al.

"Bitterness I could handle," said Uncle Nunzio. "It was the smell that was awful; I think it gave us brain damage!"

"That would explain a lot," I whispered to Ricky.

"Ma was one of them Italian women from the other side, who could feed an army on a nickel," Uncle Nunzio went on. "Set her loose in a park and she'll come home with a friggin' antipasto!"

"Ain't that the truth," said Uncle Al. "If it came out of the ground, to Ma, it was food."

"And I'll never forget the first time I saw her with that net," said Uncle Nunzio. "You remember the net, don't cha, Al? All those years, we believed we were eatin' sardines when all along Ma was snatching minnows from the creek!"

"It didn't hurt us none, though," said Uncle Al. "At least none that I can tell."

"Is he fucking kidding me?" I whispered to Ricky.

"Really," was Ricky's whispered return. "Those minnows are probably still lodged in his brain; he just doesn't know it. By now someone shoulda told him."

"Didn't hurt youse none?" our father, with incredulity, chimed in. "Hurts me just thinkin' about it." His face contorted in a manner that reminded Ricky and me of Munchk's famous scrotum look, mixed was a dash of disgust, when imagining minnows and dandelion greens together in his mouth.

"You'll never know all that goes into this gravy," our mother called out from the kitchen. The whole house fell silent when we realized that it was our mother's voice that had risen above the din. Our mother made gravy with a focus similar to that of the sentinels who guard the tomb of the unknown soldier. That she, for whatever reason, elected to join in the fray was a phenomenon of an unparalleled nature.

"Mary-nooch!" Uncle Nunzio cried out. *Mary-nooch* was Uncle Nunzio's pet name for our mother. "I been waitin' all friggin' week for your gravy! Countin' the days! Don't tell me anything I don't wanna know!"

Every time I reach for a bottle of Ortho Weed Be Gone and aim it at those pesky dandelions that manage to find their way onto my lawn each spring, I imagine poor Mama Corelli turning in her grave. *That's food that you're destroying!* she is no doubt shouting from the other side. When I was a child, one day after I picked several dandelion blooms for our mother, the greasy bald-headed Mr. Profacci told me that dandelions grow from cat piss. "Why do you think they're yellow, Corelli? Don't you know anything?" the fat prick said as his flabby face formed a scowl. And here I thought that I was bringing our mother a bouquet of bright yellow flowers. No sooner I heard Mr. Profacci bark out the words "cat piss," I dropped those dandelion blooms right where I stood. The stout man, who had appointed himself block captain, let out a hearty laugh, his hairy udders shaking vigorously as I wiped my hands on my frayed dungarees. The nonsense that we are told as children seems to stay with us forever.

Now that I know better and have also long since left behind the influence of Mr. Profacci, instead of reaching for that trusty bottle of weed killer, I'm going to venture out onto my lawn with a pair of scissors and a bag. The neighbors, as is their right, will gather and whisper, "What a shame for his wife and son that Francis has flipped his lid—and so young!" Later, my wife will follow with some cheesy *Uncle Al* reference. Despite the ridicule, out onto the lawn I shall venture. Rest in peace, Mama Corelli.

Mama Corelli died shortly after our father turned five. He has memories of Mama; few are vivid and most are vague. Like his own children, Freddy Corelli mainly knows Mama through old photographs and stories told at family gatherings and holiday dinners. However, his most lasting memory was not one that was planted in his head. It is said, of all our senses, it's our smell that has the longest memory, and every so often, Freddy Corelli gets an imaginary whiff of that rare and earthy combination of cooked greens, espresso coffee, and mothballs. Perhaps the smell that these seemingly unrelated entities can produce was typical in households where entrenched was a first-generation Mediterranean immigrant. But this is only a guess on my part.

Mama Corelli, as the story goes, was neurotic with her usage of mothballs; handfuls could be found in closets, drawers, *and*, for good measure, in the corners of every room throughout the house, including the cellar. The mothballs failed to neutralize the cicoria, the smell of which, as Uncle Al and Uncle Nunzio would later attest, permanently seeped into the woodwork and the area rugs that accented each room. Instead, along with the frequently brewed espresso coffee, the mothballs helped to produce an unusually pungent and earthy smell that our father has not smelled since the early days of his childhood, save for his imagination.

So, there you have it: Mama Corelli, armed with mothballs and all her other peculiar customs and quirks, invaded Philadelphia, where, along with her three sons, she lived at Twenty-sixth and Indiana in a neighborhood dubbed Swampoodle.

Swampoodle was once a cozy neighborhood nestled between Lehigh Avenue and the more upscale Strawberry Mansion and ranged between Seventeenth and Twenty-seventh Streets. It was dotted with stately old trees that in earlier times stood in what later became known as Fairmount Park. "From where we lived, you could walk to Shibe Park (Connie Mack Stadium)," Uncle Al and Uncle Nunzio used to boast. None of my living relatives with attachments to the old neighborhood know the reason for the odd name Swampoodle. Who knows the origins of such matters; for instance, how a neighborhood gets its nickname? Some things always were and were never questioned. Swamps are places where ill-fated men of bad character end up because of the handiwork of those of worse character. But there are no swamps in Swampoodle, and in the 1930s, folks were concerned about putting food in their own bellies, so dogs were also scarce. But one matter rang true; Swampoodle, as its name might suggest, had its share of flavor and colorful characters. For that reason, Mama Corelli, despite being an oddity and curiosity providing fodder for conversation, fit right in. Mama was just another thread within the framework of what was one of Philly's more original tapestries.

The children next door, two young boys, whose names no one can seem to remember, were terrified of Mama Corelli. "Your grandfather was friendly with those boys; *he* would remember their names," our father told me. That was all well and good, except that it was 2010 when I asked, and whatever our grandfather may or may not have remembered was fairly irrelevant. Wherever "he" happened to be by 2010, no one would dare go to pick cicoria. But thanks just the same, Dad. As always, you were a big help. It must have been Mama's tight, rigid lips that disappeared into her mouth as she aged, and which gave one the impression that she wore a permanent scowl that was the source of the boys' dread. Also, whenever Mama hung laundry in the backyard, she had the habit of yelling in Italian to whomever was in the kitchen. The quick, loud syllables gave the young boys the impression that she was angry. Whenever Mama Corelli appeared, they would gather up their toys and make a mad dash for the kitchen.

"Ma, why don't you speak English around the children?" suggested Antonio. "Maybe offer them some candy? Children love candy; you should see them at Halloween, the way they line the streets."

"Forget the candy," said Uncle Nunzio. "Invite 'em in for cicoria. You can give 'em my share. Al's, too."

"Poor little bastards 'ill have nightmares," said Uncle Al. "They'll wet the bed!" Whereas smelts and baccala were part of a once-a-year ensemble of sea creatures served every Christmas Eve, cicoria was a Mama Corelli culinary staple that was contended with on a once per week basis.

On the contrary to how Mama was perceived by the boys next door, all the children of Swampoodle idolized Antonio and called him "Uncle Tony." Whenever Antonio Corelli was spotted in the neighborhood, children were flocked around him. With interest, he would listen to their school tales, the goings on in the neighborhood, and especially to all the heroics that took place on little league baseball diamonds. All my life, I have envisioned a tall man with broad, burly shoulders, long arms, and enormously powerful hands walking down Twenty-sixth Street surrounded by a group of young boys frothing over with enthusiasm and all chirping away at once. The ability to talk to children isn't a gift but a matter of desire. Some possess it; some don't, and we are fooling ourselves when we subscribe to the theory that children are unable to know the difference. I believe that the finest qualities a man could own are kindness and the ability to listen to children. Both could be said of Antonio Corelli.

****

Skullhead, Stranger, Turd, Patty One Eye, Meat, Crazy Legs (the poor bastard's one leg was so much shorter than the other, when he tried to run he looked part revolving door/part pogo stick), Moose (every neighborhood has one) and Sixty-four, along with Mama Corelli, were some of the more colorful characters loose in Swampoodle. How some of the names came about are self-explanatory—particularly Meat, who used to boast that "size truly does matter," so we need not delve into the obvious. But Sixty-four? If you weren't aware, *Sixty-four* was a real headscratcher. Legend had it that Bobby Salino—or Sixty-four, as he was called back in the day—charmer that he was, kept careful score with his girlfriends, and he and Gina Rizzo made it to the aforementioned lofty number before he opted out. Poor Gina; had she been born six decades later and a Millennial, she could have given Bobby Salino the ol' heave-ho and kept the nickname for herself. Gina Sixty-four and damn proud of it!

Swampoodle's true legends, though, were Nails and Vincent Bronini. Nails, as the nickname would suggest, was as tough as nails—no one in the neighborhood would dare fool with him. Except for Antonio, who refused to go out of his way—he held neither fear nor reverence for the neighborhood's shadier characters—everyone feared Nails. If you lived in Swampoodle, the last five words that you wanted to hear were: *Nails is looking for you.* If you were someone unfortunate enough to have had those five dreaded words reach your ears, it was prudent that you went and found Nails before he found you. And make no mistake, he *would* find you—it was a small neighborhood, and there were no rocks to hide under. The longer Nails had to look, the angrier he was gonna be, and no one wanted to contend with an angry Nails. The results, from what I was told, were always unfortunate.

Nails grew up a Mafioso wannabe but ended up only a small-time racketeer who controlled most of the gambling action in Swampoodle and other surrounding neighborhoods. Antonio grew up listening to Poppa Corelli recount all the horror stories of the Cosa Nostra in Italy; so, he despised the fact that *it* or the *mafia* or the *whatever* successfully entrenched itself in America and served to shape the opinion others had of Italian Americans unfavorably. It mattered not to Antonio that Nails was "small time;" he didn't care for the sector of society that Nails represented. Nevertheless, he did not speak disparagingly of Nails but warned Uncle Al and Uncle Nunzio to be wary of Nails and not have dealings with him— particularly Uncle Nunzio, who liked to lay wagers. Antonio and Nails met only in passing, and when they did, each gave one another a cordial nod or tip of the hat before moving on.

When it came to Swampoodle's characters of dubious nature, Vincent Bronini was legendary; long before adulthood, he had lapped the other racers. Poor Sister Mary Veronica; she panicked at the end of fire prevention week when Vinny torched the contents in his desk. The fire escalated. It was Gina Rizzo's brother, Sal, upon realizing Sister Mary Veronica was frozen with fear, who pulled the alarm. Next, the schoolyard filled with the student body of St. Mary's, and a siren was heard blazing its way through the neighborhood. Carmine Fumo would learn the hard way that reckless and stupid are a dangerous combination when Vinny stumbled onto the keys to his "old man's" roadster and helped himself to a joyride, which resulted in him plowing through the front window of Fumo's Pool Hall. This was a stunt that had the neighborhood buzzing for days, and Nails was especially livid because the poolroom doubled as his hangout. In fact, the poolroom doubled as a hangout for many of Swampoodle's shadier characters, among them Uncle Al and Uncle Nunzio, although they were stupid, not shady. It was said that Carmine Fumo's screams could be heard as far away as the Schuylkill River. After berating Vinny in both English *and* Italian, Carmine marched him home by the lobe of his ear, twisting it and dragging him as he went along.

Like some Italian men named Vinny, Vincent Bronini's first name was shortened to Jim—it's what his closest friends called him. It seems a stretch, but so too is Margaret to Peggy and William to Bill. I once knew a Kevin who was called Barry. Evidently, the nickname for Vincenzo is Cenz. Pronounced in Italian, Cenz sounds like James, and that's how we arrive at Jim. Eventually, Vinny's surname was also shortened to Broni. *Yo Broni!* If a surname exceeded one syllable, it was doomed for a haircut and not necessarily one that was flattering. Even if you have a cool sounding name, someone would come along and screw it up, and then you were stuck with the distortion until you went off to college, joined the army, or, if you're a neighborhood lifer, died. Vincent Bronini's, a.k.a. Jim Broni's, legend grew to where his name became symbolic for all things asinine and prodigiously foolhardy. Eventually, his name was condensed into one word: Jimbroni. In Swampoodle, to be called a Jimbroni was the worst of insults, far surpassing asshole, shit-for-brains, dumb cluck fuck, etc...

"*You see that guy over there? I heard he's a real Jimbroni.*"

"*What a Jimbroni!*"

"*Jesus Christ, I married a Jimbroni!*"

It's true the old adage *birds of a feather flock together.* It was only a matter of time before Vinny found his way to Uncle Al and Uncle Nunzio, or they to him. Either way, for better or for worse, this alliance of haphazardness was destined to become part of the colorful fabric of Swampoodle.

Chapter Five
Love at First Reach

Nowadays Ricky resides in Arizona with his second wife, Judy. He and his first wife, Melanie, were married just long enough for a cup of coffee to cool, then it was splitsville. Ricky and Judy live with their daughter, Sara, and five-year-old grandson, T.J. T.J. Corelli. Kinda has a ring to it, and not a bad looking little fella either. Unfortunately, T.J.'s father, for whom T.J. is named, is currently serving a prison term on the charge of several counts of insurance fraud. This explains why T.J. bears the surname Corelli and not Stubbs. Sara didn't wish for her then infant son to go through life carrying the same name as his convicted felon father. Sara, to erase the stigma, also had her name changed from Stubbs back to Corelli. Besides, Sara Corelli sounds like a sexy pop artist no stranger to making hit records, whereas Sara Stubbs is a likely reminder of the fat girl no one wanted to sit next to in sixth grade. The result of her failed marriage saw Sara sell her house, which alone and with her soon-to-be ex-husband in prison she could not afford, and she and T.J. moved back home.

With Ricky away on business, which was often the case in those days, Thomas Jonathon Stubbs persuaded Judy—who was in the midst of a spell that left her weakened and compromised from the MS that she was diagnosed with back in 1999—in 2006, to sign documentation that left her liable for a portion of her son-in-law's insurance chicanery. Then one night, Sara calls, hysterical because the police came and carted off her husband in handcuffs. Judy, making every effort to calm Sara, heard the doorbell ring. With Sara rambling incoherently in her ear and T. J. crying in the background, Judy, in pajamas, hobbled to the front door where awaiting her were two policemen, handcuffs, and an arrest warrant.

"Sara, perhaps you should go to the police station," Judy Corelli, with as much calm as she could summon, had advised. "But before you leave, you may wanna make an effort to reach your father." As Judy was read her rights, she muttered with disdain, "This is a real Uncle Al situation." Both policemen gave her the queerest look, but Judy was in no mood to offer an explanation. Instead, she drolly added, "If I'm not behind bars, I'm sure to be a hit this Thanksgiving."

Judy was released from prison. Thomas Jonathon Stubbs remained. Occasionally, Ricky would grumble to Sara that she married a Jimbroni—a cunning Jimbroni but a Jimbroni nonetheless.

Ricky believed that the dry Arizona climate would be kinder on Judy's condition than the cold and often humid northeast corridor of the United States; though unlike its hosts, MS doesn't vacation, nor does it cooperate with such trivialities as climate change. In other words, it travels well. Thankfully, as of late, Judy has been enjoying a good stretch and is more like herself. T.J. is getting ready for school and Sara, since washing her hands of one Mr. Stubbs, is once again looking for love.

While we're on the subject of Arizona, Ricky moved to that southwest desert of a state back in 2001, the very year the Diamondbacks managed to wrestle the Series away from the Yankees, who were an inning away from another title. After Soriano homered off Schilling in the top of the eight, I was sure that Jeter and Mariano and company were destined for another title and that they would keep winning them and that I would remain bent at the waist, a helpless victim, as Uncle Al and Uncle Nunzio continued ramming Yankee success up my ass. But Mariano blew a rare save and the Yankees lost. I should have been up and twirling around my living room, rejoicing that tomorrow I could say to Uncle Al and Uncle Nunzio that the Yankees let one get away, snatched defeat from the jaws of victory, and choked! Instead, I sagged in my recliner just as miserable as if "The Bombers" had won their 27th title. Why? The Diamondbacks were in existence only four lousy years. My beloved Phillies have been kicking around since the Roman Empire, or so it seemed. Can you see where I'm going with this? Four years versus a millennium and as of 2001, the same number of titles!

And to make matters worse, one of the heroes of the 2001 Series was Curt Schilling—a former Philly! If that isn't adding insult to injury, tell me what is! There was no positive aspect in this Yankee loss; it allowed an expansion team ownership of as many titles as the Phillies. The '01 Series may have been a thriller, among the most exciting all-time, but for me, it was a lose/lose proposition. What a surprise.

Despite all the drama in Arizona, Ricky never missed nor would he consider missing Munchk's birthday. More than any holiday or anniversary, Munchk's birthday reigns supreme. It's the first day circled on the new calendar; and whether in Arizona or buried under an avalanche somewhere in the Arctic Circle, there is no such thing as a valid reason for not being available on April 19th.

For me, April 19th means it's off to Philly International to collect Ricky. I wait on the shoulder of the ramp that leads to the arrival gates because quite frankly, I'm too much a cheapskate to pay for parking. Often, I've been permitted to remain there until Ricky calls. Once, a policeman came and shooed me along. I had to wind my way through the airport, back out onto I95 South and again locate the ramp leading to arrivals. Yes, it was a hassle, but a worthwhile hassle if I can dodge a parking fee. I'm a good sport about most things; I don't mind owning, insuring, and occasionally repairing an automobile; just don't ask me to pay to leave it somewhere. It's not a hotel, there are no amenities, it's only open space. As far as I'm concerned, it's no different than air, and the same rules should apply. Naturally, my wife does not agree and reminds me. "*Francis*, you're wasting more in gas than it would cost us to park, never mind our time and the wear and tear on the car." She's right, of course; but how is a man to stand on principles if he must concern himself with logic? Can you answer me that?

Ricky and I usually spend the ride to the cemetery complaining about the Phillies and their customary poor start, and today was no different on both counts. The Phillies were off to a poor start and we were grumbling about it.

"When will they realize that, when all is said and done, the games in April matter just as much as the games in September? One hundred and ten years, and it's the same bullshit!" This was Ricky's annual gripe. I gave him an *I know what you mean* shrug but could offer no rational explanation for this yearly debacle, other than to say, "Baseball teams are no different than people; some of us like the challenge of climbing out of a hole. Look at us." Of course, this was a ballclub that's been kicking around since Grover Cleveland was president and has lost the most games in history. When you dig a hole, it's liable to be a doozy and can take the better part of a decade to crawl out of; just ask Uncle Al and Uncle Nunzio.

Once we reach the cemetery, everything stays behind: friends who borrow money, irksome coworkers, wives who make light of our pet peeves but reserve the right to have their own … ballclubs that thoughtlessly abuse our passion? And dare not mention how hard we work or how underappreciated we, at times, feel. Once through the gate and winding along a sea of crafted stonework, it's all about Munchk. We talk of the good times and of the fun we shared as youngsters. We talk, too, of how we infuriated one another and later laughed about it. As time moved on—as Ricky and I put more distance between ourselves and our childhood—it was the pranks, ultimately, that became the most endearing. I can recall clearly how Munchk's lips and nose crinkled and her eyes narrowed when we angered her. The dreaded "scrotum" look. No sooner had it formed, we knew an imaginative reprisal was in store.

"Uh, oh," Ricky uttered with fear, "I think we done pushed the evil munchkin too far. Did you see that look? It was the scrotum look!"

"We always seem to push her too far," I said. "I think Munchk is getting more sensitive in her old age. Either that or she's starting puberty, and now everything gets her pissed."

We spent the remainder of the day tiptoeing about for fear of setting off an elaborate and well-concealed booby-trap; but the imaginative reprisal wasn't realized until the following day at the school cafeteria, when we bit into our sandwiches, only to discover that the mayonnaise we expected to complement the ham and cheese had been scraped off and rather liberally substituted with toothpaste. I was sitting across from Ricky when I took my first bite. Therefore, there was no need to guess the level of astonishment that registered on my own face. In looking at Ricky, I may as well have been looking in the mirror.

I always imagine Munchk's eyes popping open at dawn, long before anyone else in the household was prepared to begin their day. Without making a sound, with pajamas and droopy eyes, she creeps across the hall to the bathroom and opens the medicine cabinet, or, better yet, as Munchk was efficient, she had taken the tube of toothpaste to bed with her that night. She may even have taken the trouble of looking in on her two poor, unsuspecting brothers before tiptoeing down the stairs. No doubt she quietly muttered to herself at the kitchen counter, while busy sabotaging our sandwiches, "This'll fix those two fuckers. We'll see who's the *gnarly little runt who should've been tossed out the window on the way home from the hospital.*"

Sometimes we laugh about it. Other times, we cry. In the end, we ponder a simple question: Why? Then we allow our eyes to travel the paths and rambling slopes of the cemetery in search of others who are standing in front of headstones—others who, sometime before leaving, may wonder the same regarding loved ones who were taken too soon.

Before leaving, we stroll the cemetery and look at dates chiseled into headstones. We are in search of others whose time on Earth was equally short as Lizzy Corelli's. We're perfectly aware of how morbid an exercise this is; though, in a sense, it enables us to depart with the assurance that Munchk has company, as, in turn, do we. There does exist a sense of comfort, albeit an unusual one, that there are others Munchk's own age with whom she could share the promise of eternity, and that there are also others like us, who have had no choice but to remain and are grieving for a similar reason. At my current age, I have had the opportunity to make several trips to various cemeteries, but it's only for Munchk that I am still striving for perspective *and* answers.

It's strange; while Munchk didn't live long enough to rail over either Gulf War, access the internet, lose her mind over Spy Gate, never mind ride shotgun in a car equipped with airbags, in many respects she seems as current as the latest technology—the latest headline (Obama Supports Gay Marriage). As I've aged and have gone along in my life and times, I've tried to imagine the woman that she could have become had fate afforded her the same opportunity as her siblings. Today was, or would have been, her forty-fifth birthday. For me, Elizabeth Corelli has become quite the ripe old sage with whom I often confer. She has been a close friend and confidant throughout my adult life. Though how I miss the dynamism that used to spring from that little body, along with the scathing wit and humor that was repeatedly launched in my direction and often struck me with the force of a sledgehammer.

"Mom and Dad knew right off the bat that you'd turn out to be a dumb bastard, Frank; that's why they named you after a dead pig that Uncle Al and Uncle Nunzio buried out in Fairmount Park!" Yessiree, Munchk kept her blade especially sharp for yours truly. Often, I wanted to strangle her. Nowadays, anyone wanting to know for whom I was named, I tell them straightforward: "I'm named after a pig that was smuggled from an Aramingo Avenue slaughterhouse and later buried out in Fairmount Park in 1938. The burial plot is on the grounds of Mount Pleasant—a mansion once owned by the infamous traitor Benedict Arnold." Although irrelevant, I enjoy tossing in that tidbit of history. You could well imagine the curious looks that I have received over the years. Uncle Al and Uncle Nunzio begged ol' Mary and Freddy Corelli to name their first son Frank. It seemed a reasonable request, and so they honored it. But my mother (not my father) had the good sense to draw the line at Frank. Although in the afterglow of delivering her first child, Mary

Corelli still had enough wits not to get talked into Crosetti for my middle name. Frank Crosetti Corelli, named after a smuggled pig that was named after a Yankee shortstop.

After the cemetery, Ricky and I head on over to the home of our childhood for our favorite: lasagna. Upon our arrival, ol' Freddy and Mary pretend not to know what day it is or why Ricky happens to be in town. Good sons that we are, we grant them their charade. Years ago, on what would have been Munchk's twelfth birthday, we pleaded with our parents to take us to the cemetery. We weren't sure what to expect or how we would feel when there. Nevertheless, and not without a great deal of reluctance—largely on the part of our mother—they broke down and complied with our wish.

"No matter how *we* feel, it's their right to go," I heard Dad softly say to Mom moments after Ricky and I were dismissed so they could deliberate in private. We couldn't hear what else transpired but assumed either Dad was very persuasive or Mom was too broken to argue.

Along with growing solemnity, all four of us—not that there was much chatter to begin with—fell silent once the cemetery came into view; not even a nervous sigh was heard. We continued in somber quietude, approaching with trepidation, wondering who would stand and who would wilt, until gathered in front of Munchk's headstone. In death, even when it's a child, there is a change in status. The departed become loftier, endowed with wisdom, for they have gained the other side and have been shown the mysteries of the universe. My kid sister was in the ground; yet she towered over me. I felt diminished in the presence of her cold stone, this monument to her too-short life, and etched in that stone were the jarring words: Elizabeth Mary Corelli … it was official, she was dead. None of us seemed anxious for words, felt compelled to speak, or knew for sure whether words during such an occasion as standing at the final resting place of the youngest one in a family would be tolerated. No one wished to be the source of interruption during another's time of ponderous reflection. The weightiness of the moment grew and seemed to separate us; each of us, despite our proximity, was on his and her own island. It was Ricky who brought us back into balance. He broke the weighty silence when he wondered aloud, "Can Munchk still be our sister?"

It was an unusual question that Ricky posed, a peculiar choice of words. Not *is* Munchk still our sister, but *can* she still be. The dead have no known facility; relationships are a two-way street. A widow can remarry; a dead wife can no longer be a wife. Are the rules different for siblings?

71

"Of course," Mom had answered in a typical motherly fashion. "Lizzy will always be your sister."

It was a comforting and predictable reply and one that could have been resting on the lips of anyone: a friend, relative, associate, or anyone who happened to be passing by; it was a stock answer to a question that was asking much more than its mere words were suggesting. Therefore, when I looked over at Ricky, I saw not sadness or anything resembling reassurance. Instead, what registered was discontent. It didn't occur to me until much later that Ricky was not in search of solace; moreover, his question was far more existential than Mary Corelli, who was burdened with emotional stress bordering on the unbearable, understood it to be. At the time, had I been more astute, I might have said to Ricky, "If a tree falls in the forest, no matter where you are in relation, it does, in fact, make a sound." Munchk, the ultimate quantifier! How can anything so universally common and natural as death keep one so utterly dynamic from being our sister? The answer: it cannot.

I suppose Mom's words, at face value, were perfectly suitable but in context, they were philosophically lacking. However, especially in those days, no one ever accused Mary Corelli of being a philosopher. Getting to the crux of a matter by way of interpreting subtext was not her strong suit. *Can* Munchk still be our sister? Looking back on that day, solving the mysteries of the physical and spiritual world probably wasn't something that should have been asked of a grief-stricken mother, less having expected a satisfactory reply. Nowadays, as a parent myself, when I look back at the four of us gathered at Munchk's grave, I realize that our mother's sorrow was immeasurable, her wound far greater than ours. Even after all these years, decades, there remains a vestige of grief indelibly etched on her face. For those who knew her back when, that vestige is especially apparent.

Before we made our departure, Mom crumbled to the ground. Her face pressed to the stone; she traced her fingertips over the newly engraved words *Elizabeth Mary Corelli*. Through the depths of unimaginable sorrow, she seemed to communicate with Munchk. Afterward, Dad helped her to her feet, and the four of us hobbled to the car. We departed with the same somber silence as we arrived.

The next year, Dad chauffeured Ricky and me to the cemetery. Mom stayed behind. The following year and the year after that, it was the same. For Mom's sake, we would pretend we were going to a ballgame or to a movie we were confident she would hate. It didn't matter whether the Padres, Giants, or Astros were in town; Dad would tell Mom, "Carlton's pitching against Seaver. I'm gonna take the boys to the game." Tom Seaver, who by then was a Red, was toeing the rubber in Pittsburgh; but Mom never challenged us, never went fact-checking behind our backs; and when Dad used the movie lie, it was always some idiotic car crash comedy that we were seeing and that he would "spare" Mom the "agony" by taking us himself. "I'm taking one for the team," he'd tell her. But it never mattered; on April 19th, Mom made certain she was too busy to come along. She would pretend not to know the date and at dawn had all her ingredients and pots and pans lined up—she would remain pinned to the stove making gallons of gravy. Come my eighteenth birthday, I had scraped together enough cash and brought myself a clunker—a real Uncle Al classic. It was no longer necessary to include Dad. From that year forward, only Ricky and I went to the cemetery.

"Mom, I see you haven't lost your touch." Ricky swooned, his words garbled after eagerly shoveling the first forkful of lasagna into his watering mouth.

"First there's perfection," Dad proclaimed, as though perfection was a commonplace result attainable by anyone owning a salt shaker. "Then, there's your mother's lasagna!"

"Well put, Dad. Who could disagree?" Then I reminded Ricky, "You can't get lasagna like this in Arizona." Mom, humbly and modestly, accepted our compliments. Then the four of us ate in peace without anyone mentioning that it was April 19th.

Since Munchk's death, Mary Corelli's combative nature hasn't merely subsided; it has whittled away to nothing. No longer does she live for confrontation. Nowadays, she could be described as soft-spoken, docile, and gentle as a lamb. Surprisingly, ol' Freddy Corelli has become the guardian and gatekeeper of the marriage. To suggest that he lives for confrontation would be a stretch, but occasionally, I have seen genuine flashes of hostility. Every marriage needs juice and fire, whether it springs forth from a set of well-measured middle-aged testicles or a crazy woman with a bleeding vagina. However, women who demonstrate spunk are always given credit for "wearing the pants" or owning "brass ones," and back in the day, Mary Corelli was notorious for having had the biggest and boldest set of testicles in the neighborhood. Meanwhile, Dad's timid jewels stayed hidden away, safe behind the line of fire; but, since Munchk, he has found himself pressed into action. *Put me in, coach!*

Not only did this role reversal seem odd, but it came as a shock; it sure took Ricky and me by surprise. Only two matters have remained consistent throughout this unlikeliest of transformations: Mom continues to be an excellent cook, and Dad, with catastrophic results, still tinkers with the plumbing, though it's been told to us that the catastrophes, no thanks to proficiency, are fewer and far in-between. If not for those two cornerstones, it would be difficult to tell them apart, never mind that they have long since reached that point when couples begin to look alike. It's strange how, over time, this metamorphosis transpires. What's more, you don't notice it happening until the process is complete. Then one day you walk into the room and realize your parents look more like siblings than a couple. I hear the same is true with pets, though I can't imagine that one day I'll resemble a ten-pound Maltese. Then again, with ten more years of *Francis* reverberating in my ears, who knows what the hell I'll end up looking like.

Going home has become a bittersweet affair. I can remember when this old house contained more clamor and excitement than walls were made to withstand. Our house was the heartbeat of the entire Corelli Clan. Everything happened at Mary and Freddy's place: birthday parties, holiday celebrations, graduation parties, and Sunday dinners. Now, it's quiet, undisturbed, and devoid of the spirit to which it had once grown accustomed—a real empty nester, featuring a TV watcher and reader. How I wish, like an avalanche, these walls could release the hilarity and riot they have stored up and have selfishly held onto for the past several decades. What a thrill it would be to once again hear all the excitement and buzzing we used to make, just like on the day of our grandfather's surprise sixtieth birthday party.

"Whoa, whoa, whoa," I heard Dad holler to Uncle Al's twin grandsons, Anthony and Michael. In a state of terror, the two tikes went tearing into the kitchen, nearly crashing into Mom's legs. Mom was busy at the stove. In other words, she had on her game face. In retrospect, Mom reminded us of Andy Pettitte on the mound, with his famous behind-the-glove glare. "You know," Dad added, when addressing the frightened youngsters, "we only have one rule in this house, so listen carefully. No one can disturb Aunt Mary when she's at the stove." Then he slowly ran his index finger across his neck to demonstrate what would happen should anyone crash into Aunt Mary's legs.

"They got scared, Dad," I told him.

"Aw, what's the matter?" Dad dropped the warning tone in favor of soothing the frightened pair.

"It's just Uncle Nunzio, Dad," I answered for my frightened young cousins. "He's up to his old tricks. He set his chest hair on fire, and little Mikey and Anthony got terrorized."

"Is that all?" Dad forced a jovial belly laugh, then hugged the terrorized youngsters and added: "Your Great-uncle Nunzio, he didn't mean to scare youse none. He does that for all the new kids in the family, and he wanted to make sure you two didn't get cheated. I hear you two are his favorites!"

That's some hell of an initiation—a crazy old uncle setting his chest hair on fire. I can remember it just like it was yesterday; Ricky and I, like Anthony and Michael, went tearing from the living room and tumbled into the kitchen, having just missed Mom's legs. Afterward, we spent most of the day hiding out in the kitchen. Occasionally, we would venture into the dining room and peek through the archway at the lively scene of Italian arms waving about in the living room. When Uncle Nunzio noticed us, he would make a funny face, and we'd go scampering back into the kitchen. After several attempts, we worked up enough nerve to venture back to the living room, where most of the family was gathered. Not Munchk. Tiny as she was, Munchk wasn't afraid of anything. After witnessing Uncle Nunzio's pyrotechnics and listening to the crackling sound that singed hair made, she took the book of matches from Uncle Nunzio's hand and tried to set more of his chest hair on fire. Everyone was so taken aback, so utterly bemused by Munchk's boldness, that all they could do was sit back and mindlessly watch a two-year-old attempt to strike a match.

Doubtless many families come equipped with nutty old uncles who insist upon providing their kin with their unique brand of entertainment while gathered for an occasion. Card tricks, cheesy magic tricks, along with retelling the same old jokes and stories are among the usual suspects. But setting one's own chest hair on fire? That's original! Absurd, but original. However, I would be remiss if not pointing out that Uncle Nunzio, like Mr. Profacci, had an abundance of chest hair; between the neck and waist he hardly looked human—ten hairs shy of a primate was what Ricky and I decided. Once we tried to determine whether Uncle Nunzio was a primate clever enough to have learned to use matches or a human being stupid enough to try and incinerate himself. It was a jump ball, but we decided on the latter. The reason being, had a primate been clever enough to employ matches, no doubt he would have discovered a

75

wide variety of uses, the least of which would have been to purposely singe his own hair. But that's just a guess on our part.

"Mary-nooch," Uncle Nunzio hollered into the kitchen, "I starvin' to death out here! Where's my lasagna, you been stirrin' that friggin gravy since Memorial Day!"

"Nunzi, you fat bastard!" hollered Aunt Dot. "You're worse than a dog; all you ever think about is your next meal. Leave our Mary alone."

Aunt Dot was Uncle Nunzio's wife and a real piece of work. Four feet ten inches tall, one-hundred percent Scotch-Irish and eyes that blazed with fury, and when those Scotch-Irish eyes blazed, they became buggy and crazed, like when Don Zimmer or Lou Piniella argues with an umpire. It was epic; we couldn't wait until someone provoked her. Aunt Dot was the only one in the Corelli Clan louder and more gregarious than Uncle Nunzio. And as is often the case with a waitress in a breakfast diner who, as a matter of a habit, calls everyone *hon,* Aunt Dot's pet word was *bastard.* "Nunzi, you bastard," was how she would begin a thought *or* tirade. There was a time when we truly believed that that was our great-uncle's name. We were kids; what did we know? We figured that Uncle Nunzio had a double name, like Jimmy John, Bobby Joe, Billy Ray... Nunzi Ubastard. Eventually, we caught on. After all, what were the chances that Uncle Al had the same second part of a double name?

And when Aunt Dot resorted to her pet word, it was never offensive, at least not when within the confines of the Corelli Clan. One could only guess how she was perceived when unleashed upon the rest of society. The Corelli men loved her, particularly our grandfather. They loved her fire. As far as being referred to as a bastard? While unorthodox, for Aunt Dot, it was a genuine term of endearment.

"Frankie, you bastard," she called to me, upon seeing that I was all duded up in my Holy Communion suit. "Get over here so that I can get a closer look at cha." Did I really have a choice? I did as I was told and went and stood beside the four-foot-ten-inch fireball. As a child, I liked standing next to Aunt Dot; it made me feel that much closer to adulthood.

"Ain't he handsome, Nunz?" asked Aunt Dot, once I was front and center and ready to be fussed over. I had every strand of hair gelled into place, and my clip-on necktie hung perfectly straight with the aid of an obnoxiously gaudy tie bar. Bear in mind we are an Italian family and not the subtle, sophisticated type that understands that Puccini is not a variety of pasta.

"Sure, he's handsome," bellowed Uncle Nunzio. "He looks just like his great-uncle, don't he?"

"Nunzi, you bastard, when the hell did you ever look this good!" blazed Aunt Dot.

Well, that was Aunt Dot. Who can explain such a phenomenon, other than to say that she was a Corelli—perhaps only by marriage but a Corelli nonetheless?

Aunt Theresa was Uncle Al's wife. She was interesting in her own right and perhaps even more so than Aunt Dot. The reason being, she had what one might allege as unique and questionable ties to Swampoodle. And if not for the advantage of being the sister of a certain feared Swampoodle character—which is a story in and of itself and one which later on will undergo its fair share of examination—like an albatross, many of those questionable ties might have clung to her, or, at too close a range, followed her throughout her life. However, having the benefit of that aforementioned and feared relation, her reputation, although besmirched, was never discussed openly. Aunt Theresa's reputation remained a private matter, discussable only with those whose lips were trusted to remain tight; for looming was always the fear of reprisal. In other words, everyone knew the truth and there were occasional snickers, but one had to remain prudent. Nevertheless, a reputation, with all its juicy morsels, can be buried only so deep—the boundaries it has enjoyed are bound to get tested. Eventually, and often with unfortunate results, *that* which we prefer to remain buried manages to wiggle its way to the surface; there's always one unexpected morsel that is particularly troublesome and stubborn and forever fighting to know the light of day.

Among ourselves, we (Ricky, Munchk, and yours truly) referred to Aunt Theresa as *Aunt Prostitute*. When others were nearby, the derogatory moniker was shortened to Aunt P. Eventually, Mom caught on, and her perceptiveness brought about an unfortunate result for Dad.

"Gee, I wonder who let *that* cat out of the bag?" Mom glared menacingly in the direction of poor Dad, who did a less than plausible job pretending not to understand the reason for her fury. Meanwhile, we didn't do so hot a job pretending not to have caught onto to the gist behind Mom's scathing witticism. Our eyes were resting on Dad, who appeared to be shrinking in his seat and was busy swallowing nervously. Shrinking and swallowing. That was all one usually managed when in the face of Mary Corelli's wrath while trapped under the weight of their own stupidity. Poor Dad.

Poor Dad will become a constant theme throughout the remainder of our narrative. You see, Freddy Corelli never *could* stand to leave a cat in a bag … *or* a prostitute. Anytime beans were spilled or a ghost was given up, one could rest assured that ol' Freddy Corelli was somewhere nearby. In defense of Dad, he didn't have a mean bone in his body, nor were his tittle-tattling ways done with any measure of maliciousness. Simply put, he couldn't help himself. Once he got to talking, the wrong words managed to find their way into his mouth. Once there, they were liberally spewed about, while eager ears, such as Ricky's, Munchk's, and mine, were waiting to collect them. The dirt on Aunt Theresa was a gem, and it led to the running joke: had Uncle Al finished high school, he would've been voted *Most likely to marry a former prostitute.*

"Hey, I think I heard the doorbell," said Uncle Al. He vigorously waved his arms as he attempted to whisper above the din. Putting a finger to his lips, he added, "Everyone pipe down, it might be Antonio."

"If it is Antonio, I hope he ain't hungry," said Uncle Nunzio. "The lasagna just went in the oven."

"Hey, Nunz, go and see who's at the door," whispered Uncle Al.

"I can't, I'm too busy starving to death."

"Nunzi, you bastard, go see who's at the friggin' door," ordered Aunt Dot.

Grumbling, my poor, starving great-uncle hobbled to the door. Upon opening it, Uncle Nunzio turned about, faced the room, then shouted, "Look, everybody, it's cousin Vito from Ninth Street! And wait'll you see the size of this friggin board of cheese he brought with 'im!"

After such an introduction, Vito, the cheese vendor from Toscana, waltzed heroically into the room, balancing a board adequate for a set of Lionel Trains, never mind cheese, whereupon he was swarmed as if Mike Schmidt entering a room filled with fervent little leaguers waving their arms for autographs while yelling *me first*. Ricky and I watched our kin stuff their mouths with a variety of cheeses, much of which we thought smelled too awful to walk by, never mind consume.

"Remember, we must save some for Antonio," cried Vito, whose English had improved dramatically since the Christmas of 1938, and who was afraid that his impressive board would empty too quickly; though judging from the size of the board, there was no danger in our grandfather getting cheated.

In the course of all the clamor and commotion brought about by what Ricky and I viewed were highly overrated clumps of curdled dairy, there sat a woman alone and in a corner. She, as she often did amid such gatherings, viewed the scene of rapacious cheese vultures with thoughtful reticence. Tall, slim, and with understated elegance, she was the closest thing that we Corellis had to a real *lady*. Better than most, and where the Corelli clan was concerned, better than everyone, she understood a thing or two about decorum. Her name is Elizabeth Corelli. She is our grandmother and the woman for whom Munchk was named.

****

As it was his daily custom back in the day, on September 1, 1939, Antonio stopped in Russo's Variety Store on his way home from work for a copy of the evening *Bulletin*. He arrived at his customary time, which was somewhere between 5:45 p.m. and 6:00 p.m. By that time of day, there remained only a few copies in the once plentiful stack for those stragglers in want of news. Today when he arrived, there remained but a single copy. As he approached and the print came into focus, it was no wonder. On the front page in big bold letters read the headline: *Germany invades Poland*—the initial act of what would shortly thereafter escalate into World War II. As Antonio went reaching for the one remaining copy, his eager hand arrived at the very same time as the equally eager hand of another. When he noticed the slim, attractive, and well-manicured hand that had attached itself to the opposite side of the newspaper, he withdrew.

"Please," he said, with a magnanimous wave of his hand. "You take it."

"Oh no, I insist," the woman said in return.

After several attempts of each trying to outdo the other's altruism, it was decided that they would divvy out the sections of the newspaper, but then afterward engaged in a mild dispute over who would bear the burden of the cost. This was a battle Antonio would not lose, as the woman, on the issue of cost, after permitting Antonio a few moments to delve into the first paragraph below the startling *Germany Invades Poland* headline, agreed to yield. All throughout the negotiation, pleasantries and warm glances were exchanged. Upon their departure, Antonio opened the door for the woman, whose overall appearance was as slender and well-manicured as her hands, with the hope that their exchange would continue beyond Russo's Variety Store. To his disappointment, the woman went sprinting off and she did so in the opposite direction of Twenty-sixth and Indiana. Antonio believed that something much more than the sharing of a newspaper had transpired, and that this woman, despite looking out of place in Swampoodle, would choose to linger by his side a while longer. Instead, she went running off and in a great hurry. It seemed that wherever it was that she was headed, she couldn't get there fast enough. It left Antonio to wonder whether his breath was bad or if he smelled unpleasant at the end of a day's work.

"I'll be damned; she couldn't get away from me fast enough," he sulked to himself.

With the long hours he worked, along with the time and trouble of looking after Uncle Al and Uncle Nunzio, who were always full of surprises, Antonio hardly had time for a love interest. But since Mama Corelli moved in, his load has been lightened. He began to consider his life, where it was headed, and the possibility of finding a nice girl with whom he could settle down. With his share of the newspaper tucked under his arm, he turned about and began his slow, plodding walk home. Never before had Antonio seen the slim, elegant woman around Swampoodle, and he wondered if he would ever see her again. He hadn't gone but a few paces in the direction of Twenty-sixth and Indiana, when he heard someone call out, "Sir." Alertly he spun around and saw the mysterious woman walking briskly in his direction, as briskly as she had run from him earlier. Throughout the day, she had heard speculations and murmurings regarding the volatility and unrest that led up to the *Germany Invades Poland* headline; and since she was a learned young woman who prided herself in keeping informed, she was anxious to get her hands on a newspaper. "I just remembered," she said, for in her alacrity she had forgotten, "my father, without fail, buys the *Bulletin* every day at four." After apologizing for the oversight, she handed over her sections of the newspaper to Antonio and again went scurrying off. Before Antonio had the presence of mind to call after her, out of the corner of his eye, he saw written on one of the paper's white margins: Elizabeth Erwin, Cumberland 9-4762.

Nothing can make a man's day or boost his demeanor more than having been acknowledged by a pretty girl, especially if it's a girl with whom he has developed a sudden interest. As a young man, I wished that whenever it was my turn to meet *Miss Right*, I, too, would experience a chance encounter and have an enchanting tale to tell; but such scenarios only seemed to have occurred back in a time called *the good old days,* when our country was innocent and its society less guarded—a time when an out-of-the-blue romantic encounter with a handsome stranger was not only permissible or possible but something a gal might even hope for. Nowadays it's difficult to imagine two people reaching for the same newspaper, assuming newspapers will continue to exist. Clunking heads while walking the mall, because both are fixated on a miniature screen while trading thumbed messages with someone at another mall would seem the more likely scenario; although, it's unlikely that anything resembling romance would follow such an encounter. I'd put my money on assault charges.

I'm not one of those salty old pricks opposed to technology but I acknowledge that it has created new levels of rudeness. *Hey moron. Yeah, you; the one who decided to put his android on speaker in a restaurant. There's a reason that they used to put phones inside booths.*

Back to what transpired following that chance encounter at Russo's Variety Store: Our grandfather always said, with tongue-in-cheek, that if Hitler hadn't invaded Poland, the opportunity to meet our grandmother may never have presented itself, and that today none of us would be around. I must say there are fewer ironies uglier than that one. That my entire existence might indirectly or directly be tied to the atrocity of Hitler invading Poland is a ponderous scenario indeed and certainly one worth chewing on; but I'm here, and who am I to argue? Besides, hopeless romantic that I am, I believe that one way or another fate would have afforded Antonio Corelli and Elizabeth Erwin another opportunity. Sorry, Adolph. You get credit for nothing.

Antonio walked home, whistling tune after happy tune. Not even the witnessing of the hopelessly reckless Vincent Bronini driving the wrong way on a one-way street caused him to frown, less miss a note.

"Hey, Uncle Tony," the imbecile called while waving from the car. "Need a ride home?"

When Antonio arrived home, he found Uncle Al and Uncle Nunzio camped out on the front porch, their shoulders slumped, their eyes a bit droopy. In other words, their mood was in direct contrast with that of his own, which had lilted past lighthearted on the way to cheery.

"Big surprise," glowered Uncle Al. "Ma's cooking cicoria."

"I'm tellin' ya, Ma could find a friggin dandelion in the goddamn Sahara Desert," grumbled Uncle Nunzio. "Sometimes I think she cooks the weeds that grow up through the cracks in the pavement and doesn't tell us." Uncle Al cringed before Uncle Nunzio added: "I think we should start keeping an eye on Ma before we all end up layin' next to poor 'ol Frank. And would you get a load-a-da way the house smells! It's worse than being at work!"

"You're in a good mood, Antonio," Uncle Al managed to acknowledge, once Uncle Nunzio was through with his tirade. "Maybe you didn't hear what's on the menu tonight."

"Yeah, Antonio, what gives?" asked Uncle Nunzio. "You and that goofy look on your face! We could see it as soon as you turned the corner."

"I had a good day today, so I'm in a good mood." It was unusual for Antonio to act defensive, and it caused Uncle Al and Uncle Nunzio to leer at him with suspicion. "What's the big deal, is it against the law for a guy to be happy? Can't a guy have a good day or be in a good mood just because it's Tuesday … or Wednesday?"

"It's Friday," Uncle Nunzio was quick to point out.

"Well, there you go," said Antonio. "That's all the more reason to be in a good mood. You should be in a good mood, too."

"We *did* mention Ma's cooking cicoria," said Uncle Nunzio. "Or maybe all this *'sudden happiness'* is cloggin' up your ears."

"And it ain't like you ain't ever been happy before, but you never looked like *this*," said Uncle Al.

"So what gives?" Uncle Nunzio continued to press. Both Uncle Al and Uncle Nunzio, while sitting on the top step of the porch, lurched forward as if prepared to further grill their big brother on the matter of his happiness. For a second, Antonio appeared ready confess but then muttered, "Ahh, you two mugs. Never mind."

Typical of a man grinning from the ninth cloud and elevated to such loftiness by the mystery of feminine charm, Antonio subscribed to the notion that he was the only one aware of such emotions, and that these new, exciting, and largely unfamiliar feelings were beyond Uncle Al and Uncle Nunzio. After climbing the porch steps, he whacked each of them on the back of the head with his newspaper, then ventured inside where his nostrils were rudely introduced to the smell of cicoria, or some unpleasant collection of urban weeds, the likes of which he dared not consider. After sauntering back to the kitchen and being careful not to allow Mama Corelli catching him wincing, Antonio stooped down just far enough to place his chin on Mama's shoulder. The playful and affectionate gesture was good for a grin but not enough to distract Mama from the business that was taking place at the stove. Antonio followed with a firm kiss on Mama's cheek before shifting his eyes downward to glance at what would pass for tonight's dinner. From the earliest days of his childhood, Antonio could remember Mama Corelli telling him, "Cooked greens are the key to a long and healthy life." He wanted to remind Mama that spinach and broccoli rabe were also green, and that most of the time, it wasn't necessary for them to eat dandelion greens. But he knew Mama would have been quick to remind him that, while spinach and broccoli were occasionally purchased and cooked, dandelion greens were free for the taking for anyone willing to trek over to Fairmount Park.

"I see *somebody* had a good day," said Mama Corelli, who brightened at her eldest son's unexpected display of affection.

Antonio rushed to the mirror, which hung in the dining room. He was curious if he could see what was so clearly apparent to everyone else. So comprehensive was he in examining himself that he never heard Mama Corelli abandon the stove and steal up behind him. She placed a hand on one of his massive shoulders and said, "Once upon a time, your father used to get that look. I remember it well. Right now, you remind me of him when he was your age. She must be very beautiful, Antonio."

"Ma, you have to excuse me," Antonio pleaded, "but right now there's a telephone call I need to make."

****

The following Saturday night, when Antonio arrived at the Erwin residence, his first and most enthusiastic greeter was one near to the floor. As he was attempting to make the acquaintance of both Mr. and Mrs. Erwin, Antonio couldn't help his eyes from shifting downward, less could he conceal the odd sense of curiosity that registered on his face.

"Your eyes aren't playing tricks on you," said Mr. Erwin. "The poor thing has only three legs."

After Mr. Erwin spoke, his eyes also shifted downward, his face registering a similar sense of curiosity as he watched his hand all but disappear, when wrapping around it was Antonio's much larger hand. Mr. Erwin took a step back to better regard this massive appendage that had taken hold of his, then suffered a twinge of disconcertion that he was about to surrender his daughter to a man whose manliness easily dwarfed his own, and Mr. Erwin was hardly an unmanly man.

"He was a stray that Elizabeth found wandering through the neighborhood a few years back," Mrs. Erwin, stepping forward, told Antonio. She had noticed Antonio's fascination for the enthusiastic creature, who on behalf of the Erwins represented the reception party, had yet to wane. "She brought him home, cared for him, and the two have been inseparable ever since. She named him Max after the boxer, Max Baer. Elizabeth figured, to have survived on the streets with only three legs, he must be a *real* fighter."

"I'll say," agreed Antonio. Then he thought to himself that Elizabeth Erwin must be *some* girl, and one with the kindest of hearts to have brought home a three-legged stray. A girl who named a three-legged dog after a boxer; boys who named a stolen pig after a shortstop; somehow there was an irony, but Antonio dared not dwell on it. He broke his momentary stupor by asking, "Elizabeth knows about boxers?"

"She's been known to listen to matches," Mrs. Erwin said with a note of pride. Mr. Erwin frowned apologetically as if to say *what self-respecting young lady enjoys the sport of boxing?* Antonio was hardly obsessing over Elizabeth having a passion for pugilists. His thoughts were of a girl and her dog—a damaged dog someone or some family no longer thought worthy. That must have been the scenario, or so Elizabeth Erwin figured. And why wouldn't she? How many dogs as needy as one with three legs would, on its own accord, take to the streets? Already, Elizabeth Erwin and three-legged Max had become compassionate and endearing figures that touched Antonio's heart. Permitting himself a peek into the future, Antonio wondered how well Mama Corelli would take to poor, old three-legged Max. What's more, how well would poor, old three-legged Max take to the smell of cicoria? Then there was Uncle Al and Uncle Nunzio to consider, not to mention Vincent Bronini, who of late had been turning up at the house far more regularly than Antonio would have preferred. Suddenly, the notion of incorporating fanciful propositions such as love and romance into his life seemed more daunting than on the drive over to the Erwins. But he knew that he was getting way ahead of himself.

When offered a seat, Antonio permitted his eyes to rove around a home that was far more sophisticated than his own. Its finery—delicate bric-a-brac and brocade material—in combination with the well-spoken Mr. and Mrs. Erwin caused him to wonder whether he hadn't stepped out of his league. What was someone who was pulled from school and shoved into a coal mine doing in a place like this?

Before Antonio was permitted to make off with the Erwins' fairest treasure, Mrs. Erwin took hold of his huge, powerful hands. Lifting them up to the level of her eyes, she examined them. Then she looked up at Antonio and whispered the word, "Respect." Antonio's nod was enough to reassure a mother.

Before leaving, Antonio again was offered Mr. Erwin's hand; then he waved to Elizabeth's three younger brothers, who were all seated in a row on the sofa and in the order of their respective ages. Talk about a family that knew a thing or two about making a good impression. And all for the sake of a first date! The Erwins indeed made *some* impression on Antonio. Incidentally, the three younger brothers sitting unnaturally erect on the sofa, along with Uncle Al and Uncle Nunzio, would become my great-uncles. Their names were Edward, James, and Richard. Collectively, along with Elizabeth, they made up a theme, having been named for royalty—the queen and kings of England. Perhaps Mr. and Mrs. Erwin had lofty expectations.

****

Many years ago, in the early days of my childhood, a typical outing for us was Mom and Dad driving a few short miles across town to Hunting Park. The place offered plenty of fun things to keep kids engaged, but the main attraction was the carousel, and what a magnificent carousel it was! In those days, there were many carousels in Philadelphia, including one on Belmont Avenue in Fairmount Park West, but we were told the one in Hunting Park, built by the Dentzel company on Germantown Avenue, which was one of five carousel manufacturers in the city, was the best there was. Last, I remember, Ricky, Munchk, and I were five, two, and six years old respectively, and we thought there was nothing better than a day at Hunting Park and riding that carousel. Dad always managed to find the biggest and grandest looking horses. He would sit high in the saddle and hold up Munchk, as if he was showing her off for the entire world to see. In retrospect, it reminded me of *The Lion King* when Mufasa showed off Simba to the rest of the pride. *Look, everyone, this is Elizabeth Corelli, my beautiful daughter!* Munchk, who never had much fear of anything, least of all her older brothers, looked so proud to be held up so high. She would smile and wave to everyone as the carousel turned around and around.

Mom would help Ricky up and onto a much smaller horse. With both hands gripping tightly to the pole, he sat proudly in the saddle. Mom stood on the platform right beside him, hands ready should he falter. I, on the other hand, was able to ride alone and I went for the tiger. The tiger didn't mimic a piston in slow-motion like the smaller horses, but it was a fierce and magnificent looking representation of the real beast. Ricky always said that I rode the tiger because it was much lower to the ground and that I was afraid to be "way up high" on a horse that went "up and down." Ricky also pointed out that my tiger was not at all a fierce jungle cat but looked more like Tony the "Frosted Flakes Tiger" and was hardly *grrrreat!* Of course, Ricky was just envious because he wasn't yet able to ride alone. The truth was I didn't care what anyone thought; I had my tiger, and I was happy.

After the carousel, we would mosey on over to another feature of the park, the lake, and rent pedal boats. Munchk wasn't yet old enough to pedal, so she rode with Mom and Dad. Ricky and I, because Mom and Dad had the disadvantage of toting along a non-pedaler, a person who was essentially cargo, challenged them to a race. We lost. Every bleeping time, we lost. We spent the entire time pumping and thrusting our legs with fury, trying to propel a craft not built for swiftness to move swiftly, until our faces were ready to explode. All we ever managed was a view of the back of Mom and Dad's head, and worse at Munchk, who, with her head resting on Dad's shoulder, sneered antagonistically to let us know that we were well behind and had no shot at winning. It mattered not how hard Ricky and I pedaled or how much will and determination we put forth; the munchkin always prevailed. What's more, even at age two, she knew how to revel in victory and in a manner that made us want to tear her to pieces.

Next, we hit the concession stand for custard cones. Dad would get a double-twist. I couldn't wait until I was old enough to order a double-twist. I settled for a single vanilla with chocolate jimmies. It was exasperating watching Munchk, at age two, lick a custard cone. Most of that cold, sweet, delicious custard ended up first on her face and eventually onto the multitude of napkins with which Mom had armed herself. What a waste! And if we happened to be at the park on a day that an American Legion baseball game was taking place, we would stop and watch an inning or two. Wooden bats, metal cleats, leather gloves, a hardball smacking the pockets of those gloves and green grass; those American Legion games were what sparked Ricky's and my passion for baseball. And it is not my imagination; a baseball diamond smells different than that pesky lawn that demands a portion of your weekend. It may not be one of the great mysteries of Western civilization, but no one can convince me otherwise. Anyway, it mattered not a lick that it wasn't a major league baseball game taking place; we were perfectly content watching two American Legion teams play ball. The crack of a bat, custard cones, pedal boats, and a ride on a carousel; whether an adult or a child, what wasn't there to enjoy about an outing at Hunting Park?

More than a place of fond childhood memories, for us Corellis, Hunting Park was a place that possessed a measure of historical significance. It was the place that Antonio Corelli took Elizabeth Erwin on their first date. I'm guessing Antonio had something more romantic in mind—perhaps Lemon Hill under the moonlight—but after meeting the wholesome and sophisticated Erwins and then learning the story of how poor, old three-legged Max became a member of the family, he figured a carousel ride along with a stroll through a park buzzing with gaiety would be more fitting. You gotta like a man able to think on his feet. Sometime between leaving the Erwins and situating Elizabeth in the car, he must have taken into consideration the positive impression such a date would make, not only on a fair-haired young woman who rescued an injured canine but on the folks back home, who were patiently awaiting Elizabeth's return and the news she had to tell.

A few years back, in between wives and feeling melancholy, I decided to take a drive on the avenue for which Hunting Park is named. The avenue winds through the park in such a way that you would think you were driving in circles. The carousel has long since been gone, dismantled, and carted away. So, too, is the lake gone. I read that the city filled it in and built a swimming pool in its stead. The ball fields and playgrounds have remained, though they are not so well maintained as I remember. It is bittersweet returning to places once so cherished and whose glory days are well behind. As I gazed out over the park and its deteriorating environs, it was hard to imagine that it was once a place where blossomed a great love, or perhaps many great loves. Nevertheless, I am living proof, although a generation removed, that love blossomed at the once great park.

Alone, I stood where the carousel once turned, and its cheerful music blared and matched the gaiety of those riding and others gathered around and awaiting their turn. Strange, but as I stood there all those years later, my nostrils filled with the smell of oily gears. I even imagined Munchk waving to me as she went by on the grandest of horses. I was seized with feelings of nostalgia and melancholy and longed for a bygone era to come alive before me, to brush up against me so I could once again understand the simplicity of its joy. Finally, I drove away, feeling happier for the memories that have thankfully remained, then sad for the current state of the once lively and well-patronized park. It was sometime around 1969 that the park began its decline. I'm thankful that I was born at a time when I was able to experience Hunting Park's golden era, albeit near the end.

Often defunct carousels are dismantled, their parts auctioned off, many of which end up in the shops of antique dealers. How sad it must be to watch the dismantling of a carousel. Weren't there happy people gathered here by the hundreds? Wasn't it just yesterday? What happened to them? It's different when a circus or carnival folds up and leaves town; you're all but sure of their return. Not so with the Hunting Park carousel. I sometimes wonder about my tiger. Perhaps he's on display in the home of some collector. If that's the case, that's not an altogether bad fate for an old

Hunting Park tiger; though, I did once read that the Hunting Park carousel was moved to Cedar Park in Sandusky, Ohio, but who knows if it's still in operation. Whatever the case, I always have an eye out for my tiger in case he's still out there … somewhere.

Antonio walked Elizabeth Erwin to her front door, hopped back into the old Dodge Sedan, which was a much lonelier and less exciting place than it was a minute ago, and went diving off, heading straight away for Lemon Hill. The dark, isolated, late-night grounds of Lemon Hill were not necessarily where he wished to be, nor did he want to be home or anywhere else where Elizabeth Erwin was not, and while in that mindset, the familiar grounds of Lemon Hill, darkness notwithstanding, was as good a place as any. Thoughtfully, he paced the grounds of the famous mansion as a full moon shone down upon the Schuylkill River. He was finding difficulty putting the loveliness of the fair-haired Elizabeth Erwin and the combined smells of cicoria, espresso coffee, and mothballs in the same thought. In the same universe! He found it no less difficult imagining his brothers in the company of the much more sophisticated Mr. and Mrs. Erwin. Antonio saw this as not merely a dilemma but a disaster waiting to happen. It was a given Swampoodle had characters more colorful and rougher around the edges than what the lovely Elizabeth Erwin was accustomed to. She didn't rub elbow with any Skullheads, Turds, Sixty-fours, Patty One Eyes, and those who thumped their chest calling themselves Meat. There were no Jimbronies in the Erwin clan, and they surely never heard of any tough guy Mafioso wannabes named "Nails."

Antonio spent the remainder of the night pacing the grounds of Lemon Hill. Occasionally he glanced up at the stars, hoping that somewhere in the expanse of celestial wonder was a solution to how his world and the world of Elizabeth Erwin could harmoniously come together. He drove away, but not without first arriving at an irrevocable conclusion: He found the woman of his dreams, the kind of woman for whom he'd gladly work his heart out and never suffer a moment of regret. He would make it work. Somehow, he would make it work. But looming larger than the shenanigans of Uncle Al and Uncle Nunzio and the disparity of their upbringings was a considerable hurdle over which he would have to climb.

****

"So, Antonio, when are we finally gonna get meet this girl of yours?" wondered Uncle Al.

"Soon enough," Antonio dismissively replied.

"Aw come on, Antonio, where are ya keepin' her locked up?" Uncle Nunzio, who was beginning to feel slighted, had asked. "If this girl's gonna wind up being our sister-in-law, don't we gotta right to meet her?"

Antonio glared at his younger brother and grumbled, "She's not locked up, Nunz. And don't worry, you'll meet her soon enough when I think the time is right."

"Jeez, Nunz," said Uncle Al. "You're right; before ya know it, we could have a sister-in-law. We better start brushin' up on our manners."

Hmm, thought Antonio, *maybe this won't be so difficult after all.* Then, on cue, Uncle Nunzio protested, "What's wrong with our friggin' manners?"

Antonio stood just inside the front door while, on the porch, Uncle Al and Uncle Nunzio debated over what about them needed to improve before acquainting themselves with one Elizabeth Erwin. That such a conversation was taking place was encouraging and made Antonio feel more confident about his brothers. Still, there remained the considerable hurdle over which he would have to climb. The aforementioned hurdle was waiting for him, where she always was at that time of day, back in the kitchen and attired in a shapeless housedress, stout shoes, and wearing her customary grim expression. Mama Corelli's grim expression may have been a permanent fixture, but she nonetheless relished the role of mothering her three sons. In those days, what other sort of life was there for a middle-aged immigrant widow?

"Hey, Ma, what do you think of this?" asked Antonio. Proudly, he flipped open a small box, which for days had been secretly housing a fiery gem.

"I think any girl should feel fortunate to receive such a ring, Antonio," said Mama Corelli. "I take it you're going to give it to that girl you been seeing?"

Antonio was reasonably adept at reading between Mama Corelli's lines. *That girl whom thus far you have been keeping away from us* was what was clearly implied.

"Ma, you'll meet her soon enough, that's a promise. Hey," Antonio added, as though no truth could more of a given, "how could I marry a girl without first bringing her home to my mama?"

"You're not ashamed of your family, are you, Antonio?" asked Mama Corelli. Her face may have been pointing downward at her stovetop concoctions, but her eyes clearly shifted to the right and over at Antonio, who was leaning in the archway between the kitchen and dining room. Her tone was unmistakably accusatory.

"Of course not, Ma," lied Antonio. "What gave you that idea?"

"This *girl*, Antonio … is she Italian?" Mama Corelli's cadence suggested that all along she suspected that Elizabeth Erwin was not of the desired ethnicity.

"Actually, Ma, she's German-Irish." Antonio's reply was matter-of-fact, his shrug of the shoulder casual, as if to suggest: *German-Irish or Italian, what's the difference; half the country's one or the other or some combination of both, so it would only make sense that Elizabeth Erwin would be as well.* Then he added, brightly, "Just like President Roosevelt." (FDR was actually of Dutch/Scottish descent.)

"I see." Mama Corelli didn't seem surprised to learn that Antonio's involvement was with a woman of non-Italian descent, but it could not be said that her tone was a happy one. As she kept her full attention on the food she was preparing, her next question was—and no qualms were made of the fact that Mama was wary of the answer— "Is she at least Catholic?" If this were a movie, it would be time to cue the suspense-enhancing music.

Antonio raced through a gamut of herky-jerky gesticulations, including a variety of goofy eye movements, idiotic frowns, and inane shrugs. Midway through his absurd display, he asked, "I'm sorry, Ma, could you repeat the question?" Mama Corelli was not amused. Finally, after contorting himself such that he would have made a pretzel vendor proud, Antonio managed to squeeze out the words, "She's Protestant." Years later, he joked, "It took a whole troop of boy scouts to untie all the knots I got myself into trying to get out those two lousy words." More so than *I'm sorry* or *I was wrong*—words with which men inherently struggle—*She's Protestant* may have been the most daunting words Antonio Corelli ever uttered.

Upon hearing the word *Protestant*, abruptly, Mama Corelli turned her back to Antonio and raised her right hand. It was her way of categorically letting Antonio know that she was through with the subject of Elizabeth Erwin and that he was also dismissed from her company.

With slumped shoulders, Antonio moped into the parlor. Once there, he took in the surrounding walls, which he owned, then the furniture occupying the space within those walls, which he purchased. How could it be that he was reduced to a child seeking approval, and worse yet was denied? He sank into his sofa, buried himself in the evening newspaper, and waited to be called for dinner.

It was seldom that Mama Corelli allowed the antics of her two younger sons to distract her such that she forgot to say a before-dinner prayer, and tonight's dinner would not commence without first giving thanks to a higher power:

"In the name of the Father and of the Son and of the Holy *Catholic* Ghost," was how Mama began.

Antonio pretended not to hear the purposeful misspeak and remained with his head bowed and staring down at his plate, upon which there was a healthy heap of spaghetti with meatballs and a side of cicoria. Subtly, Uncle Al shifted his eyes to the end of the table where sat Mama; he was grateful to look at anything *but* the dreaded vegetable. Not Uncle Nunzio. He didn't have a subtle bone in his body.

"The Holy *Catholic* Ghost?" Uncle Nunzio's face twisted as if having eaten something unexpectedly sour. "Hey, Ma, I ain't no prayer expert, but I pretty sure that ain't how it goes. At least I don't think that's how it goes. Right, Al?" Uncle Nunzio deferred to Uncle Al in matters of religion. Uncle Al managed only a partial nod. He didn't wish to openly oppose Mama Corelli, who he could clearly see was out of sorts. "There, ya see, Ma," Uncle Nunzio persisted, "it's just the Holy Ghost, not the Holy *Catholic* Ghost."

Mama Corelli brought her hand down upon the table and snapped, "Since you're so smart, Nunzio, then maybe you can bring me home a nice Italian girl who goes to the right kind of church!"

Antonio buried his face in his huge hands. Uncle Al's slender figure shrank in his chair.

"Oh, I get it," said Uncle Nunzio. "Antonio ... that girl of yours, she ain't a *paesan*, is she? And I'm bettin' she ain't no Catholic, neither?"

"No, Nunz," Antonio emphatically stated, mocking Uncle Nunzio's grammar, "she *ain't*."

"Well, she ain't no Hebe, is she?" asked Uncle Nunzio, as though the possibility at best was remote. "And I sure as hell know she ain't no colored." Throwing his hands in the air, he added, "Then what's all the fuss about?"

Rising to her feet, Mama Corelli shouted, "Nothing is ever a big deal! Everything around here is a big joke!" Leaving her plate behind and food to get cold, Mama Corelli went storming off in the direction of the porch. After a long silence, which saw three brothers pick at their food with little interest, Uncle Nunzio proposed, "Antonio, why don't you make Ma happy and bring her home a nice Italian girl," to which Antonio replied, "Being Italian doesn't make you nice, Nunz, it only makes you Italian."

"True," agreed Uncle Al. "But chances are it does make you Catholic. You'll kill two birds with one stone. She might not be the girl of your dreams, but at least we'll have some peace."

"Peace?" shrieked Antonio. "As in stealing hubcaps with that birdbrain friend of yours—Bronini—and selling them to a junkyard to make extra cash? Is that the kind of peace you're talking about? Spending the rest of your life with someone is supposed to be about love. It's not a matter of … *convenience* or trying to please everyone else."

Uncle Nunzio wasn't through putting in his two-cents and further proposed: "Hey, Antonio, what about Angela Spaticini from Twenty-first Street? Christ Almighty, she's got tits out to here! I heard *she's* lookin' to get married. I'll bet she'd say yes if you asked her."

"And I'll bet she'd say yes if *you* asked her, too," Antonio retorted. "She'd probably say yes to *anyone* who asked her." He drolly added, "Who wants a woman who'll say yes to anybody … or to any*thing*?"

"Antonio, do you actually hear yourself?" cried Uncle Nunzio. "I'd friggin' *kill* for a woman who said yes to anything! Just tell me where she lives, I'm on my way. Angela, baby doll, here comes Nunzio!" The three brothers fell apart such that it became necessary to muffle their laughter in their shirtsleeves. They surely didn't want Mama Corelli to think that they were yucking it up while she sat alone brooding on the porch. After finishing most of what was on his plate and making sure he was beyond the effects of Uncle Nunzio's humor, Antonio excused himself from the table.

"Ma, do you mind if I sit down beside you?" he asked.

Mama Corelli nodded in the direction of the vacant chair.

"Ma," Antonio began, careful to maintain the utmost respect. "I'm not Irish. I'm not German. And I'm not Protestant. But none of that seems to matter to Mr. and Mrs. Erwin. Ma, you see where I'm going, don't you?"

"It's easier for Mr. and Mrs. Erwin, Antonio," said Mama Corelli.

"How so, Ma? Help me understand."

"You were only a baby when we came here to America, Antonio. You remember nothing of the old country. Maybe in a way that's good, but also sad. Either way, like Mr. and Mrs. Erwin, America has always been your country, your home—the only home you've known. Me? I'll always be a foreigner—a stranger in a strange place. My ways are old. My thinking is old. I know that. There are things about America that I'll never get used to and because of that, I'll die in a foreign land always having felt like a foreigner. But that's my problem, Antonio, not yours. If this girl is truly in your heart, then I won't stand in your way. It's not my right."

Mama Corelli didn't punctuate her monologue with a smile as Antonio had hoped. In fact, she appeared more reflective than when Antonio first stepped onto the porch. Or perhaps it was resignation that overwhelmed her—resignation that religious and ethnical lines in twentieth-century America were eroding too quickly. Nevertheless, Antonio thanked her. After taking hold of her hand and pressing it to his cheek, he told her, "Your blessing means a lot, Ma. Maybe more than you realize."

"I've seen many changes in my lifetime, Antonio. But Poppa was always here, and we faced them together." With a sigh, Mama added, "You should go now and tell your brothers that everything will be fine, especially Alfonzo; he worries about me."

"We all do, Ma," said Antonio. "We all love you."

****

On the night of Christmas Eve, sometime between devouring all seven fishes while at the same time delighting in Uncle Al and Uncle Nunzio's misery and the beginning of the all-important dare we forget to mention *mandatory* Midnight Mass, Antonio Corelli managed to slip away long enough to slip a ring onto the finger of the lovely Elizabeth Erwin. A week later, or more specifically, on the first day of the new year, the Erwins abandoned their tradition of pork and sauerkraut in favor of Mama Corelli's lasagna.

The day began as expected, with warm holiday greetings, before moving on to light, cheery, and terribly predictable conversation, which included the questions and comments: *How was your Christmas? Did you buy everything that you wanted to buy? Did you get everything you wanted to get?* (Uncle Nunzio wanted firecrackers.) *I don't ever remember the stores so crowded. Were the holidays always this hectic?* Year after year, it's the same claptrap in every family. What followed the nonsense was soup, salad, and the aforementioned lasagna, which produced sighs of delight and ten satisfied bellies. The conversation became more relaxed: *Will Mack ever get the A's out of the cellar? Between the Phils and A's, Shibe Park was home to more than two-hundred losses last season. Did you see Gone with the Wind? Clark Gable is a dream! Will Roosevelt feel pressured into joining the fray? Did you hear, Al Capone has syphilis? It couldn't happen to a nicer guy.* Then came talk of how holidays are public enemy number one regarding the ol' waistline. The bellyaching over tight pants and dresses led to the introduction of—you guessed it—dessert and coffee.

Intermittently, because he was on edge worrying about the behavior of Uncle Al and Uncle Nunzio and Mama Corelli's numerous quirks, Antonio had held his breath for what seemed an eternity but was only four hours. By the day's end, every muscle in his rigid body felt as if they had been dragged over the world's rockiest terrain. At last, gratefully, Elizabeth turned and cried out to Mr. and Mrs. Erwin, upon realizing how much time had slipped away, "We really should get going. I must check on Max!"

With a grateful sigh, Antonio slumped in his chair. All the air that he had stored up throughout the day came thankfully seeping from his weary body, his natural color restored. With each passing day, it had become harder and harder to say goodnight to Elizabeth, but not so on the first night of 1940. "Right, we can't forget about poor, old Max," he readily chirped. Right away, he made a dash for the coat closet. He assisted the Erwins with their winter wears, then clumsily ushered them through the door.

"Gee," Uncle Nunzio remarked, "we weren't too anxious now, were we? Christ, Antonio, for a second there, I thought you were gonna bearhug the whole family and carry them to their car."

"All right, all right, so maybe I was a little anxious," admitted Antonio. "But it's not like I don't have good cause to be. Remember, it's not every family that's gotta stolen pig buried out in Fairmount Park."

"He's gotta point, Nunz," said Uncle Al.

"What's all this I'm hearing about a stolen pig?" Mama Corelli, who was busy with the dishes, called out from the kitchen.

"It's a long story, Ma," they called back to her all at once.

"It's always a long story with you boys," said Mama Corelli, who didn't feel nearly as slighted as her words might have suggested. But she was correct; there were stories that, if not necessarily long, were too unpleasant for a mother's ears and therefore never got told. Our grandfather was always covering for Uncle Al and Uncle Nunzio, while at the same time trying to keep them flying straight. He had lofty aspirations.

On the first day of 1940, the Corellis, if indeed such effort existed, put their best foot forward. It could even be said that Uncle Al and Uncle Nunzio were charming and that Mama Corelli was not viewed as too much an oddity; although, at the table, there was one anxious moment. It took place right at the time while the food was being passed around. Antonio caught Mrs. Erwin's curious eyes wondering about the mothballs that were strategically piled in each corner of the house. In fairness to Mrs. Erwin, who *wouldn't* wonder about a matter so odd as piles of mothballs placed in every corner of a house? You'd be odd not to question the reasoning be-hind a matter that curious. Uncle Nunzio, who also noticed Mrs. Erwin's roving eyes, whispered covertly, while subtly poking his elbow in the direc-tion of Mama Corelli, who was busy playing the role of hostess, "It's to ward off the evil spirits." With a good-humored wink and smile, he added, whispering, "She changes them every month. If they're not fresh, the evil spirits can get in, and we can't let that happen." Uncle Nunzio ended with a playful roll of the eyes and comical shrug, which caused Mrs. Erwin to quickly cover her mouth. She didn't wish to laugh out loud, then feel obliged to explain herself. Mrs. Erwin removed her hands, revealing a warm, friend-ly smile, which served to reassure both Antonio and Uncle Nunzio that everything was fine and that no family was without its quirks. With a nod that expressed both gratefulness and, of all things, admiration, Antonio acknowledged Uncle Nunzio for his quick thinking and always present hu-mor.

****

The wedding bells rang beautifully as they often do during the sun-ny month of June. With all the planning and preparation, Antonio had only insisted upon one thing: He wanted the wedding party photographed atop Lemon Hill. Elizabeth's only stipulation was that she have at least one photograph taken with her holding poor, old three-legged Max.

The Schuylkill sparkled with brilliance under the June sun and William Penn, who every day of the year stood regally atop the Philadel-phia skyline, under a cloudless blue sky, loomed beautifully, as if a senti-nel keeping a watchful eye on the happy gathering at Lemon Hill.

Aside from guests of the Erwins, the church was jam-packed with Swampoodle's usual suspects, including Skullhead, Stranger, Turd, Patty One Eye, Meat, Crazy Legs, Moose, and Sixty-four. On Sixty-four's arm was his latest conquest; though it was widely believed that the fling would not live up to his name. With Uncle Al and Uncle Nunzio posed proudly as tuxedoed groomsmen and accounted for, Mama Corelli made certain that Vincent Bronini, during the church ceremony, was seated right beside her, her hand clutching his arm just in case. Many in the church were uniquely attired. In other words, there were some in Swampoodle who had not the means less the sense to leave the house well matched. Nails, con-versely, was not one who had such difficulty. Aside from being the most feared, he was also known as the neighborhood fashion plate, modeling himself more after the flamboyant Al Capone, rather than the more busi-ness-attired Arnold Rothstein. Nails saw himself as a compelling figure who

enjoyed showing off his haberdashery while strutting through the neighborhood taverns and pool halls. He sat in the last pew of the church as one
would when expecting to make an abrupt exit. He was flanked by two of
his shady looking associates. But what made the marriage of Antonio and
Elizabeth an event to remember was the young boys of Swampoodle flock-
ing to the church and clamoring to shake hands and congratulate their
Uncle Tony. Because it was Saturday, many of the boys were still wearing
their grass and dirt-stained little league baseball uniforms to go with their
dirt-smudged faces.

"I had no idea that I was marrying the neighborhood hero!"
crooned the new Mrs. Corelli.

The following June, Elizabeth was with child. As she was entering
her third trimester, Hollywood and Universal pictures released *The Wolf
Man* starring Claud Rains, Ralph Bellamy, Bela Lugosi, and Lon Chaney Jr.
Bing Crosby crooned Irving Berlin's dreamy masterpiece, *White Christmas.*
1941 also saw Joe Di Maggio hit safely in fifty-six consecutive games and
Ted Williams post a batting average of .406. But the most compelling event
of the season, if not the decade, or even the century, from an American
perspective, was Japan's bombing of Pearl Harbor. Shortly thereafter, Antonio discovered in his mailbox what tens of thousands of other men
across the country by then had discovered: a draft card. How ironic, that the
very world-concerning matter that brought Antonio and Elizabeth together that day in Russo's Variety Store, would come to separate them.

It was clear the war would not be over in the next three months;
therefore, Uncle Al and Uncle Nunzio were in for the pep talk of their lives.
Antonio wanted to know beyond all certainty that, in his absence, life at
Twenty-sixth and Indiana would carry on smoothly and without incident.
"That's my wife, *your* sister-in-law in there," he reminded them on the
porch after dinner. "And that's *your* nephew or niece that she's carrying—
our family's next generation. I'm counting on both of you."

"We won't let you down, Antonio," they promised.

Antonio Corelli had no memory of his first crossing of the Atlantic; therefore, he had no conception of its vastness. This time would
be different.

Chapter Six
Life is But a Dream

Following six weeks of basic training, Antonio, since he drove a rig for a living, spent the next two years in a unit that drove army supply vehicles all over the continent of his birth. He was already three months into his tour of duty when he finally received a photo of baby Fred. It was some experience, and a quite surreal one at that, to have first laid eyes on his son, his own flesh and blood, by way of a photograph while halfway around the world. He wept openly.

Antonio could tell from the feel and weight of the envelope that it contained more than a letter, that it was a letter accompanied by photographs. He hesitated before tearing it open; he needed to better prepare himself for what he was about to discover once he broke the seal. *Was it a boy or a girl? Should I be nervous or overjoyed? Was it healthy and had all its infant parts? I hope he or she looks like Elizabeth.* It wasn't every day a man is an ocean removed from loved ones when learning that he has just become a father. He gazed over at his fellow soldiers, some of whom already were blessed with a child, including O'Malley, who barely had time to get acquainted with baby Grace before being shipped out for duty. All is fair in love and war.

"It's a boy!" cried Antonio. "Seven pounds ten ounces! And his name is Fred … after my father!"

"Well, let's have a look at the little chipper," said Kowalski, who left behind a wife and a two-year-old son.

"Yeah, Corelli, pass it around," bellowed Dugan.

"Christ, would ya look at the mitts on this kid?" said O'Malley. "Tell me *he* don't take after his old man?"

"He'll be out there shaggin' fly balls like DiMaggio in no time," said Dugan.

As the story goes, Dugan never passed on an opportunity to mention his hometown Yankees and their famous center fielder. In the beginning, it would cause O'Malley to cringe with envy. O'Malley was from Boston and, worse, he was a Braves fan. Thus far in his lifetime, the Braves had lost 100 games five times, and in a recent campaign lost a staggering 115! Nevertheless, O'Malley tried to boast that, while the Yankees had Joltin' Joe, the Boston Braves had the great Rogers Hornsby. But that didn't work with ol' Dugan, who knew baseball inside and out. Dugan was well aware that Hornsby played only one year for the Braves, in 1928, when O'Malley was but a ten-year-old. Then there was Kowalski, who was from the south side of Chicago and a fan of the White Sox, otherwise known as the hitless wonders. Despite the White Sox owning his heart, Kowalski knew enough to give Dugan the lion's share of the stage whenever the conversation shifted to baseball, which was most of the time. And who could blame ol' Dugan? It wasn't his fault that he was born in the Bronx. Unlike Uncle Al and Uncle Nunzio, Dugan had every right to take pride in The Bombers, even if it rankled his brothers in arms.

With the news of baby Fred, there were cheers, handshakes, and well wishes all around; but more importantly, for a few fleeting moments, men who hailed from various parts of the country had all but forgotten why they were thrown together. It was seldom that such moments were afforded, and these men were grateful for any reason that enabled them to feel as if the war didn't exist, battles weren't looming, and that the world was once again normal, or whatever normal meant to a generation that understood a thing or two about sacrifice and inconvenience. But such euphoria didn't last for long. *Welcome to the world, baby Fred. Oh, and incidentally it's at war with itself.* Later on, when he had a moment to himself, Private Corelli read:

Dear Antonio,

I didn't believe it was possible that anything in this world could make me happier and to feel more alive than holding you, my dear husband. Then I held your son. I don't have to tell you that he is beautiful. That, you can plainly see for yourself. What I will tell you is, every waking moment, I hold him close and tell him all the wonderful things there is to know about his father. Funny, but it seems I never run out of things to say. Fear not, dear husband; your son will know you. He will come to know you as though all along you were here in the flesh. And when that momentous day arrives, when your son first lays his eyes upon you, in his heart he will know for sure, that is my father.

With more love than mere words can express,
Mrs. Elizabeth Corelli

I have many treasures chests at my home. No, not chained and padlocked trunks salvaged from shipwrecks and filled with gold coins, but albums filled with the photographs of those who are no longer around to sit at our table and share Sunday dinners and holidays. Carefully preserved in one of those albums is the letter our grandmother wrote to our grandfather back in the winter of 1942. Right beside the letter on the next leaf is a photograph of our grandmother in a rocking chair. Resting peacefully in her arms is baby Fred. Resting, but not quite as peacefully, on the arm of the rocking chair is poor, old three-legged Max.

Antonio had bought the rocker for Mama Corelli. It was a *welcome-to-Philadelphia* gift, and his way of expressing to Mama: *you're still the chief, and we, your sons, are your subordinates.* Mama Corelli willingly yielded her throne to Elizabeth when mother and child came home from the hospital.

Just below the rocking chair photo is another gem; it is of our grandfather and my personal favorite. Ricky's too. Antonio is in uniform with his long arms and huge hands draped over the shoulders of O'Malley and Dugan; Kowalski snapped the picture. The two soldiers are standing unnaturally erect, with their arms folded tightly to their puffed-out chests in an effort not to appear dwarfed while flanking Private Corelli. Their efforts fell dismally short. They were substantially dwarfed by Antonio's height and impressive appendages. Dangling from the mouths of Dugan and O'Malley were lit cigars; Antonio had his cigar in the hand that was draped over Dugan. O'Malley and Dugan appear happy to be sharing in the good news of healthy baby Fred *and* for the opportunity for cigars and a joyous moment. As it was captured in the photo, the magnitude of Antonio's joy was immeasurable. I had taken a digital photo of the original and downloaded it onto my desktop—yes, I'm old fashioned and still prefer a desktop. I emailed the photo to Ricky, and ever since, we have used it as wallpaper.

I don't recall whether our grandfather was in Italy, France, Belgium, or Germany when he received the news of baby Fred. I'm not sure I ever knew the answer to that question, and anyone who might have known is no longer around to ask. Nothing like allowing the family history to go to the grave. Perhaps I should have penned this novel years ago when I thought I didn't have the time. Then again, does it really matter which country Antonio was in when he received the news of baby Fred? What does matter are the eyes that look back at me each and every time I boot up my desktop—eyes that have never failed to teach me the sheer joy of being alive.

Antonio Corelli was not a wanting sort of man. He asked for little and was never one to wish his time away. In other words, he was never heard droning on *I can't wait for this* or *I can't wait for that.* He didn't live for that car he always wanted to drive or that vacation he longed to take; he simply lived, and sitting across the table from Mrs. Elizabeth Corelli was what he lived *for.* Whether as a son, husband, father, uncle, or grandfather, he was your classic *If you're happy then I'm happy* kinda guy. Walking away after having a conversation with Vito, the cheese vendor, and learning that his friend and *cousin from Toscana* was in good health and spirits was worth more to him than any earthly possession. Where have you gone, Antonio Corelli...

Meanwhile, as Dugan was painstakingly pointing out to Corelli, Kowalski, O'Malley, and to anyone else who willing to listen to him drone on about the virtues of a true champion, versus also-rans such as the Phillies, A's, White Sox, Cubs, Red Sox, and Braves, back in Philadelphia baby Fred had replaced Mama Corelli as the family's new version of Flat Stanley. And although the family's new arrival was considerably more maintenance than a small brown paper bag with facial features drawn on it, the newbie was nevertheless photographed in Fumo's Pool Hall, many of the local taverns, the racetrack, and just about anywhere else one would never suspect an infant to turn up. The reason was, on Saturdays, so that Elizabeth could have some well-deserved time to herself, it became the custom for Uncle Al and Uncle Nunzio to take baby Fred off her hands for a few hours.

"You two know about babies?" she had asked. One could only imagine the misgiving with which Elizabeth filled and the level of trepidation that quaked in her voice when Uncle Al and Uncle Nunzio first presented her with the idea.

"Know about babies?" Uncle Nunzio began, as though slighted over the question. "Why, sure we do. Hell, I was once a baby myself. Al, too, if you can believe it." The "Al, too" was added while slyly poking his brother in the ribs with his elbow. *Straighten up, I think she may actually be buying it.* Naturally, Uncle Nunzio's claim, regardless of how sincere he seemed slighted, did little to inspire Elizabeth's confidence.

"Baby, my ass," retorted Uncle Al. "*I* might've been a baby, but this animal's been shaving since when he was in diapers."

"Whadda you want from me, I was a manly looking kid," cried Uncle Nunzio. "Unlike *some* people I know."

"Manly, my ass," Uncle Al again retorted. "You were a chimp! Still are."

"That's enough," said Mama Corelli, whose hard glare stifled the banter, which was hardly serving to boost confidence in the new mother. Finally, Elizabeth deferred to the more seasoned Mama Corelli to arbitrate.

"All right," Mama told Uncle Al and Uncle Nunzio. "But remember that's my grandson. Have him back in this house in three hours, not one minute later."

"Relax Ma," said Uncle Nunzio. "What's the worst that can happen? We sell ol' Freddy here to the gypsies. Look at this face; we'll make a fortune!"

"Three hours!" Mama Corelli threatened.

"Actually," muttered Uncle Al, as they were nearly through the door, "the worst that could happen is 'ol Freddy ends up next to poor ol' Frank."

"Who's Frank?" asked Elizabeth, who's ears were sharper than Uncle Al had expected.

"It's a long story," Uncle Al alertly replied.

"*A very* long story," added Uncle Nunzio. "Remind us, we'll tell you later. It's a real kick in the head." His last remark was combined with a dismissive wave and with one foot already on the porch.

"Everything is a long story in this house," Mama Corelli shot back, before again reminding Uncle Al and Uncle Nunzio of their time limit.

For Mrs. Corelli the younger, that initial Saturday would be the longest three hours of her young life. Said Uncle Nunzio to Freddy on the day of our grandfather's surprise sixtieth birthday party: "You shoulda seen your mother that afternoon when we made it home. She was so relieved I thought she was gonna cry. But after that day, she trusted us; didn't she, Al?"

"Nunzi, you bastard," bellowed Aunt Dot, "Elizabeth still doesn't trust youse!"

It was some hodgepodge of humanity that lived at Twenty-sixth and Indiana: One infant, two Jimbronies, an immigrant whose eccentric customs should not be explained unless the goal was to be humorous, and a young woman, who, although lovely and served to provide a striking contrast, came packaged with, of all things, a three-legged dog. A comic in search of material need not have looked further than Twenty-sixth and Indiana.

Without Antonio, whose presence within the home had served as a buffer, there did exist a measure of tension. Impervious to this tension, naturally, were baby Fred and poor, old three-legged Max. The tension may have been slight but enough to make everyone aware of it less relaxed. After all, Elizabeth and the remaining Corellis, minus baby Fred, were two entities which under no circumstances would have otherwise come together, never mind have come together under one roof. Eventually, and effectively, each in their own way learned to use Baby Fred and poor, old three-legged Max as a cushion and distraction to ease the existing tension. An infant and a three-legged dog, although unwittingly, replaced Antonio as unlikely but effective buffers. It just goes to illustrate, whether within a family unit or out in society, we all have a role to play—even those wholly unaware of having roles can possess influence and an innate dynamic.

Elizabeth did consider moving back with the Erwins, though she did not intimate as much to Antonio; she wouldn't while he was overseas. The admission slipped out years later during a lighthearted moment. Then one morning she awoke and realized, *I'm Antonio's wife. I'm Mrs. Corelli. For better or worse, Twenty-sixth and Indiana is my home.*

Eventually, the antics of Uncle Al and Uncle Nunzio grew on the new Mrs. Corelli. So, too, did the strange customs of Mama Corelli, although the mothballs had to go. Not from the drawers and the closets; in those places they were safe and could remain. It was the little round, white balls that were piled in corners that were becoming problematic, as Elizabeth was finding them in the mouth of poor, old three-legged Max. Also, it was only a matter of time before baby Fred started crawling, and Elizabeth figured it best that the mothballs were not so accessible. "It's much easier," she tactfully explained to Mama Corelli, "to put them away, rather than to teach Max that they're not toys and that he shouldn't put them in his mouth." Elizabeth cringed when she first approached Mama Corelli on the subject of her mothballs. She knew how Mama felt about her mothballs and prayed that breaching the subject wouldn't escalate into one of those *It's either me or the dog* confrontations. But if poor, old three-legged Max was not sufficient in forcing Mama to make her mothballs scarce, the soon-to-be crawling baby Fred was Elizabeth's ace in the hole. Mama certainly wouldn't want anything to happen to her first and only grandson over a silly superstition.

"You really done it now, Max," said Uncle Nunzio. "The evil spirits'll be comin' through the walls in no time. Yeah, Maxi old boy, it's all downhill from here, nothing but bad luck in your future."

"Bad luck?" cried Uncle Al. "As it stands, the sonofabitch has only three legs! How much unluckier can he get?"

"He could go blind," said Uncle Nunzio.

"Good point," said Uncle Al.

Despite continually going out of his way to try and win her heart, Mama Corelli had no time for poor, old three-legged Max. Whenever Max hobbled into the kitchen, which was often, Mama would scold him with a barrage of expletives, then shoo him away. But ol' Max was not a mutt to give up easily. No siree. He would drop to his belly, place his snout on the floor, and with his droopy ears and droopy eyes, he would look as pathetic as can be. *Okay, Mama, see if you can resist me and my three legs now.*

"Ma, you realize you don't have to use Italian when you curse at Max," said Uncle Nunzio. "He won't understand you any better if you use English."

"He understands me just fine," Mama hollered from the kitchen. Then she unleashed another tirade to inform her youngest son that the use of Italian expletives was for Elizabeth's benefit, not Max's.

"Maybe Max is Italian," said Uncle Al. "Ya never know."

"Sure. And maybe he's also Catholic," retorted Uncle Nunzio.

"Dumb bastard probably gets off on the smell of cicoria," said Uncle Al. "I bet that's why he hangs out in the kitchen."

"Figures," said Uncle Nunzio. "It would take a three-legged old mutt to wanna sniff such garbage."

"What are you two mumbling about in there?" Mama Corelli hollered from the kitchen.

"It's a long story, Ma," they both yelled back.

"Of course, it is," said Mama.

****

With Antonio an ocean away, it later became the belief that baby Fred, in his tender years, fell too much under the influence Uncle Al and Uncle Nunzio. Though it could be said that any influence from his uncles, no matter how insignificant, would have been too much. (Incidentally, with living standards being what they are nowadays, which has resulted in almost everyone in a middle-class household having their own room, television, laptop, notepad, and other preferred handheld devices—which has further resulted in no one needing to share anything—it would seem odd to find someone born into a situation where already entrenched was a grandmother and an uncle ... or two. That was not the case, however, in 1942. The term *family* must have meant something entirely different back in *the good old days*.) A steady diet of Uncle Al and Uncle Nunzio must have adversely affected the way Freddy Corelli was wired. How else could it be explained that he reached adulthood a frustrated plumber? Whoever heard of anything so preposterous? A frustrated chef, musician, writer—any one of those could be explained as they are lofty vocations requiring lofty aspirations. But a plumber? And don't get me wrong, I have a healthy respect for plumbers, but something frightening must have occurred during one of those one-hundred-and-eighty-minute Saturday jaunts.

Ricky, Munchk, and I never could quite figure how Dad ended up a used car salesman who longed to tinker with pipes, the disastrous results notwithstanding, but we knew enough to know that asking would have resulted in an explanation so inane we would have regretted it. Maybe there *was* no relationship between Dad's outcome and his uncles' influence. Maybe Dad was nuts all by himself, although it would be cruel to suggest someone was nuts without *some* validation. Uncle Al and Uncle Nunzio blamed their *admitted* shortcomings on having to inhale and then eat cicoria; not that they were foolish enough to dare to suggest that had Mama Corelli been less ethnic and resourceful, versus more continental and fanciful in her relationship with cuisine, that she might have raised scientists.

Back in the days of our youth—and particularly while assembled at the dinner table, which was a time when we all had one another's undivided attention—like most American boys, Ricky and I hoped to talk baseball with our father. Isn't that what red-blooded American fathers and sons are supposed to do? If not fully engaged in the fundamental activity known as having a backyard catch, shouldn't they spend their free time *talkin'* baseball? Dad, to his credit, did the best he could to accommodate us, but somehow, he managed to steer the conversation back to his favorite subject: Plumbing. "The true blood and guts of every household," he would proclaim. "The pipes in your house are no different than the arteries in your body. And God help you if either of them gets clogged; it's either a heart attack or flood."

"Is he fucking kidding us?" asked Ricky, when we were on our way to the neighborhood courts, with a basketball in tow.

"I'm afraid not," I replied. Though, secretly, I had to admit that Dad's analogy of a house and its copper pipe infrastructure to the arteries of the human body was one of his better moments. I also had to admit, this time aloud, that Dad was adroit at beginning with baseball and ending with plumbing. He had become the master of the segue; his transitions were smooth and, to his credit, despite how irritating, usually on point.

"Ya can't stop them Cincinnati Reds," Dad said of the *Big Red Machine* of the mid-1970s. "Once their offense gets going, it's like gushing water. Ya either have to close up the pipe or deal with the flood; but ya can't close up the pipe unless ya first find the shutoff valve, and good luck with that because it ain't like ol' Sparky Anderson is gonna tell you where it is." (Sparky Anderson managed the Reds in the 70s.)

"Please, Frank, tell me we're adopted," pleaded Ricky, when once again we were on our way to the neighborhood courts.

Gushing water. Now there's an area where Freddy Corelli had some expertise. Yes, he may have known a thing or two about Pete Rose, Joe Morgan, Johnny Bench and the rest of the Big Red Machine, but no one knew gushing water better than our father. No one! And without any further ado, we have finally reached the place in our narrative that was promised earlier. Plumber Fred, take it away!

Growing up, we lived in a corner row house. When you live on a corner, not only do you have a front patio and backyard but also some ground on the side. Mom was the steward and sole decider of how our home's exterior should look and how it was used. Trust me, this was a fact that never reached the point of a discussion never mind a debate. There were never any power struggles within the Corelli domain; Mary Corelli reigned supreme, and her reign went unchallenged.

The front patio served as Mom's asylum from having to contend with one, two, three, and sometimes four children. The backyard was where plum tomatoes that would eventually get turned into the world's most fabulous gravy were grown. The ground on the side was designated for Mom's flower garden. Every year she planted zinnias from seed, which mixed beautifully with the established perennials she planted when she and Dad first moved to good ol' Bennington Street. One mid-June Sunday morning, well before Uncle Al came clanking down the street in his monstrous contraption and before the equally monstrous Mr. Profacci bent over to retrieve the morning paper, Dad, who for whatever reason woke earlier than was his custom, took his coffee outside and noticed the foliage looked a bit fatigued. It was hot weekend and Dad, playing the part of the dutiful husband, thought he would do Mom a good turn by watering the tomato plants, newly sprouted zinnias, and wilted perennials, thus allowing

Mom a morning of leisure. "I'm up, so I may as well," he said, but we were too engrossed in television to care about what might happen to flowers when denied water. As luck would have it, when Dad turned the knob attached to the spigot, he discovered that the spigot had developed a hairline crack—no doubt a result of the harsh winter or the cumulative effect of many Northeast winters. Instead of entering the hose, the water came spouting through the aforementioned crack. Clearly, this was an instance when ordinarily a man would grumble and wheeze; perhaps let loose a few expletives. Not Dad. A cracked spigot brought forth a rush of adrenalin, as it gave him an opportunity to tinker. Off he marched, straightaway to the basement, to locate his trusty pipe wrench. When he returned, he adjusted the wrench to grip the spigot and began turning it. Some difficulty was expected. After all, it was an outdoor fixture, the threads of which potentially were rusted onto the flange. But Dad had no trouble turning his wrench. In fact, to his surprise, it turned with minimal effort—perhaps too little effort. You know what they say when things seem too good to be true?

"This'll be a simple job," said Dad. "One, two, three, lickety-split. All I have to do is pop on a new spigot, and we'll be good to go." That was Dad; everything was either *lickety-split* or *in a jiffy*. Whenever Mom heard *lickety-split* or *in a jiffy*, she'd go reaching for her frying pan and gravy pot and line up all her special ingredients. The reason? Mom's gravy making and Dad's plumbing repairs had in common one glowing feature; they were all-day affairs. The similarities ended there, though, as no two simultaneous efforts, whether worldwide or in the same room, ever produced such opposite results—and not occasionally but every blessed time. It was during these times that Mom was pinned to the stove and Dad was playing Mr. Fix-it that Ricky and I would take off for the day, usually for the basketball courts. Neither of us cared to witness Dad's angst when things got screwed up, or Mom's wrath when the inevitable occurred.

Munchk, on the other hand, would remain right there at Dad's side. She played the role of the cockeyed optimist and would hand him the tools and lend moral support. Munchk wanted so badly for Dad to succeed just once before a plumbing repair escalated into a catastrophe. She longed to utter the words, "I told you so," followed by, "All those other times were just bad luck; Dad really *does* know what he's doing."

"Better wear a life preserver, Munchk," we would whisper on our way out the door.

We always imagined sweat pouring from Dad's brow, his anxiety mounting with each turn of the wrench. "This'll finally do it," he had had too many occasions to pray. Meanwhile, the water had risen to a mere whisker below the nose of his fiercely loyal apprentice.

All right, maybe that was an exaggeration; but there *were* instances in our childhood, when our house was akin to the Titanic with the way it filled with water. Thankfully, it never sank.

Little did Dad know, it wasn't just the spigot that he was turning with his "trusty" wrench, but also the flange *and* the interior copper piping. By the time the amateur understood what was happening, he held in his hand the spigot, which had rusted onto the flange, which, in turn, was still connected to a twelve-inch copper pipe. There was approximately a five-second delay between Dad wondering, "Gee, what's that sound?" and realizing, "Oh shit, that's water gushing in the basement!" By the time he collected his limited wits and went stampeding through the house on his way to the basement and shutoff valve, which was situated in a closet well barricaded behind old junk, he was already standing in ankle-deep water.

Since we're on the subject of basement closets, ours, I suppose, was like most—a place where fascinating items seen on television, that were once believed could make life worth living, remained in unsightly piles. Most of these items were used only once before banished to the closet and never again resurrected. Some, though, were given numerous tries by Dad, who was determined to prove that, with due diligence, a particular item could work that way it was shown to have worked on television. But most often the only time these well-advertised wonder-gadgets ever get disturbed or moved is on the day of a yard sale, or when an imbecile needs to reach the shut-off valve before turning the basement into a subterranean water park. Dad quickly emptied the closet as the water continued to gush and rise. Haphazardly, he tossed the old junk onto the floor. Some of it sank; some of it floated.

"What's with all the commotion!" Mom, who was launched from her bed when she felt the house shake, which was the result of Dad stampeding through the living room, had hollered.

Mom was accustomed to sleeping in on Sundays. She was not pleased. Dad tore through the living room as if his hair was on fire. Ricky, Munchk, and I were watching television and munching on cereal. He blew past us with such alarming speed, his eyes wild with frenzy, we hadn't the chance to ask regarding what was clearly a crisis, though judging from his level of agitation and known history, there was little mystery. We abandoned our bowls and went outside to investigate and found stuck together and laying on the ground a knob, spigot, flange, and copper pipe. *Can you believe he actually did it again?* was the incredulous thought that transpired between Ricky and me. Munchk, who didn't appreciate the clear message in our silent exchange, glared at us with narrowed eyes and a crinkled-up nose. It was the dreaded scrotum look! The look I usually received following the conclusion of a chess match, when Munchk appeared poised to reach under the table and rip off my nuts dare I act smug after having placed her in checkmate.

"Never mind the commotion, Mare! (Dad never enunciated the 'y' in Mom's name.) Just go back to bed!" he hollered back. He was pleading for Mom to not take another step, never mind open the basement door and peer down the stairs. Mom was already in the kitchen by the time Dad had finished emptying the closet to where he could reach the shutoff valve. Objects were floating around the basement.

Meanwhile, Munchk could see the wheels turning in our heads. I am perfectly sincere when saying that the furthest thing from our minds was to add insult to injury, but inflating the inner tubes we used to float in the ocean down the basement was a real gas. You gotta take advantage of your opportunities.

Mom rolled her eyes as only she can, then went rummaging through the kitchen cabinets for her frying pan and gravy pot and then lined up all her special ingredients for a day of culinary arts. The thrill of floating around the basement was short-lived. Ricky and I toweled ourselves off, laced up our sneakers, and collected our basketball. It was off to the courts, and, given the enormity of the flood, our estimated time of return was dinnertime, and even that was optimistic. At the moment, though, our real concern wasn't returning to a dry house but making it to the end of the block before Uncle Al showed up in his monstrous contraption hollering *Who wants to go for a ride!* The dutiful Munchk had gone to the basement to help Dad deal with the flood.

Meanwhile, I barely had one sneaker laced when I heard the doorbell ring. My shoulders slumped, and my head sagged. So did Ricky's. All hope was lost. Who else could it be but Uncle Al? We heard Mom holler, "I'm busy in the kitchen. Would someone please answer the door!"

With Mom pinned to the stove and Dad detained down the basement, I should have jumped up and made for the door. Instead, I remained on the edge of my bed sulking, and those few seconds of wallowing in my *Oh shit, it's Uncle Al* gloom was all that was needed, as the ever dutiful Munchk came scampering up the basement stairs. As she went trudging for the door, she made squishing sounds along the way, her little feet thrusting water through the soles and canvas of her sneakers. For this, I should have felt a twinge of guilt, that I bucked a responsibility I ought not have and in doing so took Munchk away from where she was really needed—with Dad. But then I figured, let her get the door; it's high time she experienced Mr. Profacci's greasy, bald head and his hairy udders when he bends his scantly robed and rotund figure to retrieve his newspaper. Let *her* try and hold down her cereal after becoming acquainted with such gruesomeness, then later have the fat, miserable bastard unwittingly trigger a nightmarish slumber!

"Where's yer old man?" I heard Uncle Al ask Munchk.

Munchk let out a sigh as though the last thing on earth that she wanted was for Uncle Al to involve himself in Dad's latest plumbing catastrophe; that would otherwise be known as the blind leading the blind. Nevertheless, Munchk stepped aside and permitted Uncle Al to pass.

"For cryin' out loud, Lizzy, your shoes are soaking wet!" cried Uncle Al.

"Mom's in the kitchen," said Munchk, hinting to Uncle Al that she had no time to chit-chat less regard the condition of her canvas sneakers.

"Oh, I'll bet she is," said Uncle Al, delighting in the aroma of sautéed onions and garlic. Before he had the chance to exhale and with his eyes all aflutter, Munchk alertly took off for the basement.

"So, what's my favorite nephew up to this morning?" was how Uncle Al cheerily greeted Mom. Uncle Al was expecting Mom to say *Your favorite nephew's still sleeping*, so that he, in typical Uncle Al fashion, could retort using a disdainful roll the eyes. Uncle Al was surprised when Mom rather drolly remarked while nodding in the direction of the basement door, "Why don't you go and have a look for yourself."

"So, my favorite nephew's up bright an' early?" said Uncle Al. "Tackling a project, is he?"

"You have no idea," said Mom.

Uncle Al made it only halfway down the basement steps before abruptly turning tail and heading back to the kitchen.

"I j-just remembered, Mary," he stammered as he went racing by the stove, "I f-forgot to put money in the collection box. Can't cheat the church, ya know. It's a sin. T-tell Freddy I'll catch up with him another day." As Uncle Al went rumbling through the living room, I heard him mutter, "Christ Almighty, there's stuff floatin' down there!"

Mom couldn't help but laugh. Uncle Al did precisely what she expected Uncle Al would do. Who knows what our great-uncle actually had set aside for this Sunday's agenda? Clearly, his intention was not to race back to church to locate a receptacle into which to toss whatever spare change might have been jingling in his pocket. Perhaps his agenda involved emptying the classic beanbag ashtray that was positioned on the dashboard of his pickup truck? Or maybe this was the day he finally intended to repair the infamous sodomite spring, which dwelled under the passenger seat? What his agenda did *not* involve was aiding his *favorite nephew* in the task of ridding a basement of who knows how many gallons of water. For Uncle Al, that was too much like work; and Sundays, like the good book says, was not set aside for work. But far be it from yours truly to blame or disparage Uncle Al, especially when I was perfectly willing to abandon a catastrophe in favor of the neighborhood courts, which is precisely where I would be heading, once Uncle Al was back in his truck and clanking his way down Bennington Street.

Later that day, when Ricky and I returned just in time to enjoy rigatoni smothered in the world's greatest gravy, Munchk was not smiling. She was not particularly pleased that Ricky and I used this worst of all Sundays for a day of leisure, that we bailed out on her and Dad, abandoned them, while they worked tirelessly, marching bucket after bucket from the floor to the wash tubs, hour after hour, until the remaining water could be handled with a mop. Her unfriendly body language and terse manner in which she addressed us, not to mention the dreaded *scrotum look*, told us all that we needed to know. We were, in a word, fucked.

The following day came the toothpaste-in-the-sandwich episode. One could only imagine our surprise when our teeth pierced through the bread on the way to achieving the sandwich's innards. But the worst was yet to come. You see, we wrongly assumed that Munchk merely disposed of the mayonnaise when swapping it for toothpaste. Silly us, always underestimating our baby sister. You'd think by then we could gauge the range of her maleficence—the depths of her vengefulness. Toothpaste in the sandwich? Please! The evil munchkin prankster was just getting warmed up.

Munchk was well aware that my first class following lunch was Algebra 1; for Ricky, it was History. We arrived at our respective classes only to discover that smeared all over the binomials that took me two hours to figure, and a two-page report on the Stamp Act, which took Ricky the better part of a day to write, was the aforementioned mayonnaise—the very same mayonnaise that was *not* in our sandwiches, the result which only moments ago hastened my brain to send a message to my taste buds and alert me: "Hey, asshole, just in case you were wondering, this ain't mayo!"

Indeed, the very same mayonnaise that I imagined had been scraped from our sandwiches with a knife, wiped into a napkin and promptly discarded, caused quite a stir in two classrooms. When I arrived home, Munchk made sure she was right there to greet me with the most satisfied grin I had ever seen anyone wear. She then gave me a pat on the behind and said, "So, tell me, Frank, how was your day? I sure hope it was better than the day *I* had yesterday." A moment later, Ricky had to endure more of the same. I suppose we got what we deserved.

****

There is nothing extraordinary about a bathroom faucet. It's a bathroom faucet. No big deal. By the mid-1970s, indoor plumbing had been around for nearly a century. Turn a faucet on, and presto, you get water. Turn it off, and the water stops flowing. Most generally, that's how this simple but effective modern-day mechanism works. But faucets get old, *and*, as is the case when anything reaches a certain age, they lose some of their effectiveness and dependability. In the case of a faucet, particularly one that has been used with regularity by five people over several years, it can develop a slow drip, perhaps even a leak.

There's nothing exceptional about a leaky faucet. It's a common enough occurrence, and one which every household occasionally has suffered. Often, as I learned in more recent times, a new washer will do the trick; but if the problem persists and one is not adept at household repairs, a licensed plumber should be called … not a car salesman who thinks he's a plumber.

I have learned that among us there are those who allow themselves to become obsessed when a faucet develops a drip, and to the extent where a drip will haunt them and ruin their sleep. Such a person might lie in bed at night, when all is quiet and still, and listen for the pitter-pattering of the persistent drip as it pelts the drain stopper. After a while, such a person will begin to anticipate the pelting, then wonder whether or not the last drip will indeed be the very last. After all, it can't drip forever—can it? That's about the time that *leaky faucet psychology*, if there exists such a condition, kicks in, and the affected person imagines that the drip is getting louder … drip … Drip … DRIP. (What a pity Edgar Allen Poe didn't live in an era with indoor plumbing.) If you are unfortunate enough know such a person, you will know for sure they have gone off the rails when come morning time, you discover them standing in front of a sink with a stopwatch and timing the intervals of the drip … drip … drip. Then Dad, as only he can, took such lunacy a step further by placing a measuring cup under the faucet. He stood there, for who knows how long, staring at his stopwatch, until the cup collected one fluid ounce of water. From that one fluid ounce, he was able to determine how many gallons of water we were losing per week, per month, per year, or until they voted Carter out of office. Dad explained all this mathematics to us one night while we were assembled at the dinner table. He must have figured that the only way to get hungry, growing boys to sit still long enough to listen to such mindless bullshit was when feeding them. Admittedly, despite the inane methodology, Dad's calculations were impressive. On the way to the courts afterward, Ricky and I jibed about the world's most impressive word problem: *If a leaky faucet drips one ounce of water every seventeen minutes, how many gallons of water will it waste per year and, at two cents a gallon, at what cost?* Mmm, a complex word problem, to which a highly stimulated Ricky answered, "I got it, I got it, don't tell me. WHO GIVES A FUCK! The answer is, WHO GIVES A FUCK!!" Hey, Dad, how 'bout them Cincinnati Reds?

When Dad returned from the plumbing supply store, he was beaming as only a man might when in possession of something guaranteed to make him the envy of Bennington Street.

"Look, Mare," he cried, hardly able to contain his excitement, "all chrome! And with separate levers for the hot and cold. No more of that cheapo knob-in-the-middle business. This time we're going first class!"

"How wonderful," cried Mom, clearly mocking the level of enthusiasm Dad had displayed. Then she made for the kitchen, where she went reaching for her frying pan and gravy pot and lined up her special ingredients. Dad was hardly discouraged by Mom's lack of interest and went racing up the stairs, his new toy tucked under his arm. He tore open the box as would a child on Christmas morning having gone for the gift most anticipated, the one that was sure to inspire the lauding of Heaven and instantaneous release of unbridled euphoria—the one that would be the first to become familiar with the basement closet. Dad dropped to his knees and flung open the vanity doors below the sink, eager to put himself to work.

"Oh, *Lizzzzeeee*," called Mom. The accentuated cadence was Mom's way of reminding Munchk that she had better stick around.

"Yeah, Mom, I know, I'm going." Munchk sighed and began to climb the stairs.

The maven plumber and his midget apprentice. Can life get any shakier? Though I'm being entirely unfair to Munchk; it was hardly her aspiration to become an apprentice to a wannabe plumber, especially on, of all days, a Saturday. I couldn't say with any certainty what Munchk's plans were that day. No doubt, when she woke, like any student who wakes on Saturday morning, she felt the thrill knowing the entire day belonged to her. Poor Munchk.

"The damn knob on the shut-off valve won't turn," those of us below heard Dad grumble. Mom was at the stove. Ricky and I were at the dining room table with our baseball cards. To Dad's credit, he did try to disable the water supply before dismantling the old faucet. He knew that much.

"Maybe it needs some oil," Munchk respectfully advised him.

"The damn thing's too old and rusty," Dad told her. "Oil won't do. I'm gonna go grab my pipe wrench. That'll give me enough torque to loosen this baby."

Munchk swallowed nervously. Who wouldn't? The last seven words she wanted to hear, or anyone would want to hear, especially when the task at hand was swapping out one faucet for another, was, *I'm gonna go grab my pipe wrench.* These were not words that inspired confidence, especially with the memory of the basement irrevocably etched in everyone's mind. Munchk also realized that the configuration of the knob of the shut-off valve was not exactly compliant with a pipe wrench.

"Dad, while you're at it, maybe you should also grab a pair of pliers and a bucket," Munchk advised. Dad wasn't sure what purpose a pair of pliers and a bucket would play in the changing of a faucet; but to his credit, he took Munchk's suggestion without question and returned with the requested items *and* the dreaded pipe wrench. As it would come to pass, not questioning Munchk, who was resolute when making her requests, would be the only thing Dad did right all day.

If I may defend poor Freddy Corelli—and I do not advocate that a pipe wrench should have been introduced, nor involved during any stage of the project, let alone plucked from the toolbox—it should be noted that until clearly visible on the surface, the wearing of a metal pipe or any weakness it has accrued over time is difficult to detect, especially for an amateur. Nevertheless, and with confidence, Dad adjusted the wrench, placed it on the knob of the valve, then gave it a healthy yank. What's worse, he proceeded to yank the wrench before having made a preliminary effort to estimate how much torque was required to loosen an old valve knob. Instead, he simply, mindlessly, and, as it would come to pass, regrettably yanked. Perhaps a display of manliness was what Dad had in mind. It is not all that uncommon—or so I'm told, for I have only a son—for a father to want to appear strong and heroic while in the presence a daughter; though not in retrospect or otherwise would Dad admit to having such motives.

Plumbers and heroes notwithstanding, as we should have expected, the metal tore like tissue paper. In the grip of Dad's *trusty* pipe wrench were the knob, valve, and a twisted piece of metal, which served as the pipe which provided the faucet with good old-fashioned Philadelphia H2O. Through the jagged end of the piping still jutting out from the wall gushed the aforementioned water. Lots and lots of water! Dad's eyes bulged with astonishment. He froze, and his mouth fell agape. The water gushed with such force that it pelted Dad's crotch as he remained kneeling on the floor in front of the sink; his stupor, one of incredulity.

"Dad!" cried Munchk.

Several gallons of water gushed forth before Dad was released from his stupor. He got to his feet, then came lumbering down the stairs in pants so laden with water that it made an otherwise simple maneuver a cumbersome strain. When Dad reached the landing of the stairs, he continued on with a tiptoeing side-to-side gait—the sort of gait one might use when having pissed themselves and did not wish to have the affected parts of their pants contact their skin. On the way to the basement and main shut-off valve, in the kitchen, Dad quickened his idiotic tiptoeing side-to-side prance. He hoped that Mom, who was already well involved with her gravy making, wouldn't notice the condition of his pants nor the squishing sounds that his shoes made as he hopped along, not to mention the puddles that were left in his wake.

"Looks like the dam broke again," I drolly remarked.

"Nice pants, Dad," Ricky added.

Before Dad managed to reach the shut-off valve—not the one dedicated to the bathroom sink; that one he was unable to locate, so he made for the main valve and shut off the water source to the entire house save for the outside spigot—Munchk had the presence of mind to take the pair of pliers and pinch close the end of the jagged pipe. It didn't stem the flow of water entirely, but enough to where whatever trickling persisted was managed with the bucket she so brilliantly requested. The water stopped trickling altogether, when Dad, not without an effort, twisted shut the main valve.

Poor Dad; if he had his druthers, along with access to the necessary instruments, he might have hung himself or, at the very least, spent the rest of his life hidden away in the basement, perhaps behind the old

114

junk in the closet, occasionally tapping on the ceiling to signal for bread and water. Either scenario seemed kinder than having to resurface only to walk by Mom, who, despite the commotion, remained busy at the stove; she was pretending to be oblivious. There were instances when Mom acting oblivious was more effective than her famous confrontations; it made you more nervous, if for no other reason than it was out of character. Mom never as much as looked our way when, from the dining room table after completing a Carew for Yastrzemski trade, Ricky and I began humming, "Row, Row, Row Your Boat."

Months later, when the faucet debacle was well behind us, Mom confessed to having to bite down on her cheeks to keep from laughing out loud. You see, she didn't always run roughshod over Dad or tear him a new one. Ol' Mary Corelli did have *a* subtle bone in her body, and feigning ignorance was one way she, on rare occasions, would intimate to Dad the level of her anger. And at times, she could be clever, and that was when she was at her best and most amusing, and the faucet episode gave her a golden opportunity.

While Dad remained in the basement deciding *how* or whether he *should* show his face … or hang himself, Munchk remained in the bathroom where she worked diligently on the flood. Gallon after gallon, one bucket at a time, water was swept into a pail then dumped into the bathtub. Meanwhile, I was attempting to coax Ricky into parting with one of his two Johnny Benches for a Catfish Hunter, thus ignoring the efforts of our dutiful baby sister. And yes, we knew we were fucked. It was a given. For that matter, so too was Dad if he didn't soon get his sorry ass up from the basement.

This was one instance when I honestly did sympathize with Dad. We all have had dreams of being in a public place—for me, it was the classroom—only to discover that we were naked and left to agonize over how we could sneak away and make it all the way home without being seen. I imagined that Dad was suffering similar anxiety, down the basement, alone and with nothing but his own stupidity for company, while he fitfully calculated a way to make it to the bathroom to help Munchk without first being seen by Mom. What a dilemma! And the best was yet to come. Before the cleanup reached the point where Munchk was able to manage with a mop, some of the water found spaces between the mosaic tiles where the grout had long since gone missing. Incidentally, did I fail to mention that the kitchen is directly below the bathroom? And that the stove is directly below the sink? I'd like to exaggerate and say water came pouring down on Mom. In truth, it came down a drop at a time and in approximately three-second intervals. The reason I say the intervals were "approximately" three seconds apart, Dad wasn't there to time the drips with his trusty stopwatch.

Nevertheless, Mom did something that under no circumstances she had ever done before, at least not to our knowledge. She abandoned not only the stove but the kitchen entirely while making gravy. This was an act of unparalleled magnitude, and it seemed so unnatural that it caused Ricky and I, as we were about to execute the trade of two Bill Madlocks for a George Brett, to wonder whether Mom had gone off the rails or foresaw her death and was about to drive herself to the nearest hospital. In our own chaotic and dysfunctional little world, Mom abandoning her pot of scarlet-colored delight was an event that would rank alongside a guard at *the tomb of the unknown soldier* should he one day say, "Fuck this," and abandon his post to go grab a coffee at a nearby Starbucks. But Mom wasn't gone long from her post, and when she returned, she had in her possession, of all items, an umbrella.

I've seen many a strange occurrence in my life and times, but not before, nor since, have I witnessed anyone working at a stove underneath an umbrella. This was Mom's subtle or perhaps *not* so subtle way of categorically stating, *"Yep, my husband is an asshole all right. I married a real Jimbroni."*

After Dad, in his bedraggled state, worked up enough nerve to emerge from the basement, Mom pretended not to notice the drenched pants and the shoes that squished when he pathetically slinked on by. Dad, who was on his way *not* to install a new faucet—his original aspiration would not come to fruition until a licensed plumber replaced the torn away pipe and valve—but to assist Munchk with what remained of the flood, pretended not to notice the umbrella. I learned something that day. There is nothing more amusing than watching people attempt to ignore that which is glaringly obvious. I can say firsthand that, when such ignorance is performed well—and on that day, two virtuosos were at the very top of their game—there is nothing more hilarious.

When Mom was all through with the long and laborious process of yet another otherworldly culinary delight, and it came time to boil water for the rigatoni she had planned to serve, she took her pot and placed it at the top of the stairs. Once again, her attempt at subtlety, when her real aim was to be overtly scathing, was masterful. Her point was, and I shall paraphrase a famous nursery rhyme: *Since you once again fucked up the plumbing, this time leaving me no source of water with which to continue, go and fetch me a pail of water... you asshole!*

Begrudgingly, Dad did as the Gibraltar-sized hint suggested; he took the pot not up a hill, as does Jack in the famous nursery rhyme, but to the spigot outside, which, a while back, was replaced by a licensed professional. Luckily for Dad, this spigot was separate from the main valve, thus leaving us an available source of water. People have been known to occasionally borrow a cup of sugar from a neighbor but never a pot of water. Dad filled the pot and rather sheepishly returned it to Mom, who was still sporting her umbrella. He also appeared aggravated, for, when outside at the spigot, he had to endure one of those smug sourpuss smirks from Mr. Profacci, who, along with Mrs. Profacci, had just returned from dinner. *Fucked up again, ay Corelli,* his satisfied smirk had clearly conveyed. Mr. Profacci delighted in the misfortunes of others. He enjoyed anything that provided him the opportunity to unleash his smug, smirky puss—it wasn't just Uncle Al's truck that lit up his life.

Dad came through the dining room with short, careful steps, and with both hands firmly grasping the handles of the pot. God forbid he sent a couple drops of water flying from the pot onto the carpet. We couldn't have that! As Dad passed the dining room table, where I lightened my collection of one of its three Carlton Fisks for a Nolan Ryan, we heard him grumbling about "fat bastards" who patronize "all-you-can-eat buffets" and how they stand in lines holding trays onto which they eagerly await the opportunity to "pile greasy, disgusting food." Dad closed by adding, "I'll have the last laugh when that fat bastard has a heart attack."

At the end of what began an eventful day and stubbornly remained such, once we were all assembled for dinner, with each forkful of rigatoni, Dad swooned and declared Mom a "culinary goddess." He knew that he had fucked up and would have to spend however long it took for a licensed professional to fix the plumbing with his lips puckered and stuck to Mom's ass, which was a familiar theme and one of the few matters he managed with any level of proficiency. You'd swear that Mom had an imaginary altar that followed her around; and there was Dad, scampering not far behind, trying his darndest to keep pace so that he could take advantage of every opportunity to kneel and smooch. Shamelessly, poor Freddy Corelli would grovel before and praise his wife; however, the lower he groveled and the loftier his praise, the more he was ignored.

Meanwhile, at dinner, while Dad was receiving the silent treatment, Ricky and I were getting the famous *scrotum look,* which was Munchk's version of the evil eye. It was amazing how one so slight of form, so diminutive, could seem so menacing, but somehow, she owned the facility to strike fear in the heart of others—their age and size notwithstanding. Perhaps it was her fearless nature or ability to take hold of the moment that made her seem more in control of a given situation than those around her. Whatever the case, it was impossible to guess what trick Munchk might have up her sleeve; but, as sure as Ricky and I were sitting there, her vindictive wheels were already in motion.

Later on, that evening, Mom further humiliated Dad, this time by way of another one of her not so subtle gestures, which saw her take her toothbrush, paste, and bathroom cup to the outside spigot. The message was loud and clear to the neighbors, particularly Mr. Profacci, the fat prick, who was peeking through his blinds, and also for all those who happened to be passing by: *Beware; this is the sort of thing that can happen when you marry a moron.*

On the following morning, Mom awoke to her slippers placed at her bedside, her bathrobe neatly folded on the nightstand, and a pot of water waiting for her by the bathroom sink. Meanwhile, Ricky and I awoke with trepidation and fear of reprisal. When passing through the hallway, we peered into the bedroom of the evil munchkin and found her peacefully sleeping, or so it appeared. Being grades behind and her first class not beginning until nine, it wasn't necessary for Munchk to wake until it was nearly time for us to leave.

"I'll bet she's faking," whispered Ricky.

"Could be," I said, "but she looks asleep to me."

We crept downstairs to the refrigerator to see if our sandwiches had been tampered with. To watch us unwrap them, one would think it would have been more prudent to call the bomb squad or that we had involved ourselves in a matter better suited for national security.

"Mine looks okay," I said. "How 'bout yours?"

"So far so good," said Ricky.

After rewrapping our sandwiches, we flipped through the pages of our school books, searching for signs of sabotage, be it mayonnaise, missing pages, etc.…

"Nothing," I reported.

"Same here," said Ricky.

Mmm, I thought. *Munchk is either slipping or planning something really elaborate later on when least expected.* It was when Ricky and I were loading our schoolbags with our un-tampered lunches and un-sabotaged books that we heard Munchk stirring. We decided to wait for her appearance before making for the bus. We were hoping to gauge her mood, holding to the notion that, provided with a few minutes of interaction, we might gain some insight into what sort of vengeance was on the horizon. When she reached the kitchen, she appeared exceedingly drowsy, like someone who had been up all night surreptitiously tinkering away.

"Good morning, Frank," was how she cheerily greeted me. Her cheeriness, although an effort, seemed genuine. Then she gave me a pat on the behind. That was the signal! The friendly pat on the behind! We were already fucked; we just hadn't figured out how!

"Have a nice day," she called to us as we went for the coat closet.

Munchk's prank didn't quite register until Ricky and I had already followed through with having placed both arms in the sleeves of our coats. With a mixture of stupefaction and disgust, we gingerly peeled away our coat sleeves from our arms, then let our outer garments drop to the floor. Smeared all over our arms and much of our shirts was a smorgasbord of every imaginable condiment: mustard, ketchup, relish, horseradish, mayonnaise, Cheese Whiz... A1 fucking Steak Sauce! We made a mad dash to the kitchen sink to rinse off. I arrived first.

"There's no water, Frank, you moron," Munchk reminded me. "Remember the flood? The one I all but cleaned up by myself?"

"Jesus Christ!" I cried out, as Ricky and I stood in the kitchen and, with bulging eyes and mouths agape, regarded one another's appearance.

"Uh oh, that's not the bus I hear, is it?" wondered Munchk. She was lounging comfortably with a bowl of cheerios in her lap and her little feet dangling over the arm of a chair. "You two had better start running."

I didn't know who I was angrier with, Dad or Munchk. Ultimately, our current predicament began with Dad. But Munchk was wearing this self-satisfying smirk, one of unparalleled smugness, which I had not the time to wipe off because a bus needed to be caught.

"Jesus Christ is right!" cried Ricky as we grabbed our school bags and then went tearing down the street. We resembled a painter's palette and smelled like a day-old hoagie in the cool morning air as we sprinted for the bus. Our only saving grace was that the school bathrooms had running water and paper towels. Still, we had to sit in our respective classrooms in wet shirts that reeked from a multitude of condiments. The evil munchkin really stuck it to us.

Every family has its own dynamics—its inner-workings—otherwise known as all the quirks that make it unmistakably *your* family. We don't always appreciate these dynamics, but, as time goes by, we learn to love it, even depend on it. If nothing else, Dad's plumbing catastrophes helped to reinforce the roles and stations within the household. Mom reigned supreme, whereas Dad, and I am being generous, was a distant subordinate. In fact, to suggest that Dad was second in command to Mom would be the equivalent of suggesting that Bruce Seldon finished second to Mike Tyson—Iron Mike KO'd Seldon in the first round.

Munchk was Dad's ever-reliable sympathizer—a real Freddy Corelli apologist. As his apprentice, not only was Munchk able to anticipate Dad's debacles but also predict the heights to which they would escalate. Hence: the call for pliers and a bucket. It was during the times of those debacles that, right or wrong, for better or worse, Ricky and I would foolishly try and elevate our status to somewhere alongside that of Mom's. The result was always the same; our baby sister was *Johnny on the spot* with regards to providing our comeuppance. At the time, it never seemed fair that Dad's screwups should result in episodes such as Ricky and I biting into toothpaste-loaded sandwiches; though I suppose poor Dad had all he could handle with Mom's verbal and often times psychological abuse. The last thing this sorry member of the junior varsity needed was having to contend with the diabolical pranks of an evil munchkin. Looking back on it, despite having greater numbers, the men in the household were no match for the women. They whipped our ass every time.

****

When Antonio stepped off the bus appearing quite fit and trim in his uniform, but also looking as if he misplaced his razor; perhaps it was only fitting, as he set his sights in the direction of Twenty-sixth and Indiana, that the first thing he should see was Vincent Bronini driving the wrong way on a one-way street. Nothing says "welcome home" like friends up to their old tricks. Antonio smiled. He didn't approve of recklessness and stupidity, but it warmed him the notion that good ol' Swampoodle hadn't changed and there was an indication that home was still home-sweet-home, a place he belonged.

"Hey, Antonio, welcome home!" the imbecile called from the open window of his car, as he was intersecting Lehigh Avenue by way of Twenty-second Street. "Wanna ride?"

"No thanks," Antonio called back. "I'm gonna enjoy the fresh air. Besides, I need to stretch my legs. But it's good to see you, Vinny."

Little did Antonio know, he and Vincent Bronini had a common destination; though had he known and had the Jimbroni been driving in the right direction on the one-way street, Antonio would have passed on a ride. He had spent much of the day cooped up on buses and trains bringing him homeward. And it was true, he did desire fresh air and stretching his legs; but more than anything, he wished to reacquaint himself with the feel of old and familiar sidewalks under his feet and the sight of old and familiar signs in store windows along the avenue. He would walk tall and proud and feel the sights and sounds of the bustling neighborhood all around him. But Swampoodle wasn't so bustling as he remembered. Perhaps things *had* changed, and he had not returned to the same place. Everything looked the same. It even smelled the same. But where was all the buzz—the buzz that routinely froths in a community where folks are close-knitted, enjoy the commonality of how they worship and background, *and*, as was often the case in Swampoodle, were related? Nowhere in sight were boys in grass-stained baseball uniforms parading the sidewalks celebrating a victory. Nor were folks seen shuffling in and out of Nicastro's Tavern, Delvecchio's Deli, Martin's Apothecary, Pazienza's Bakery, or the local five-and-ten. There was only a smattering of folks, none of whom Antonio recognized, nor did they recognize him. Even at Fumo's pool hall—the neighborhood's most notorious hangout, which doubled as Nails' headquarters and featured characters ranging from Nails' lackeys to Uncle Al and Uncle Nunzio—as Antonio observed, when he peered through the window, the crowd was unusually sparse. With mild bewilderment, he shrugged at his own reflection in the window, then headed home to the welcoming arms of Elizabeth and his first ever meeting with two-year-old Freddy Corelli. Along the way, he was saluted by a passerby—the man was an old neighborhood fixture Antonio thought he recognized but whose name he could not recall if indeed he ever knew it. The man was the first and last to acknowledge Antonio's uniform before he turned onto Twenty-sixth Street. It was there, a few paces from home, that he became enlightened to the reason for the mysteriously silent pool hall and quiet midday streets. On a banner that was long and wide enough to eclipse the second story of three row houses were the printed words: *Welcome Home, Antonio.* On the porches and sidewalks in front of those houses, and also spilling into the street, stood people whose count could not be estimated by their lone and overcome onlooker, other than to gawk and wonder: *My*

121

goodness, there must be hundreds! As Antonio approached, he saw among the notable gathering the faces of Turd, Moose, Skullhead, Patty One Eye, Meat, Stranger, Crazy Legs and Sixty-Four, along with many others, who ordinarily would be occupying the pool hall and taverns of Swampoodle. Even Nails made a cameo appearance. Antonio also spotted amid the gathering his always smiling cousin from Toscana, Vito, the cheese vendor. But what truly warmed his heart was all the ball caps, grass-stained uniforms, and dirt smudged faces that earlier were thought to have been missing. The children of the neighborhood, although grown up a bit, were gathered in force to welcome home their Uncle Tony. With a broad smile and with one eye always on Elizabeth, who from the top step of the porch did her best to remain poised and patient, Antonio acknowledged each and every one of the boys as they rushed to gather around him.

"My goodness," he bellowed, "you guys are practically men. I could hardly recognize youse!" What followed were a dozen or so young men hollering out, "Do you remember me, Uncle Tony? Do you remember *me?*"

It took some time, but Antonio was finally permitted to wind his way through the enthusiastic crowd and up onto the top step of the porch, where waiting for him was a woman known for her poise, who launched herself into his burly arms.

"My goodness, what a kiss!" said Uncle Nunzio at our grandfather's surprise sixtieth birthday party. "We thought they were gonna make up for the whole two-and-a-half years right in front of the whole neighborhood!"

"Yeah," said Uncle Al, "but by the time the smooch ended, there wasn't a dry eye on the block, and everyone was cheering. Even the two young boys next door, who were scared shitless of Ma, came out to cheer."

"Those two weren't the only ones scared shitless, ay Freddy?" teased Uncle Nunzio. "I think it was a whole week before you could look at your old man without needin' your diaper changed."

"I have no memory of that," claimed Dad. "As far as I know, it could all be lies. Go on, Mom, tell 'em."

Our grandmother smiled demurely, then shrugged as if to say: *I'm sorry, son; I'd like to rewrite history on your behalf, but I cannot.*

Little Freddy Corelli stood on the porch positioned warily behind Mama Corelli, where he hoped to remain hidden away. Through fearful eyes, and while holding on tightly to Mama Corelli's hand and housedress, he watched helplessly his mother in the process of being devoured by someone whom he perceived as a huge, hairy stranger. It mattered not how many stories he was told of the brave soldier fighting for his country overseas; this was not a scene for which little Freddy Corelli was prepared. To poor, little Freddy, the long arms, hulking shoulders, huge powerful hands, rugged, unshaven face, along with the uniform that commanded the adulation of many were utterly monstrous. Every young child has his or her own notion of the boogieman—who this universal phantom is and what he might look like—and for poor, little two-year-old Freddie Corelli, the boogieman turned out to be his own father. Sensing this, Antonio made a funny face, hoping it would break the ice or draw a smile from the frightened youngster, but the boogieman's funny face caused little Freddy to further retreat behind Mama Corelli's stoutness. Meanwhile, down below and pawing away at Antonio's leg and wanting his fair share of attention was poor, old three-legged Max.

"Max, you remember me?" cried Antonio. The boogieman lifted up Max and his three legs so that they were face to snout. Max, in turn, friskily licked Antonio's unshaven chin. Antonio hoped that the canine's affectionate display would bring forth his terrified son.

"Freddy, say hello to your Poppa," urged Mama Corelli. "He came from Europe—all the way from the other side of the world just to see *you*! What do you have to say to that?" Mama Corelli lifted up little Freddy as though preparing to offer him up to his father, but the frightened toddler recoiled, threw his arms around Mama's neck, and held on for dear life. Antonio held up a hand. It was to let Mama Corelli know that the joys of fatherhood would have to happen in their own sweet time, that this long-anticipated meeting could not be forced. Antonio Corelli was the world's greatest son, brother, and husband; and now, to be any kind of father, he would first have to convince a toddler that he wasn't, of all things, the boogieman.

Antonio went back out into the crowd, where once again he was embraced by Vito, the cheese vendor, and several others. The good cheer and genuine affection with which he was surrounded warmed him more than he could express, but it did not prevent him from becoming preoccupied with the brand-new Cadillac that was parked in front of his house. As he recalled, in Swampoodle, only Nails, the flashy gangster wannabe, owned a Cadillac. Since the United States first became involved in World War II, Nails had made his way through the ranks, having become a bigger deal in the rackets. Antonio, with a roving eye, managed to dissect the crowd and saw that Nails had gone. So too had his two associates who, like bodyguards, had him well flanked. But the Cadillac remained. When Antonio asked to whom the Cadillac belonged, the answers he received ranged from long-winded to fragmented, and most were convoluted. He didn't wish to spoil the good mood that pervaded Twenty-sixth Street, so he resisted accusing anyone of talking in circles.

Meanwhile, Mama Corelli served spaghetti and meatballs, and neighbors poured homemade red wine from gallon jugs. Twenty-sixth and Indiana had become a genuine festival—a block party for the ages! Not an altogether bad way for a soldier to get reintroduced and reacclimated into civilian life; and aside from welcoming someone beloved, it gave folks a chance to celebrate the end of a war. And as our grandfather once told us, "There's no event more worthwhile of a celebration than the ending of a war won by the side fighting for freedom and the rights of man." Antonio spoke nothing of the conflict itself but volumes of the friendships he made along the way—particularly the friendships he gained with Kowalski, O'Malley, and Dugan.

"You two birds woulda loved 'ol Dugan," he told Uncle Al and Uncle Nunzio. "The guy couldn't shut up about DiMaggio and the Yankees— it's all he ever talked about. Like you two, he's a real frontrunner—couldn't spare an ounce of love for the underdog."

By the time the global conflict ended, Antonio knew more about "Murderer's Row" and "The Bronx Bombers" than anyone living outside of the New York Metropolitan area. Even the more obscure names such as Earl Combs, Mark Koenig, and Bob Meusel were irrevocably etched in his brain. As far as 'ol Dugan was concerned, Gutzon and Lincoln Borglum were remiss for having omitted the faces of Yankee managers Miller Huggins and Joe McCarthy, when chiseling into Mount Rushmore; never before, according to Dugan, was so egregious an oversight committed. Naturally, the first thing that Uncle Al and Uncle Nunzio wanted to know from Antonio was, did he meet Joe DiMaggio? They knew full well that the great Yankee center fielder, along with other baseball greats, Hank Greenberg, Ted Williams, and Bob Feller, was drafted into the war.

"I met plenty of *paisans*," Antonio told them, "but none that played baseball, at least not for a living."

As the supply of food and wine dwindled, so too did the crowd, and yet the brand-new Cadillac had not budged. Antonio couldn't say why he was so obsessed with the vehicle, other than such a large, shiny, expensive machine looked out of place on Twenty-sixth Street. Unless matters changed in a way he had yet to learn, the eye-catching automobile was well out of the financial reach of all who, despite the dwindling supply of food and wine, had remained. His intuition was screaming that something about the car was amiss; yet he managed to set aside his misgivings in favor of mingling and thanking everyone for taking the time to welcome him home. He looked on as Meat strolled away with Turd, Moose with Skullhead, Stranger with Patty One Eye, Sixty-four with a young woman new to Antonio.

At the same time, Vincent Bronini drove off, thankfully in the right direction. Alone at last, Antonio, Elizabeth, and poor, old three-legged Max stood on the porch overlooking the quiet sidewalk and street, while there sat, provoking Antonio's obsession and fanning the fires of his curiosity, the mystery vehicle, this uninvited guest, who made a masked appearance and was stubbornly clutching to its anonymity, refusing to reveal itself. Antonio was beginning to suspect that, in his absence, Uncle Al and Uncle Nunzio graduated from dead pigs to new cars but dismissed the notion, preferring to believe the pep talk he delivered before going off into the army meant something, that it wasn't heard and readily forgotten, but resonated and carried influence that was sustaining. No, Uncle Al and Uncle Nunzio, once unsupervised, had not reverted back to their foolhardy ways, but were true to their word and did as promised and looked after Elizabeth and child. Or had they?

Come evening, Antonio made repeated trips to the window; each time, he peeked through the blinds and continued to obsess over the mystery vehicle. His instincts were warning him to be wary, that the shiny new Cadillac represented trouble—if not for him then for someone. On what would end up his final trip to the window, something distracted him. Instead of peering through the blinds, he turned away from the window and toward Uncle Al.

"I see you took up smoking," he said. Uncle Al replied by making an indecipherable noise that was part *yes* and part *grunt*, to go along with what appeared an ineffectual shrug. From the feeble sound and gesture, Antonio gathered that Uncle Al began smoking for lack of something better to do. It was also becoming clear to Antonio that his obsession with the Cadillac was making Uncle Al a nervous wreck.

"You think that maybe he shoulda taken up the clarinet, instead?" Uncle Nunzio's snarkiness took Antonio by surprise. So too did the zealousness with which he defended Uncle Al. "Who knows, Antonio, maybe Al could become the next Benny Goodman. What do *you* think? Do you think that's possible?"

"All right, Nunz." Antonio glowered. "Since you're such a smart guy, why don't *you* tell me about the Cadillac?"

"Enough already with this friggin car!" protested Uncle Nunzio. "It's all you been thinkin' about since you got here! Now, little Freddy 'ill be asleep any minute, and you haven't seen your wife in two-and-a-half years. For Chrissake, go say goodnight to your son and take Elizabeth out on a date. And while you're at it, stop worryin' about that damn car!"

"Fine, Nunz," said Antonio, "I'll take Elizabeth out on a date. I agree with you; it's what I should do. But don't think for one minute this conversation is over."

"Hey, Antonio, do ya smell that?" hissed Uncle Nunzio. He pointed into the air and was alluding to the earthy mixture of cicoria, mothballs, and espresso coffee that often hovered thickly in the house. "It means you're not in the army anymore. And just in case you were wondering, we've been doing just fine these past two-and-a-half years without you."

Antonio and Elizabeth made it to Hunting Park just in time for the evening's last carousel ride. Antonio left the house having been humbled by Uncle Nunzio, and now the prevailing obsession was not the Cadillac but wondering whether there was any credibility to his youngest brother's assertion, that his presence at Twenty-sixth and Indiana would not be nearly so vital post World War II as it had been prior. He forced himself, while strolling the park, to regard only Elizabeth and concluded that she looked just as beautiful as he remembered, but she seemed sturdier, that over the past two-and-a-half years she gained strength—it was not only evident on the surface but emanated from within. Motherhood had catapulted Elizabeth's status; she was more woman than the woman Antonio said goodbye to thirty months ago, and he bounded alongside her as would a child striving for equal footing, to catch up in both distance and time.

Uncle Al and Uncle Nunzio also appeared to be in good standing, or as good a status as one could hope. Mama Corelli had aged accordingly but she was still energetic enough to cook spaghetti and meatballs for a welcome-home committee large enough to have blanketed the sidewalk and spill into the street. Even poor, old three-legged Max had a little bounce remaining in his three legs. Everything seemed to be pointing toward what Uncle Nunzio was sharp in suggesting, that life at Twenty-sixth and Indiana had carried on quite nicely without the guidance of Antonio Corelli. As he, with Elizabeth, continued to stroll Hunting Park, he tried to reconcile the notion that his house was no longer a ship over which he needed to assume command, but rather a place into which he should allow himself to gradually dissolve and assimilate.

Separated by two-and-a-half-years, along with pondering the role of a returning soldier, for Antonio, holding Elizabeth's hand felt strangely new and exciting, and the onrush of strangeness and excitement helped him to forget all about the brand-new shiny Cadillac parked in front of his house. A war involving sixty-seven nations waging battles on three continents had been fought and would affect the globe going forward for the foreseeable future, and yet Antonio Corelli found himself right back in Russo's variety store, where he and Elizabeth went reaching for the same lone copy of a newspaper. He was having his first date all over again and was more nervous the second go-around. As the two strolled through the park, with Elizabeth bringing Antonio up to speed on family and neighborhood affairs, something strange occurred to Antonio: Since the day of their chance meeting, he and Elizabeth had spent far more time apart than together. In fact, they had known one another for only a fraction of their lives and had been in the company of one another for only a fraction of that fraction. The unsettling notion led Antonio to wonder whether the war had erased what little equity had been built and that he would need much more than a welcome-home party and a date at Hunting Park to discover whether or not he and Elizabeth were the same people who bumped into one another, then two-and-a-half years ago were forced to say goodbye. What was more, it all seemed so insignificant when juxtaposed to what was the most epic war in human history. As he would learn in the days ahead when contacted by Dugan, O'Malley, and Kowalski, he was standing in a crowded boat filled with men experiencing the same sort of rocky transition.

"Even with you gone, Freddy's first word was still *dad*," said Elizabeth.

"His mother wouldn't have had anything to do with it, would she have? Really," Antonio ironically added, "I'm impressed that without any coaching, he just happened to blurt out the word *dad*. The kid must be a genius!"

"Okay, maybe he had a *little* coaching." Matching Antonio's irony, Elizabeth added, "I might have mentioned the word *dad* a time or two, but only in passing."

For Antonio, the notion of little Freddy was all at once sobering, exhilarating, and terrifying. Like thousands of other men, who either left pregnant wives or cooing infants, Antonio returned to the life of a child in progress—a little person, who was already walking and talking and, moreover, already knew how to make cognitive decisions, including who he thought was scary.

The lights of the carousel remained on, and the music would continue to play until all the receipts were counted and the patrons had filed out of the park. The buzz of the park was beginning to wind down when Antonio and Elizabeth strolled over to the lake. All the pedal boats were docked and tied, and so the glimmer of park lamps and moonlight on the lake was undisturbed. Antonio asked for "just a few minutes" on the lake. The man in charge of the pedal boats was about to hiss at the idea, for the boats were tied, the park was minutes from closing time, and he wanted to go home. Then he noticed Antonio's uniform. Following a moment of reflection, he decided in favor of honoring the request of a recently returned soldier and his wife, who had chosen Hunting Park as their first postwar outing.

"Take all the time you want," the man said, after scurrying to untie one of the boats. "Just tie her up when you're through." Antonio tried to slide the man a little extra coin for his kindness, but the man refused. Acknowledging Antonio's uniform, he said, "You already paid more than your share. Tonight's fare is good for the whole season." Then the man saluted both Antonio and Elizabeth and went on his way.

"Ah, what a nice gesture," said Elizabeth. "You seem to bring out the best in people."

"I'm sure it was only the uniform," said Antonio. "I doubt very much that I had anything to do with it."

"Perhaps," said Elizabeth, though she was hardly convinced of Antonio's humble assessment of himself. I, for one, am inclined to agree with the woman who would one day become my grandmother. No doubt the uniform was a factor, but our grandfather had an innate facility to bring out the best in everyone.

They pedaled out into the middle of the lake and rested under the stars. There, Antonio expressed his concerns that Elizabeth had a two-and-a-half-year head start regarding the endeavor of parenting, while he was virtually clueless and was about to be thrown into the lion's den. "I don't even know where to begin." He frowned with consternation. "Even a rough outfit like the army gives you three months of basic training."

"You can begin by not thinking too hard about it," Elizabeth told him. "Do whatever comes naturally. Your goodness will take care of the rest."

When they arrived home, where they would share a bed for the first time in thirty months, gone from the front of the house was the Cadillac. Once entering the house, Antonio discovered that gone too was Uncle Al. The mystery was solved. Antonio assumed, correctly, that these two events were hardly coincidental and as connected as any two occurrences could be. Little Freddy was sleeping peacefully, not in a bassinet or crib but in a trundle bed, to which he had long since graduated. Elizabeth went and kissed little Freddy on the forehead. Antonio remained behind, standing in the doorway, where he pondered the immeasurable significance of a child's first two-and-a-half years. Mama Corelli was also sleeping peacefully. Antonio returned to his throes of contemplating the issue of Uncle Al and the Cadillac when he went to Mama's bedside and placed a kiss on her forehead. He looked in on Uncle Nunzio, who was also sleeping, or so it appeared. He elected not to disturb his youngest brother, nor would he eagerly await Uncle Al's return. Instead, he put the car and how it might have legitimately or illegitimately been acquired from his mind. He went to Elizabeth. Tomorrow, however, would be another day.

"When I got home from the slaughterhouse, he had that look in his eye—the one we dreaded," said Uncle Al, at our grandfather's surprise sixtieth birthday party. "Then, when he started to talk, he was real calm—too calm. I thought for sure I was a goner. You see, when Antonio hollered at us—meaning Nunz and me—within minutes, everything was back to normal. But when he talked calm, he'd have us shakin' in our shoes. And not that he ever woulda, but when you look at Antonio, then Nunz and me, all it woulda taken was one swat."

"I thought for sure Antonio was gonna send us to the cellar for the coal shovels and that we were gonna get chauffeured to Fairmount Park," said Uncle Nunzio. "You see, he assumed, and why wouldn't he, that Al wasn't in on it alone, that *I* must've had something to do with that Caddy. At the time, all I could think of was, if we were lucky, he'd let us stick around long enough to have dinner. It was gonna be our first time reunited at the table, and for the occasion, Ma spent the whole day in the kitchen making lasagna."

"Nunzi, you bastard, you never changed!" hollered Aunt Dot. "If you're thinkin' at all, you're thinkin' of food."

"Ain't that the truth," said Uncle Al, who, after returning to the point, went on to add, "I thought for sure I'd be diggin' my own grave that night—that I was doomed to lay next to poor ol' Frank the pig."

"So that's your Cadillac sitting outside?" Antonio began. He wanted Uncle Al to willingly and of his own accord reaffirm what he already knew. Uncle Al swallowed nervously, which Antonio took to mean *yes*. Uncle Al didn't dare wait for Antonio to petition an explanation. He began by telling Antonio, "I been dating Theresa Scoli."

"I see," said Antonio, though he couldn't imagine how Theresa Scoli tied in with the automobile in question. What's more, he was warier of Theresa Scoli than he was of the Caddy and infinitely more curious how Uncle Al became interested in such a girl.

"It just kinda happened," said Uncle Al. Then he shrugged to imply, *how does any romance begin?* It was both an ineffectual and defensive gesture, but Uncle Al had a point; the origin of a romance, like getting shit on by a bird, just kinda happens.

"Is it serious?" Antonio asked.

"Kinda," said Uncle Al. The one-word reply dripped with weakness and apology.

"Have you thought it through?" Antonio set aside the role of the calm but supremely in-charge interrogator in favor of a brotherly tone. "Are you really sure you want Nails for a brother-in-law?"

Uncle Al shrugged to indicate *not really*, but it didn't change his feelings, and he was in love with Theresa Scoli.

Antonio pulled his chair closer to his Uncle Al and asked, "You *do* know about her, don't you, Al?"

Uncle Al lowered his eyes, then told Antonio, "That's all in the past. She's different now."

"For your sake, I hope so. I really do. But now tell me about the car."

Theresa Scoli had informed the gullible, pussy-whipped, and often foolhardy Uncle Al, "I'm used to being chauffeured around in luxury cars, not crummy old Dodges." So, what did being put on notice prompt Uncle Al to do? He surely didn't have enough handy cash to run out and buy a "luxury car." Nor was he in good enough standing to ask a reputable lending institution for a loan. Besides, Antonio was not around to cosign for a loan—not that he would have regardless, and no sane dealer of "luxury cars" would have dealt with Uncle Al at his current age and income. Smitten and without resources, Uncle Al, after making an appointment, went slinking into the back room of Fumo's Pool Hall, where waiting for him was Nails—the only one in all of Swampoodle with enough cash handy to cover the cost of a Caddy. Naturally, the rate of interest on a Nails loan was hardly favorable; but what did Uncle Al know about interest rates? An interest rate is nothing more than a pesky detail when you're a young man with stars in his eyes. Theresa Scoli scoffed at the notion of Uncle Al borrowing money from her brother, who still made it his business to look after Theresa, despite them having had a falling-out.

As the story goes, one afternoon, Nails returned home and discovered Theresa, his seventeen-year-old sister, well compromised by a young man who was into Nails for a healthy sum of money. Word had it the young man bet the house on Max Schmeling, who, to the dismay of German Americans, was knocked out in the first round by Joe Louis. Talk about backing the wrong horse! Worse, not only had he yet to make good on even a portion of his debt, but was brazen enough to make Nails' sister his latest conquest. Though, to be fair, the term "conquest" might not be applicable in this instance. Theresa Scoli and Danny Giorno were believed to have been in love.

When Nails walked in on the scene, Theresa and Danny separated and recoiled, which was a natural reaction when a man and a woman so well engaged get walked in upon. Nails did not utter a word. Nor did anything that resembled anger flash in his eyes—or so the story goes. Instead, he casually strolled across the room over to where, on the floor and situated in a corner, sat a vase—a handmade and hand-painted Chinese artifact it was said to have been. Nails removed the pussy willows from the vase and, with care, he laid them on a nearby table. With Danny Giorno flustered with worry and clumsily hopping his way back into his trousers, Nails jammed his fist inside the vase. After turning upon the awkwardly hopping Danny Giorno, Nails promptly beat him to within an inch of his life, being careful not to kill poor Danny, as he owed plenty of money. In other words, it was Danny Giorno's stupidity that saved him. Had he bet mere chump change instead of the house on Schmeling, Nails' associates might have been out gravedigging that night.

When Nails was through with his pounding and thrashing, blood spouted from every orifice of poor Danny Giorno's anterior. A multitude of welts and bruises were also placed on his appendages. Nails then dragged the battered and bloody young man across the floor, wrapped his hands around the radiator and, his fist still in the vase, he bludgeoned Danny's knuckles. Afterward, Nails calmly removed his fist from the vase, wiped the artifact clean of Danny's blood, then returned it to its place of display. He handled the pussy-willows with equal care.

131

With the battered and semi-conscious young lover sprawled and motionless on the floor, and a hysterical Theresa kneeling at his side, Nails rang Fumo's for his associates. He ordered them to scoop up the foolish young fellow and dump him on the doorstep of the nearest emergency room, then he headed straightaway for Nicastro's Tavern. Before leaving, he instructed Theresa that, upon his return, he shouldn't see a single drop of blood or any sign that a beating had taken place.

Theresa Scoli truly did care for poor Danny Giorno and wept openly while he lay nearly beaten to death in her living room. Her revenge, though, would not be a rash, sudden, or haphazard affair. It would be calculating and doled out incrementally over many months. As Theresa was straightening up what had been a massacre and scrubbing out bloodstains, she vowed from that day forward to fuck everyone owing Nails money. It would be a test of wills between brother and sister and one which would see Theresa, many times over, recreate the scene with Danny, with the notion that she could fuck more men than Nails had the energy and strength to bludgeon. It was a daunting undertaking that Theresa Scoli had set down before herself, but she would go on to cover every losing bet in Swampoodle—or at least every losing bet within reason; she didn't include the nickel-dimers betting the afternoon baseball game. After all, a girl has got to have standards. She covered the more substantial bets; and in an inner-city neighborhood, where folks gathered in pool halls, taverns, and on street corners, finding out who bet on what and how much was as easy as finding out what was for dinner in your own house. As Theresa would learn, the heavier betters were also the chattiest; they simply couldn't help bragging about how much money they were able to risk. It was as if the bigger gamblers, particularly the goombahs, couldn't wait to brag to the working stiffs how much dough they could afford to lose. Though, big or small, the running joke of all those giving Nails their action was: if you won you lost, but if you lost you won. Not that anyone bet to lose or admitted having been hard-up enough to have done so. Though, it was fairly well documented that Theresa Scoli wasn't an altogether bad consolation prize for a poorly laid wager.

Poor Nails; he was faced with the prospect of having to beat up all his heavy gamblers, have them beaten up by his associates, quit the rackets, or deal with the disgrace of having a slut for a sister. One thing was sure. Nails had no intention of getting a *real* job, nor would it have been good business practice to leave welts and bruises on the bodies of his heavier betting customers—especially the ones who paid promptly. And so that was how the king of the neighborhood, or so he liked to think of himself, was confounded by his own sister. Of course, for fear of reprisal, no one dared mention Theresa Scoli's exploits too loudly, as there were plenty of ears in the neighborhood loyal to Nails. In fact, loyal ears notwithstanding, Theresa Scoli became a means for settling heated disputes in taverns and on street corners. *I'm telling Nails you fucked Theresa* would get anyone to fold and submit to being wrong, when in fact they were right. Theresa Scoli's vagina had half the neighborhood on edge, and it defeated Nails far more soundly than he had beaten Danny Giorno. It took a while (nearly two years), but Theresa's anger toward her feared older brother subsided, and with the absence of anger went her highly irregular method of revenge. Danny Giorno, unfortunately, had long since moved on. Enter Uncle Al.

Antonio managed to sell the Cadillac. He placed an ad in the local newspaper, and within a day a pharmacist from Strawberry Mansion, a bordering neighborhood, was ringing his phone. He didn't get the full purchase price, but he came close enough to where he could make up the difference.

"If Theresa is serious and has the best intentions, she'll have to take you as you are—crummy old Dodge and all," Antonio told Uncle Al. Then Antonio strolled into Fumo's Pool Hall with an envelope filled with cash. He made straightaway for the back room—Nails' office or headquarters. Mr. Fumo didn't mind Nails and his associates commandeering his back room, as Nails not only drew a crowd but the kind of crowd that loved shooting pool, and not just a rack or two—these were gambling men who would shoot for hours. The sign on Fumo's front door might have read: *Monday thru Saturday, noon to 10:00 p.m.*, but it wasn't unusual to see lights on and clouds of cigar smoke hovering and to hear balls cracking north of midnight, and with large sums of money riding on several games.

"Forget the back room," said Uncle Nunzio, at our grandfather's surprise sixtieth birthday party. "By the time ol' Fumo was through countin' his receipts, he couldn't a cared less if Nails put his *own* name in the window."

"Ain't that the truth," said Uncle Al. "Fumo's was a gold mine. The only time it wasn't hoppin' was the day Vinnie drove his old man's car through the front window. I hear he's still kickin', ol' Fumo, that he's retired and living in Boca Raton."

"Yeah, and he's got Nails to thank for it," said Uncle Nunzio.

Despite not having first arranged a meeting, Antonio did not first stop and ask Mr. Fumo if it was okay to pay Nails a visit, nor did he inquire whether or not the racketeer was available. He thought to himself, *I'm handing him cash; I'm not gonna wait around to be told when I may do it.* When he entered the back room, Nails' associates stood not out of respect but in anticipation of having to rough up someone they believed was acting too boldly. When he realized that it was Antonio, Nails waved off his eager henchmen.

"What's this?" asked Nails when Antonio handed him the cash-filled envelope. "I don't recall you placing any bets." He thumbed through the stack of bills, then added, "I'd remember if someone bet *this* kinda dough."

"It's not a gambling debt, it's all the money that my brother owes you," Antonio told Nails; though his good sense had told him that Nails hadn't mistaken the money for anything *but* what was owed for the Cadillac. Nails rocked on his chair and said, "The Army must pay really well nowadays." A derisive chuckle was added. Then he glanced over at his associates and said, "Maybe you boys oughta think about joining up?"

The laughter that gushed from the two henchmen was as scathing as Nails' remark. *It's one matter to get drafted into the Army, but only a sucker would join.* The laughter burned in Antonio's ears. He glared over at Nails' associates and remarked, "It takes honor to serve your country. It's not for everybody." The remark served to stymie their laughter and straighten their smirks. Then Antonio turned to Nails and added, "My brother will no longer be coming to call on Theresa with the Cadillac. The car had been sold."

"I see," said Nails, who, at the moment, saw Antonio as a high-minded ingrate that was meddling in his affairs. When Antonio turned to leave, Nails added, "Incidentally, Antonio, it wasn't an interest-free loan."

"How much interest are we talking about?" Antonio asked the racketeer. "He borrowed the money just three weeks ago."

"Fine, forget about it," said Nails. He waved his hand at Antonio in a manner that displayed a loss of patience and disdain over the whole affair. Again, Antonio turned to leave. This time Nails said to him, "If Al ended up marrying Theresa, I was gonna waive the debt and make the car a wedding present."

"If or when my brother ever does anything to deserve that kind of generosity, I'll be the first to reward him," said Antonio.

"Fine." Nails' tone was conciliatory. Then he added, "Far be it from me to barge into family affairs."

You can't blame a guy for trying. After all, if there was one thing Nails knew, it was that Theresa's reputation preceded her, and a woman of such ill repute would have a helluva time marrying, especially if she remained in the very area where her exploits were legendary, assuming the matter of marriage wasn't already out of the question. Anyway, the old saying *There's a sucker born every day* was what Nails must have been mulling over after learning the reason Uncle Al requested a meeting in the back room of Fumo's Pool Hall. Nails knew that he could use waiving the debt on the Caddy as an incentive—a real ace in the hole—in exchange for a promised hand in marriage. As it turned out, there would be no need for any schemes. Perhaps Uncle Al had a *Jesus* moment and made it his mission to save Theresa Scoli. Whatever the reason, not only did it work but did so for decades thereafter.

When Antonio closed the door to the poolhall's infamous back room, he heard Nails' associates jump up and complain, "How do ya like that guy, waltzing in here like he owns the place." And, "He's got some nerve. We oughta go after 'im and teach 'im a lesson!" But Nails never said a word. No doubt he decided that it was prudent to let sleeping dogs lie. If he had someone who was potentially Theresa's future brother-in-law roughed up, it might have launched her into another spiteful fuck-fest. This was not a road that Nails wished to walk down again. Once was more than enough. Antonio and Nails were not friends, but they were two men with sibling issues; and on that front, they understood one another.

As I write these words, the year is 2012, and if our grandfather were alive today, he would have reached the ripe old age of ninety-four. Maybe it's best that he didn't live so long, that I have no memory of one so strong and capable—who once and with confidence strolled into a lion's den—having to surrender his driver's license, going about with a walker, or needing assistance getting into and out of a chair, among other issues that often accompany living to an advanced age. Fortunately, or unfortunately, depending on one's perspective, Antonio Corelli did not stick around long enough to need a nursing home, an assisted living facility, nor for a second did he become a burden to anyone. And wouldn't that have been a *real kicker*, a man, who once housed three generations, including a three-legged dog, having been packed up and carted off for institutional living—the last stop on the train before the graveyard. I would like to believe had his life come to that, where such action was necessary, one of us would have come forward and taken him in. That's what I *like* to believe. But in all likelihood, that's not what would have happened. I would have sighted my wife's career and son's activities as factors, *or excuses*, for not taking in our grandfather. Ricky would be armed to the teeth with factors, *or excuses,* such as Judy's health and having to occasionally babysit T.J. whenever Sara had a date. Mom and Dad are still living in the house of our childhood, and those two-story row homes can be a real nightmare for the elderly. And when we have exhausted all our plausible excuses and have emptied our chamber of the lame ones, we are quick to point out, *But, Grandpa, you'll be around folks your own age—those of your generation with whom to talk over the good old days. And there'll be activities!* Yes, let us dare not forget the activities. We certainly do our damnedest to convince others what's truly best for us is also what's best for them. At times, we may even have ourselves fooled that we are genuinely acting in the best interest of loved ones. I once heard the late great George Carlin say, "Parents are among the most full-of-shit people on the planet." That statement could also be extended to children, grandchildren, or just plain old human beings in general. As I stare at the photo of our grandfather—with his long, burly arms and huge, powerful hands draped over the shoulders of O'Malley and Dugan—I realize that it's all moot, that had Antonio Corelli lived to a ripe old age, he would not have inconvenienced anyone. Instead, he would have recognized his needs long before anyone else had, then followed through with the necessary arrangements. No doubt, he would have taken matters into his own hands just as he had that day back in the mid-1940s when he strolled into the infamous back room of Fumo's Pool Hall to confront Nails and his associates. Antonio Corelli was not only part of but stood head and shoulders above most of what Tom Brokaw dubbed "The Greatest Generation." At one time or another, we have all been asked the question: If you had the chance to meet anyone in history, who would it be? The few times that I've been asked, my reply was simple: "I already got that one covered." When asked, "What do you mean by that," I grin and leave it at that.

****

After us men took turns doling out additional and well-deserved praise to the chef, Ricky and I dismissed Mom and Dad to the comforts of their living room and stayed behind to wash and dry dishes. It was the least we could do after having our bellies filled with superior cuisine. Dad, oddly enough, elected to remain—not to assist in or oversee dish duty, but to intimate to us his concerns for the Phillies. It was April 19th, Munchk's birthday, and our beloved boys of summer were off to their usual lousy start. Dad maintained that, despite not quite three full weeks into a 162-game grind, this was not the Phils' customary slow start to a season, that they were no longer the same team that rattled off five con-secutive division titles.

"I'm not sensing the magic the way I used to," he said. "If they dig themselves too big a hole, I'm afraid they'll get stuck in it."

"Relax," we told him. "So long as they can send Hamels, Halli-day, and Lee to the rubber three outa five games, the odds are in their favor."

Dad was a tough sell; he was convinced that either the much-improved Nats or Marlins would overtake the Phils as the new boss of the eastern division; and not once did he mention the "P" word. Slyly, Ricky shot me a look. *Maybe there's hope for Dad, after all.* As it would come to pass, not only were Dad's concerns not typical Philly pessimism but they were prophetic; although he was wrong about the Marlins; after a quick start, they plummeted to the cellar. Utley and Howard's seasons were derailed with injuries, and Halliday and Lee pitched like a couple of imposters. The Phils finished in the middle of the pack, eighty-one and eighty-one.

Last summer Mom complained to me, "Anymore, your father lives to watch the Phillies. Two-hundred bucks a month for a thousand channels and all we watch is Comcast Sports Network. It wouldn't be so bad if Harry and Richie were still doing the games. Sarge and McCarthy, with all their yammering, can make you batshit crazy." I reminded Mom that every minute Dad was in his recliner and glued to the fifty-four inch flat-screen that Ricky and I purchased and set up back in 2009, the year after the Phils won the Series—Dad was a real bandwagoner and wanted a new TV to watch a winner— was time not spent reaching for his pipe wrench and all the other tools with which he went to war against the house. "More trips to the living room and the remote control and less to the basement and toolbox; I can't imagine a healthier trend," I told Mom. We laughed, then reminisced the days when be it by television or radio, every night we invited Harry Kalas and Richie Ashburn into the living room.

It had been a typically subdued April 19th. Mom and Dad pretend-ed not to know the date. Ricky and I made every effort not to mention anything that would remind either of them of Munchk. Dad's pretending today, as it always had been, was mainly for Mom's benefit; he knew darn well what day it was. He never intimated as much to Ricky and me, but we could always tell what Dad was thinking; he wasn't exactly the hardest guy to read; often his body language spoke as loud Mom's words did back in her confrontational heyday.

So, there we had sat, four people, enjoying the world's greatest lasagna, pretending. Imagine the likelihood of Ricky, who resides three time zones to the west, happening to turn up in the neighborhood. What were the chances? And what were the chances that Mom, who supposedly had no idea of the date and that we were coming to visit, happened to make enough lasagna for four? But the real kicker was how fascinating it can be for everyone in a room to know an absolute truth but dare not speak of it. We truly are a fascinating and complicated species—not just us Corellis, but folks in general. Ricky has maintained that our transition from caves and jungles to the internet was entirely too swift, that on the evolutionary scale, our emotions are ninety-seven centuries behind our intellect. That's a really cool way of saying that no matter how sophisticated and technologically advanced we become as a society, our emotions will doom us to the same mistakes. So, since there's not much chance of that ninety-seven-century gap closing in our lifetimes, Ricky and I will engage Dad for as long as he wants to bitch about the Phils and we'll continue to grant the April 19th charade. Incidentally, dessert tonight was four pieces of tiramisu. What were the chances?

During the course of the evening, we did manage a laugh, albeit a subdued one, when Ricky reminded us of Uncle Al's twin grandsons, Michael and Anthony, and how terrified they looked on the day of our grandfather's surprise sixtieth birthday party when planted on Uncle Nunzio's lap for a picture. The ill-advised maneuver came right on the heels of Uncle Nunzio setting his chest hair on fire, therefore producing an unfavorable result, which any moron could have predicted. Nothing like having both legs pissed on by twin toddlers. Our cousins didn't appear to have any lasting damage from the experience, and eventually, Uncle Nunzio became their favorite. After Ricky's retelling of the decades-old anecdote, Mom laughed politely, then quickly returned to the forlorn look that we have all grown accustomed to seeing.

It's been seven years now since Uncle Nunzio has left us. I miss my old great-uncle. Despite a limited vocabulary, he had a way with words, and I say this with fondness, for nobody could tell a story like Uncle Nunzio. So expressive and gregarious he was, there were times I thought he would fall over from how dramatically he waved his arms about when regaling us with a slice of the past. Within the Corelli clan, he was the last of our grandfather's generation to leave us. He remained a terrific portal to the Swampoodle days and was the life of the party right up until the end.

Bright and early the following morning I'll drop Ricky off at the airport. Our goodbyes will begin with him reminding me of the open invitation he extended when he first moved to Arizona. I'll tell him that a weekend in late autumn when the weather isn't so godawful hot, would work. More often than not, I follow through. Ricky, more often than not, packs up his family and comes east to spend Christmas in Philly. Then it's on to April 19th and another year without Munchk and another year of pretending. God, how I wish that one year we would all break down and cry, scream, or even blame one another. Anything would be better than pretending.

****

At dinner, Antonio made sure to sit directly across from Uncle Al. His expression was stern but not menacing. He nodded to let his younger brother know that the situation between him and Nails had been dealt with. After dinner, Antonio handed Uncle Al the keys to the Dodge Sedan.

"If Theresa Scoli truly cares for you, it won't matter if you show up riding a mule," he told him.

"I guess you're right, Antonio." Though Uncle Al sounded and appeared a bit sulky. He was bothered for having made trouble for Antonio so soon after returning from overseas. And gone would be the feeling he was the prince of the neighborhood rolling around in a shiny new Caddy. The fantasy was over. It was twelve midnight, and Cinderella's grand carriage turned into an old Dodge.

For Antonio, the damage control upon returning from Europe was just beginning. Later that week after stepping off the bus and about to head straightaway for the dinner table, he spotted Uncle Nunzio sitting on the curb, his head of wavy black hair buried in his hands.

"Nunz, what's the matter?" he asked.

"Nothing's the matter, Antonio." Uncle Nunzio sulked. "Just go on home; I'll be fine."

"Everything okay with that nice girl you were telling me about? What's her name?"

"Her name's Dorothy, and I was gonna ask her to marry me."

"Was? What happened? What's stopping you?" Antonio sat on the curb alongside Uncle Nunzio and draped a long, burly arm around his shoulders.

"Ahh, forget about it," said Uncle Nunzio. "It's not important. Not anymore, it ain't."

"Hey Nunz, whudda you say we go for a stroll around the neighborhood. I been thinking maybe we haven't spent enough time together since I came home. I bet between the two of us we can figure something out."

Antonio helped Uncle Nunzio to his feet. They hadn't gone but a few plodding paces before Uncle Nunzio opened up about how, for months, he had been putting money aside each week, the goal being an engagement ring for his Dorothy.

"When I held all that money in my hand, I couldn't resist." Poor Uncle Nunzio, he was drenched in regret. "They said Mr. Smarty Pants was a cinch in the third. I already done pretty good in the first two races, so I was feeling good about myself, like I couldn't miss. You ever feel it so strong in your gut, like no matter what you can't miss? So, I took the winnings from the first two races and all that money I had put aside—every damn dime of it. Hell, I didn't even save myself enough to buy a lousy hotdog! I'm tellin' ya that sonofabitchin' horse shoulda blew away the field. Instead, he looked like Ma was riding him—like instead of oats, he ate a tray of lasagna!"

"You used to bet pocket change on the Yankees. I see you've come up in the world."

"Yeah, I've come up in the world, all right." Uncle Nunzio's sulky self-deprecation brought his legs to a halt. Then he added: "Hey, Antonio; what I said the other night, about the way things were going all this time you been gone…"

"Forget about it," said Antonio, then he took a long, powerful arm and with it he hooked Uncle Nunzio closer to his side. "Look, Nunz," he added, "I got some money coming to me from the Army. I'm not saying we're gonna walk out with the biggest rock in the store, but we'll see what we can do about putting a nice ring on your little Dorothy's finger. One thing, though, Nunz," and with both his massive hands Antonio took firm hold of Uncle Nunzio's shoulders. "You bring me home your pay every week—I don't wanna hear any excuses. I'll slide you a little money from time to time so you can treat that girl of yours real nice, but that'll be the extent of it. I'll hold onto your money until I think the time is right. Understood?"

"You bet Antonio. I'll do whatever ya say."

Bright and early Sunday morning, little Freddy Corelli worked up enough nerve to come tiptoeing into his mother and father's bedroom but stood what he determined a safe distance from what he believed was his slumbering father, otherwise known as the boogieman. When Antonio, who had been playing possum, opened an eye, little Freddy went scampering through the hallway back to his room.

"What a shame I wasn't able to frighten the Germans so easily," said Antonio. "I might have ended the war two years ago."

"Your little visit to Fumo's Pool Hall the other day has been the talk of the neighborhood," said Elizabeth. "Maybe you're becoming too scary for your own good."

"Do *you* think I'm scary?" asked Antonio.

"I think you're perfect," said Elizabeth. "Soon, so will Freddy."

On cue, little Freddy—who evidently decided since his mother survived the night lying beside the boogieman, it could be that the boogieman wasn't such a bad fellow after all—came scampering back through the hallway and went leaping up onto the bed. Actually, Freddy came up a bit short and was about to take a header into the side of the mattress, but Antonio alertly caught him under the arms while in flight and pulled him up and onto the bed.

"Well, well, now, it's finally nice to meet you, son," bellowed the boogieman. A moment later, poor, old three-legged Max came hobbling into the room.

"Now we're really a complete family," crooned Elizabeth.

That afternoon, Antonio loaded up the old Dodge Sedan with the whole family, including poor, old three-legged Max, a picnic basket, and his future sisters-in-law. He headed for Lemon Hill.

"This has been our tradition since we came to Philly," he told Theresa and Dorothy.

That Sunday was a day that would get talked about for years to come—not for any particular incident or haphazard but for its harmony and perfection. I can see them just as clearly as if I had been a passerby that day in Fairmount Park. And had I been, I would have witnessed seven adults, one child, and a three-legged dog sprawled out on blankets around a picnic basket under a blue sky—seven adults, a child, and a three-legged dog in no particular hurry to do anything other than to share a day. My generation doesn't understand what it means *not* to be in a hurry. Unfortunately, my son's generation will understand it even less. We've become the hopeless—an army of drones conditioned to a world that's only a touch or click away but fails to notice life within an arm's length—pseudo-masters of the universe enslaved by pocket-sized devices. I suppose that I could make an attempt at a Sunday picnic; although it's doubtful I would get through the day without caving in to the temptation to check my smartphone for baseball scores or fantasy football updates. My weakness would prompt my wife to whip out her hand-held device of choice for a session of Angry Birds or Candy Crush. Meanwhile, our son would have already sent and received forty text messages, bitching and getting plenty of feedback for having been kidnapped by two morons who still believe family time in America has some redeeming value. Welcome to American Picnic circa 2012.

Back to the mid-1940s: It was said that our father never left our grandfather's side that Sunday and that he had held onto his hand most of the day. Said Uncle Nunzio, when observing father and son at last conjoined, "Either our little Freddy is shrinking, or Antonio's hands are getting bigger." Within the Corelli clan, our grandfather truly was a freak of nature; aside from being built like an NFL tight end, he had a head on our grandmother, who was tall but in a willowy sort of way, and Uncle Al, who was all lank and no meat. I also have a photo of our grandfather, who, from behind, had his arms wrapped around Dad; his hands are covering Dad's torso from his belt buckle to his neck. The photograph was taken at Lemon Hill. It was Dad's eighteenth birthday!

It should also be duly noted, on that special Sunday in the mid-1940s, Dorothy, who years later we came to know as the fiery Aunt Dot, and Theresa, who years later we would call Aunt Theresa but snicker among ourselves Aunt Prostitute, held up rather well under the scrutiny of Mama Corelli. Theresa Scoli had the right last name, went to the right church, and wasn't too shabby looking. In both motive and frequency, once upon a time, she was Sixty-four run amok, but as far as Mama Corelli was concerned, she was batting a thousand. As for Aunt Dot? She was Catholic. A blazing ball of Irish fire, but Catholic nonetheless.

After they ate, the men lounged and yawned. The women doted over Freddy and fussed over poor, old three-legged Max. Then Dorothy proposed, "It's such a beautifully day; let's all go for a walk in the park."

"Good idea," said Uncle Nunzio. "And while we're at it, I'll show you the family plot."

"Nunz!" Antonio glowered, his eyes glaring as to remind Uncle Nunzio: *have you forgotten that Ma's with us?*

"The family plot?" followed Theresa.

"It's a long story," said Uncle Al.

"In this family we have nothing *but* long stories," grumbled Mama Corelli.

Chapter Seven
The Magnificent Number One

Tuesday, October 4, 1977: It was game one of the League Championship Series between the Phils and Dodgers. Last October, Schmidt, Carlton, and the gang were dispatched in three straight games by Rose, Bench, Morgan, and Perez, otherwise known as The Big Red Machine from Cincinnati. After a 162-game grind, Philly had geared up for its first playoff appearance in twenty-six years. It all went so quickly—a blur you wanted to slow down but were powerless to do so—three games in four days, all possessing little drama. It seemed one minute, Ricky was reaching for his lucky jersey and the next, we were preparing for a long, mournful winter. Often in a playoff series, there's either a play or an at-bat or pitch, where the fortunes of either team can swing one way or another. That was not the case in 1976, at least not in the National League. And what made the all too expedient result even more unbearable was that Dad, "the resident expert," had predicted the aforementioned outcome in a haughty, know-it-all fashion. His attitude was difficult to swallow. What was sports if not an escape from the hard-bitten realities of life into a realm where sometimes David does emerge victorious over Goliath? Isn't that the whole point of watching and why it grips us? Anyway, in 1977, against Lasorda's Dodgers, we were confident in a better fate.

Back in the mid-70s, major league baseball didn't have six divisions and a wildcard which created the divisional playoffs; and the Championship Series, or Pennant as it was known back in the day, was only a five-gamer. Unlike a seven-gamer, a whole lot is riding on game one of a five-gamer—there's a lot more pressure. Uncle Al and Uncle Nunzio came by to wish us luck. They seemed sincere but then followed their well-wishing by reminding us that the Series between the Phils and Dodgers was moot, as the winner would merely provide fodder for the Yankees. Leave it to Uncle Al and Uncle Nunzio; they were masters at nearly saying the right thing. Then Uncle Nunzio further reminded us, "Back in our day, there were no divisions, only leagues; the majors had none of this *let's give the second-best team a chance* nonsense. Ain't that right, Al?"

"That's right; back when the Yankees were winning championships by the dozen, you had a come in first to play in the Series."

While awaiting the first pitch, Ricky was munching on Wheat Thins, eating them straight from the box. He wasn't hungry; we just finished dinner. What's more, Wheat Thins were hardly his favorite, but they were what he was munching on the night the Phils clinched the division title, and baseball fans, like the players themselves, are known to be superstitious. Meanwhile, Munchk was wearing a pink t-shirt stained with whatever she was eating (you guessed it) on the night the Phillies clinched the division title. As for myself? I was beyond superstitious. Not *above* it. *Beyond* it. In fact, I had what one might referred to as reverse superstition. In other words, I didn't trust my own karma. Therefore, I didn't eat a particular food or sport a specific garment for fear that I might adversely influence the outcome of the game. So, there we sat, three superstitious loons on pins and needles, our hearts in our throats, sharing the living room with our mildly interested father and even less attentive mother, awaiting the game's first pitch. All that remained between us and *Play Ball!* was the singing of the National Anthem.

I may regret going on record saying this, but I never cared much for the singing or playing of our National Anthem before an important game—especially a game in which I'm emotionally invested. For me, the anthem represents three more minutes of anxiety and to consider how I might feel should the game not end favorably. Worse yet, while the song is being sung or played, aside from the camera zooming in on the soloist, be it a vocalist or musician, it also zooms in for close-ups of the players, and sure enough, there are always some whose countenance reveals a measure of genuflection. I don't want to see the players on *my* team genuflecting. I don't want them wasting even one-tenth of a single second on the notion *win or lose we're still one nation under God*. Bullshit! They have the entire off-season, if they are so inclined, to run around saluting flags, gazing at monuments, or paying homage to national and religious symbols of their choosing. I want to see game faces—menacing scowls reassuring me that the men in the uniforms representing the City of Brotherly Love are gonna beat the tar out of those ding-blasted Dodgers. This is war, goddamnit!

The game was rolling along as well as we could have expected. The Phillies raced out to a five-one lead. With Carlton toeing the rubber, give me one reason why I should not have felt that game one was already in our hip pocket? You can't. But then came the bottom of the seventh. There was already a man on base when Carlton walked the next two batters. You could count on the hand of Mordecai Centennial Three Finger Brown how many times Steve Carlton walked the bases loaded; it was like spotting a goddamn unicorn, but that's precisely what he did in the seventh inning of game one. And despite all the nervous fidgeting that was going on in the living room, it never occurred to any of us that Ron Cey would, or could, hit a grand slam off the game's best pitcher. More to the point, who hits grand slams in the playoffs? I had watched every pitch of every inning of every playoff game and World Series since 1970 and had yet to witness a ball leave a yard with the sacks loaded. But that's exactly what Ron Cey did—he went ahead and did the unthinkable—he took Carlton deep at Chavez Ravine, otherwise known as Dodger Stadium.

A sick feeling gathered in the pit of my stomach as I watched all four Dodgers, including Ron Cey, who I would spend the next several years despising, cross home plate with jubilation. Ricky closed up the box of Wheat Thins. Then, with a mixture of gloom and astonishment, he set the box on the floor beside his chair and pushed it away as though it was an unseemly entity filled not with snack food but nefarious intentions. Munchk pulled the front of her shirt away from her body as if she owned a genuine fear the material would bake into her skin. With her mouth agape and eyes registering shock, she stared down at the stained garment as though all along she was unwittingly enshrouded with an evil that had conjured and cajoled to gain her trust through means of trickery, then, in the end, betrayed her. After the quartet of Dodgers returned to the dugout, Dad, amid the hovering despair, made an idiotic plumbing analogy that was hardly amusing less relevant and prompted me to consider what I might have done had we kept hidden in the household a loaded gun. We hadn't a loaded gun, only tools which, in Dad's hands, seemed like weapons. In a moment of sublime satisfaction, an image of me beating Dad with his own pipe wrench was what I conjured. It would have been the perfect scenario: Mom, who by the third inning tired of the game, pinned herself to the stove and made gravy. The subsequent event of the seventh inning would have sent Munchk running wildly into the kitchen yelling, "Mom, you better come quick! Frank's beating Dad to death with a pipe wrench!" Mom would do what Mom always does when involved with her gravy—ignore everything entirely, including murder and grand slams by the opposing team.

The Phils managed to scratch out two runs in the top of the ninth inning and were able to hang on for a seven-five victory. Ricky claimed having ingested enough Wheat Thins to where they continued wielding whatever supernatural properties he believed they possessed. Munchk claimed never for a second having doubted the mystical powers of her pink, food-stained shirt. Dad followed by claiming that water, no matter the situation, always seeks its level; then in his own convoluted manner, he managed to illustrate how that was relevant to the Phils coming from behind to win. Dad notwithstanding, game one at Dodger Stadium all but purged the memory of last October's wham-bam-thank-you-ma'am treatment we were treated to by The Big Red Machine from Cincinnati. We all, including Mom, who completed another pot of perfection, went to our beds smiling.

The next day Uncle Al and Uncle Nunzio—somehow, they must have gotten a whiff of the gravy—came to visit, and we were right there to remind them that *our* Phillies were on a collision course with *their* Yankees and that they had "better watch out!" The Yankees were in a fifteen-year World Series slump and hadn't been crowned champions of baseball since 1962, the year that I was born. Uncle Al and Uncle Nunzio relished pointing out, with far too much delight, the Phils had yet to win the World Series … ever! They also deemed it necessary to add to their history lesson: "They ran the wrong team outa town. They shoulda kept the A's around and sent them other bums packin'." (The A's departed Philadelphia in favor of Kansas City in 1955, before arriving in Oakland in 1968.) Then Uncle Nunzio *wrongly* pointed out *again*, "The only decent ballplayer youse ever had around here was Vince DiMaggio, and youse only had him around for one lousy year!" Then he turned to Uncle Al and said rather supercili-ously, "I seem to remember we had a DiMaggio on our team. Didn't we, Al?" Uncle Al, who played right along with the charade, said, "Sure, I remember. I think his name was … wait, don't tell me, it's on the tip on my tongue…" then he snapped his fingers to help summon the answer and exclaimed, "Joe! His name was Joe!"

"I think you're right," the agitating Uncle Nunzio bellowed, keeping up the charade. Then a self-satisfied grin formed on the face. I wasn't asking for much, just words that could wipe away his grin. There weren't any. What was worse, his tone became even more supercilious when adding, "*Joe* DiMaggio, Frank. Ever hear of 'im? Youse ever had any ballplayers on your team like that?"

Like a moron, I allowed myself to get baited into a dispute over which team had more all-time greats, the Phils or Bombers, and began rattling off the names Richie Ashburn, Robin Roberts, and Jim Bunning. Uncle Al and Uncle Nunzio were quick to dismiss all three as also-rans that never won anything. Despite their meager and what any baseball historian would agree was an invalid assessment of those great players, my argument, in the face of hearing rattled off a whole laundry list of Yankee greats, felt hollow and unsupported. It was true, Ashburn, Roberts, and Bunning were amongst the greats, but I never saw Richie Ashburn play a single game; he retired from baseball the year I was born. Robin Roberts retired in 1966, a time before I knew what baseball was. I did see Jim Bunning, who would one day get elected to the United States Senate representing Kentucky, pitch one game near the end of his career, but I was too young; therefore, I have no lasting memory. But Uncle Al and Uncle Nunzio? They saw all the greats: Micky Mantle, Whitey Ford, Yogi Berra, Joe DiMaggio ... even Lou Gehrig!

It was just our luck; we had a father to whom pipes gave an erection, a mother who stirred gravy, and a grandfather whose pastime was playing chess and listening to opera. The only two in the clan able to work up a passion over hardball long ago gave their allegiance to a team in another city. Nevertheless, the way I see it, it's better to have those with whom to get heated over a passion then not have anyone at all with which to share a passion.

Tonight didn't go so swimmingly. The Phils were chased from Chavez Ravine, having taken a seven-one whoopin'. The night started out okay; they grabbed a one-zero lead in the top of the third inning, but the Dodgers answered quickly with a run of their own in the bottom half of the inning. Then lightning struck again. This time it was Dusty Baker with a fence-clearing bases-loaded swat. The look on our faces revealed the notion that hitting grand slams on consecutive nights in a playoff series was as plausible as Moses parting the Red Sea, among other Biblical phenomena. I was grateful Dad had to work that night; I could not have endured his commentary. Biting into a toothpaste sandwich, or shoving my foot into a shoe in which a glob of horseshit was secretly planted would have been more endurable than listening to Dad yammering on about drains and pipes and how Dusty flushed the bases.

And speaking of toothpaste and horse manure, Wednesday, October 5th marked the last day the evil midget prankster donned her pink food-stained t-shirt. For good measure, she took a pair of scissors to it. It wasn't quite as spirited a maneuver as driving a wooden stake through the heart of a vampire, but it was along the same lines. As for Ricky? He lost all confidence in Wheat Thins. The notion that confidence and Wheat Thins were ever linked together was sheer lunacy. So is not eating them for thirty-five years and counting. As for yours truly, I didn't go on despising Dusty Baker the way I did Ron Cey. Specifically, I didn't spend the next three decades referring to the Dodger outfielder, who would later become a major league manager, as Dusty Fucking Baker; although initially, I had planned to. But after reflecting upon game two, I realized that had Dusty struck out and left the bases loaded, we still would have lost three-one. Dusty Baker's blast turned out to be the icing on the cake, whereas Ron Fucking Cey's grand slam was emotionally jarring and I believe speeded up my mortality by at least a month and likely two.

I did my darnedest to keep up the spirits of Ricky and Munchk. "When you start a series on the road, the best that you can hope for is to gain a split," was what I told them when there was one out in the ninth inning and no sign of a rally brewing. Ricky understood the rationale—he was a ballplayer himself and a good one—but Munchk was not one for splits. She was an all or nothing kind of girl and wanted the life crushed from the Dodgers while they were still in Los Angeles, and then promptly polished off once their plane landed in Philly.

"Jeez, take it easy, Munchk. We'll get 'em back on Friday," I said, though, secretly, I was very much in line with Munchk's line of thinking. I would have preferred the Phils' foot squarely planted on the Dodgers' throat with three opportunities to deliver the fatal blow.

And now comes the hard part, the travel day following a loss. Minus sleep (though who can sleep after a playoff loss), all that's available to fill this intolerable gap of time is a crescendo of anxiety, anticipation, and fretfulness pulsing thirty unbearable hours. Why no medication is prescribed for such occasions is a real headscratcher. This is America! Those who live in cities where baseball, basketball, and hockey are played—sports whose outcomes are determined by a series—understand this; for no doubt, there has been plenty of opportunities to experience the agony of defeat and what it can do to your health. I would have allowed myself to be paraded around the neighborhood naked in the bed of Uncle Al's truck if it meant that game three could have been played Thursday. I was a wreck!

Thursday came and went and did so without a single plumbing mishap to distract us from the seven-one drubbing through which we had agonized. You can't count on Dad for anything! However, Uncle Al managed to come by Thursday to collect a container of the world's greatest gravy. Uncle Al and Uncle Nunzio saw Mom's gravy as a birthright. We

149

were grateful Uncle Al brought along Aunt Prostitute. She was always good for a distraction, as she gave us the opportunity to snicker for a minute or two; though Mom was quick to thwart our fun with one of her menacing glares. Mom was afraid the reason for all our whispering and giggling was too obvious, and she was sensitive where Aunt Prostitute was concerned. Later on, Mom, for the umpteenth time, lambasted Dad for his "loose lips" by shouting, "If it leaks, you're so keen on fixing; why not start with the one below your nose!"

The earth turned and Thursday passed. We knew that it would, though its departure introduced what we would come to know as *Black Friday*. No, not the day following Thanksgiving—a day that begins with folks who, by the hundreds, will camp out in parking lots in front of large chain stores such as Best Buy, Toys R Us, etc....—a day that sees pushy, reaching, twisting, grasping morons position themselves for what's sure to escalate into a stampede, and all in fear that, should they fail to produce the year's hot ticket item to place under the tree, they might come home sometime between Christmas and the New Year and find their fragile wunderkind dangling from a ceiling fixture by way of their own bed sheet. *Dear Mom and Dad, I told you that I really wanted that new game system, but I guess you didn't believe me.* The Black Friday I'm talking about is relevant only to Philadelphians and took place in October. *This* Black Friday was a day that will live in infamy—not to suggest that its placement in history should rank alongside that of the bombing of Pearl Harbor; though at the time, you could not have told that to two teenage boys and their sister.

Game three of a five-game series is what's known as *the swing game;* afterward, the winner will have a decided advantage. We all sat nervously through a scoreless first inning. Not a single word was exchanged—not of baseball, plumbing, nor of anyone's peculiar behavior regarding their chosen superstition. We feared the baseball gods might frown upon the feeling we wished to emote, so we remained silent and believed we were wise in doing so. Then came the top of the second. With Steve Garvey on first base, Dusty Baker, our game two nemesis, whacked a double. Garvey, not the speediest guy the diamond has ever seen, tried to score. Admittedly, the play was close. It is now 2012, thirty-five years later, and Ricky and I are still waiting for Steve Garvey to touch home plate. The Phils argued the awful call, but in those days, there was no replay challenge. Umpires didn't huddle; the manager's only recourse was to state that he was playing the game under protest, which amounted to nothing more than a feeble way to vent, as plays were not revisited never mind overturned. Right or wrong, teams and their fans had to live with the decision on the field and life went on. Superstitious loons that we were, we figured the play was either a precursor of things to come or that sometime before the twenty-seventh out was recorded, the baseball gods, who *some* believe exist and were known at times to be reliable, would put things right. I was all but certain of the latter and was nearly proven right, as the Phils took a five-three lead going into the ninth inning. But it was then, in the ninth inning, when I learned the harsh life lesson: there are no such things as baseball gods, just evil maniacal pranksters lurking about with forbidding senses of humor, who are appallingly careless regarding the hearts of young baseball fans.

There were two outs in the ninth inning, and Vic Davalillo was down in the count no balls and two strikes. Let me repeat that: There were *two* outs and *two* strikes in the *ninth* inning; one lousy strike shy of recording all twenty-seven outs. With Steve Carlton toeing the rubber on Saturday, we were as good as in the World Series and well positioned to tell Uncle Al and Uncle Nunzio where they can stick the Bronx Bombers and their lordly Joe DiMaggio. Ricky and I began to act pompous and casual, adopting the notion that the Dodgers were a mere stepping stone—a minor distraction while blazing a path to bigger and better things. Then, of all things, Vic Davalillo laid down a bunt. A two-strike bunt in the ninth inning! Who does such a thing? Well, not only did it surprise Ricky, Munchk, and me, along with the sixty-thousand-plus fans who had jam-packed themselves into the stadium and the multitude watching on television but alas the Phillies! The result of this unappreciated trickery saw Davalillo standing at first base.

"No big deal," said Munchk. "Garber'll get the next guy." Gene Garber had a corkscrew windup and side-armed delivery and was part of a Phillies bullpen that included Ron Reed, Warren Brusstar, and Tug McGraw. All four relievers had winning records and earned run averages under three. I thought the same as Munchk; of course, Garber would get the next hitter.

Dodger manager, Tommy Lasorda, sent Manny Mota up to pinch-hit.

"Manny Mota?" said Dad. "Jeez, that guy's ancient. If he were a metal pipe, he would have rusted through already."

I was surprised; not only did Dad know Manny Mota, but that Mota was one of the games' elder statesmen. Manny Mota was currently thirty-nine and would soon retire as baseball's all-time leading pinch hitter. I looked over at Dad, intending to acknowledge his baseball awareness with an admiring nod, but then he went and fucked it up by adding another asinine plumbing analogy.

The corkscrew, sidearmed-hurling Gene Garber quickly got ahead of Mota, no balls and two strikes. Again, we were one strike away from Saturday, Carlton, and the likelihood, if not a certainty, of playing in the World Series. Yes, the World Series, after a twenty-seven-year drought, would return to Philly! What's more, we were one strike away from telling Uncle Al and Uncle Nunzio what they could do with their pinstripes and Yogi Berra, Tony Lazzeri, Frank Crosetti (the ballplayer not the pig), Phil Rizzuto, and all the other *paisans* who played in the Bronx. Then Manny Mota promptly delivered a line drive that took Greg Luzinski all the way back to the left field wall.

It had been the custom of Phils manager, Danny Ozark, to replace Greg Luzinski with the younger, swifter Jerry Martin, when taking the lead into the ninth inning. The name of the game was "protect the lead." But this was *Black Friday!* The ball caromed off Luzinski's glove. Vic Davalillo scored, and Manny Mota went to third base on a throwing error. I watched Ricky wince and Munchk squirm. Munchk's confidence was waning. She looked over at me as if to say, *Frank, can't you do something to stop this? Are you really gonna just sit there and do nothing?*

Poor Munchk; she wanted that Series more than anything— every bit as much as Ricky and I wanted it, and she wanted reassurance. I'd have eaten toothpaste sandwiches for a month. Hell, I'd have put toothpaste on my chocolate ice cream and spaghetti if I thought it could change the outcome and deliver to Munchk the victory she so desperately desired.

Next, Dodgers' second baseman Davey Lopes hit a hard ground ball that took a bad hop. Those goddamn Astroturf seams, they bite you in the ass at the most inopportune moments. The ball caromed off Mike Schmidt's knee, conveniently over to Larry Bowa, who alertly rifled a throw to Richie Hebner at first base. The replay showed not only was Lopes out but clearly was out. Mom, who thus far hadn't said a word regarding the game one way or the other, leapt to her feet as if, had she been in the stands, she might have charged the field and torn apart umpire Bruce Froemming limb by limb. Luckily, she was home and only available to let loose a fiery barrage of expletives, beginning with, "What is he, fucking blind!" and ending with, "Jesus Christ, is he fucking blind!" Dad looked over at me with one of his goofy, apologetic shrugs. *Now you do you under-*

stand why we don't bring her along to the games? Poor Mary Corelli, she really couldn't be trusted in public.

Bruce Froemming was a fine umpire, but to this day, I have no idea what he could have been thinking. I suppose our brain is not a foolproof mechanism that every time without fail processes action precisely as it unfolds. But that's my forty-nine-year-old rationale talking in 2012, not my devastated heart in 1977.

Bruce Froemming must have known how egregious his call was but couldn't reverse it. Reversing bad calls was not a practice in the 1970s. Froemming must have been praying for a Phillies comeback in the bottom half of the ninth inning—not only to put things right but to exonerate him of any blame should the Phils go on to lose the Series. But that's not what happened; and after Davey Lopes came around to score what would end up the winning run, my juvenile mind was left to wonder how a just God, assuming He has a sense of fair play, could permit such a tragedy.

Saturday's ballgame was played through a downpour. The Phils lost the game and the Series. It was an altogether different feeling from last October. Then, our team wasn't expected to emerge victorious over the mighty Big Red Machine from Cincinnati—a team for the ages. This year was different. Victory was not only attainable but was placed on a silver platter for the taking; and through the means of some evil twist of fate, it went up in smoke—or, as Dad put it, down the drain. As Ricky, Munchk, and I were trying to process the profundity of our despair, Dad rolled his eyes and with a contrived sigh said, "There's always next year," which is a baseball euphemism for *fucked again.*

It took me years to forgive Bruce Froemming. I might have forgiven him sooner had Munchk lived long enough to see the Phillies play in and ultimately win the 1980 World Series. To this day I have maintained that great as the 1980 team was—and they were truly terrific, led by Pete Rose—the 1977 team was even better. That's an opinion shared by many; though it's an opinion based on baseball merit alone. Regarding my own supposition, I've always needed to believe in my heart that the '77 team was better—that it was and shall remain an incontrovertible truth that Munchk saw the best team the Phillies ever fielded. Looking back, I suppose a part of me died that October—the part that could only belong to Munchk and a baseball team that came of age during the tenderness of our youth. It's kind of ironic, I should think, baseball and life. Two outs and two strikes in the ninth with Carlton going on Saturday; it seemed so attainable, as near certain as certain could be. And then the moment passed us by, an unseen force keeping our arms pinned to our sides, disallowing us to reach. Young, beautiful, frightening witty—a lightning rod of irrepressible energy, with everything seemingly pointed in the right direction to lead a charmed life. If the stars were aligned for anyone, they were aligned for Munchk. And then one day they were not. I guess it isn't *just a game* after all.

As it would come to pass, the 1977 postseason would bring to an end the New York Yankees' fifteen-year World Series drought; they beat the Dodgers four games to two. Perhaps it was fitting that New York, after a year of being terrorized by David Berkowitz, the infamous Son of Sam, should be afforded the right to exhale by way of celebrating a championship; maybe given the circumstances, a World Series title meant more to New Yorkers. Reggie Jackson hit three first-pitch dingers in consecutive at-bats in what would end up the sixth and deciding game. And Reggie's success didn't end with mere World Series heroics. Not by a long shot! This is America—a place where being prisoners of the moment leads to swift capitalism. The ticker tape had yet to be swept from Broadway, and Reggie's name was already on a candy bar. Ricky, Munchk, and I refused to try it. No matter the lengths that others went to try and entice us, we would not allow anything named after a New York Yankee to pass by our lips. "So, help me," scowled Munchk, "next year if anyone tries to put a Reggie Bar in my Halloween bag, I'll shove it up their ass!" I didn't feel quite *that* strongly about it. My feeling was simply this: Between Hershey, Mars, and Nestles, there was plenty of chocolate at the drugstore from which to choose; I didn't need to tickle my palate with Mr. October.

As expected, Uncle Al and Uncle Nunzio came by to gloat. I lost count how many times they mentioned Reggie Jackson, but it far exceeded the point ad nauseam. Weeks later, Uncle Al had a pile of crumpled up Reggie Bar wrappers surrounding the beanbag ashtray on his dashboard. "Best candy bar on the market," he crooned.

"I hope his teeth rot out," hissed Munchk. "Then let's hear him flap his gums about Reggie Jackson."

Munchk didn't fuck around. Not when it came to baseball. Harsh and acerbic as she could be, she did have a point. I watched Reggie Jackson win three consecutive World Series titles earlier in his career with the Oakland A's. Back then, Uncle Al and Uncle Nunzio wouldn't have known whether Reggie Jackson was a tight end for the Baltimore Colts or a point guard for the Boston Celtics. The Yankees were not contenders in the early 1970s and only had one *paisan,* a utility player named Frank Tepedino, so their interest in baseball had dwindled. Now, suddenly, they were once again experts, and knew everything there was to know about Reggie Jackson, and yammered on with Reggie Jackson *this* and Reggie Jackson *that*... On that note, fuck Uncle Al *and* Uncle Nunzio! And Reggie Jackson too! And while we're at it and just for good measure, the same to Joe DiMaggio! On second thought, if someone does try and slide a Reggie bar into my Halloween bag, I *will* shove it up their ass!

Munchk had not the heart to listen to Uncle Al and Uncle Nunzio and all their gloating. Nor had she the heart to stick around and defend her beloved Phils, less listen to me feebly do so on all our behalves. She retreated to her bedroom. Ricky stood by my side, and together we went toe-to-toe with Uncle Al and Uncle Nunzio, despite our beloved team not having provided us an adequate supply of ammunition. In retrospect, one might have thought Donald Rumsfeld was there urging us, "You go to war with the army you have, not the army you might want or wish to have at a later time." But our poor Phillies have had as many last-place finishes as the Yankees have had first—a fact that's difficult to ponder never mind admit. Why does God hate Philly? It wasn't long before Ricky and I tired of what was an exercise in masochism and grabbed our basketball and headed for the courts. Along the way, we wondered how we would begin to fill a void left by a baseball season that ended in such heartbreak. It was only October. April seemed so far off.

****

The 1977 season was the most memorable of my lifetime—Ricky's too. That year we saw a total of twenty-five games at the old Vet. Some we saw with Dad, most we saw on our own, and twenty-one of them ended in favor of the home team. That's knowing how to pick 'em! We spent every cent we made mowing lawns and washing cars on public transportation, tickets, and hotdogs. Even after all these years, the smell of cut grass and steam that rises from hot, wet car metal and street tar reminds me of ballgames; and there are instances, inexplicably—I could be in an elevator—when I'll get a mouthwatering whiff of a Veteran Stadium hotdog. At one point, Ricky and I had an eleven-game winning streak. Superstitious loons that we were, we didn't see it as mere luck, but that our physical presence in that old concrete doughnut was transversal, connecting astral energy to the planet surface, or more specifically to the dugout accommodating the home team. And as much as our wallets allowed, we made sure that our positive karma was present on nights the Phils played The Big Red Machine, the Dodgers, and Bucs.

Munchk begged to come along. Mom wouldn't allow it. She insisted that Munchk was too young to be out riding public transportation at night. I wasn't sure whether Mom was fundamentally opposed to the idea or simply the impropriety of how it would appear. After all, we couldn't have Mary Corelli's daughter spotted on a bus or train after dark. What would the neighbors think? Either way, Munchk would argue that she would be well protected by her big brothers—the same two that repeatedly were confounded and brought to their knees by clever pranks.

"Oh, sure, Munchk, we'll protect you. Won't we, Ricky?" The tongue-in-cheek tone, the roll of the eyes, the condescending sneer—I had the whole package down pat; it was our only revenge.

"Goddamn you, Frank!" Munchk hollered. "I hope you get hit in the head with a foul ball! Never mind," she went on to add. "It's too late for brain damage. I rather you take one in the nuts!"

"Lizzy, watch your tongue!" snapped Mom.

"Foul balls don't reach the seven-hundred level. If you'd ever been to the stadium, you'd know that," I haughtily told Munchk. The seven-hundred level seats were known as *nose bleeders* and the only seats that Ricky and I could afford.

"Oh yeah, Frank," Munchk fired back. "Well, it wouldn't much matter if you were sitting in the one-hundred level. You couldn't catch a cold, you clumsy prick!"

"Lizzy!" yelled Mom.

Even had my offer been a sincere one—to provide Munchk the necessary protection against evildoers lurking about on units of public transportation past dark—I don't believe Mom would have budged on her position. Poor Munchk. She was relegated to the house and her radio; for back in the day, home games were only televised on Sundays.

It was mid-May. The Dodgers were in the midst of their first East Coast trip. Since it was months before the ill-fated Series in autumn, I had no more reason to despise the Dodgers than I had any other National League rival. Lasorda's boys were just another team trying to unseat the Big Red Machine as kings of the National League.

It was a tough night for players and fans alike; two rain delays totaled better than two hours. That thinned the crowd, which was fine for us folks way up in the cheap seats. It gave us a golden opportunity to creep down to the lower levels, but put a damper on home field advantage. When play resumed, enthusiasm was a bit soggy. I always found it odd that the more money folks pay for seats, the less willing they were to wait out a rain delay. But how else would a couple of kids who mowed lawns and washed cars for spending cash get a chance to crash the party? After the first delay, we parked ourselves in the last row of the three-hundred level—the closest we had ever been. What a view! I urged Ricky to keep his cool and act as though we had been there all along. Even on the nights when we came with Dad, our best seats were row one of the six-hundred level. God bless the rain! And then it rained again. The crowd thinned even further. There were only a few thousand who chose to remain, and they scattered themselves throughout the lower levels. We repositioned ourselves to row one of the field boxes along the first base line. We made it to the big time! We were standing field level, able to bend over the fence and touch the turf. So what if the seats were soaking wet? We tried to act natural, like kids of privilege used to such luxuries as field boxes. We failed. I'm fairly certain we resembled a couple of bourgeois American tourists inside the Roman Coliseum. After my head was through swiveling and I remembered that a game was taking place, I got to thinking, *I can't wait to tell Munchk, to rub her nose in it. Let the evil midget prankster sprinkle itching powder in all my underwear or smear condiments in my favorite jacket; ol' Frankie boy is in row numero uno!*

I was having one of those self-agrandizing Ralph Kramden/George Costanza moments. Things were going my way, and it made me as pompous as the day was long. Then it happened—the worst part of the night. Perhaps it was poetic-justice for my wanting Munchk to understand the meaning of envy. And no, what happened was not an egregious call that cost us the game by an umpire who was already up past his bedtime. Some baseball fans—myself included—have been known to accuse umpires of manipulating rain delayed and extra-inning games for the sake of beauty sleep. I wish I could say that was the case. What happened was worse. Infinitely worse.

I suppose that I could be accused of having been entirely too enthralled with my new vantage point and it caused my mind to go adrift. Indeed, it is fair to say that I lapsed into somewhat of a reverie. And yes, I heard the public address announcer's careful syllables as he announced: "First baseman, Steve Garvey." I may even have noticed Steve Garvey standing up at the plate. However, I could not have told you the count, how many men, if any, were on base, nor how many outs, if any, had been recorded. It seemed that the closer I got to the field, so dipped my concentration, my baseball awareness. I did not see Steve Garvey check his swing.

157

It's common knowledge among baseball fans that when a right-handed batter checks his swing, the ball travels to the first base side. Often, it reaches the stands. While in the throes of my reverie, it seemed only seconds that I was foolishly musing over the size of a cavernous concrete doughnut otherwise known as Veteran Stadium, from the position of its floor, when a missile was launched in my direction and was coming straight for my head. I had never seen a projectile travel with such velocity, nor possess force so potentially damaging as it sought its lackadaisical target. For what couldn't have been more than a split-second, I froze. While locked up in a frozen state, having become the proverbial deer in headlights, I watched a white, round missile zero in on its target—its seams, which tightly stitched together cowhide covering a ball of yarn that if undone would stretch for a mile, became larger and larger.

For those accustomed to sitting in the seven-hundred level of the old Vet, the one item that you could safely leave home was your mitt. Line drives did not travel to the seven-hundred level. Hits of any kind did not reach the seven-hundred level. Mitts were worn only by those occupying lower level seats; although often I witnessed brave souls in boxes spear *a real screamer* with a bare hand. While trapped and frozen in that smallest measure of time known as a split-second, I gave the employment of my bare hand some consideration, but very little. As it would come to pass, I did the unthinkable. I, Frank Corelli—a young man who holds *that* which takes place on a baseball diamond in utter reverence, when seeing an official major league baseball hit his way by a perennial all-star no less—ducked. That's right, I ducked; and a man sitting three rows in back of me ended up the beneficiary of the treasure launched from Garvey's stick.

Immediately, jeers were heard from the smattering whose resolve was stronger than the rain. Despite watching the man three rows behind me scramble for the baseball, my brain experienced a five-second delay, as it took that long to realize it was upon me whom the jeers were raining down. Had there been forty-thousand in the stadium, as there was before the first delay, such cowardice might have gone largely if not entirely unnoticed. But at midnight with the Vet filled to only one-twentieth its capacity, my lack of valor was as glaring as an error that let in a go-ahead run, and it received similar treatment.

When I recovered from my debacle, I turned to Ricky and pleaded, "Whatever you do, don't dare mention this to Munchk." I could imagine all that I would have to endure should Munchk come to learn that I ducked a foul ball. I may as well plant myself in front of a firing squad!

The result of Steve Garvey's at-bat was the furthest thing from my mind. As the inning wore on, I grew more paranoid thinking Munchk was still up listening to the game, and that up in the announcer's booth, Harry Kalas and Richie Ashburn were carrying on about the kid in the Larry Bowa jersey that ducked a foul ball. *She knows, goddamn-it! She knows!* Like a moron, I looked up at the announcer's booth with the notion that I could read lips from a hundred feet away. I spotted Ashburn in his Geoff-cap and pipe. *You're the one*, I was sure he was saying, as he puffed his pipe. God, was I paranoid—terrified that Munchk would somehow find out that I ducked the ball.

"Hey, Frank, did you ever get that ball signed? You know, the one you caught off Garvey's bat?" asked Uncle Nunzio at our grandfather's surprise sixtieth birthday party. "Wait, just a minute. I almost forgot. You ducked. Ain't that right, Al? Our boy here ducked?"

"That's the way I heard it," said Uncle Al. "So, I guess it must be true."

"Of course, it's true," said Uncle Nunzio. "The fans of them bums, the Phillies, are no different than the team; they can't catch. Ain't that right, Frank ol' boy?"

"Nunzi, you bastard," hollered Aunt Dot, "leave poor Frankie alone! He's a good boy. Ain't cha, Frank?"

Just how in the hell is one supposed to respond to such patronizing horseshit? *Indeed, Aunt Dot, I am a good boy—a very good boy—I am, I am. And by the way ... fuck you!* At times, it was hard to determine who was more irritating, my Jimbroni great-uncles or their idiotic spouses. Though, more often than not, Aunt Prostitute did not rush to share her opinions. She may have been lacking sense but was smart enough to understand that she was lacking. When the banter reached a certain level, as it often did, instead of throwing gas on the fire, she would recede into the background.

It truly wasn't Ricky's intention to betray me regarding the ducking incident. In his excitement to describe to Munchk our field box experience, it just came blurting out. I guess Dad had to pass his loose lips onto someone.

"We were *this* close to the action," he cried, then held up his thumb and index finger an inch apart to indicate our proximity to the field. "Frank was almost killed by a foul ball! You shoulda seen it! He ducked just in the nick of time!"

"I'm sorry, Ricky," said Munchk, "I'm not quite sure I heard you right. Tell me again what Frank did?"

159

There's nothing worse than the sinking feeling that comes upon you the second when realizing you're fucked. And it doesn't matter from how many different angles you look at the board; checkmate is checkmate. Right before my eyes, I watched Munchk transform from a sulky brat—who was once again left behind and relegated to her room and radio—to a menacing tower of strength who would channel all her effort and surplus energy into to making my life miserable.

The clock read 2:10 a.m. when Ricky and I came creeping into the house from nine innings of actual baseball and two rain delays. We figured there was no way in hell Mom would make us go to school the next day (it was already the next day) and that she would be a good sport and let us sleep in. By 2:10 a.m., I was too damn exhausted to change and decided to sleep in my clothes. Ricky did the same. I peeled back the sheet and fell into bed. As soon as I hit the mattress, I heard a sound that was part crack part splat.

"What was that?" asked Ricky.

What was that? I knew exactly what *that* was; Munchk planted an egg in my bed. Maybe, for good measure, she planted two. I reached back and felt the goo all over the seat of my blue jeans. Strangely enough, I didn't give a damn. It was 2:10 a.m.; I was too tired to give a damn. I didn't bother getting up, nor did I give a thought to cleaning the mess never mind changing out of my pants. Besides, had I changed out of my pants, I would have felt the disgusting egg goo against my bare skin. I remained as I was, in my clothes, on top of a crushed egg … or two; and as I lay there, I laughed myself to sleep.

I guess Munchk figured that I failed her by not being persuasive enough with Mom when she begged to come along, and the old egg-in-the-bed trick was her means of pointing out the error of my way. It wasn't the first time that I had been victimized by an egg. Boys are accustomed to thoughtlessly tossing their book bags to the ground when shedding them from their shoulders, and without any regard for what, aside from books, might be inside. Fool me once, shame on you. Fool me twice … fuck it. But I have Munchk to thank for what a cautious and vigilant adult I have become. I'm a classic *look-before-you-leap* kinda guy. I'll probably live to be a hundred-and-fifteen.

As luck would have it, Mom came bursting into our bedroom at 6:30 sharp and proceeded to parade about with guns blazing or trumpets blaring, take your pick; but she did enter our domain with the promise of fresh coffee and a hot breakfast. It was remarkably uncharacteristic, as I observed with one eye closed and the other half open, for this ordinarily intense, combative woman to display such folly. She marched around our bedroom tootling a pretend bugle, all for the sake of letting us know that we should have been more conscious of life and its responsibilities and had come home after the first rain delay. It was then that I realized the reason why Munchk planted eggs in my bed. When she saw that it was midnight and we had yet to return from the Vet, any chance of her accompanying us, her brothers, who displayed a blatant lack of responsibility, was gone.

Back to Mom: I was okay with the army revelry; given the circumstance it may even have been fitting. But when she decided to tackle John Philip Sousa's *Stars and Stripes Forever*, which she flubbed miserably, it made me wish that I hadn't ducked and that Garvey got me right between the eyes.

I'd like to cite the example of strength, discipline, and determination that our grandfather had thus far exhibited in his life and times as factors that inspired me from my bed and onward to a productive day. That's what I'd *like* to cite. Instead, it took me imagining that I was the frail and fair Mrs. Profacci lying next to the rotund, greasy, baldheaded, and abundantly hairy Mr. Profacci, that launched my sleep deprived body from the bed and crushed egg upon which it had been resting. How brave a woman was Mrs. Profacci? And isn't it amazing the thoughts that can run through a mind that's been deprived of proper rest? On that note, I think I'll take Mom up on her offer of fresh coffee and a hot breakfast. Not to suggest that there are other options on the table; I am *going* to school. It is not a debate. If I'm lucky, maybe I'll catch a glimpse of Mr. Profacci bending down for his newspaper. I can't think of a better way to prevent an early morning boner from poking through my bathrobe. What a life. All this, plus Munchk. Who knows, maybe by the time I return, Dad will have flooded the kitchen.

Over fresh coffee and a hot breakfast, and while staring blankly at the front cover of the sports page, it occurred to me that I might avoid additional Munchkafied retribution by offering to take the evil midget prankster to a day game. After all, we couldn't have our *delicate little treasure* encountering misfortune while riding public transportation after dark. It did occur to me, however, that Munchk might perceive a day game scenario as a cheesy way of me avoiding standing up to Mom on her behalf. The perception was a possibility but a risk that I was willing to take. Moreover, my musing over the accommodation occurred only moments before Ricky and I revived ourselves by way of recounting for Munchk our field box experience, which led to Ricky inadvertently blurting out that I ducked. It was all out in the open—my rain delay, field box, and foul ball debacle. As for additional Munchkafied retribution to which a moment ago I had alluded and hoped to avoid? Forget about it! And I'm not talking a casual, unavailing, innocuous and ineffectual *never mind* type of *forget about it*, but a bonafide Joe Pesci gangster movie *forget about it.*

****

For afternoon games, it's advisable to wear a ballcap. Battling glare and an unrelenting midday sun for nine innings can be a real pain in the ass if you're not prepared. I have a ballcap—a nice red one with the Phillies' white logo prominently sewn in the front. I once wore this modest treasure, which I purchased at the stadium with my hard-earned dough, proudly. However, nowadays, no longer can I wear it proudly or otherwise, away from the house or inside; for written across the back of the ballcap in black magic marker are the words: *Beware, there's an asshole under this thing!* My ballcap sits unaccompanied on my chest of drawers, collecting dust. No longer does it adorn my head at the schoolyard or basketball courts. It doesn't see daylight except for the few rays of sun that manage to break through the window. It stays hidden away, banished to my room, no less stationary than the rug, furniture, and wallpaper. I also have a batting helmet—a shiny red one which would also serve well against the harsh day game elements. Luckily, it's plastic. So, let's say, for instance, someone took a black magic marker, and on it, they wrote *Belonging to A Dunce;* it could easily be wiped clean.

Off we went—Ricky, Munchk, and I with my shiny red batting helmet to a Sunday afternoon game in mid-June. Sundays were give-away days; kids fourteen and under would receive the item du jour. Sometimes it was something really worthwhile, like a Phillies calendar, bottle-bat replica, or shiny red batting helmet. Other times, it amounted to nothing more than a crackerjack prize, such as a kazoo. *Lucky us.*

"Come on," I said, "we're gonna sit between home and first, the last row of the seven-hundred level."

"Why so high?" complained Munchk.

"'Cause I'm not gonna run the risk of getting stuck in front of a six-year-old blowing a fucking kazoo in my ear for two goddamn hours." Munchk shrugged, which I inferred to mean *good point.* Then she somewhat agreeably added, "The last row it is."

By the time Steve Carlton began toeing the rubber in the top of the first, Veteran Stadium had transformed into a goose convention minus the droppings. Thousands of children were honking away on kazoos, blowing them until hypoxic, their faces inflating until blue. Carlton must have been grumbling on the mound, "What the fuck was management thinking? Let one of those morons come down here and try and pitch amidst all this bullshit." Then, sure enough, Enos Cabell, the game's second batter, sent the second pitch of the at-bat soaring over the right-field fence. Munchk glared at me as though it was the fault of the kazoos, and that I possessed the power to silence twenty-thousand kazoos, but to spite her, I elected not to. Then came the fourth inning. Not only had we yet to score, but Cabell took Carlton deep again.

"Goddamn it, Frank!" hollered Munchk. "With eighty-one home games to choose from, you bring me to kazoo day! So, help me," she threatened, "if Cabell homers again and we get shut out..."

I sank in my seat, contemplating my fate, as it would no doubt come to pass, should Cabell homer again and the Phils manage to go scoreless through all nine frames. Thirty-one years later, over a beer in a sports bar, during game two of the World Series between the Phils and Rays—a Series the Phils would win—Ricky and I joked that Munchk was not merely a prankster but a terrorist. It isn't normal, I would imagine, for baby sisters to possess the capability to strike fear in the hearts of older brothers unless portrayed as a wraithlike figure in a cheesy horror film. Munchk was a rare bird.

There were two men on base with one out when Tim McCarver stepped up to the plate in the bottom of the fourth. Since he became a broadcaster for FOX, Philly fans have lost their love for ol' Timmy McCarver, the once popular battery mate of Steve Carlton. Many fans sense a hint of anti-Philly sentiment whenever Tim's behind the microphone and there are red pinstripes scattered about the diamond. Some maintain that the once popular catcher, who enjoyed plenty of fan support at the old Vet, is still bitter for having been left off the 1980 post-season roster; although after twenty-one seasons in the majors, three World Series appearances, two which yielded rings, the notion that Tim was bitter over 1980 should be chalked up as faulty reasoning. But you see, we in the city of brotherly love, in case you haven't heard, can be a bit touchy and sensitive. Anyway, I do not share the widespread opinion of the Philly faithful; for on a warm summer Sunday afternoon back in 1977, when down two runs, with thousands of kazoos blaring and an evil munchkin sitting two seats away from me with her arms folded and face fixed in a scowl, Tim McCarver sent a fly ball soaring over the right-field fence, and in doing so saved me from a world of misery. Munchk leapt to her feet with a hardy cheer that resounded over the blaring kazoos. The Phillies took a 3-2 lead which they would not relinquish, and I have loved Tim McCarver ever since.

We boarded the Broad Street subway following what was, despite the blaring kazoos, a satisfying 7-3 victory. Carlton went the distance and chipped in with a homer of his own. I sat beside Ricky on a bench that was facing the aisle and had its back to the subway platform. Munchk sat on the bench directly across from us. She smiled at me. I interpreted her smile as a pleasant way of telling me, *thanks, Frank, for bringing me along.* I returned her smile. A moment later, she let loose with a giggle. It was uncustomary for Munchk to giggle; shy gestures were hardly in her repertoire. I shrugged, partly out of curiosity, but also to suggest that her smile was gratitude enough. Any more of a display than that, I would feel embarrassed. In other words, regarding our relationship, it would be best not to switch lanes or make sudden turns. But it wasn't until a moment later, when what began as a shy giggle, or so I thought, became animated laughter.

I'm no different than the next guy in that I find it annoying when someone is laughing and I'm not aware of the reason. It makes me think that I've become the butt of an inside joke. Next, Munchk pointed in my direction and made an effort to speak, but her words came out a garbled mess made indecipherable by laughter that now reached the point of hysteria. Meanwhile, my mild amusement reached indignation; though, had I become the butt of some secret joke, Ricky wasn't in on it. Not only was he not laughing but he seemed equally confused by Munchk's behavior. It was not a put-on. I reached the point of demanding an explanation for laughter that was out of control and for no apparent reason, but I became distracted by the subway doors sliding shut and the chugging of the engine. It was at that precise moment that I sensed a hand reaching into the open window—the very window in front of which I was sitting. Before I could fully grasp what was happening, a young boy, who looked to be Munchk's age and built as slight, was standing on the subway platform and in a tantalizing manner was dangling my shiny, red batting helmet just inches from my reach. *Looky here at what I got,* was what the insolent little fucker's actions were more or less screaming to me. Not only did the little bastard dangle my helmet in an outstretched hand while shaking his little tush, but then—after having narrowed himself to strut crookedly, like someone who was kicked by a horse—he began to gyrate ala Sammy Davis Jr. as Mr. Bojangles. It was one matter to fall victim to an *ah-ha, gotcha* moment, but then to have no recourse? I was livid, at the boy and at Munchk, who, by then, was doubled over on the floor of the train in a fit of laughter. I turned back to the boy and foolishly went lunging for the open window, reaching as far as it would allow. From his advantageous position on the platform, he continued to dangle my helmet; his strutting became more turkey-like, while I continued to flail in frustration, my face pressed to the glass.

I don't recall the exact expletives that were launched from my lips that day in the subway car, but it's a fairly safe bet they were colorful and ascended to a mighty decibel. In other words, I didn't leave the subway car having made any friends. Nowadays, whenever I see my poor Maltese puppies in the bay window working themselves into a frenzy, I know it's because the neighborhood cat has plopped down in the middle of the lawn and is looking back at my poor pups as if to say: "So whatcha gonna do about it, tough guys? Bust through the window?" I don't scold my pups for the horrendous racket they make. I cradle them, and with affection and understanding, I tell him, "I know what you're going through. I've been there. We're more alike than you could ever imagine."

As the subway rolled away, I pulled my arm back to create the necessary space it took to stick my head through the window, that way I could continue shouting, however in vain, colorful language at the prankster. He was no longer dangling my helmet and strutting about like a turkey. The little bastard actually placed my helmet on his head and waved goodbye to me—a helpless, frustrated moron yelling in vain. Munchk laughed all the way to 15th Street, where we boarded the Frankford/Market Street line. By then Ricky joined in the fun. By the time we reached Erie and Torresdale (our stop), my anger subsided, and I was able to see the humor. Thirty minutes ago, had I been able to get my hands on that boy, I might have given him a thrashing he would not likely forget, and, God help me, I would have enjoyed it. But, after several stops on two units of public transportation, I was able to see the humor and the boy's actions as a harmless prank that sent three people home laughing until their sides nearly split. Besides, it was Sunday. Why shouldn't a day that began with Uncle Al's monstrous pickup truck and Mr. Profacci's hairy udders end with the theft of my shiny, red batting helmet? Easy come, easy go.

God knows how many bumper-to-bumper traffic jams, bridge openings, and gaper delays I have thus far endured in my adult life, and I have managed to get through each and every one of them with a smile, and all because of the unexpected way that kazoo day ended. As I gaze out at all those motorists growing angrier and angrier over their current dilemma and at a world known to cause such inconvenience—sitting in traffic has a way of negating the better angels of our nature—I think to myself, *you poor bastards; have you nothing with which to occupy your minds other than your own frustration? Have you no resources? No memories to call upon able to produce a smile?* And then I see Munchk, her slight form and all the sparkle and vigor of youth, doubled over in the aisle of a subway car, then tossing herself about on the bench with laughter that could not be controlled had she tried. And then there I am, some thirty years later, stuck on some highway and laughing right along with her. Can you see me, sister? I'm still laughing with you.

****

It's high time I got back to that October to April void to which earlier I had alluded. By the time Ricky and I returned from the basketball courts, Uncle Al and Uncle Nunzio had gone. In truth, it wasn't the silly Reggie Jackson homage that I found so irksome; if those two old coots wanted to go down on Reggie Jackson, so be it; that was fine and dandy with me. What I did find irksome, and to the extent that I wished them blindness so that they could never watch another game, was their belief that since the Yankees beat the Dodgers four games to two in the Series, and the Dodgers beat the Phils three games to one for the Pennant, the Yankees would have beaten the Phils in a sweep. Now how's that for sideways rationale? *Great* uncles my ass!

"Easy pickins," said Uncle Al, dismissing our Phils as nothing more than a bunch of also-rans that didn't belong on the field with the Yankees.

"Yeah, well, if anyone would know about easy pickings, it's Uncle Al," was what I whispered to Ricky. Mom, who was nearby and able to read my impure thoughts, shot me a hard glare. I looked back with pleading eyes: *Our team wins 101 games, and Uncle Al is permitted to dismiss them as unworthy, but I'm prohibited from snickering about Aunt Prostitute? Is that how it works?* Mom had a way of glaring at me that made it seem as if it was my fault that Uncle Al married the most prolific fornicator ever to hail from Swampoodle.

"Yeah," said Uncle Nunzio, who couldn't resist piling on, "it woulda been nice watching Reggie take ol' Carlton deep. Maybe next year, Frank, your boys'll finally hit pay dirt. But I wouldn't hold my breath." And that's when Ricky and I decided we heard enough and went for our basketball.

By Thanksgiving, the sting of defeat was somewhat eclipsed by an event unrelated to the world of sports: I was "going steady," as we called "relationships" back then in the 1970s, with Karen Crawford, a girl widely thought the prettiest sophomore at Frankford High. Long, shiny hair can be captivating. Long, shiny hair that bounces with each step can cause a guy to walk into things if not into oncoming traffic. It was unanimous, Karen Crawford from the front was eye candy. From the back she was pure poetry! Karen could have been the Breck Girl circa 1977, as those tumbling, bouncing locks by themselves seemed to possess more confidence than any one person could imagine possessing; and her pretty little turned-up nose and winning smile announced to the world: *Look out, here I come!* Most teenage girls, if they don't have a valid reason to feel self-conscious regarding their appearance, will invent one. There was no point in Karen pretending, even if only for the sake of others. She was dealt a royal flush, and every girl knew it; and I, Frank Corelli, with my own two hands, got to hold that royal flush and enjoyed my enviable status. And not to oversell it, for a sophisticated species must place a premium on character, but Karen had, what we used to call in the 1970s, a body that didn't quit. Nowadays, as I welcome each friend request on Facebook, I'm noticing that many of us have bodies that didn't quit and are showing no signs of quitting. This would be a good place to insert LOL, but I'm not much for text-speak. Back to the 1970s.

So how did yours truly land such a beauty? Let's just say ol' Frank Corelli wasn't entirely devoid of looks and charm. He had a few things going for him.

"Frank, you sorry ol' Phillies fan, you! I didn't think you had it in ya," the gregarious Uncle Nunzio bellowed, regarding my then eleventh-grade beauty queen, when we were all gathered for our grandfather's surprise sixtieth birthday party. By the day of the party, a sunny Saturday in September, Karen and I had been an item going on eleven months, which was lengthy for a high school romance, particularly when juxtaposed to the duration of the average current-day marriage. "Those two'll never break up," I used to hear others comment.

Ricky and I had a helluva time watching our old great-uncles trying to charm my stunner of a girlfriend. Karen played the game like a pro; she had them believing they were savants of romance and acting as chivalrous as Lancelot as they ate from her well-manicured hand.

When I approached Mom with the idea of inviting Karen to the surprise party, she was agreeable. Karen had already spent time in our grandfather's company and, like most, thought he was as grand a guy as she had ever known. Though, no sooner had I extended the invite—one that was readily accepted—I felt a pang of regret, when imagining poor Karen overwhelmed by a house filled with boisterous Corellis. I envisioned poor Karen suffering through an afternoon of strange people doing strange things, such as Uncle Nunzio setting his chest hair on fire. It was not the sort of scene that in any way could benefit a high school romance. I became fearful that, instead of enjoying herself, Karen would spend the day clinging to me as one would on their first trip to an asylum. And far be it from me to suggest that a clingy Karen Crawford was a nuisance, but under the circumstances, such as a house party, it could have made for a strained afternoon. As it would come to pass, I didn't give Karen nearly enough credit. She dispelled my fears in no time, mingling with my kin as though nothing came more naturally. She was even brave enough, when urged by Vincent Bronini, to sample some of the more pungent slices from Vito the cheese vendor's tray.

"Brave girl," I said to Ricky. Then Aunt Dot stole up from behind us and asked, "Frankie, she's yer girlfriend, is she?"

Why must older relatives ask redundant questions in patronizing tones? I wanted badly to inform Aunt Dot that Karen was my press secretary, or was here to work on a plumbing issue that Dad, earlier on, made worse—or, better yet, she was a perfect stranger who was hungry and, when noticing all the cars parked out front, concluded we had food. But I was a *"good boy"* and held my tongue. "Yes, Aunt Dot," I respectfully replied, "she *is* my girlfriend."

"She ain't too shabby, there, is she, Frankie?" Aunt Dot observed.

"No, Aunt Dot," I replied, my respectful tone coming apart and lapsing into irony, "she *ain't* too shabby. *There*, nor anywhere else." Fortunately, the sarcasm was lost on my poor old aunt. I turned back to Ricky and checked my watch. It was about time for Uncle Al and Uncle Nunzio to regale the crowd with one of their anecdotes from yesteryear. Sometime afterward, Uncle Nunzio will set his chest hair on fire. Karen handled both scenarios like a champ.

Karen and I were only an item for a month when she decided that Ricky would be a perfect match for Sherry Mills—Karen's best friend and neighbor and, like Ricky, a freshman. I thought it was too close for comfort: best friends dating brothers, a collaborative love life; but of the matter, I was *informed* not *consulted.* When we first went about as a foursome, it felt strange, awkward, bordering on the incestuous. I didn't recall feeling that way while watching Felix Unger and Oscar Madison date the bubbly Pigeon sisters, but Ricky and I were not bubbly women reading a cheesy script, and Karen and Sherry were hardly *The Odd Couple*. In other words, Ricky was fine when it came to going to ball games, hitting the neighborhood courts, and partaking in other brotherly type activities that required high-top sneakers, but I didn't care to get too directly involved in paving the way for his love life; nor did I wish to witness his love life from too cozy a proximity nor have him witness mine. Nevertheless, I took the manly way out, having stepped aside to allow Karen to do whatever weaving and manipulating that was required to get her and Sherry Mills on equal ground. As I would come to learn, best girlfriends are in much better standing as girlfriends when each has a love interest to consider. That's a fact.

So, that's my story. Ricky's, too. We filled a cavernous void and healed our broken hearts over a baseball team that was derailed earlier than it should have been by way of the opposite sex. Ahead was a long, frosty winter, but we would keep warm with an eye on a horizon that would bring forth spring training and the understanding that once again the grass would grow and baseball would be back in the headlines. But what about Munchk? She was too young yet to get involved in our gender in the manner with which we involved ourselves with hers. But I should have known by then not to underestimate our kid sister. Munchk had her own plan and method to fill a void and heal a broken heart. Interestingly enough, it would involve her oldest brother, and in the not too distant future, she would blaze a path that would make history.

****

We didn't grow up in a neighborhood nearly so colorful as Swampoodle, but Juniata Park did have its share of quirks. A block from our house was Ferko Playground, and from our bedroom windows, we had a view of *it*, the courts, and surrounding ball fields. It was a nice feature until Mom condemned you to your room and all you could do was sit with your chin on the window sill and stare out at all that you were not permitted to enjoy. I use to pray for rain, but the rain never came; and to make matters more unbearable, Munchk would antagonize the imprisoned by flitting around the driveway like a goddamn sparrow, flapping her arms and chanting:

> *I'm free! I'm free! I'll flap my wings and fly away.*
> *I'm free! I'm free! At the playground, I shall play.*

Then off she would go, flapping her way through the driveway on her way to the park. Her arms never fell off, nor was she ever struck by lightning. God doesn't answer prayers.

Juniata Park is so small there's no sign on the City Hall courtyard map of its existence. We are the only neighborhood without representation. I once questioned a city official and was told the map predated the neighborhood. I knew he was full of shit—just a guy in a hurry, who wanted a twelve-year-old out of his way—but I was a kid and didn't want to act too bold. I should have had Munchk with me. The only sign of our existence is Hunting Park Avenue, which also runs through a dozen other neighborhoods. In fact, it winds its way past where the Hunting Park carousel and my tiger once turned, then travels on to Fairmount Park not too far from where Frank the pig was buried, and it dead-ends at the Schuylkill River. Despite the snub, you can rest assured that we were a neighborhood with a proud boy's club and a darn good string band!

Joseph A. Ferko, the fellow for whom the playground was named, led the Ferko String Band. I don't recall a rivalry or territorial battle between the Ferko and Juniata Park string bands, but I hardly had my finger on the pulse of such matters as acrimonious banjoing. But I can say with certainty that our very own Juniata Park String Band was an essential institution to our humble hollow; for year after year, and in grand style, they punctuated a parade whose purpose was to ring in a new little league baseball season.

Most neighborhoods make a big to-do over the beginning on a new baseball season. And why wouldn't they; with buds in the trees, birds a chirpin', cowhide smacking leather and every sign of spring, you need something to announce it, to ring it in. By noontime, after the last church service, folks begin to line the sidewalks of our cozy little hollow—two and three deep they are standing. This tight, enthusiastic gathering is waiting for the parade to pass. First comes the ball teams and their coaches— the little leaguers (seven to nine-year-old) are followed by the big leaguers (ten to twelve-year-old) and all the teams march proudly behind their team's banner. Every team's record is zero and zero. Hope springs eternal.

If you were one of the two boys holding the banner, it meant you were one of the top players. Twice I carried the banner, as a nine-year-old Twin, then twelve-year-old Brave. Ricky played for the Celtics. It was the team's inaugural season, and the whole team was comprised of first-timers. It didn't matter how many games those woeful Celtics lost by twenty runs or better, Coach Beisel had nothing but encouraging words to share—he never failed to find the silver lining, despite going winless. That year my Twins thumped Ricky's Celtics 62—5. In my first at-bat, I hit a hard grounder right through Ricky's wickets. It was while digging hard for second that I came to learn that Ricky knew the expletive phrase *you mother fucker*. "Next time get your glove down," I called to him while standing safely on second. He gave me one of those sulky, pissy shrugs, as though I hit the ball to him on purpose. The following year, every one of Coach Beisel's players returned a year older, stronger and wielding a boatload of confidence. And did they not go all the way to the Championship Series? Hell, yeah, they did; and Ricky whacked three doubles in the clincher.

The ballplayers are followed by riders on horseback tossing fistfuls of penny candy to the sidewalk, where young, eager hands will be quick to scavenge the ground. I can remember, as a youngster, waiting for the candy to be tossed; you'd have thought it was gold. But what I really couldn't wait for was being old enough to wear a uniform and march in the parade. *That* was my first boyhood dream.

Ladies and gentlemen, the Juniata Park String Band! The string band was what those who didn't have a son or grandson marching in the parade stood for and patiently awaited. Every block had a character that had already been hitting the Schmidt's or Ortlieb's; and upon hearing the strains of *Golden Slippers, Oh Those Golden Slippers* strummed in the distance, those beer guzzlers would begin to gyrate, working themselves up to the moment when the band turned onto their street. They would unleash their inner Fred Astaire and dance (and sometimes stumble) alongside the players—sometimes, if drunk enough, they would weave their way through the formation. I never quite understood it. What was it about *Golden Slippers* that turned the neighborhood drunks into Fred Astaire wannabes—or, as was the case on our street, with Mrs. Profacci, a Ginger Rogers wannabe? Though, who could blame poor Mrs. Profacci for all that she consumed? If I had to carve out a space next to Mr. Profacci and his hair udders, I surely would have twisted off my share of caps. She was like clockwork, Mrs. Profacci, every night taking to the patio, armed with a bottle of Seagram's and ginger ale—no doubt working up her nerve for beddy-bye.

The parade winds its way through the neighborhood, and it ends at the ball fields. Waiting in the middle of the diamond is a platform around which the teams will position themselves. On the platform is a podium set there for guest speakers whose speeches, year after year without fail, can only be described as longwinded drones of humdrum through which we must agonize. But then came the year when somehow, we managed to rope the Flyers head coach, Fred Shero, into an appearance. We were all very excited when learning that the leader of the Stanley Cup champions, our very own Broad Street Bullies, would be in our midst. We were all preparing for magic words of inspiration that would change our lives. After all, it was Fred Shero! The architect of the team that brought Lord Stanley's Cup to the city of brotherly love! No magic words of inspiration were uttered nor heard. Coach Shero spoke only briefly regarding the spirit of competition, then vanished faster than Keyser Soze.

The day's final speaker is always some councilman or local politician, who, after patronizing us by reminding us of what a good community we are—strong and vital to the city of Philadelphia—will go on to speak of funds that will never get appropriated for projects that will never come to fruition. *Raise your hand if this sounds familiar.* Nevertheless, everyone claps. Despite blowing smoke up a community's ass, the speaker is confident of applause, as no one wants to ruin the spirit of a day set aside to celebrate a community and its children.

In the spring of 1978, Councilman Whoever—after several times patting himself on the back while spouting his lofty intentions—in closing, congratulated the Juniata Park boys club for opening their little league baseball enrollment to girls. This produced not polite but uproarious applause. Mixed in, however, with the overwhelmingly favorable response, were a few jeers from morons holding to the notion that their sons were future major leaguers, and that allowing girls to assimilate into the league would devalue the competition, therefore thwart their progress. *Darn those girls; they ruin everything!*

On the first Saturday of the past December, at 8:00 a.m. sharp, Munchk was standing outside the door of the boy's club, birth certificate in hand. Munchk was one of only two females raring to sign-up, and between both genders, she was the first in line. Did some of the boys give her a hard time? Naturally, it was to be expected, but it wasn't anything she couldn't handle. After all, it's Munchk we're talking about; for her, a little razzing from boys was the equivalent of a picnic with butterflies instead of ants—it was hardly a distraction less a deterrent.

Gabby Kearns, who was a year older and a grade above Munchk, also handled the razzing with ease. Although Gabby had no intention of becoming a ballplayer; she carried her birth certificate to the boy's club because she was informed of a recent entitlement. For Gabby, it was all about the women's liberation movement and making the big statement. Gabby was pretty and popular, and she figured she could use her influence to pave the way for dozens of girls owning the desire to spend their summer donning ball caps and flannels. For weeks, girls at school and in the neighborhood followed Gabby like sheep. Many who had yet to place a hand inside a mitt, throw a ball, or swing a bat, were talking baseball and how Juniata Park's little league would soon be monopolized by long hair and tits. Munchk came home fuming that she was lumped in with the rest of the Gabby's disciples and was not given credit for having a mind of her own.

"I hope the very second she steps into the batter's box she gets her period!" Munchk scowled.

"That's a bit harsh, even for you," I told her.

"Goddamn it, Frank!" Munchk fired back, "Gabby's taking something that I love, something that *we* hold sacred, and turning it into a fucking circus! I hope she's unprepared and bleeds all the way down to her stirrups!"

I suppose Munchk had a point. Gabby Kearns went political and chose baseball for her platform—her holy cause—whereas Munchk's desire was to develop into a genuine ballplayer willing to work hard and become an asset to the team that drew her name.

To Gabby Kearns' dismay, that Saturday morning in early December, she found herself surrounded by boys, boys, and more boys. Occasionally, Munchk would glance back and grin victoriously, when noticing Gabby, her head swiveling nervously, fretting in the hope of spotting on the horizon other females making their way to the club. After Munchk gave her name and flashed her birth certificate, she exited the club only to discover that Gabby had drifted further back in line; her eyes still roving about the landscape in search of the sheep that she believed would follow her.

Poor Gabby Kearns; she learned the hard way that most people talk a big game but are a little short when it comes to follow-through. In the end, her once galvanized disciples decided that there were better ways to spend the summer. Gabby's dream of ponytails and nail polish scattered about the diamond was over. To her credit, though, she remained in line and sometime that morning threw her name in the hat. Come Monday morning, dozens of girls showed up at school armed to the teeth with all sorts of excuses—some were lame, others were creative, most claimed to have been sick.

"I guess you all must have drunk from the same water fountain?" said Munchk, brimming with sarcasm. By lunchtime, little league baseball, as it pertained to the girls, was no longer a hot button topic. By Tuesday, it was forgotten altogether. The moral of the story: For many, just knowing there exists an opportunity for a prize is better than the actual prize itself.

****

Of the four seasons, which are equal in length (or so says the calendar), it's the winter that seems to drag its feet and act reluctant to introduce the next season. A long, frosty winter is also good for helping us to forget certain matters, to blot them from our memories, especially those we would prefer to forget. I could well imagine Gabby Kearns, who by the springtime had yet to purchase a glove, was more than mildly surprised when she received a phone call from her coach informing her of the team's first practice. Christmas to Saint Patrick's Day is a sizable chunk of the calendar. For a twelve-year-old, it's an eternity. Poor Gabby received the very news a pseudo-activist doesn't wish to hear. It's showtime, darlin'! It's showtime!

Gabby Kearns won't be alone, though. Every team has one boy who, when stepping into the batter's box, resembles a deer in headlights, a frozen stick in the mud, and appears that any second, he might soil his uniform. We've all seen him, that poor, terrified boy, whom nothing short of a locust swarm could pry his bat from his shoulders... *that* one. Well, the Juniata Park little league Pirates "one boy" need not feel so bad; for alas, he shall have company.

The long, frosty winter had no such effect on Munchk. Unlike Gabby Kearns, all Munchk could talk about was leather, cowhide, and wood; by the first of the year, she had worn us out. There were days we tried to hide from her, but we didn't exactly live in a mansion. And with Munchk, there was no pretending to be asleep; if you tried, the result was a wet finger in your ear—or, if she felt too ignored or shoved aside, she might ring out a wet rag of ice-cold water on your face.

Spring could not get here fast enough. Munchk came home from signups all charged up, and before lunchtime, it was off to the sporting goods store in search for the perfect mitt.

"You're coming too, right, Frank?" Trust me, it was not a request. But then, in a more deferring tone, she added, "You have to help me pick it out."

I didn't count on Munchk picking out a mitt costing me a portion of my Saturday. I pretended that giving up an hour or so of a coveted day was a colossal inconvenience. *How can you possibly think I don't have better things to do?* Hey, every so often, one must flex a little attitude. Posturing aside, it was my duty to lend Munchk my expertise. So, I went along. But did I really have a choice in the matter? Munchk was frothing over with excitement and about to transform into an avalanche, the likes of which would crush me had I refused her. I did bother mentioning, "Why not use *my* old mitt? I don't use it much nowadays." It was true, I didn't use my mitt much anymore. I had been playing ball since the age of seven, and back in my seventh year, whenever Dad wasn't selling cars or tinkering with pipes, we would take our mitts and a ball out into the yard. I could tell that Dad hadn't played much ball as a kid; his mechanics were *that* poor. Nevertheless, I was glad for whatever time that he was able to spare for what in those days was a fundamental father and son activity; however, I couldn't groom Ricky as a catch partner fast enough.

To be fair, Dad hadn't much grooming as a child when it came to playing ball. With our grandfather and great-uncles raised by immigrant parents in a poor coal-mining town, ball playing was hardly a priority; though I do remember hearing about a secondhand mitt that Uncle Nunzio came by. It had either gotten misplaced and therefore never made it to Philadelphia or made the trip and afterward was sold; I never got the story straight. But by the time Dad was of a ball playing age, even had poor, old three-legged Max been equipped with a fourth leg, he would have been too old to go chasing after balls that a young Freddy Corelli might have thrown. Therefore, in his youth, Dad didn't do much catching *or* throwing.

Within our humble little neighborhood, I was considered a good ballplayer but didn't get much playing time as a high school freshman, so I didn't see any sense in continuing. Looking down the road, I saw myself making the junior varsity squad but as a second stringer with little or no chance of landing a spot on the varsity. But even if I had not voluntarily derailed my baseball career, my idle mitt was too big for Munchk's little hand. Ricky's glove was no more suitable; though had it been, he would still need it come the spring.

Ricky turned out to be a better ball player than yours truly. I was bigger and stronger and could hit for distance, but Ricky made more contact and was slick with the glove. The hard ground ball I hit that scooted through his wickets back when we were little leaguers must have left one helluva an impression; to the best of my knowledge, it never happened again. Ricky figured not only to make the freshman team but was forecast to be the starting second baseman. With that being the case, it was off to the sporting goods store to find a little league mitt to fit a very little hand. I never saw Munchk this excited. She examined mitt after mitt, inhaling the fresh leather deeply when she held it up to her nose. "Best damn smell in the world," she said.

"I agree, it's the best smell; but I think we can skip over the first basemen's mitts," I told her, as I looked down my nose at her diminutive size. "It's a fairly safe bet that first base won't be your position."

"Well, then, what about this one?" Munchk asked. "It must be a second basemen's mitt; it's signed by Joe Morgan. What do you think, Frank? Do you like it? Maybe I can try out for second base."

Munchk was hardly what you'd call a timid or delicate soul. Nevertheless, I was careful not to burst her bubble by telling her that the only time she would ever set foot on the field was when her team was either up twenty runs or down twenty runs. Even then, it wouldn't be until the last inning, and most likely they would stick her in right field. At the little league level, those players with a miserly endowment of ability were stuck in right field; it was where they were figured to do the least amount of harm. The kid whose mind was more on the Twinkies and Tastykakes waiting for him after the game, than the game itself, was sent to right field. So, too, was "Mr. Coordination," otherwise known as the kid who, if he ever managed to put his bat on the ball, it would take a miracle for him to achieve first base without first getting his leg tangled and taking a header on the baseline. Every little league team gets stuck with one "Mr. Coordination." Of course, none of this describes Munchk. Munchk, if nothing else, was hardly short on agility. But she would be the only girl.

"Second base? Sure, I don't see why not," I lied. "How's it fit?"

"Like a glove," she replied, before taking another moment to inhale the fresh leather.

"Then Joe Morgan it is," I said.

When we arrived home, I took possession of Joe Morgan, oiled him up, placed a ball in his webbing, tied him up with string, and placed him on the shelf right in between my Bobby Bonds and Ricky's Fred Lynn. "There," I said, "come springtime, it'll be all broken in—soft, supple, and comfortable as an old glove." Munchk appeared a bit sulky. She wasn't expecting so shortly after his arrival that Joe Morgan would get shelved; though she seemed to understand. "Don't worry," I told her, "you'll be on the field shagging flies before you know it."

Since the end of last season, Bobby Bonds had been shelved— his only activity was collecting dust. Little did I know I would soon resurrect him, and when I did, he would see more action than he ever had in the past.

The very Monday following signups and the acquisition of Joe Morgan, upon my arriving home from school, I discovered Munchk perched on the front steps. Her hair was tucked under a ballcap, and she was wearing a hand-me-down hooded sweatshirt that she pilfered from Ricky's closet. Despite her slight form swimming in the well-worn, over-sized garment, I could tell that she was antsy. On her left hand was Joe Morgan. In her right hand, she was gripping a baseball. Sitting on the steps right beside her was Bobby Bonds. "I can't wait, Frank," she said.

It hadn't occurred to me until that very moment that yours truly was awarded the task of working with Munchk—to train her and turn her into a ballplayer before the arrival of spring.

"You *do* understand it's December?" I told her. "And that we're supposed to be jingling our bells and partaking in fun winter activities, like telling obnoxious children there's no Santa Claus?"

"It's not that cold out, Frank," she said, ignoring my humor.

"I agree, it's not exactly a winter wonderland … yet. But there's a reason they play winter ball in Puerto Rico and not Philadelphia." I could see that my rationale penetrated, but it didn't prevent her from crooning out my name in a manner that was part shout part moan. She would not stand for me wasting precious daylight with idle chitchat. I looked down at Munchk and saw a young girl willing and determined—someone who would stop at nothing to become a ballplayer. I also envisioned her inviting the neighbor's bulldog to slobber on my toothbrush, if not sticking it up his ass, should I refuse. I excused myself just long enough to go inside and call Karen Crawford and explain to her my new assignment. I told her that I would meet her sometime after dinner.

My only saving grace, in the matter of having a catch with a rock-hard object in the country's chilly Northeastern corridor, was that it was December; therefore, only an hour or so of daylight remained. What's more, I figured Munchk would tire from chasing her own misses, and our initial practice session would be over in a matter of minutes. As it would come to pass, I did not know my kid sister nearly so well as I thought.

Munchk followed me through the breezeway and around back to the driveway. I marked off fifteen yards. A reasonable distance for a first catch, I thought. My first toss was a real lazy lob with plenty of arc, which Munchk effortlessly caught in the webbing of her glove.

"Frank, I'm not a five-year-old!" Munchk gripped the ball and promptly fired a chest-high missile that exploded into my mitt. For a fleeting moment, I thought that I was back in the field box with Garvey's check-swing foul ball bearing in on me and ready to take off my head. A satisfied grin formed on Munchk's face. She knew not only did the velocity of the throw take me by surprise, so too did the accuracy. With a slight bend of the knees, and while bouncing from side to side on the balls of her agile little feet, she awaited my return throw. My second toss did not have nearly the arc as the first, but it was still not to her liking—a fact she had no trouble letting me know. I didn't believe it possible, but her second return throw had more velocity than the first. I could hear the rock-hard object hissing through the chilled December air. POP! Again, the ball exploded into my mitt. *Okay,* I thought. *If this is what you want, here it comes, ready or not.* I reared back and fired the ball with the same velocity I would have had it been Ricky positioned fifteen yards away. Not only did Munchk spear the baseball in the webbing of her mitt, but she made it look as routine as a ham sandwich … minus the toothpaste, of course.

I could see the wheels turning in Munchk's head—her thoughts were loud and clear: *This ain't Gabby Kearns you're throwing to but a real ballplayer. Gabby can keep her tits and ass; I've got Joe Morgan!* She then pounded her little fist into the webbing of her glove. Adorable as she may have looked in her ball cap while swimming in a sweatshirt that came to her knees, she reminded me of a bull seconds before the gate is lifted. She had that *you better get out of my way or I'm going right through you* look. For the next hour, we fired chest-high lasers, one after another, right on up until dark. And thank goodness for the faltering sun, as my poor right arm felt like it was about to fall off. I kept looking up at the sky, urging the sun to go down. *Hurry, you intergalactic dawdler; what's taking so goddamn long?* Had my arm faltered before Munchk's, it would have meant my everlasting disgrace. Forget the sun going down; at that point, only a supernova could have saved me.

"So, how'd you think I did, Frank?" Munchk asked as we were making our way through the breezeway. *What do you think of your kid sister, now? Huh?* At the very least, there should have been a note of redundancy in her tone. But when I looked down at Munchk, I saw eyes swollen with hopefulness, the sort of hopefulness that must have been in the eyes of poor, old three-legged Max when luckily he stumbled upon eighteen-year-old Elizabeth Erwin. *Is it possible she doesn't know? Can it be that she needs to be told?* Up until then, I had loved Munchk, if for no other reason than she was my sister. But on that chilled December afternoon in 1977, by the time we cleared the breezeway, I had fallen in love with her. "I think you're gonna be a ballplayer," I told her.

Later on, that night, I explained to Karen my new after-school routine—a fixed routine that would span the winter months and continue on until the early days of springtime, when Munchk would have an entire team with which to practice. I cringed when I told Karen the news. I thought for certain she would object and say something to the effect: *what's the point of us going steady if you're gonna spend all your free time with your kid sister?* And who could have blamed her had that been her attitude? What moron lands the prettiest girl at school, only to snub her in favor of turning their back driveway in a winter camp for baseball? Karen surprised me. My cringing was for nothing. She judged it a gesture of magnanimity an older brother helping a kid sister fulfill an ambition. "Most guys I know wouldn't take the time and trouble," Karen told me. "Lizzy's lucky to have you for a brother."

It never occurred to me that by helping Munchk, I would also win points with Karen. Talk about killing two birds with one stone! And I had every opportunity to take the low road and inform Karen: *the only reason I'm helping Lizzy is to avoid living in fear of being terrorized by a variety of clever pranks.* But the truth was, I wanted Munchk to succeed. Come springtime, I wanted her, should she be so inclined, to march into school and show all those girls, who had merely talked a big game—but, as it had come to pass, decided celebrating their pubescence was the preferred course of action—what can happen when one challenges themselves and dares to be great.

The very next day, again, I found Munchk perched on the front steps awaiting my arrival. Again, she was accompanied by Joe Morgan, Bobby Bonds, and that same round, hard rock—that tightly wound and stitched object that only a day ago left my hand stinging like a sonofabitch. "How 'bout today we work on ground balls, Frank," she said, and around back to the driveway we marched. Today we stood a little further apart than yesterday. I began the session by rolling a little dribbler that stopped and settled just inches in front of the tips of Munchk's shoes. She reached down, picked up the cold, rock-hard orb with her bare hand, and began to inspect it as though she was searching for deficiencies and imperfections. Then she fired it such that, had I not been wearing a mitt, it surely would have taken my hand off.

"All right, all right, I get the picture," I called to her.

Next, I looked to my left, then feigned as though I was going to roll the ball in that direction. When I saw Munchk off balance and leaning that way, I threw a hard grounder to my right. She nearly recovered in time. She came close. But close is not close enough. The ball went scooting past her, mere inches out of her reach; it went bounding along the cold cement. In a fit, she slammed Joe Morgan to the ground, hollered out a barrage of expletives that reminded me of someone on a train who had his hat pinched, then went sprinting after a ball that didn't stop rolling until it reached the end of the driveway. When she returned, she was huffing and puffing; and despite the crisp December air, her face was ruddy and glistening with perspiration. The hair that began the session tucked neatly under her ballcap came loose; some locks were swaying about, while others were stuck to her well-perspired neck and cheeks. She had a wild look about her, possessing eyes that blazed with anger mere words would be inept to express. I had seen that look before. If looks could kill, there would have been a Frank Corelli chalk outline in the driveway within the hour.

"Goddamn it, Frank!" Munchk hollered. "What the fuck did you do that for!"

"Munchk, don't you know you're not supposed to end a sentence with a preposition?"

"Fine! What the fuck did you do that for, you asshole!"

With some trepidation, I advanced toward Munchk. Slowly I tread and with hope that by the time I reached her, a portion of her anger would have subsided. It hadn't. Nevertheless, I risked putting my arm around her and calmly explained, "Before a batter steps up to the plate, he won't be so accommodating as to inform the fielders ahead of time where he plans on hitting the ball." Still somewhat in the throes of her fury, Munchk seemed poised to fire a sharp response, but the words never came. *My* words, thankfully, pierced her cocoon of anger and sank in, and this led to her somewhat sulkily shrugging and lowering her eyes. She returned to her position, knees slightly bent and on balance—never again was she not on balance. I can't say that thereafter she never bobbled a ball or misplayed a hop, but that chilly December afternoon marked the last time she had cause to go sprinting down the driveway in pursuit of a ball. Fool me once...

For days, we worked on grounders: grounders to the left, grounders to the right, along with choppers that had to be charged and then short-hopped. Soon she began to remind me of Tank, the neighbor's bulldog, with how quick and instinctive she could pounce on a ball. Indeed, Munchk was like a canine blessed with the ability to move laterally, and all her throws had terrific velocity, the majority right on target. It was uncanny how such a slight arm was able to whip a ball through the air with such speed and accuracy.

"Imagine that coach … what the hell was his name, the bastard," Aunt Dot tried to recall at our grandfather's surprise sixtieth birthday party.

"The bastard's name was McConnell," replied Uncle Al.

"That's right," Aunt Dot continued. "Imagine that McConnell bastard sticking our Lizzy in right field. And he calls himself a baseball coach?"

"What'd ya want from the poor sonofabitch," Uncle Nunzio chimed in. "It was the first time he had a girl on the team. But give 'im credit, it didn't take him too long to figure out he screwed up. Christ, our little Lizzy was like a friggin vacuum cleaner at shortstop!"

"Boy, ain't that the truth," added Uncle Al. "No sooner our Lizzy was where she shoulda been all along, those Cubbies were the best team in the league. That wasn't no coincidence, ya know!"

"But let's not forget, Lizzy had a darn good coach; and a more devoted one no ballplayer ever had," Karen Crawford reminded everyone.

"Sorry, Frankie," said Aunt Dot. "We didn't mean to slight you none."

"Yeah, congratulations, Frank," said Uncle Al. "You turned our Lizzy into the best fielder in the whole damn neighborhood."

"Hey, Frankie ol' boy, it's a shame you can't coach the Phillies," Uncle Nunzio decided to add. "Maybe if you did, them bums might finally get to the Series!"

Leave it to Uncle Nunzio to deliver a compliment, while at the same time taking a dig at my beloved baseball team. I guess he thought he was being clever when taking digs at the Phils, and so he never missed out on an opportunity. He pounced on those opportunities as alertly as Munchk pounced on grounders. Anyway, I was reluctant whenever it was suggested that I take a portion of the credit regarding the level of success to which Munchk had ascended on the diamond. Sure, I might have had something to do with it; no doubt, my winter tutelage had served Munchk well once springtime rolled around; but, as the old adage goes, the cream rises to the top. Munchk had the agility of a mongoose. One way or another, she would have become a ballplayer, regardless of my efforts; I just happened to be in the right place at the right time. There were instances, though, when I allowed myself to believe—especially upon noticing Munchk's savvy and alertness when she took a lead at first base, or the intensity she exhibited when pounding her little fist into the webbing of her mitt from the position of shortstop, or the determination and focus that so clearly registered on her face while digging in at home plate—that she was somehow an extension of her oldest brother. Yeah, I permitted myself moments of folly, but those moments were both sobering and brief; for when I held myself up to Munchk, there was one glowing disparity: She was utterly fearless! Not to suggest that I approached the game timidly, but that Munchk was uncommonly fierce; she played every game and every play of every game as though her life depended on it. Watching Munchk was like watching how others imagine themselves.

****

I don't remember the day or date, only that it was sometime in mid-January when Munchk came bursting into my bedroom and yelling, "Frank, wake up! There's no school today! Look out the window, there's six inches of snow on the ground!"

When you live in a northern town, snow in the wintertime is what you live for, and that enough of it should fall to necessitate the cancellation of school. Six inches of snow was predicted, and we got every inch of it and then some. Despite Munchk frothing over with excitement, I managed to keep my eyes closed and feign being asleep. I did this while envisioning a day of snow frolicking with Karen Crawford, followed by hot chocolate and an activity that would not require scarves and mittens or any other cold weather barriers. I was hopeful. But my blissful vision was rudely interrupted when I felt Munchk's boney knees poking into my lower abdomen, thus applying pressure to my bladder. Her dagger-like fingers were digging into my shoulders as she attempted to shake me awake.

"Come on, Frank," she urged. "Mom's got French toast waiting for us. Then we have to shovel the driveway so that we can practice!"

"*Munchk*," I began, "if you don't remove those boney knees of yours, I'm gonna end up pissing all over both of us." No sooner had I finished grumbling about the position of Munchk's boney knees, her words registered. I looked over at Ricky and thought, *shovel the driveway? Practice? Is she out of her fucking mind!*

Munchk may very well have been out of her mind, and it led to her lying awake last night wondering how we could practice should it snow, and sure enough, she came up with a solution. The gift of an impromptu day off and how I imagined spending it would not be a reality—not until much later in the day. I looked up at this human ball of fire that was my kid sister. Who could resist anyone so determined? How could I, after seeing excitement flash in her eyes, deny her? Perhaps after all is said and

182

done, I will have frolicked, sipped hot chocolate and, if Karen and my weary bones allow it, have achieved some level of intimacy. But first and for certain, I am doomed to a snow shovel followed by the sound of a frozen hardball exploding into my mitt.

Not a moment too soon, Munchk removed her boney knees and allowed my strained abdomen to relax. Then she hopped off the bed, dashed to the window, and after throwing open the sash, she cried, "You see, Frank, it's not even that cold out! Now get up, you lazy shit!"

"Munchk, there's snow on the ground," I reminded her. "It must be cold."

Naturally, it was cold, but Munchk did have a point; the air always feels somewhat milder moments after the snow has finished falling. It's as though along its fluttery journey from the clouds to the earth, the snow removes the bite from the air and smothers it against the ground. Besides, last winter Ricky and I, along with other lunatics not hot to trot for sledding, brought snow shovels to the basketball court. Somehow, though— keeping in mind that basketball is a sport played in winter—the notion doesn't seem nearly so asinine as clearing snow from a driveway for the purpose of tossing around a hardball.

"Be thankful she doesn't want batting practice," said Ricky, his tone suggesting that I have been reduced to the role of Munchk's lackey, "or she'd have you up at the park shoveling the field."

"Wouldn't that be one for the ages?" I said. "I can just see the headline: MORON SHOVELS BALLFIELD SO SISTER CAN TAKE BATTING PRACTICE." Although, I shouldn't begrudge the notion; we have to get our "five minutes of fame" somehow.

True to Munchk's word, Mom had French toast ready and waiting, along with links of breakfast sausage and fresh coffee. By then, Dad had already brushed off his car and was dashing through the snow.

"Does Dad really believe that there's a chance in hell he's gonna sell a car today?" I asked Mom. She shrugged to indicate that it wasn't likely, but went on to add, "You never know, maybe some lunatic had his mind made up from a week ago that today was the day he was going to buy a car—or, maybe some poor fellow's car just went on the fritz, and he has to have a set of wheels by tomorrow or else he can't get to his job. Either way, your father feels it's his duty to be there."

"Nice try, Mom," I said.

I wasn't being flippant, only acknowledging that every family in given situations adopts a routine. Whenever there was snow on the ground,

Dad, like his hair was on fire, would scurry off to work—he couldn't get away fast enough. Mister Eager Beaver would wander around the car lot and showroom up until the time he figured that Ricky and I had finished all the shoveling, then he would come wandering home. That was Dad's typical snow day: escape before breakfast, dodge all the work, and return in time for lunch. A breadwinner's delight.

We owned three snow shovels, one for each member of the family brandishing a penis, but Dad's shovel never left the basement, let alone got introduced to snow. Dad didn't care much for snow, was not a fan of the sort of activities snow provides, and the notion of shoveling weather he didn't ask for but was heaped upon him by nature, made him wince in dismay. For Dad, there was no sound more sickening than a snow shovel scraping against a cement sidewalk—the second he heard it, he would begin reaching for his back, then run for cover. Ricky and I didn't mind shoveling snow; and after making quick work of our place, we would shovel for our next-door neighbor, never forgetting to shovel a portion of their backyard to accommodate the bodily functions of Tank, the bulldog. Afterward, Mom would urge us to go and help the Profaccis, citing, though not necessarily in these words: Mrs. Profacci, aside from a possible hangover, was too frail for the backbreaking task of snow removal, and Mr. Profacci was a fat bastard who would likely fall down the steps should he attempt to rid them of snow.

When we made our way across the street to the Profaccis, we prayed that Mrs. Profacci would answer the door. She was a good sport and gave us five dollars to split, whereas cheap old Mr. Profacci, with his greasy, bald head and hairy udders, handed over three bucks. Even at that, it pained him to pull those bills from his fold. You never saw a sonofabitch take so long to count to three; you'd have thought he was handing his car keys to drunks. And then there were those instances when he would give us the ol' *my wallet is in my other pants* excuse, and then act put-upon when having to retrieve it. He would purposely take forever, with the hope that Ricky and I would tire of waiting outside in the cold and leave without getting paid, but we always hung in there, if for no other reason than to witness how painful it was for that miserly old prick to part with his cash.

Today, Ricky would spend the morning hours around the front clearing off cars and shoveling his way to a nice payday, Mr. Profacci notwithstanding, whereas I'll be spending the morning around back digging a hundred feet of driveway … for love! However, I must admit to Munchk's credit, she was, and I shall quote a recent commander-in-chief, "shovel ready." No longer was Dad's shovel a mere ornament that year after year hung on the wall in the basement as a shrine to his laziness—a store-condition apparatus sure to fetch the sticker price at a yard sale—it would receive a workout for the ages.

It took a while, most of the morning, but Munchk and I conquered the driveway. Throughout much of our long and laborious effort, Tank, the bulldog, either whimpered, barked, or growled—I'm guessing he was a fairly intelligent and sane creature utilizing whatever sounds he had available for the purpose of challenging the validity of what must have appeared, even to a dog, a foolish undertaking.

"Maybe he doesn't care for snow," said Munchk.

"What should the snow matter to Tank?" I grumbled. "It's not as if the lazy prick has to shovel it. Once he's through with his business, he can go back inside whenever he pleases."

"Maybe that's the problem, Frank. Poor Tank can't squat to go because the snow is too deep."

"It serves him right for being a dog," I hissed while straining with a heavy heap of snow. "I guess we all have our cross to bear."

"Frank, look," my sympathetic young sibling pouted. "He just tried to squat, and his ass hit the snow. The poor boy must think that if he goes, his turd will ride up his tail. Come on, Frank, go and make a spot for him."

"I thought that was supposed to be Ricky's job," I protested.

"Who knows how much longer Ricky will be around front," said Munchk. "Poor Tank needs help *now*. Come on, Frank, have a heart."

As usual, I did as Munchk requested; and no sooner had I carved out an ample spot, Tank the bulldog dropped an impressive specimen.

"Hey, Frank, would you mind throwing a heap of snow over that thing so we don't have to look at it all morning?"

I glared over at Munchk. With no lack of derision, I replied, "Yes, right away."

And then it hit me: This runt, who once scoured the neighborhood with a bucket and trowel in search of horse manure to plant it in my sneaker, was all of a sudden repulsed by a dog turd? Granted, it was a healthy specimen and ripe as a sonofabitch, but hardly anything that should have inconvenienced a gatherer of equine waste. Although, Munchk was right about one matter; no sooner had Tank relieved himself, he ceased whimpering, growling, and barking, and was reduced to a docile creature seemingly disinterested in our bizarre endeavor.

When I returned my attention and energy to the drudgery of shoveling, I tried to keep my thoughts on Karen, my end of the day reward; though try as I might, my prevailing thoughts were of our next-door neighbor, Mrs. Profacci, and others handing Ricky five bucks, while I would end the day broke and exhausted. How I prayed that it would be Mr. Profacci who answered the door when Ricky went for his pay, and when seeing Ricky was alone, the misery old prick would slide him a measly buck and a half. I suppose being stuck in a driveway all morning long shoveling, for the right to have my hand pelted in the ice-cold air by a rock-hard baseball all afternoon, did little to enhance my otherwise sunny disposition. The other foul thought that crept into my beleaguered head was the *so-called* Blizzard of '44. This suspect event occurred eighteen years before I was born; yet I can remember it as though I had been there to see it firsthand. The reason being, every winter from the time that I was old enough to understand English, Uncle Al and Uncle Nunzio told and re-told the story of the legendary Blizzard of '44.

"Talk about a winter wonderland?" Uncle Al would drone on. "You never seen nothing like it!"

"Yeah, Frankie ol' boy, we had to dig out all of Twenty-sixth Street, your Uncle Al and me," said Uncle Nunzio, "and all we had to work with was a couple of coal shovels. Can you imagine? Coal shovels in a blizzard?"

"But what could we do?" moaned Uncle Al. "Your father was hungry, there was no food in the house, and one of the boys next door was sick and needed a doctor."

"We worked like dogs in that blizzard," Uncle Nunzio would go on to allege. "But with your grandfather away in the Army, the whole block was depending on *us*. We had to come through for them."

I have always found it very difficult to believe that my grandmother, Mrs. Elizabeth Corelli, a most capable and organized woman, would have allowed the household to run down to the bare bones. But even if it was partly true, on hand was the ever-resourceful Mama Corelli—the "MacGyver" of food. Mama Corelli could have taken paint chips and toaster crumbs and somehow managed a meal. As for the boy next door? I have no reason to doubt that he was sick and would have been in dire straits without medical attention, but I always have.

Without fail, but not without first making sure that their level of heroism was fully understood, that indeed they had rescued all of Twenty-sixth Street from impending doom with coal shovels, Uncle Al and Uncle

Nunzio would go on to explain how the harshness of a Scranton winter made Philly in January seem no more daunting than a day at the beach.

"You Philly creampuffs don't know the meaning of the word cold," Uncle Nunzio would drone on, as if he wrote the book on what it means to be inconvenienced by winter. This from a man who, if he singed off half his chest hair, would still resemble a gibbon.

"I was forty before I owned a winter coat," claimed Uncle Al. "And even then, I hardly wore the damn thing."

Imagine growing up amid such greatness? Such heroism? It's a wonder I didn't become a Navy Seal. But I did shovel a hundred feet of driveway, and all for the sake of my kid sister becoming a ballplayer. With that in mind, I have two thoughts for my great-uncles. *Up yours*, Uncle Al! And *up yours*, Uncle Nunzio!

Occasionally, I glanced over at Munchk, only to discover that she was holding up remarkably well. As we were nearing the end, having agreed that enough space was carved for an adequate workout, I couldn't imagine there'd be many throws in that right arm of hers—not after having taxed it as she had. But when given a chance, Munchk usually found a way to prove me wrong, if for no other reason than to shatter my meager expectations.

Once every last remnant of the storm was eradicated, you'd think that Munchk would have taken a moment to sigh while gazing at the massive heaps of snow that our hours of labor had produced. The sight of numerous heaps piled higher than our heads was surely worth a moment of reflection, or so I thought. Munchk heaved her shovel the way one would a javelin, then made a mad dash toward our house. The shovel pierced a heap of snow, the pole and handle sticking out like Excalibur. I had hardly a moment to ponder the place, the imperceptible well, from which she drew her surplus energy when she reappeared and went trotting back to the driveway with Joe Morgan, Bobby Bonds, and a ball. She casually flipped me my mitt, and we went to work, and work we did. Once the first popping sound of the ball against my leather mitt rang in my ear, I no longer dwelled on the Blizzard of '44 or how much money Ricky was pocketing. Not even Karen crossed my mind. All my focus was absorbed by Munchk, her fieriness, her determination—it was difficult not to get swept away in it. I became impervious to the nip in the January air, the cold rising up from the cement. All that remained was an aspiring ballplayer and me, repeatedly firing a rock-hard object while walled in by snow. I once remember hearing someone say, "You can always tell the winners at the starting gate; they have a certain look about them." Munchk had that look—that day, and every day. Who would have ever guessed she'd be so short for the world?

****

Despite my exhaustion, I did manage to spend the evening with Karen. We strolled the winter wonderland mitten in mitten, occasionally stopping for the thrill of a kiss and an embrace. We did what aspiring young lovers do to feel warm on the inside during times of bitter cold. Though, every time I opened my mouth to speak, what gushed forth was praise for Munchk. I had spent hours hauling heaping shovelfuls of snow, piling it eye-high, toiling like never before, with Karen as my inspiration. Yet between kissing, cuddling, and nuzzling with our numb noses, I frothed on and on about my determined kid sister, how remarkable it was that one so diminutive could move God knows how many tons of snow, and afterward possess the fortitude to field and fire a frozen hardball with the agility and precision of Larry Bowa and Davey Concepcion. Surprisingly, it enlivened Karen to see how spirited I became while touting Munchk's ability. God, she was a good sport; and as genuine as she was beautiful. Lucky me.

After I came wandering home, I ducked my head into Munchk's bedroom and found her weary little body perfectly still under her bed covers and her eyes about to droop shut. I wanted to tell her that she was magnificent and that any team would be lucky to have her. Instead, I smiled and closed her door. I wasn't sure if my reason for not revealing my thoughts was because I didn't want her to feel satisfied—that there were yet greater heights within her reach, or I simply didn't know how. Perhaps it was a little of each. To this day, I still couldn't say for sure. While lying in bed, I heard Ricky musing aloud about how he planned to spend his hard-earned money; but to be honest, I really wasn't listening.

****

The winter thawed and, despite the countless hours spent with my pint-sized protégé, I was still going steady with the uniquely understanding Karen Crawford. Also, Ricky and Sherry Mills were still an item. It appeared that both romances would not only survive the school year but spill into the summer. That winter featured two more snowstorms requiring a shovel, and Ricky was *Johnny on the spot*, making himself all the spending cash good old Bennington Street provided. As for yours truly? I was in the business of grooming the finest ballplayer the neighborhood would ever see. It didn't pay a *red cent*, which was an axiom that Aunt Prostitute applied to most, if not all, of Uncle Al's ventures. However, there *were* dividends; hard work, in some form, yields its rewards. I had gone the entire winter and spring without having been the recipient of a prank, and during all that time, not a single blistering insult was hurled in my direction. My kid sister was an angel with a mitt on her hand and a ballcap for a halo.

The last of the snow melted and with it went the winter. In its stead came the introduction of green grass and the promise of warmer days. Soon that green grass would begin to grow and provide Ricky with an even steadier source of income. Not so for ol' Frankie boy, as green grass and warmer days meant that it was time for batting practice. Munchk was no different than any other aspiring ballplayer; she couldn't wait to wrap her little fingers around the handle of a bat and whip it through the air.

Some have maintained baseball is boring. Often, I've been made to listen to the assertion that our grand old game is too slow. I'm reasonably certain that those sharing these *invalid* opinions have never swung a bat having made ringing contact in just the right spot on the barrel and at a precise instant. To open up the hips and bring down the bat from the shoulder into a wrist-breaking swing at an exact point in time is mechanical perfection. Moreover, its result, when successful, is a crack of the bat—a sound that can be every bit as stimulating as a Beethoven symphony. Once this sound and feeling are experienced, it is never forgotten, no matter how many years have come to pass. Boring? Only the unenlightened would subscribe to such drivel.

When I turned onto Bennington Street, right away, I noticed Munchk. It was clear that she was antsy and nearing the end of her patience, as she had waited an hour on the front steps. Waiting alongside her was Bobby Bonds. Tucked away in the webbing of Bobby Bonds was a brand-new hardball. Munchk also had her fingers curled around the handle of a bat inscribed with a replica of Pete Rose's signature—her chin was resting impatiently on the knob. From the end of the street, I could see excitement flash in her eyes when she noticed I had turned the corner. She was raring to go, as unsettled as a bronco introduced to caffeine. She leaped the entire set of steps in a single bound, equipment and all, and met me on the sidewalk.

As I was getting nearer to this tempest called Munchk and about to get swept up in its vortex, I began to reminiscence the days, which were not all that long ago, sitting in a classroom on pins and needles, on what were many a fine spring afternoon, counting the minutes until the dismissal bell rang. The elementary/middle school was five blocks from our home; yet on those afternoons, while watching the hour hand of the clock slowly creep its way to the highly anticipated three o'clock hour, I could smell my mitt—its leather was blasting through my nostrils when I yearned for those acres of green grass and freedom that awaited me. Anticipation can sure play tricks on the senses. And while we're on the subject of anticipation, I took it upon myself to temper Munchk's enthusiasm; the notion being that it would take several swings and misses, resulting in mounting frustration, before she got her timing down and made anything that could qualify as solid contact. She needed to be warned and prepared. Once again, I underestimated my youngest sibling.

We have all seen numerous youngsters, for the first time, try on a pair of roller skates and go about for hours as if on stilts, painfully striving for some level of proficiency to raise their recreational repertoire by a single activity. Then there are those rare few who take off as if they were born with skates on their feet. I suppose some of us are just lucky, naturals blessed with the ability to take to things as a fish takes to water. That was Munchk. With her, you could throw out the manual. Whatever she tried—whatever the endeavor happened to be—it seemed as though she had been doing it since birth and as second nature as breathing. Nevertheless, as we were making our way to the ballfield, I preached the fundamentals of hitting: Keep your back foot planted, your shoulder locked in, and whatever you do, don't turn your head! Not once did she glance upward as I spouted off these and other instructions. Her eyes remained fixed straight ahead on the ballfield, her steps quickening. With each uttered instruction, Munchk managed only a nod to let me know she was aware I was speaking, though she was hardly hanging on every word. Up until that point, she had seen hundreds of ballgames and thousands of at-bats. Where she was concerned, how to stand in the batter's box was not exactly one of life's great mysteries. Still, I felt the need to visit and revisit how one should conduct themselves standing at the plate. After all, you may watch it a million times, but you cannot know the batter's perspective until you bat.

Munchk did as I instructed or as she had already known to do; she stood in the batter's box with her back foot planted in a small gully which she took ample time to carefully and meticulously carve. Her front shoulder appeared locked in; her bat was cocked behind her right ear as she awaited the first pitch. She also choked up two inches and was gripping firmly, but not *too* firmly, Pete Rose's handle. As I began my wind-up, I watched her nose crinkle up and her eyes narrow. It was the dreaded scrotum look—that all too familiar mask of menace—a look that in the past caused me a world of fretfulness while awaiting my often and at times well-deserved retribution. Indeed, the dreaded *keep-me-up-all-night-wondering-and-all-day-looking-over-my-shoulder* scrotum look was present at the ballfield. It had been months since I last made myself scarce during one of Dad's plumbing catastrophes, so there was no logical reason for me to fear Munchk. Nevertheless, I envisioned a line drive launched from the barrel of Pete Rose—a real screamer that would deliver a clear message to my vulnerable and unprotected nuts. I also had another consideration as I began my wind-up: my age and size versus that of the young, diminutive female batter awaiting the pitch. With that in mind, I slowed my wind-up and tossed the ball toward home plate in such a fashion that it traveled in a non-threatening, ineffectual arc—a real lazy, looping sort of toss it was—the sort of toss that would have failed to produce a sound against leather had there been someone squatting behind home plate prepared to catch it. As the ball rolled off the tips of my fingers, the batter's eyes ceased from being tightly narrowed and relaxed into a disdainful glare. Also, her nose un-crinkled. Then the young, diminutive female un-cocked her bat from behind her right ear and lowered it to her side so that its head was resting on the ground. She followed the flight of the ball with those disdainful eyes, then reached out with her free hand and allowed the feeble toss to settle into her palm. The young, diminutive female batter, with what appeared to be some thoughtfulness, examined the ball. Then, with astounding velocity, she fired it back to the pitcher. In no uncertain terms she was informing the pitcher that it was not Gabby Kearns in the batter's box. She also reminded him, "That's not the way that Fat Danny O'Rourke is gonna pitch me. He's gonna fire it as hard as he can, right under my chin, and I need be ready for it!"

Danny O'Rourke—or, as some dared to call him, "Fat" Danny O'Rourke, went on record boasting that he would strike Munchk out on four pitches. At first, he claimed that he would require only three pitches to send her back to the dugout but then amended the claim, having decided that he would waste the first pitch by firing it right under Munchk's chin—a glaring reminder that she was a girl playing a man's game and that she didn't belong. Well, as they say, it's a dog-eat-dog world; and, from the traditionalists to the groundbreakers and all those in-between, everyone feels they have to make a statement or show the world they have something to prove.

Munchk went about the business of additional landscaping at home plate, focusing mainly on deepening the gully into which she had planted her back foot. Then she gave the plate a good thump with the bat head, before re-cocking the lumber between her right shoulder and ear. Again, I went into my wind-up. Munchk re-crinkled her nose and re-narrowed her eyes. I never saw such a look of determination.

I didn't do much pitching in my ball playing days; mostly, I played first base but knew the proper mechanics of pitching. I went into my leg-kick, remembering to keep my back straight. Next, I opened my hips and squared my body to home plate or *dish* as some like to call it nowadays. I pushed off the pitching rubber and planted my front foot with my toe pointed toward the plate. What followed was my arm whipping forward. The ball felt good rolling off my fingertips; I was empowered, in control. I watched as the round, white projectile went tailing in on Munchk's hands, and with a touch more velocity than I had intended. The speed and location notwithstanding, with surprising adroitness, Munchk managed to clear her hips, draw in her hands, and whip the bat's barrel through the inner half of the strike zone. She did this with alarming quickness and, in the process, made ringing contact. *Nothing like the crack of a bat!* The ball traveled on a line to where, if a shortstop had been well positioned, it would have been caught. But what was more important, Munchk was all over a pitch that should have been too difficult for someone with limited experience to handle; and not only did she hit it but she hit it solidly. No siree, there would be no teetering on stilts for Munchk; she would skate with the agility and tenacity of a roller derby pro! Why would I have expected anything less?

Well, ol' Frankie boy took off after the ball like an obedient Labrador retriever. I was a few strides into my gallop when I realized that batting practice as it was presently being conducted was not my brightest maneuver. Later on, it was described as, "a real Uncle Al operation." *Hey, did you hear the one about the moron who brought only one ball and no fielders to a batting practice?*

Despite not expecting Munchk to spray line roves all over the goddamn field, supplying myself with only one ball, thus ignoring the old Boy Scout motto *Be Prepared*, was one matter. Showing up with no fielder was dumber than stealing a dead pig. Like a moron, I sprinted all over the field, chasing liner after liner, playing the part of the ever-loyal retriever; the only thing missing was a stick in my mouth. With each retrieval, my trips back to the mound became slower and slower. I was afraid the widening intervals would affect Munchk's timing, but I had to allow myself time to recoup the energy necessary to throw a ball lively enough to where the effort wouldn't produce frowns from a young, diminutive female batter who would prefer getting hit with a pitch than mollycoddled into thinking she was better than she was. What kept me going, instead of keeling over from exhaustion and resenting my own stupidity (the latter was underscored by Munchk's success), each time I trotted back to the mound she had that same look, which was of a prize-fighter with something to prove and who couldn't wait to prove it—to herself, to me, her peers, to everyone. In spite of my exhaustion, I got caught up in the spirit of her ambition. Yessiree, Munchk was gonna show Fat Danny O'Rourke, Gabby Kearns, and whoever else might have gone on record as being a detractor that her motive for donning flannels and stirrups was not to further the feminist movement or pave the way for other females aspiring to become ballplayers—she was an *individual* not an activist—but to simply become a ballplayer herself. Some may have mislabeled her as having been a young girl with lofty intentions or having high-minded motives. The truth was simply this. Munchk loved baseball; it was in her blood. Her desire wasn't to be close to the game but part of it. She could not have cared less whether another female on Earth shared her ambition or walked in the path she had hoped to blaze; she was all in, regardless; no one was ever more committed to an endeavor, and yours truly was with her every step of the way, shoveling driveways and chasing line drives. The next day it was off to Rennell's, one of those local catchall stores, for the purchasing of as many baseballs as we could afford. Also, for the time being, Ricky, despite Sherry Mills not being nearly as understanding as Karen Crawford, would have to curtail his romancing and grab his mitt.

"You gotta take one for the team," I explained to Ricky. "Team Corelli needs a fielder." I wouldn't go so far as to say Ricky scoffed at the notion, but he was quick to turn the table on me, citing that he would allow himself to be recruited as long he could pitch and I did the fielding. I thought it was rather cheesy of Ricky to lay down conditions, so I didn't bother disclosing that yesterday, I took one off the kneecap. Munchk kept her front shoulder so well locked in, and brought her hands through the strike zone with such mechanical perfection, she tended to hit a lot of balls up the middle, which was a nightmare for a pitcher. I figured, screw it; let Ricky and his stipulation find out for themselves.

Ricky, thus far, had not been involved in the process; therefore, he could not imagine how grooming a female, particularly one Munchk's size, could be anything but an exercise in futility. He grumbled a bit on our way to the ballfield but forgot all about Sherry Mills, romance, and whatever else might have been on his mind when he witnessed up close his younger sibling in action. It didn't take long before Ricky was as swept away as I was in the spirit of Munchk's ambition.

****

The calendar jumped a month, and Munchk came dragging through the front door after practicing with her team, the Cubs, looking sulkier than I had ever seen her. I assumed she misjudged a fly ball, mishandled a grounder, or was overanxious and struggled with the bat, and her teammates didn't hesitate to let *the girl* know it and had gone about it in a fashion typical of young boys. But I would learn that was not the case at all—that her sulkiness stemmed from nothing that occurred during practice, but from having requested either number 10, 20, or 21 (numbers worn by Larry Bowa, Mike Schmidt, and Bake McBride) but instead was issued number 1. Uniform day was always a pain in the ass, with everyone clamoring to wear the same number as their favorite Phillie. Half the Cubs had clamored for 10 or 20, but those uniforms went to those players whose physiques could adequately fill them. Naturally, that left out the littlest Cub. The numbers stopped at 20, so there was no 21. Most, if not having received their first choice, settled for and received their second. Not Munchk. The littlest Cub was out of luck. What's more, her uniform came to her by way of default, as the uniform with number 1 was the only uniform suitable for her diminutive size.

"But that's great, Munchk!" I told her. "Number one is the best number to have."

"Bullshit, Frank, it was the only number left," she complained. "They were passing around uniforms left and right, and I ended up with the only one nobody else wanted."

"Munchk, don't you get it?" My voice was ringing with excitement. "You'll be wearing Richie Ashburn's old number!"

That was all Munchk needed to hear, that she shared something with the great Phils broadcaster and former gold glove center fielder and batting titlist. She brimmed with pride and afterward showed off her new digs to everyone, including the Profaccis and Tank the bulldog. But, as luck would have it, it was gravy day, which meant Uncle Al and Uncle Nunzio would be coming by. I spotted them marching toward the house; each was carrying an empty container which Mom would generously fill.

"Christ, they're like dogs, they can smell food a mile away," said Ricky.

"If nothing else, they have a sense of smell," I drolly remarked. Mom never failed to give Uncle Al and Uncle Nunzio the heads up when it was gravy day; she would not have wanted them to miss out. You see, Aunt Prostitute wasn't exactly a culinary artist, and Aunt Dot, who did know her way around the spice rack, never mastered a good Italian gravy. To listen to Uncle Al and Uncle Nunzio, Mary Corelli's gravy far surpassed the nectar of any known divinity. "Mary-nooch," Uncle Nunzio lauded when Mom permitted him a taste from the wooden spoon, "this is all the proof we need that God's a Dego!"

"I thought you'd didn't believe in the Man Upstairs," said Uncle Al.

"I don't," said Uncle Nunzio. "But if there was a Man Upstairs, he'd be a *paisan*. Ain't that right, Frankie?"

"Number one?" Uncle Nunzio intoned with a sneer, once the dynamic duo arrived and saw Munchk proudly wearing her uniform jersey. "Richie Ashburn?" His face further twisted when he turned toward me. I had just finished bucking up Munchk's spirits. "Come to think of it, I seem to remember another number one; he played around the same time as Ashburn. What was his name, Al? You remember…"

After pausing to think it over, which was all part of the charade, Uncle Al chimed in with a resounding, "Billy Martin!"

"You're right, it was Billy Martin!" said Uncle Nunzio. "Ever hear of 'im, Frank? If my memory serves me right, I think he mighta won a World Series or two."

"Oh, he won more than one or two," said Uncle Al, who knew damn well that I didn't need any reminding of how many times Billy Martin walked off the field a World Series winner.

"Come to think of it," said Uncle Nunzio, "Martin still wears the number one, even though nowadays he don't play ball but manages."

"Yer right," said Uncle Al.

"Hey Frankie ol' boy, tell me again who won the World Series last year," Uncle Nunzio smugly requested. "I gettin' old. Sometimes I have trouble remembering." Uncle Nunzio ran a hand over his wavy locks, which by then had turned mostly white. Then he lurched forward with an ear pointed in my direction, urging me to loudly remind him who were the ultimate victors of the 1977 season.

Munchk didn't stick around to listen to the two vaudevillians run through their predictable material. She slipped away to her room, leaving Ricky and me alone to handle our great-uncles, much in the manner that we usually abandoned her in the times of Dad's plumbing catastrophes. In her absence, we gave Uncle Al and Uncle Nunzio all that they could handle, but, in the end, we simply couldn't find a rational way to leap over the twenty-one World Series titles the Yankees had thus far amassed, especially in the spring of 1978, when our beloved Phils were still bankrupt. Once again, we were reduced to spectators gritting their teeth in frustration, while our front running uncles beat their chests on behalf of a team that was currently a contender and historically unapproachable. On that note, fuck Billy Martin!

****

By twelve o'clock, the late churchgoers had already returned from Mass and had dissolved themselves into the gatherings that lined the many streets that made up the parade route within the neighborhood. Some streets were lined not just two but three-deep with many waiting to spot their children, grandchildren, hear the string band play, or, in many instances, scramble for the penny candy tossed by those riding horseback. There came a cheering from the crowd as the first banner turned onto our street. The seven-to-nine-year-old little leaguers headed the parade and were proud to do so, to be the frontrunners. For them, to march in the parade was still a big deal. The seven-to-nines always received the more enthusiastic waves from the crowd, and the crowd's enthusiasm was well returned. There were shouts of *"Hi, Mom"* and *"Hi, Grandma"* from seven-year-olds unable hold themselves to a mere wave.

I can remember my first opening day march; I thought if the neighborhood were one block longer, my right arm would have fallen off. I waved excitedly when I spotted Uncle Al amid the crowd; for at age seven, riding around in the back of his pickup truck was still a world of fun. I waved excitedly when I spotted Uncle Nunzio; for at seven, I was at too tender an age for him to torture me regarding my dismal home team and how they rated alongside the lordly New York Yankees. I waved excitedly at Aunt Prostitute; back then, I knew her only as Aunt Theresa. Next was Aunt Dot, who was so short and fiery one felt obligated to match her enthusiasm. I waved to Dad, Ricky, and Munchk, who was held high by Dad; I yelled "hi" to Mom. Then I nearly leapt out of my cleats; for at the end of the block and standing head and shoulders above the crowd was our grandfather. Posed next to him and leaning on his ample arm, her cheek resting on his hulking shoulder, was our grandmother.

Next came the ten-to-twelve-year-old little leaguers. The waves from the crowd were only a drop less enthusiastic, but the returns ranged anywhere from meager to nonexistent. Some among the marchers managed to tip their caps. For a hotshot twelve-year-old ballplayer, a tip of the cap was a gesture that must be considered generous. Mixed in with the occasional tip of the cap were plenty of lazy nods, *what the hell are you looking at* smirks, and mock salutes. You could always tell the ones who were at the beginning stages of puberty; they had an aversion to doing anything conventional. Munchk managed to wave to the crowd as she marched by; but, as Ricky and I observed, she already had on her game face.

"Christ," I said to Ricky, "she looks like she's about to chew the leather of her glove and spit it out."

I can remember marching in the parade at age twelve: I winked at Mom, but ignored Dad altogether, as he had installed a basement dehumidifier and elected to trail the hose into a bucket instead of the washtubs. "It's free water, Mare! I'll use all the water the bucket collects on your garden!" Some days passed. Mom's zinnias were wilting. She couldn't imagine why. When she went to the basement to run laundry and grab the above-mentioned bucket, as Dad had fallen down on the job, her shoes went squish. Ricky and I nearly gagged to death we laughed so hard, and as the result, our cleats were tossed into the neighbor's yard where Tank gnawed them to pieces. Next I nodded to Aunt Prostitute and Aunt Dot. I wanted to flip Uncle Al and Uncle Nunzio the bird for having numerous times disparaged my beloved Phils, who, by the spring of 1975, had made great strides and were playing better ball than the Yankees. Wisely, I held myself in check, having delivered an eye-rolling upward nod that could only be interpreted as, *screw you guys!* Then in the background, his form towering above the multitude, I spotted our grandfather. Holding on to his ample arm, her cheek resting against his hulking shoulder, was our grandmother. I raised my hand high above my head and was swaying it back and forth as though waving farewell from a ship that wasn't to return for many a day.

Next came the men and women on horseback. To the delight of the many young hands that came prepared to scramble and gather, they tossed fistfuls of penny candy into the crowd. Unfortunately—this is prone to happen when beasts are permitted to partake in human activities—a horse left behind a parting gift for the string band, which would soon appear and whose strains could already be heard. One would think that playing music while marching in a tight formation was difficult enough without having to sidestep piles of manure. Every job, I suppose, has its pitfalls.

From across the street, I noticed Mrs. Profacci was beginning to gyrate, as *Oh, Dem Golden Slippers* was all but upon us. When the string band turned onto Bennington Street, with all their pomp, flashy colors, and blaring banjos, Mrs. Profacci grabbed hold of Mr. Profacci, seemingly unconcerned that his rotund figure hardly allowed for anything that might qualify as a dance step. As she did every year, Mrs. Profacci pulled the poor, ill-equipped Mr. Profacci along, refusing to allow his stoutness, greasy bald head, and hairy udders to discourage her from whooping it up alongside the band. And whoop it up she did! She dragged poor Mr. Profacci along for several yards, then began strutting and high-stepping her way around his impressive circumference. Like the Earth around the Sun, she revolved and revolved, having repeated the maneuver numerous times by the end of the block. What was even more impressive, along the way not a single drop of precious liquid was spilled from her glass. What balance! And to his credit, Mr. Profacci, who at first scowled, got caught up in the spirit of the moment. With outstretched arms and a slight bend at the knees, he went about as though he were mimicking the mummer's strut. Either that or he was sleepwalking while suffering from hemorrhoids.

Thankfully, or regrettably, depending upon one's perspective, the Profaccis lived toward the middle of the block. Some say the old gal made an ass of herself. But I believe that from time to time a person is entitled to let loose and make an ass of themselves, and do it without caring what anyone else thinks. So what if she already had a few? Not every matter in society, despite how fashionable it has become, requires us to micromanage and act hypercritical. All the poor woman did was embarrass her husband—the same man who on countless mornings treated the neighbors to the sight of his rotund form wrapped in an undersized bathrobe. Anyway, while the Profaccis were doing their thing, Uncle Nunzio and Aunt Dot were also strutting and high-stepping alongside the string band, and Uncle Al, who was looking on from the sidewalk and clapping, cheered them on.

During this time of pomp and festivity, which saw adults acting too much like children to be considered adults, and children acting too cool to be considered children, who should remain safely tucked away behind the crowd, making every effort stay inconspicuous, but Aunt Prostitute.

Theresa Scoli Corelli, aka Aunt Prostitute, always recoiled whenever she found herself in a crowd. No doubt she was wary that someone from her Swampoodle days might be lurking about and recognize her. For that reason, she lived her life as discreetly as she could. *Hey, I remember you; you're Theresa Scoli,* were the seven words she most dreaded, along with the subtle wink and smile likely to follow such an acknowledgment. Despite all the behind-the-back snickering that went on in our household, I did have empathy for my great aunt. We all drag through life our share of regret; some more than others.

Following the string band came several decorated cars representing local businesses. As always, the cars held up the rear of the parade. From within the cars, there were plenty of friendly smiles and enthusiastic waves, though their appearance was somewhat anticlimactic. After all these years, no one yet figured out the local business folks should begin the parade, not end it. Nothing like saving the dullest for last.

Many followed the parade to the park, where it spilled onto the ballfield and surrounded the platform that was set up for guest speakers, who, as always, did their best to subdue an otherwise buzzing crowd waiting to hear two words: PLAY BALL!

In no time flat, the seven-to-nines were fidgeting. The ten-to-twelves were beginning to yawn. Even the adults were showing signs of restlessness and faltering postures. Then Councilman Whoever gave the neighborhood a big, congratulatory pat on the rump for renaming its boys' club the Juniata Park Boys and Girls Club. All at once, all eyes went roving the landscape in search of Munchk and Gabby Kearns. And depending on who you talked to, the girls were either perceived heroes or villains. From within the sea of uniforms, I spotted Danny O'Rourke. He was poking his head upward in an effort to locate the Cubs and their *token female*—the same female he went on record proclaiming he would strike out on four pitches. Fat Danny O'Rourke, who, by twenty-first century American standards, would only be considered husky, sneered in Munchk's direction. But Munchk had her eyes fixed on Councilman Whoever, and she didn't notice Danny, nor anyone else, acting rudely.

And while we're on the subject of Fat Danny and huskiness as it may relate to the twenty-first century, I have recently been informed by my wife—who made what for her was a plausible attempt at diplomacy—that it isn't just my Facebook friends that have expanded their anatomical boundaries. *Thickening around the middle* was the precise term she used. It rang with such pretention that it left me wishing she had called me fat instead. Either way, this so-called "thickening" has led to a woman, who by nature seeks control, substituting my nightly dish of ice cream with low-fat cottage cheese mixed with some dietary vanilla-flavored yogurt. Cottage cheese and yogurt. I'm sure any day now I'll begin sprouting a vagina.

At last, and not a moment too soon, the speakers exhausted themselves. Afterward, the platform was broken down and carted away to wherever it gets stored until next spring. The string band went marching off, still in their formation, and they provided the crowd with the parting gift *Take Me Out to the Ballgame*. Lastly, the horses were trotted back to the stables, where they would remain until next Saturday when once again they would be available to rent by the hour. During this time of transitioning from ceremony to baseball, families began to stake their claim to the multitude of picnic tables that were situated beyond the outfield fences. Soon the smell of lighter fluid, burning charcoal, and sizzling hot dogs would fill the air. Then two men appeared with elongated devices on wheels. These devices neatly dispensed the bright white chalk used for marking baselines. Coaches were busy penciling in line-ups in scorebooks and players were tossing balls all over the outfield. Finally, the umpire pulled his mask down over his face and hollered, "Play ball!"

I watched the Cubs starters, with more energy and excitement than their youthful bodies could contain, sprint onto the field and take their respective positions. My vigilant eyes surveyed the field, shifting from third to first, then the outfield, but Munchk was not among those sprinting out to positions. It occurred to me she might be pitching, but I don't recall her telling me that Coach McConnell gave her a mound tryout. Perhaps Munchk wanted to surprise me.

Like a maestro, who makes his way to the podium after the musicians have settled and tuned their instruments, the pitcher is often the last to take the field. And why shouldn't Munchk be the pitcher? She had as good an arm as anyone—could fire it with the best of them. But then I saw the very long and lean Bobby Jones, maestro-like, make his slow but confident strut toward the mound. Bobby Jones had the physique of someone you'd suspect could get knocked over by a peashooter, but also owned a long right arm that mimicked that of a whip when he unfurled from his windup. He was all knees and elbows, and the ball came out of his hand as though it was launched from a slingshot. Bobby Jones could make a catcher's mitt pop. I suppose if I were the coach, he would have been my choice for a starting pitcher as well.

When I took to the stands, I positioned myself directly behind the Cubs dugout, out of the sightline of Munchk's peripherals; I didn't want her to see the level of disappointment that registered on my face that she was not among the eight position players who, with pride and with exuberance, sprinted onto the field. I groomed a helluva ballplayer, at least as good as any of the starting eight, especially the sad sack right fielder, who I could tell was praying a ball wouldn't get hit his way. I can't say that Munchk was the slightest bit preoccupied with my whereabouts; her full attention and focus were on what was taking place on the field; her head was nowhere but in the game.

As much as I was disappointed, I was also angry at Coach McConnell for having failed to recognize Munchk's ability—or worse, he *had* recognized her ability and was choosing to ignore it. Perhaps he intended to punish her, for he might have been among the small but stalwart camp hardly in favor of girls in baseball uniforms; perhaps he even cringed way back in December, when he drew the name Elizabeth Corelli from the hat.

My speculating only served to feed my anger and disappointment. If Munchk had performed at the team practices even half as well as she had in a shoveled driveway during the frigid winter months, then she must have turned heads. They couldn't deny her forever. Though I should have anticipated that being a groundbreaker would come with a price—anything worthwhile has its price. Being as good as the boys won't be good enough; Munchk'll need to clearly outperform the boys to win a starting position. But time and again, whenever I underestimated my youngest sibling, whenever anyone dared to sell Munchk short, she went plowing forward, obliterating boundaries and finding ways to prove me and everyone else wrong.

I was paying little if any attention to the game. My eyes remained fixed on the back of Munchk's uniform and the number one, which seemed disproportionately large for the size of the jersey onto which it was sewn. I imagine that Richie Ashburn and Billy Martin had traveled through baseball's ranks having heard the words *too small to be a ballplayer*. I could only hope that Coach McConnell, gender aside, didn't feel that way about Munchk—that her ambition, along with all the hard work and determination she put forth to fulfill it, wouldn't result in her becoming a mascot to a bunch of boys around whom, on a bad day, she could run circles—that she would be given fair chance to prove she belonged.

The stands were packed with generations of Corellis, along with others whose only interest was to see "the girl" succeed or fall flat on her face. In my head, I was preparing my postgame pep talk—my consolation speech should Munchk's number not get called, and she winds up riding the pines for all seven innings. Although I had no clue what should be said to someone who, on numerous occasions, shoveled many tons of snow just for the right to compete in a little league baseball uniform. *It's only one game, Munchk. Don't get discouraged. It's a long season, there'll be plenty of time for you to shine.* Yeah, maybe that's what I'll tell her.

****

The year was 1967. To the displeasure of many, the United Stated found itself knee-deep in an infamous quagmire known as The Vietnam War. On a happier note, the Beatles, in an answer to the Beach Boys' groundbreaking *Pet Sounds* album, released the equally groundbreaking *Sgt. Pepper* album. United Artists released the critically acclaimed film *The Graduate,* starring Dustin Hoffman. Also, to the delight of Uncle Al and Uncle Nunzio, along with millions of New Yorkers, Yankee slugger Mickey Mantle belted his 500th home run. But in our own little corner of the world, with the entire family present, our house frothed over with excitement as it awaited the arrival of the first-ever female Corelli born on American soil.

"Jeez, it only took us three generations to grow a potato instead of a carrot," said Uncle Nunzio in what was his customary gregarious and comedic manner. It was Aunt Dot, though, who later satisfied my curiosity regarding my great-uncle's vegetable allegory. *"Girls get potatoes and boys get carrots."* What would we have done without Aunt Dot, who I imagine was grateful that Uncle Nunzio never tried to torch the foliage in his carrot patch the way he had his chest hair.

As far as Ricky and I were concerned, Mom could go off and have a baby every week. While she was away at the hospital delivering Munchk and then preparing to come home (in those days it wasn't delivery on Monday and home on Tuesday), we moved in with our grandparents for a week … and were taken to Hunting Park every day! Carousel rides, pedal boating, ice cream cones—it wasn't too hard to take. Ricky and I were shining examples that if you give children exactly what they want, all day and every day, they tend to behave. It's what's otherwise known as the inmates running the asylum; it works well in the short term.

Dad walked in holding a Coaster Seat, which contained the main attraction—what everyone had been on pins and needles waiting to see. He placed the seat on the coffee table, and the family positioned itself around its newest arrival.

"Everyone," announced Mom, "I'd like you all to meet Elizabeth Mary Corelli." Mom and Dad's eyes began to well up.

Elizabeth Mary Corelli? Jesus Christ! This crinkled, discolored-looking little turd that can't do anything but lie there like a useless lump gets nine whole syllables, whereas yours truly can do all sorts of stuff and goes by plain old Frank? And aside from the nine-syllable name was the manner in which Mom announced it, like she just voided her womb of a future wunderkind, who upon drawing her first breath begun her ascension to a throne. So it's fair to say that my impression of Munchk was not a particularly favorable one.

I thought Elizabeth was a fine sounding name for our grandmother. After all, the former Miss Erwin was a grandmother. But to pin such a mature sounding name on our newest arrival? The four-syllable word sounded like a bunch of L's and Z's that no doubt would get scrambled and stuck in the new arrival's throat whenever it came time for her to try and pronounce it. And then there was that wishy-washy consonant blend at the end. This was a name that will surely take years for the new arrival to learn, was what I thought. I could just imagine her first day of preschool: My name is Z-L-ZA-TH. Not a moment too soon, Uncle Nunzio blurted out "Lizzy." All at once, you could sense everyone in the room thinking, *Mmm ... Lizzy Corelli ... sounds kinda catchy.* From that moment forward, the newest arrival was Lizzy Corelli, the apple of everyone's eye.

At first, when everyone gathered around the new arrival, they oohed and ahhed. What followed was a variety of idiotic sounds and gestures as they all leaned in for a closer peek at this new thing Uncle Nunzio dubbed Lizzy. I learned that day that it's really no great wonder animals, when in their infancy, progress so much faster than humans. Uncle Al, who was holding a stuffed cow, nuzzled the black and white material against the new arrival's chin. Then, after asking the new arrival, "What does the cow say, Lizzy?" he proceeded to moo like a bovine that just had a corncob shoved up its ass. Ricky and I walked away. We didn't find the new arrival, or *thing* called Lizzy, nearly as impressive as did the rest of our clan. And how in the hell was Uncle Al able to determine that the crinkled lump sitting on the coffee table, who seemed oblivious to her kin and all their idiotic shenanigans, had our grandmother's eyes? Our grandmother declined the notion and was quick to suggest that the new arrival's eyes resembled those of her mother. Our grandmother wouldn't dare take credit for any assets the new arrival might have possessed.

"Well, at least she didn't inherit those mitts," teased Uncle Nunzio as he gave our grandfather a friendly poke with his elbow.

"Thank goodness for that," said our grandmother; but then she lifted one of our grandfather's impressive hands to her mouth and kissed it.

Regardless of how highly anticipated her arrival, Ricky and I figured that it would be years before this sibling of ours could contribute anything of interest to our existence. With that in mind, we left the room. From the basement, we heard Uncle Nunzio call out, "Hey, Mary-nooch, enough already with all this baby business. Let's get crackin' with some spaghetti, I'm starvin'!"

"Nunzi, you bastard, where's your manners!" hollered Aunt Dot. "Leave Mary alone, for cryin' out loud; she just had a baby!"

"I'm only teasin'," said Uncle Nunzio. "But it's gettin' to be that time of day."

Uncle Nunzio adored our mother. Though it mattered not if he was teasing about his hunger or need for pasta with the world's best gravy. With already having two young, rambunctious boys in her stable to look after, and an infant on the way, Mom anticipated the struggles. Days before going into labor, she made gallons upon gallons of what Uncle AL and Uncle Nunzio dubbed *the lifeblood of our family.* Mom wouldn't need to make another pot of gravy until Munchk was old enough to pronounce all nine syllables of her name backwards!

As the story goes, Munchk was walking within ten months of her much-celebrated birth—two whole months before Ricky and I managed our first tottery steps. This was a fact, once she was made aware of it, by who else other than Dad, that she never let Ricky and me forget it. Munchk became quite adept with the many ways which she was able to work into a conversation, or incidentally mention, the gap in our times learning to walk. *Frank, I'm so sorry to bother you because I realize you're still practicing, but would you mind bringing me over that thingamajig,* was an example of how I was repeatedly enlightened concerning her infant agility. Being the youngest sibling and female, I suppose it was her privilege to try and pull Ricky and me down a rung or two whenever she saw an opportunity. And no one was able to fight for their own space or air with more ferocity than Munchk! And you guessed it; Munchk was talking up a storm well before Ricky and I were able to utter anything that could qualify as a language. There was hardly a need for speculation when it came to what was on Munchk's mind. With both her tongue and legs, she ran and talked circles around our entire clan.

"She's jackrabbit fast," Uncle Al was often fond of saying. "You couldn't catch 'er if you had a net; and if you did, why that Lizzy, she'd talk her way right on out of it, God bless her."

"Yep, she sure is something else, our Lizzy," Uncle Nunzio would always add. "A human blur in a ponytail."

When Munchk got to school, she would routinely challenge the boys in her grade to a foot race, but sulked because she never had any takers. No schoolboy—especially back in the early 1970s, with Bobby Riggs already having lost to Billie Jean King in the battle of the sexes as it was played out on a tennis court—was willing to risk the embarrassment of losing, Heaven forbid, to a girl. This was also true of the boys in the next grade higher, who despite the advantage of age and size, stood a better chance of winning. It made me laugh to think that all those poor boys were terrified of my baby sister. But who could blame them? Munchk, as Uncle Nunzio pointed out, was a human blur in a ponytail—a rare being with too many electrons per atom, and a fiercer competitive you would never find.

Nowadays, Munchk has been the center of attention in gym class and has been befriended by all the boys considered fit and athletic. They all marvel at her superior speed and agility; however, for the remainder of the school day, which is spent in classrooms and in street clothes, their focus and fascination shifts to the girl who recently has become Munchk's rival, Gabby Kearns and her budding womanhood. Munchk was not showing signs that puberty was anywhere on the horizon.

I felt a tremor; it came from the stands. This is nothing remarkable; anyone who has ever sat on stands is aware that the slightest movement, such as someone stepping on or getting up to step off, can send vibrations throughout. But then the tremor became more dramatic, as if it was being produced by a stampede of cattle, horses, or some other species that finds it necessary to rumble about in herds. The terrain was shifting, voices were crescendoing, I was disoriented, enveloped by chaos. Then I felt a hand firmly grip my shoulder. The hand in question belonged to Ricky. "Frank! Frank!" he shouted. "You missed it! You missed it!"

No longer in the throes of a stupor that took me back to Munchk's first day home from the hospital and beyond, I looked up. When I did, my eyes found Munchk sprinting in from the outfield with ball in hand. As it was described to me by Ricky, along with several others, all greatly animated and talking at once: A hard, sinking line drive was hit out toward the right-center field gap. To all those in attendance (minus yours truly), it appeared, with certainty, that the ball would find open space and drop in for a safe hit. In little league, line drives swatted toward the gaps usually find open space before rolling all the way to the fence. The end result usually sees those on base scoring easily, and the batter huffing and puffing after legging out a standup triple. But this was not the case on opening day of 1978.

At the crack of the bat, Munchk was off—she had read the flight of the ball perfectly. Afterward, there was a mild debate over who traveled faster, Munchk or the ball. "It was like a missile intercepting a torpedo!" someone in the crowd had bellowed. She ran the perfect route, taking just the right angle; her extraordinary agility took it from there. Naturally, her detractors claimed that she was lucky, that it was a one-in-a-million catch that would never be duplicated. But Munchk was hardly lucky, nor was it a mere matter of her speed that made the catch possible. Simply put, Munchk had a ballplayer's instincts. She reached down at the end of her run with her glove turned toward the infield so that the ball found its way securely into the webbing. Her momentum took her into a shoulder roll and then back to being square on her feet. She then raised the ball with her bare hand high above her head to show the umpire that she had made a good catch. When Munchk got back to the dugout, I looked across the way at Uncle Al, Uncle Nunzio, and our grandfather. All three were buzzing over Munchk's catch like it was the most impressive feat they were fortunate enough to have witnessed. And how ironic that Coach Donnelly, when he called her number, stuck Munchk in right field, where he figured she would do the least amount of damage to the Cubs chances for an opening day victory. Nobody was happier about the catch, though, than the long, lean Bobby Jones. He damn near jumped out of his cleats as the catch kept the game tied going into the sixth inning.

Munchk didn't get a chance to bat in the top of the sixth inning, nor was a ball hit her way in the bottom half of the inning. Then came the seventh and final inning and what the whole sixth and seventh grades had been waiting for—the duel between Fat Danny O'Rourke and the littlest Cub. Danny's claim that he would strike Munchk out on four pitches got everyone's attention. And why wouldn't it? Nothing like a little trash-talking to spark interest; though whenever Munchk was asked to respond to Danny's bold prediction, she would calmly reply, "We'll see what happens come opening day." Some had tried to egg her on, hoping she would let loose with a sharp retort that they could carry back to Danny, but she refused to be provoked.

Danny struck out the first batter in the top of the seventh. I was nervously wringing my hands and had no control over the butterflies that had taken up residency in my stomach, as I watched Munchk taking her practice swings in the on-deck circle. Worse, the next batter hadn't an ounce of consideration for my condition and all but proved it by lunging at the first pitch. His over-anxiousness caused him to get too far out on his front foot, and the result was a weakly tapped ball, which the second baseman handled with ease. That meant it was showtime, and Danny O'Rourke was rolling along with ease. Karen Crawford took hold of my nervous hands, but she was nervous as well. Together we nervously watched Munchk stroll on up to the plate. She used the bat to carefully measure the distance from the plate to where she was comfortable positioning her front foot. Next, she proceeded to place her back foot into the gully which had been repeatedly worked over since the first inning. She tapped the plate with the bat head, then cocked the bat behind her right ear. She was ready.

Often, I've wondered what goes through the mind of a prize-fighter seconds before the bell is about to ring. Fear? Anxiety? Perhaps he's thinking to himself, *what the hell am I doing here?* Then again, it may be none of the above; for those are the feelings that are shared by the onlookers—the ones who stand off to the side to cheer and hope, and to either live or die with their beloved champion. Champions, or those with the heart of a champion, do not fear failure; they're too busy existing for the moment to consider the consequences of failure. It's the rest of us whose burden it is to stomach the anxiety. It is us timid souls that cannot imagine or can only dream of being in their shoes, who feel the pressure.

Danny O'Rourke did as he said he would do—he reared back and fired a high hard one that came bearing in on Munchk's head. Nowadays such pitches are referred to as *a little chin music* or *a purpose pitch*. Such pitches are designed to make a confident batter uncomfortable at the plate, to give them second thoughts about striding into a pitch; but because Danny, who as a rule had good control, made his intentions known well ahead of time and to the whole neighborhood, Munchk was not impressed. If Danny had kept his mouth shut, thus keeping the element of surprise on his side, Munchk might have become wary and altered her batting stance.

Most batters, when having their head thrown at, will either dive out of the way, hit the deck, or some tangled combination of each. Not Munchk. With her back foot having remained firmly planted in the gully, she uncocked her bat and simply leaned backward, her neck slightly receded. While in this position of subtle retreat, she watched a pitch that was far too close for comfort travel right underneath her chin. Despite all the disapproving jeers from the crowd, she didn't look to the umpire or opposing coach with the idea of having Danny reprimanded for his blatant tactics, nor did she glare back at Danny less show any signs of that she was intimidated. Instead, she rather coolly reassumed her batting stance as the ump called "Ball one." Again, Danny reared back; this time, he fired a hard one right down the middle of the plate. Munchk looked the ball all the way into the catcher's mitt. The umpire raised up and with emphasis called, "Stee-rike one!" I peered in at Munchk, praying, wanting desperately to know for sure whether or not the moment was too big for her, the lights too bright. I got my answer. The mouth that creased into a self-satisfied smirk told me all that I needed to know. Munchk had Fat Danny O'Rourke sized up—she had him well timed.

Danny reared back and fired his third pitch. Just like his second effort, it was a hard one right down Broadway. Munchk had no intention of watching it go by; there was no need to look over another strike or to see what else Danny may have in his bag of tricks. Besides, with two outs and no one on base, there was really no point in trying to work the count and running the risk of getting behind. Munchk pulled down her hands and whipped the bat through the strike zone, making ringing contact. What a beautiful noise! There's something about the crack of the bat that has kept folks coming back to the grand old game for over 100 years and counting. However, it wasn't but a second after hearing the beautiful noise that I yanked my hands free from Karen Crawford's warm grip and placed them in an area where I would least want to experience blunt force. Call it a kneejerk reaction, but I felt poor Danny O'Rourke's pain—me and all the other male members of the crowd. Munchk's line drive hit Danny square in the nuts, and so hard that the ball caromed all the way back to Shorty Scroggins, the catcher. The littlest Cub went streaking down to first base, having made it well ahead of the Shorty's throw.

I couldn't begin to count the instances while falling asleep, waking, or driving to and from work, I was jarred by the crack of Munchk's bat, only to cringe half-expecting a white, round missile to find its way to my nuts. It mattered not that it wasn't me or any of the other male members of the crowd that was left vulnerable after delivering a pitch; Munchk made an impression on all of us on opening day of 1978, and especially poor Danny O'Rourke.

"How 'bout the way that poor chubby bastard went down on opening day," recalled Uncle Nunzio at our grandfather's surprise sixtieth birthday party. "He was no match for our Lizzy, that's for damn sure."

"Ain't that the truth," followed Uncle Al. "Our Lizzy's one in a million, she is. She really showed that chubby little bastard who's boss."

"Yeah, well, ya can't say the little bastard didn't have it coming to him," Aunt Dot chimed in. "Especially after throwing at our Lizzy's head the way he did. Imagine such a sonofabitch as that … whatshisname…?"

"Danny O'Rourke," I said. "But you have to give him credit for remaining in the game. I don't know many who would've had the guts to take the mound after getting hit like that. I know *I* would've asked out of the game."

"What choice did he have?" Karen reasoned. "After boasting that he would throw at Lizzy's head, then strike her out on the next three pitches, he had to save face by toughing it out."

"Karen's right," Ricky added. "It's a dog-eat-dog world, and if you're gonna go around beating your chest, you better be able to back it up with more than just hot air."

"Yeah, but I bet he wished he hadn't tried hangin' around," said Uncle Nunzio. "Our Lizzy drove the poor bastard crazy on the bases. She was like 'The Scooter' himself, Phil Rizzuto. How 'bout it, Al?"

"Yep," Uncle Al readily agreed, "for anybody who knows baseball, Lizzy sure woulda reminded them of the ol' Scooter running them bases."

"You're too young, Frank," said Uncle Nunzio. "You never gotta chance to see Rizzuto play. What a shame that them bums the Phillies don't have a savvy base runner like The Scooter. Just imagine how much better off they'd be?"

As I had learned repeatedly throughout the years, it wouldn't have mattered if we were discussing baseball, Watergate, or the virtues of dandelion greens, Uncle Nunzio somehow managed to ram the Yankees up my ass. And on that note, there's only one thing to say: Fuck Phil Rizzuto!

Uncle Nunzio and Uncle Al were right about one thing; Munchk indeed was a terror on the bases. She began dancing off first base as confident as she was in gravity that second base was hers to be had. Ruthless competitor that Munchk was, she took full advantage of poor Danny O'Rourke's wobbly state, brought about by the mincing of his testicles. Munchk went dashing off on the next pitch, diving in headfirst and well ahead of Shorty Scroggins' throw. She arose from the cloud of dust created by her headfirst slide, looking like an inspired warrior, the full front of her uniform covered with infield dirt. Vigorously, she banged the dirt from her uniform. Once Danny O'Rourke went into his stretch, she began to dance off second base with the same confidence and menace as she had while leading off first. Danny tried to look Munchk back to the base, but it was clear he was at her mercy; all he could do at that point was grimace in pain and "tough it out" as Karen, months later, would remark. Munchk vigorously clapped her hands, then with equal force and menace brought them down on her narrow thighs—she displayed the sort of competitive drive one does who can't have the game come their way fast enough. I couldn't tell whether her rapidly repeated hand-knocking and thigh-slapping was meant to encourage the batter or torture poor Danny. She took off for third base. Again, she went diving in headfirst—again creating a cloud of dust from which she would successfully arise. She had the base so well stolen Shorty Scroggins didn't bother making a throw. At that point, poor Danny was so flustered, beet-red, and rattled he fired the next pitch into the dirt, three feet short of home plate. The ball skipped off Shorty's mitt; he should have tried to block it instead of trying to catch it on a hop. The result? The ball went bounding far enough toward the visitor's dugout that it allowed Munchk to come streaking home with the go-ahead run—a run that would eventually prove to be the game-winner.

The bottom of the seventh inning stayed to the script, or as the script should have played out after Munchk had so brilliantly seized the moment. Long, lean Bobby Jones mowed them down one, two, three, with two strikeouts and a weak ground ball that was tapped right back to Bobby Jones himself. Though, I must admit, I wasn't exactly hanging on every pitch. I lapsed into a sort of reverie, having allowed myself to bask in the success of my youngest sibling's debut as a ballplayer. Munchk left her mark on opening day of 1978, and in a huge way.

My great-aunts and great-uncles, along with my grandparents and the rest of the Corelli clan, went wandering off after briefly congratulating Munchk on the success of the team and her personal performance. They would leave her behind, not wanting to dare step into a spotlight meant only for the littlest Cub, and plenty of adulation was coming her way. It was a while that she remained surrounded by her delighted Cub teammates, busily and graciously accepting their praise. Coach McConnell also had plenty to say, in particular, about Munchk's command on the base paths. "That's how you play the game," he bellowed to the team in their postgame huddle, "with no fear!"

Aside from receiving well-deserved praise from her teammates, and afterward by her sixth-grade peers, Munchk had another motive for wanting to remain behind at the ball fields and not catch up to her departing family; she had a vested interested in the next game, which, incidentally, would involve the Pirates and *their* token female.

If truth be told, Munchk couldn't wait to witness the wilting of Gabby Kearns, should Gabby have the opportunity, or misfortune, to stand in the on-deck circle. Munchk would wear a celebratory smirk when witnessing Gabby's trepidation upon approaching the plate, never mind the panic that would register on her face should a ball get hit in her direction should she be called upon to man a position. It could surely be said of Munchk: she was a girl who knew a thing or two about reprisal but she wasn't necessarily vindictive; although, should Gabby Kearns fall flat on her face in her baseball debut, I hardly think Munchk would be disappointed, especially with Gabby's flop coming on the heels of her own glowing success. *Those perky twelve-year-old titties didn't do you any good today.*

Baseball is serious business, and only those who take it seriously belong on the diamond. That would just about size up Munchk's thoughts on Gabby Kearns, tits, and baseball. But Munchk hardly disliked Gabby; and I would even go so far to say that, in a way, she admired her. And there was plenty to admire; Gabby was smart as she was pretty, but Munchk didn't take kindly to Gabby becoming a pseudo pioneer for feminist causes by way of the grand old game. If Gabby had chosen another platform, Munchk might have been right there at her elbow leading the charge. But baseball to her was sacred and not to be fooled with—not for the sake of women or any other group or sector.

As for yours truly, my little league interest began and ended with the littlest Cub—the magnificent number one. If not for Munchk, I doubt very much that I would have gone anywhere near the ball fields today; there would have been no point in putting myself through the agony of listening to the guest speakers and all their tedium. Like most fifteen-year-olds without a dog in the show, I would have stuck my head out of the window just in time to see the string band pass and called it a day. Like the rest of the Corelli clan that left Munchk to her reverent teammates and peers, I, along with Karen in hand, walked away, leaving behind the smell of freshly cut grass, burning charcoal, and tapped kegs of beer, which, as we observed, were emptying much too quickly. Ricky and Sherry had the same idea and were trailing not too far behind. The four of us were heading for home. Since last flooding the basement, Dad, although he couldn't bring himself to part with the furniture, transformed the area into a recreation room so that we could entertain friends and was guilted into adding a television.

Speaking of Dad, when our quiet, peace-seeking quartet arrived, he was still buzzing over the game. I never saw him so animated; not even over a leaky faucet had I seen him this aroused. And he kept bellowing the same unimaginative superlatives: "Great!" and "Unbelievable!" headed the shortlist. You would think that on behalf of his daughter he could have come up with an apt plumbing analogy. Poor Danny O'Rourke darn near lost his pipe before ever having had the chance to use it for anything other than taking a leak, and the best that Dad could manage was *great* and *unbelievable.* Mom finally managed to settle him down, but by then, we were already settled into the basement and had shut the door. I stretched out onto the sofa, and a long, weary sigh came seeping out. It was hardly the kind of sigh that anyone would mistake to mean *mission accomplished* or *job well done*; instead, it had the resonance of exhaustion. What's more, the season had just begun! For yours truly, though, the season began way back in early December, just as the temperatures were turning frigid. As I lie there staring up at the ceiling, Christmas seemed an eternity ago, just another event that occurred in the last calendar year. While others had gone to their closets and attics to dig out their *'tis the season* adornments to enliven their homes, I was the in driveway firing a hardball through the icy air. No one needed to warn Frank Corelli about Jack Frost and where he might nip. Admittedly, I was burned out. I could have gone the remainder of the summer without hearing about baseball or watching a game—little *or* major league. And if someone had buried my mitt in the backyard and not given me a clue where to dig, or threw it into the neighbor's yard so that Tank could chew it to pieces and piss on it, that would have been ay okay by me.

Before Karen took a seat beside me, I caught her examining the wooden legs of the sofa. It was a cheap, skirtless sofa, the kind that had exposed legs. Dad had picked it up, along with the matching love seat, at a yard sale and transported both pieces home by way of Uncle Al's pickup truck. "They're still in good condition, and I got 'em for a song," he boasted to Mom, who wasn't too thrilled with what was essentially trash-picked furniture but at a yard sale cost. Karen wasn't so interested in the sofa's legs as much as she was the visible watermarks that were the remnants of last year's flood. I told her that the sofa was old and that the wood finish must have worn away. So what if the finish was worn away evenly on all eight legs of both pieces? It's *possible.* And how should I know why the watermarks on the legs were at the precise level as the watermark on the one wall that Dad had yet to panel? What do I look like, a flood insurance inspector? Besides, doesn't everybody have a father who occasionally floods the basement?

Before Karen could delve into a subject which I was in no mood to discuss, I pulled her closer. I wanted the delight of her soft, warm, sun-kissed skin, while at the same time savoring the scent of her lovely hair, which had become even more perfumed from all the hours spent in the sun. Lying indolently beside all this loveliness, it was difficult to fathom that—through the shortened days of the bleak December, the snow-laden January, a brighter but more frigid February, and the swirling winds of early March—I had allowed a frozen hardball to explode into my frozen mitt and to sting my poor frozen hand. With more than a little help from my exceedingly determined kid sister, together we turned baseball practice into baseball boot camp for the ages. I once told my son and his droopy-eyed friends—when one wintery afternoon they were all together and cozily piled in my family room and playing video games—that on three separate occasions I shoveled a hundred feet of driveway for the sake of grooming my kid sister into a ballplayer. They all looked at me with the same doubt and skepticism with which I must have looked at Uncle Al and Uncle Nunzio when they boasted of singlehandedly ridding all of Twenty-sixth Street of the blizzard of '44 with mere coal shovels. Maybe those two old coots were telling the truth after all.

I tried to wall off all thoughts of what I knew a hardball to feel like when zipped through icy air, any thoughts at all involving extreme measures to achieve goals, in favor of surrendering to loveliness and comfort. Then something came over me—something quite unexpected—and it left me with the inconceivable notion that Karen Crawford was not so lovely as I knew for certain she was just a moment ago. Sherry had been particularly frisky since our arrival; perhaps she had too much sun, and the effect now had her blanketing Ricky; their love noises were hovering about unpleasantly and causing the room to seem terribly crowded. The notion of joining them and ratcheting up the unabashed noise, with the proximity being what it was, I likened to an all-inclusive hillbilly roll in the hay if not an act of incest, and neither the former or latter left me feeling particularly amorous. I closed my eyes and willed my being, however unsuccessful, to grow numb while wondering whether I should take Karen by the hand and make a swift exit. But then it occurred to me, Ricky might feel the same way—that the basketball court was where we excelled as brothers, not romancing girlfriends a few short feet apart from one another. I suggested that we make use of the deck of cards resting atop the television; and when he was permitted enough air, Ricky readily agreed. I had the impression that had I suggested baking brownies while listening to the Bee Gees, he would have agreed.

I proposed Pinochle. I knew full well that Pinochle would get voted down, but I wanted Karen to think that I knew a complicated adult card game. Thank goodness no one called my bluff. We ended up playing five-hundred rummy. The girls kept meticulous score. Ricky and I could not have cared less about the lousy hands that we were dealt or which place we were in at any juncture during the game. Moreover, when as a foursome, Ricky and I passed on idiotic attempts to elevate our respective statuses by bludgeoning one another's ego the way young men often do when exposed to the company of females. We were beyond such bush-league junior varsity bullshit. I suppose we have Munchk to thank for that; with all the years of having to watch one another's back over a prankster of a sister, in no way were we rivals. And speaking of the devil—as I was looking over a hand of cards that had no relation to one another, other than they were in my hand—I heard a pair of cleats scraping the cement of the front steps. In a matter of seconds, Munchk had pranced her way through the house—I could hear the high-spiritedness in her pounding steps. She flung open the basement door. My repose was over.

Like a whirling dervish, Munchk came rumbling down the basement stairs wanting to know had I seen her "Game saving catch!" and how "Fat Danny O'Rourke flopped like a limp turd!" I informed her that I had witnessed both events—I didn't bother confessing that my visual of the former came by way of Ricky's thorough description—but that we could discuss her success, in detail if needed, later on when the time was right. I told her this while escorting her back to the stairs, which I hoped she would readily climb. I also spoke to her like an elder would a child thoughtlessly encroaching on adult time, and went about it a touch too superciliously. In retrospect, it was a mistake. Who am I kidding? I knew right away it was a mistake! Nevertheless, it was fascinating how readily after months acting as comrades in arms—with balls, mitts, bats, and snow shovels as tools and an unshakable desire to succeed as our directive—we reverted back to our old roles of irresistible antagonist and arrogant prick, with yours truly assuming the role of the latter.

"Later shmater," said Munchk. "There's nothing more important than talking baseball and no better time than the present." Sinuously she slipped under my arm, then proceeded to drag me back to the card table. I didn't *recall* asking how Gabby Kearns fared in her one and only plate appearance, but I received an earful. The poor female Pirate was called out on strikes after never removing the bat from her shoulder. In the batter's box, she became the proverbial deer in headlights.

"That isn't news," I said with a note of exasperation. "We both knew that it would happen." I followed by assuming a demeanor of disinterest for Gabby Kearns and all things baseball, hoping Munchk would take the hint, which would lead to a departure devoid of any drama or defiance. But, as was often the case, my youngest sibling was persistent, and her persistence led to my frustration, and my frustration led to her becoming agitated. Finally, I slammed my dismal hand of cards on the table and went lunging after Munchk. I picked her up and began to carry her off. I made it to as far as the steps, when she hollered out, "Don't waste your time on him, Karen; his prick is too puny! I'll betcha you didn't know he has to masturbate with his pinky finger!"

Upon hearing such defamation of my manhood, I figured to hell with it. Instead of lugging her up the stairs, I carried her across the room, flipped open the lid of the washing machine, and stuffed her feet first inside the drum. Then I turned to the others and signaled that it was time to go.

"Goddamn you, Frank!" Munchk hollered, struggling to get her knees above the lip of the machine. "Get me out of this thing, you lousy fucker!"

"Have a nice night, Munchk," I pleasantly called back while waving to her.

"You know, Frank," Munchk began to retort, but not until her face formed the infamous and always dreaded scrotum look, "you're more brainless that a fart and uglier than the streaks in your own underwear!"

Although false, I secretly applauded Munchk's denigration of what I believed was a worthy penis, figuring it just might rouse Karen's curiosity enough to want to investigate the validity of such a claim. After all, seeing is believing. And had Munchk stopped there—at my penis—who knows how the evening might have progressed and what secrets might have gotten unlocked. But she did not stop *there*, and the result was a predictable one; Karen's face creased up into what was clearly a wince of disgust. Having your personal hygiene called into question, regardless of how false, was one matter. Having it called into question with your girl standing right beside you was another matter altogether. Occasionally forgetting to brush one's teeth before beddy-bye, or to wash one's hands after taking a leak (keeping in mind that men are occasionally known to whiz outdoors) might be considered a mild offense, but hardly an egregious breach of hygienic protocol worthy of causing unredeemable shame. But streaks in the underwear? That, my friends, could be a deal breaker! Once again, Munchk landed a well-placed dagger.

****

The summer passed swiftly as summers will often do. Swiftness aside, the summer of 1978 didn't come and go without its share of moments. I was never the sort to kiss and tell, but sometime during the summer swelter, after the sun went down on the soft grass beyond the outfield fences, and with the strains of Gerry Rafferty's *Baker Street* heard from a distant radio, Karen Crawford came to learn that there was nothing puny about ol' Frank Corelli. Still, I was no less a novice. Karen, too. A clumsy, scared experiment urged on by summer heat, she and I became. Maybe it was July, it could've been August; we lost our dungarees down to our sweaty skin and together embodied the throb of young love searching for

215

an identity, enshrouding itself in its own desperate impulses. Overwrought by the tenderness of our age, we went feeling our way through the long night—a cultural sojourn that spanned the end of the Vietnam War and the dawn of Ronald Reagan. Love, rock and roll, summertime, and the seventies. No four things ever went together so well, and were alive within their collective thickness.

It was sometime in early summer when Coach McConnell acquired the necessary wisdom it took for him to realize right field was no place for someone with the agility of a mongoose. Munchk's new home was where it should have been all along: shortstop, the position she was born to play. He also, in his infinite wisdom, decided it would be most advantageous for the batter that made the most contact, and was by far the speediest runner, to bat leadoff. Munchk in a position to quarterback the infield, and in the slot in the order that awarded her the most plate appearances, instantly made the Cubs a formidable opponent. But something else was happening, something beyond the fundamentals of the game. Having one of only two females in the league, and her success elevating the team to unexpected heights, the Cubs became the talk of the neighborhood, the one true phenomenon of the summer of '78. Here and there, murmurings of "The Cubs are playing tonight" could be heard throughout a given day. Munchk and the Cubs sure drew the crowds. Hell, had it occurred to them, they might have gotten away with charging admission. As for yours truly? My baseball burnout ended when I saw Munchk, from her new position of shortstop, quarterback the infield. "Watch for the bunt" and "Guard the line, he's a pull hitter" were among the many instructions she routinely relayed to her teammates. She was constantly communicating with the second baseman to see who would cover the base should someone attempt a steal. There seemed no end to her baseball acumen; and *my*, how she ran the bases! She also mastered the art of the drag bunt, and at times would fake the bunt and swing away. She drove opposing coaches and pitchers crazy!

Lost, however, in all the Munchkamania, was the fact that Ricky had had himself a fine freshman season. Between hits and walks, he averaged getting on base twice per game. Hell, he even taught himself to become a switch hitter, albeit it was a weapon he held in reserve until the season finale, and he played second at least as superbly as Munchk played short. That Ricky would sooner than later wear a varsity uniform was never a question. To his credit, though, he didn't begrudge any of the adulation that was being heaped upon his sister. Like everyone else, he got swept up in Munchk's success.

Perhaps the *most* notable happening of what was shaping up to be an eventful summer belonged to Uncle Al. His pickup truck, unfortunately or thankfully, depending upon who you asked, bit the proverbial dust.

"It's like saying goodbye to a long and trusted friend and knowin' you're never gonna see 'em again," Uncle Al moaned.

I thought that my great-uncle's sentiments over a hideous contraption that years ago should have seen the confines of a junkyard was a bit histrionic. But then I got to thinking; the relationship between Uncle Al and his truck, if indeed the term *relationship* was suitable, began with Dwight D. Eisenhower and ended with Jimmy Carter. That's a span of six presidents! Never mind that one president was assassinated, another didn't seek reelection, another resigned, and one served only two years; that ding-blasted machine saw pompadours, hula-hoops, pet rocks, and the invasion of disco! Hell, it damn near outlasted the Cold War! By today's standards, Uncle Al and his truck had far outdistanced the average marriage in years, and, in many cases, affection. When putting it in those terms, I suppose it isn't all that unreasonable for a man to feel a fondness for a vehicle, no matter its looks.

Uncle Al, moments after the tow truck began driving off with his former vehicle tightly secured, went running wildly down the street, his arms flailing about as he yelled, "Wait! Wait!" At first, neighbors thought Uncle Al wanted a last look and feel, and to further express undying gratitude to a vehicle that served him so long and well (God forbid a sentiment should go unspoken), or that his delaying of a long-overdue junkyard extradition was so that Aunt Prostitute could once again experience the spring in the passenger seat poking up her ass. But none of the above happened to be the case. Instead, Uncle Al's desperate arm-flailing, hand-waving sprint was to rescue the beanbag ashtray that had been sitting on the dashboard for the past twenty-four years. From *On the Waterfront* to *The Deer Hunter*, and from the Judy Garland to the Barbara Streisand remakes of *A Star is Born*, it sat there collecting ashes and butts. Who is anyone to question or quantify sentimentality?

The following day, Uncle Al went and broke the bank. Afterward, he and Aunt Prostitute came rolling home in a brand-new Oldsmobile Cutlass Supreme, considered by many to be a fine automobile in its day. Of course, Dad gave him a sweetheart of a deal. But the offer had always been on the table; however, Uncle Al was not a man who took kindly to change. In the end, though, the once drunk-rolling, pig-stealing roustabout from Swampoodle, along with his wife, who came dangerously close to going too far to the bad, would finally ride around, if not in style, in reasonable middle-class luxury. Despite a new car in the family, Ricky's fine freshman season, and my sexual awakening, it was Munchk, who already made the summer of '78 memorable, that would provide the grandest thrill.

Our little league seasons were divided into two halves, with the winner of each half playing for the neighborhood championship. If it so happened that the same team won both halves, then the team with the second-best overall record was awarded the opportunity to play for the title. I'm sure Coach McConnell was kicking himself for not batting Munchk leadoff and playing her at shortstop a few games earlier than he had. Had he done so, the Cubs would likely have taken the first half. But he didn't, and now the Cubs found themselves deadlocked with the Hawks, their opponent on the last day of the season. The winner would advance to face the Bears, winners of the first half, in the championship.

Long, lean Bobby Jones was just as sharp as he had been on opening day—perhaps even more so. The game saw tight pitching and plenty of defensive gems from both sides and was tied at two runs apiece heading into the seventh inning, when Coach McConnell's son, Ian, whacked a leadoff triple. Ian came dashing into third base standing, all smiles and was pumping his fist. Victory was within reach and with it a shot at the championship. And if I tell you, you couldn't have knocked the grin off of Coach McConnell's face if you told him that his house was on fire, it was the truth. In fact, I doubt very much that he would have heard you, as no bearer of bad tidings could have possibly overshadowed the pride with which he beamed over his son's timely three-bagger.

All the Cubs needed to do was to get Ian home, and they had all three outs with which to do so, before turning the bottom half of the inning over to long, lean Bobby Jones, who would be poised to nail down the victory. But, as luck would have it, the next batter, Stump O'Leary, was overanxious and, as a result, he went down swinging on three straight pitches. On the way back to the bench, Stump slammed the head of the bat into the dirt. From the stands, I saw Coach McConnell cringe. He managed to grab hold of the next batter, Timmy Travers, before he began to make his way from the on-deck circle to home plate. Coach wanted to make sure that Timmy was settled enough to hit. Despite his nervous eyes finding open space somewhere in-between the hand knocking Ian McConnell and deep breathing pitcher, Timmy assured Coach McConnell that he was ready. However, whatever plan Timmy might have had prior to stepping into the batter's box flew from his head upon taking his stance. He was so far out in front of the first pitch, the bat went flying from his hands, helicoptering its way toward Ian McConnell, who had to hit the deck to avoid getting clobbered. The crowd collectively inhaled, then sighed. Coach McConnell winced in agony. The next pitch Timmy managed to hold onto his bat but was no less out on his front foot. The result was a weak pop-up in the infield. There were two outs, a man on third and the season was hanging in the balance. The stage was set for Munchk.

As cool as a cucumber, Munchk went strolling up to the plate. I was nervously wringing my hands together and squirming about in the stands. As she had all summer long, Karen was right beside me, assuring me that Munchk would succeed, but I could sense she was also growing nervous.

The stands had in them Corellis of every generation. Aside from our family, it seemed half the neighborhood was on hand, along with all the soon-to-be seventh graders, and everyone was on their feet and chanting *Liz-zee, Liz-zee, Liz-zee*. Even Fat Danny O'Rourke and Gabby Kearns were among those wildly chanting. The chanting seemed to surge and swell, its collectiveness becoming greater than the sum of its parts. Those on the field, and those enveloping the field, slipped into an alternative reality, a heightened state producing a rarefied and singular moment owning the capacity to wall off the rest of existence. This is the beauty of sports; it allows us to exist in a bubble, an impenetrable membrane, and embrace those rarefied moments only *it* can provide.

Perhaps a bit anxious, Munchk, who hit more than her share of balls up the middle, got out in front of the first pitch and lined it foul several feet to the left of third base. Everyone in the stands ducked the oncoming missile, including yours truly, the most infamous ducker of them all. There was one among the crowd, though, who did not bother ducking. Not to suggest that his reflexes were not in good standing. They were. But not everyone is the sort who ducks.

At the end of the stands stood a very tall and powerful-looking man—perhaps more powerful than his soon-to-be sixty years would suggest. For sure, this was not the sort of man who makes a habit of ducking. A man who, when not quite an adult, left the bosom of his home for the rat race of a big city, and in doing so unburdened his parents by taking along his two unruly brothers to look after and support, was hardly the type to duck. After the ball sailed over the heads of all those who did duck, this man stuck out a huge powerful hand. A moment later, the crowd winced when hearing a hideous thud, as the projectile smacked against the man's palm, and in his palm, it stuck.

Antonio Corelli hardly had the type of childhood that allowed for games of catch; therefore, he didn't know not to use his palm, especially when catching a hardball. He also was not one to call attention to himself; yet he couldn't resist a satisfied grin over making a catch that took him by surprise. Perhaps his plan was to merely end the flight of the ball by knocking it down and preventing someone not paying attention from getting injured. It would have been just like our grandfather to do such a thing. He took a moment or two to examine the ball, then his hand, which went on stinging for several minutes; then he tossed the ball back into play.

I never did ask our grandfather what ran through his mind in that brief moment in which he examined the ball and his hand, though I wished I had. Years later, when looking back, I have become inclined to believe that, while standing next to our grandmother, surrounded by family, and enveloped by the spirited chants of children as the apple of his eye was standing up at the plate with the season hanging in the balance, what ran through his mind was the day of December 26, 1938, and that if he had any lingering regrets, they were vanquished right there and then at the ballfield. How, during such a moment, could the day after Christmas forty years ago not have crossed our grandfather's mind—a day for which he would spend a lifetime trying to own up to. Surely there were several moments throughout the years that caused him to wonder about the world had he been more pigheaded than Poppa Corelli and entered that coal mine. But this wonderfully tense moment some forty years later at the ball field, if not standing out from all others, must have ranked near the top. I suppose we all did our fair share of wondering what if December 26, 1938 had a different outcome. I know I sure did.

Had there been time before the next pitch held him captive in the present, I'd like to think that our grandfather's mind had drifted back in time to a day spent on the grass of Lemon Hill, with Mama Corelli, his beloved Elizabeth, little Fred, poor old three-legged Max, Uncle Al, Uncle Nunzio, and their soon-to-be wives, Aunt Dot and Aunt Theresa. It would have been just like our grandfather to ponder that it was a long, hard climb to the top of the hill, but that even if the world allowed only a second to sit and gaze out upon its many wonders, it would have been well worth the journey.

My moist and nervous hands ceased from strangling themselves. All my anxious squirming came to an abrupt halt. These maddening exercises were each thwarted by the same occurrence—the crack of a bat—the wonderful crack of a bat. The glorious sound brought Karen and me, along with the multitude, to our feet. I watched the pitcher's neck jerk violently toward center field as the ball went soaring over his head. The shortstop and second baseman also jerked, but the ball's velocity and trajectory turned them into helpless spectators. The centerfielder, who reacted well to the crack of the bat, came dashing in toward the diamond, but the ball found green grass well before if found brown leather. Ian Donnelly came sprinting home with what would prove the winning run. The magnificent number one had come through once again.

Chapter Eight
The Best Laid Plans

Munchk and the Cubs went to the championship and put the exclamation point on what had already been, mostly due to them, an eventful summer. However, no sooner had the worthy champions finished celebrating their title, before we knew it or wanted to know it, a new school year was nearly upon us and with it would mean a swift reorganization of priorities. It was time for Joe Morgan and Bobby Bonds to be tied up and shelved. It was also time for love affairs to suffer rules of engagement in the event we wished for the trifling matter of education to accidentally seep into heads made indolent by summer heat and animal impulses. And if you happened to had been a resident of Philly come Labor Day of 1978, it was once again time to turn whatever attention could be spared to the major league ball club, which for the third consecutive year was poised to make a run for the Pennant. I prayed the third go-around would be the charm. To have a lover and a team playing in the World Series—as a high school junior, you can't get much more on top of the world than that. September also brought about another much-anticipated event, if you were a Corelli. Of course, I would be referring to our grandfather's surprise sixtieth birthday party.

On the morning of the big event, Mom sent me running to the market for ricotta cheese—the very same ricotta cheese that yesterday, Dad forgot to buy on his way home from work.

"Make sure you get the regular and not the low fat," Mom called to me as I was partway out the door. "Uncle Nunzio can tell the difference, you know, and he'll cry about it all the way until Christmas! And Lord knows we wouldn't want that!"

Mom was sure right about that; with his first steamy forkful, Uncle Nunzio would know the difference. If there was one thing we all learned *not* to do, it was screw with Uncle Nunzio's food. If you didn't have all the right ingredients and decided, as a culinary artist might, to adlib, he knew it right away—there was no tricking him. If you tried to trick him, he would appear utterly forsaken, like a child whose birthday came and went without so much as a card or mention, and then afterward was found wandering in the woods, a pitiable soul all alone and unloved. I suppose if I grew up eating weeds, as he had, the right ingredients of a well-anticipated lasagna would be a big deal, and perhaps enough to ruin my day.

Knowing it would be hours yet before Mom's gravy was ready to layer into and pour over however many trays of lasagna she planned to prepare, I decided to take my sweet old time, stopping first for Karen. We strolled the neighborhood, with yours truly wondering what the new school year would bring and Karen obsessing over re-matching Sherry Mills, as her and Ricky's romance did not survive the summer. She ran by me a list of those she believed were worthy candidates for poor, unloved Sherry, beginning with: "What do you think of Conner Livingston?" and ending with, "Well, then, what do think of Danny McGinley?" Everyone on her list received the same indecisive shrug. Not only could I not cite a single asset any of them possessed, I really wasn't listening, for the simple reason that I didn't give a rat's ass. We were already two-hundred years beyond *The Enlightenment* and even longer beyond Queen Katherine of Aragon pawned for the sake of an advantageous alliance. Matchmaking on such an insignificant level as high school romance seemed to me a trivial affair unbecoming to masculinity, though I wisely kept this thought to myself.

Upon returning to the house, we discovered that Uncle Al and Uncle Nunzio had already arrived. No matter the affair, they were always the early birds, afraid that they might miss out on something. If they didn't live in another neighborhood, I would swear the exhaust fan above our stove could somehow channel the aroma of food to their respective front doors. Whenever a meal was on the line, Johnny-on-the-spot, whoever he was, had nothing on my great-uncles.

"Mary-nooch, do me a favor and promise your Uncle Nunzio that when he kicks the bucket, you'll fill his casket with gravy! Gallons and gallons of gravy! And throw in some meatballs and garlic bread!" Uncle Nunzio cried out his plea while peering over Mom's shoulder and down into her four-gallon pot. "When it's time for me to go," he added, "I want a real dego send-off. No foolin' around." Uncle Nunzio punctuated his demand by planting a playful kiss on Mom's cheek, but Mom never for a second took her eyes away from the stove. Afterward, he hollered, "Hey Freddy, better check the plumbing. You'll wanna make sure everything's in working order. Don't worry, Al and me will keep yer beautiful bride company."

"And remember," Uncle Al warned, "there'll be a good sixty people crammed in here today, so you better make sure the toilet's flushing!"

"For Chrissake, not the toilet!" Mom hollered. "Anything but the damn toilet! Don't even mention the word! Now both of you, out of the kitchen!"

It mattered not how many times Mom lambasted Uncle Al and Uncle Nunzio, or whether it was even deserved, they adored her. Where they were concerned, Mary Corelli could do no wrong.

Family and friends were beginning to arrive. Soon our home became livelier and more animated than I could ever remember; and in the past, we surely had our share of lively gatherings. There were times when Uncle Nunzio all by himself could qualify as a gathering. One by one by two by four, whether from all around town or upstate, folks came piling into our modest-sized dwelling. To all those making the trip, Antonio Corelli was a vital person. Aside from all he did to care for his family and friends, once a year he made a trip to Scranton to check on the few relatives who chose to remain in the old coal mining town. And he wouldn't think of making the trek without first gathering as many provisions from the Italian marketplace as could be loaded into his car.

Today was a thrilling day for me. It was the day that I would finally get to meet the colorful, sometimes infamous, and often talked about gang from Swampoodle. Uncle Al and Uncle Nunzio did the honors. They led me around the room, and I shook hands with Meat, Crazy legs (who wore a corrective shoe that evened out his legs), Moose, Skullhead, Stranger, Vincent Bronini (Jimbroni), Turd (who, unfortunately, didn't act like shit but bore a resemblance), and Sixty-four (who by then was married thirty-seven years and had long since stopped counting). Heck, I even shook hands with Nails, and despite all the stories I was told, and whether or not they were an exaggeration, I wasn't the slightest bit intimidated. In truth, Nails never amounted to anything more than a small-time racketeer with whom our grandfather, following the Cadillac incident, reached a level of cordiality. Lastly, I was introduced to a man named Pasquale Benvenuto.

"Back in the good old days, we called him 'Patty One Eye,'" said Uncle Nunzio. Jovial laughter followed. "But now that we're all grown up and reasonably civilized, it's just plain old 'Pat.'" I could tell from Uncle Nunzio's laughter and by the manner which he put his arm around Pasquale Benvenuto, this was a man for whom he had a great deal of affection. But honestly, Patty One Eye? I grew up hearing about the poor neighborhood kid who had only the use of one eye, but I never imagined that one day I would be shaking his hand.

Perhaps my generation—partly because of social evolution and the indoctrination of postmodernism and political correctness—developed an acute case of oversensitivity; therefore, I found it appalling for someone to be dubbed for a body part that went missing, didn't function properly, or, in the case of Pasquale Benvenuto, no longer worked. Though I suppose poor Pasquale Benvenuto should be grateful that he didn't have a missing limb, or worse, was discovered to have been impotent. A missing limb might have left a kid in the 1930s friendless. And God knows the torture an impotent young man would've had to endure not just in the '30s but in any era. I didn't bother to ask Pasquale Benvenuto how he lost the use of his eye, nor did he seem too keen to offer. I was interested, but not enough to burden him with a question that must have been asked more times than he cared to remember. What's more, I was under the impression that Pasquale Benvenuto was not the sort of man who deemed it fitting to discuss the origins of a handicap at what was supposed to be a happy occasion. Why let such a trifling matter as blindness spoil a party? Anyway, for the remainder of the day, I addressed a man once dubbed "Patty One Eye" only as "Mr. Benvenuto." In my fifteen-year-old mind, I had enough conceit to believe I could single-handedly wash away nearly sixty years of insensitivity—if indeed Pasquale Benvenuto was that long with only the use of one eye. Indeed, yours truly was patting himself on the back, thinking he was showing those with less understanding a thing or two about decorum. Yessiree, my generation may have passed sensitivity training, largely because it learned to blow heaps of euphemistic language up its ass; such as substituting *handicapped* with *challenged*—nowadays no one is actually *blind* or *deaf*, heaven forbid, they're *impaired*—and along the path to enlightenment, we also managed to learn a thing or two about manipulation and passive-aggressive bullshit. What better way to drown insensitivity? How clever. But maybe it wasn't as complicated as all that. Quite possibly *"Mr. Benvenuto"* was nothing more than yours truly sticking it to Uncle Nunzio for all the years that he rammed the Yankees and all their folklore up my ass. Patty One Eye? I think not, you simpleminded Yankee-loving prick. Learn some etiquette. It's *Mister* Benvenuto!

Regardless of my motives—and because Meat was still Meat, Moose was still Moose, Skullhead was still Skullhead, Turd was still Turd, and Sixty-four (despite his wife of thirty-seven years never learning the real reason for the numeral nickname) was still Sixty-four—a young man once called "Patty One Eye" seemed appreciative of "Mr. Benvenuto."

Colorful nicknames enduring half a century notwithstanding, it was fascinating to observe all these old friends from another time and place, and of another generation, come together and interact. They seemed so thrilled that they were all still around and knew one another—it was pure poetry coming to life and unfolding right before my eyes. They were boisterous and jovial for sure and, *oh*, the stories they told! My life and times, by comparison, seemed deadly dull. It led me to wonder, forty plus years from now, would I have the same friends? Would I even care to have the same friends? And when and if we were to reunite, would we laugh and hug and tell colorful stories? In a way, it saddened me that I didn't have the opportunity to grow up in a harsh and gritty inner-city neighborhood in depression-laden America; that only through such circumstances could such long-lasting and endearing ties be formed. I didn't know it at the time, but I was observing, albeit a small sample size, of what years later Tom Brokaw would dub, despite their social insensitivities, "The Greatest Generation."

Depression and war: The U.S. signed the Paris Peace Accord and withdrew its last troops from Vietnam on March 29, 1973, the year I turned eleven, so I couldn't even pretend to have brushed up against what many of the guests in my home had come to know—what for years had been their daily reality, their routine. The best that I could do was learn of such matters as economic calamity and world war from the other end of wide and safe gaps known as decades. Sure, my generation would come to know of war and would even learn of its ramifications; but, in the last decade of the twentieth century and thus far a decade-plus into the twenty-first, divisiveness stimulated by 24/7 cable news cycles, the internet, and social media, would pit Americans at one another's throats over provocation versus justification. Death by politics. The days of unifying and sacrificing for a cause are over; an unfortunate byproduct of too much enlightenment and information doled out by too many sources. Our lives would carry on through Desert Storm, the hotbed that became Afghanistan, Operation Iraqi Freedom, and the decade-plus residuals that would follow two of these three efforts, without a single interruption, as *We The Privileged* continued piling into stadiums, theaters, and malls while wielding smartphones and agonizing over upgrades whenever we weren't too busy screaming at one another over the issues of gender and race. Despite the admiration I have for our grandfather and the life he has led, *his* life, if given the opportunity and regardless how I've romanticized it, would be something from which I would run. The good old days took stamina, too much stamina. Technology has engulfed everyone born after World War II and condensed them into one massive generation. Let's dub it, "Generation Self-absorbed."

None of this applied to most of the guests mingling in my home. Above all the din that was frothing in every room, I could hear admirers of our grandfather saying Antonio *this* and Antonio *that*. Every time our grandfather's name was mentioned, it was with reverence and affection. It made me very proud that such a man was our grandfather. I permitted myself to mingle through the crowd, hoping to not only *hear* but to *involve* myself with all the colorful anecdotes which were being retold with such sparkling vigor. I wanted to be washed over with the memories of *The Greatest Generation* and come out at the end of the day with a sense that their memories were also my own. It was when Turd and Sixty-Four decided to remind Vincent Bronini of the time that he stole his father's car and promptly drove it through the front window of Fumo's pool hall, that there came a knock at the door. Everyone fell silent, thinking that it might be our grandfather. After Vito, the cheese vendor, who Uncle Nunzio announced as "Antonio's cousin from Toscana" came waltzing through the door, Vincent Bronini reached for the same ear with which Mr. Fumo used to drag him home.

"Old man Fumo really did a number on me that day," he recalled. "After all these years, I still can't sleep on my left side. But there's not a thing wrong with my nose; I know good cheese when I smell it!"

Within seconds, beginning with Vincent Bronini, Vito and his impressive tray were surrounded. Cheese is a magnet for Degos. It remained to be seen how much of it reached its destination, the dining room table. Maybe one day I'll come to understand cheese. My only contact with the variety of foul-smelling, hardened chunks of dairy was to gingerly place a few slices on a small plate and deliver them to our grandmother, who was far too reserved to join the rapacious vultures that were clustered in the dining room.

Soon after the cheese tray was picked over, there came another knock at the door. I was told that a few of the Swampoodle little leaguers would be sharing this special day—that they were thrilled to have been invited and wouldn't dare miss it. When I first learned the news, I had a vision of young boys in grass and dirt-stained uniforms and smudged faces excitedly calling out "Uncle Tony" as they ran to surround our grandfather and together went strutting through the neighborhood. Imagine my surprise, when men a half-generation older than my father came through the door. Our grandmother was especially delighted, after so many years and with fondness, that these men each remembered poor old three-legged Max. But these Depression/World War II little leaguers were not only anxious to reunite with their Uncle Tony, but also to meet his famous granddaughter.

"I heard that she was a real sensation," one remarked.

"And that she runs like Ashburn," another brightly chimed in.

"She's the best darn ballplayer this neighborhood's ever seen," boasted Uncle Nunzio. "Only she runs more like Rizzuto."

"Still with 'The Bombers,' ay Nunz?" His name was Carmine Bocelli, once a helluva shortstop. "And nowadays, aside from Lou Piniella, they don't have a single *paisan*."

I looked at Ricky and shook my head. Not for anything can Uncle Nunzio help himself. Next, I saw Uncle Al glance down at his watch. He sounded unusually anxious when he said, "Antonio should've been here by now." Uncle Nunzio agreed, but then decided it was time to set his chest hair on fire.

"Might as well singe it all, Nunz," said Uncle Al. "It might be years yet before we have any new kids come into the family." Uncle Al was right, our middle generation had bore all the fruit it intended to bear. It wouldn't be until Ricky's daughter, Sara, came into the world, that Uncle Nunzio would again have an opportunity to torch his chest hair, and by then it would all turn white.

"Yeah, why not?" said Uncle Nunzio. "Let's give the kiddies a real show!"

Every Corelli child from Dad on down has had the opportunity to witness the singeing of Uncle Nunzio's chest hair. It's been well document-ed, though, that no child was ever so frightened from the experience as Dad. Most, just as Uncle Al's twin grandsons, Anthony and Michael, were about to do, scurried away and went tumbling into an adjoining room, only to return for a pyrotechnic encore once the initial shock had worn off. But not Dad; he remained scared stiff. He stood with his mouth agape, his eyes bulging, and not only did all the color drain from his face, but for hours was unable to move or speak. Fearing he was about to faint, Mama Corelli alertly scooped little Freddy up and carried him out to the front porch where, for the remainder of the afternoon, he lay in her well-endowed lap clutching her stout housedress. Uncle Nunzio's initial performance would not see an encore. He was also afraid that little Freddy wouldn't snap out of his stupor by the time Elizabeth returned and consequently would receive an earful, although the younger Mrs. Corelli was hardly one for raising her voice.

"You really done it now, Nunz," warned Uncle Al. "And if you think our sister-in-law is gonna be trouble, just wait till she writes Antonio and tells 'im you scared his son into a coma before he ever gotta chance to meet 'im. I sure as hell wouldn't wanna be you!"

"You, sonofabitch," cried Uncle Nunzio, "you're the one who told me to do it! You said it would make 'im laugh!" And that began the long line of Uncle Nunzio's *welcome to the family* initiations. You'd have thought it would have ended at one.

Little Freddy didn't slip into a shock-induced coma as Uncle Al had predicted he might, but he did spike a temperature. He also spent the next several days clinging to Mama Corelli and Elizabeth. However, he must not have had an abundance of confidence in the safety his mother and grandmother tried to provide, because he would go tearing into the next room whenever the bestial Uncle Nunzio made an appearance. During this brief period, whenever little Freddy did try and speak, it was in whispers to poor old three-legged Max.

The house finally settled following Uncle Nunzio's latest welcome to the family initiation, when came another knock at the door. Strange, but I was able to sense reluctance, even reservation, in the knocking. It seemed to me whoever it was at the door did not expect to feel welcomed, that their presence, for reasons I couldn't begin to fathom, would go unappreciated. As my eyes traveled around a room that turned quiet, it was clear that others shared my intuition, and it led to my finding myself enveloped in a cloud of misgiving. It hovered thickly.

It was Dad, this time, who made for the door, having weaved his way through what only moments ago was a jovial scene. Upon opening the door, he glanced back at a room that remained fixed in place and silent, save for a few anxious murmurings. On Dad's face was a mixture of curiosity and foreboding that, in its own way, surpassed the level of reluctance and reservation that I imagined existed in the knocking; only Dad, at that point, saw who was at the door. The ill-at-ease mixture that filled Dad's face set forth a chain reaction of similar looks that carried through the house and made its way to as far back as the kitchen, where Mom, for only the second time in my memory (the umbrella episode being the first) abandoned her gravy; she was ladling it over several pans of lasagna. I didn't actually witness Mom leaving her post, but I could feel the weight of her presence; I knew she was nearby, perhaps as nearby as right beside me, and

I was nowhere near the stove. I had my eyes fixed on Dad, who by then was standing outside. Either Dad didn't wish for whoever it was to step inside, or the unknown party elected not to enter on their own accord. I was unsure which scenario, if either, was the case, and this prompted me to take a step closer to change my vantage point. In doing so, I was able to see past the screen and over Dad's shoulder. My new position also enabled me to make out the figure with which Dad was sharing the front step. Judging from the manner in which Dad's head was moving, it must have been more than one police officer speaking to him, though I was only able to spot one sharply cornered and well-creased hat. For a moment, I felt a sense of relief, having leapt to the conclusion that the officers had come to either arrest Nails on charges of racketeering or to get their palms greased. What else could it be? It seemed perfectly logical that law enforcement, if its goal were to rankle Nails, would wish to do so while he wasn't entrenched within the confines of his home turf.

Despite Dad having his back to everyone, and the storm door, which was partially screened, eclipsing a portion of his form, his posture revealed another reality—that whatever business the officers had for knocking on our door and interrupting our celebration, had nothing to do with Nails and his nefarious business dealings. I looked on as Dad seemed to be shrinking in the presence of the policemen. Then he doubled over in a manner that one would after having the wind knocked from their core. One of the policemen—the one who, from my vantage point, could be seen—placed what appeared a consoling hand on Dad's shoulder. In doing so, he shattered the confidence of all those who, like myself, were in a position to observe. Moments later, the two policemen walked away; I listened as the heels of their shoes echoed on the cement steps. I dreaded their departure—it brought forth the sort of sinking feeling that accompanies impending doom. But they had gone, and all that remained was for Dad to return to his family and friends and to reveal whatever it was he had learned.

The storm door seemed an effort, but Dad managed to fight his way through. Weakened, aged, the color drained from his face the way it had all those years ago when he was a frightened child in the presence of Uncle Nunzio, and also on the day the smartly uniformed but unshaven Antonio Corelli came marching home to Twenty-sixth and Indiana to the bosom of his family, Freddy Corelli was a man struggling with unspeakable thoughts—thoughts that would take years to process never mind reconcile, but nevertheless needed to be uttered in the present. Only he knew the words.

The space around me grew narrow, I felt myself spiraling, but to where I did not know; and what's more, these illusory distortions left me with the sensation that, had Karen not taken firm hold of my arm, I might have drifted right on out of the world. At first, I found Karen's actions wearing; for I would have preferred to drift away and, in doing so, take along with me whatever peace an unforgiving world might endow. How dare Karen prevent this! Despite her grip and my feet planted firmly on the floor, I had a peculiar sense that I was looking downward while hovering just below the ceiling. My only interpretation of Dad's words, which reached my ears in muffled distortions, came by way of observing others in the room; though everyone seemed so distant in my ever-narrowing scope.

From above, my eyes managed to penetrate the long narrow corridor. At the end, I saw Uncle Al. He was collapsed on the living room floor; his slender form, from the position of its hands and knees, was involuntarily shaking in a violent rocking motion. I watched my poor great-uncle's mouth fall agape; he was trying to cry out, to set free immeasurable sorrow and torment, but these crushing feelings would stay stuck in his throat, quelled by the shock and horror of what his nephew revealed. His wife, my dear self-effacing Aunt Theresa, knelt down at his side. She wrapped her slender, coddling arms around his waist and, with a cheek pressed to his back, she was forced to mimic his rocking. Not until that moment had I witnessed a human soul so shattered, so destroyed. Aunt Theresa spoke not a word, but through the warmth of her embrace, she hoped to provide, if possible, a vestige of reassurance that Uncle Al was not all alone and lost in what seemed a treacherous world where no one was safe. It was all she could do.

Space grew narrower, the corridor had lengthened. I was spiraling further away. I struggled but managed to penetrate beyond the shock-ravaged faces in the crowd to where my eyes fell upon Uncle Nunzio. He had fistfuls of his hair, and with those fistfuls, he was violently jerking about his head. His dissonant cries and shrieks were every bit as dreadful as Uncle Al's quelled sorrow and torment. So too were Aunt Dot's.

Not too far from the grief-stricken pair, I watched Vito, the cheese vendor, attempt the sign of the cross on his person. Our cousin from Toscana, who I had met earlier on in my childhood when our grandfather took us for an outing to the Italian Market, was shaking—his hands were trembling terribly. That this dear old friend of our grandfather might have been praying was a crude assumption on my part. Meanwhile, our grandmother rose to her feet and faced the window. At first, I assumed her eyes went searching for the two policemen—who only moments ago had occupied the front step—and, if spotted, she planned to chase them down, for she didn't fully trust Dad's conveyance of what was told him, that possibly he had gotten it wrong. *I* was wrong. She stood and faced the window, as she was unable to breathe for how unbearable the scene had become; it degenerated such that it necessitated her looking away. I wanted to remain fixed on my grandmother, to not look at anyone else. Amid a room that was unraveling, she was the only one who managed a vestige of poise. It was my belief that if I stayed with her—if I managed to somehow keep her in my sights—for whatever it was worth, I might salvage my sanity. Instead, my eyes, compelled by a force unknown, went in search of Mom. No longer could I sense Mom's presence and I found this unsettling. What was stranger yet, I discovered she had returned to the kitchen, where once again she busied herself at the stove. Her face was blank, her actions perfunctory. No one went near her. No one questioned her.

****

It should have been the perfect day. Every last detail was well thought out and accounted for. With every invitation, there came a response, and not a single regret was among them. No one who was deemed worthy of an invitation would consider missing our grandfather's surprise sixtieth birthday party.

Originally, the menu entrée was set to be baked ziti until Uncle Al and Uncle Nunzio clamored for lasagna.

"It's Antonio's favorite," Uncle Al and Uncle Nunzio had both cried.

"No, it's your favorite," said Mom. "But that's okay."

The time, place, number of guests, and full menu were set. The only remaining issue was how to make sure of our grandfather's arrival. To accomplish that, we would need a plausible reason to ensure his appearance, reasonably close to a prescribed time, but without arousing his suspicion. That ruled out him and our grandmother coming for Sunday dinner. A planned Sunday dinner only two days before the day of his actual birth would surely get his wheels turning. I know mine would. That's when the littlest Cub once again stepped up to the plate.

"I'll have Grandpop take me out shopping for new school clothes. Trust me," Munchk told us, "I can milk it for as long as you need me to."

The plan was more than plausible; it was perfect—a true stroke of genius from the littlest Cub. Even had the Pope himself been scheduled to arrive in Philadelphia that day, our grandfather would not have refused

Munchk an accommodation. No doubt, she would drag him from store to store, trying on garment after garment, shoe after shoe, and all the while keeping a close eye on the time. And as was always the case, our grandfather would not begrudge a single second of a day spent with Munchk, including the time spent at the register. Indeed, the plan was both plausible and perfect ... until the drive home.

They almost made it. They came close. It's known that most accidents occur within just blocks of the home, and on that fateful day, a painfully accurate statistic was increased by one. And it wasn't any consolation to learn that the accident was not the fault of our grandfather's—that they hadn't perished by his error. It was Munchk, who, despite being launched through the windshield and only moments before succumbing, possessed the fortitude and presence of mind to inform the policemen of their destination. Our grandfather must have been aware that Munchk was no longer beside him in the car. The driver side door was pushed open, and he was discovered outside the car, having attempted to crawl over to where Munchk lay. He perished not quite having reached her twisted body, and moments before the policemen arrived.

I don't recall the crowd whittling down, or any specific group or person leaving our house that day—not the old Swampoodle crowd, the Depression/World War II little leaguers, the Scrantonians, including eighty-two-year-old Nico Botticelli, who taught a youthful Antonio Corelli to play chess, or Vito, the cheese vendor. It wasn't until the day turned as dusky as the gloom that enshrouded our house, that I looked up and noticed that all that remained was family, minus Dad and our grandmother. It was Dad and our grandmother, I was later told, who assumed the task of identification. Neither Uncle Al, Uncle Nunzio, nor Mom could bear such a task. No one would blame them. And how ironic that the frightened little boy, who once ran and hid from the returning soldier, would one day step forward to make such a dreadful confirmation.

Later that night, Ricky and I collected our basketball and headed for the courts. It seemed a strange reaction given the circumstances, but stunning and instantaneous tragedy compels each of us differently. The lights of the courts were timed to go off by nine o'clock, but we played straight through until midnight and well beyond, and during all those hours we exchanged not a single word. The court was our universe—a silent ninety-four by fifty-foot cosmos, save for the sound of the ball smacking against the blacktopped concrete and echoing throughout the dark, desolate park. How we wished to remain in that cocoon of a universe, that

233

undisturbed ether, until order was restored to a biospheric plane that betrayed us, or order, as we once knew it, had a chance to prevail. We played and played until, despite our emotions, our ravaged bodies were too weary to fight off the sleep that they so desperately needed—merciful sleep that, for a few hours, would smother unbearable sorrow. But that was only one night. Hundreds like it would follow in ponderous unrelenting succession. As was the case next week, next month, and next year, when morning came, we woke to discover that our reality was unaltered, that we merely escaped it by immersing ourselves in merciful slumber.

In our grandfather, the Corelli clan had its very own ocean, an unwavering force upon which it could rely. Within Munchk, emanated the light by which it saw the world. They were the strongest and brightest threads in a tapestry that was our family. With them gone, all that remained was a dull, lifeless cloth with tattered stitches that knew only sorrow and tragedy.

In the ensuing years, I saw a great deal of our grandmother. Mrs. Elizabeth Corelli was never without the poise and elegance we had all come to expect. She was a lady until the very end. In her waning years, she often spoke of the old days and especially of a chance meeting in Russo's variety store, when young Elizabeth and Antonio went reaching for that lone remaining copy of a newspaper. The story was always my favorite; I couldn't hear it enough. There were many stories told of those Depression and World War II days in Swampoodle, and Uncle Al and Uncle Nunzio surely provided their share. Conversely, nothing was ever said about Munchk; her name was never mentioned at what became our subdued holiday dinners. I suppose the sixty years that our grandfather was awarded was much easier to reconcile than Munchk's eleven-plus. When we gathered together, we were all hoping Mom would offer something up—a word, a glance, any sign that would get us going. Everyone had so much they wanted to say on behalf of the littlest Cub and her life and times; but the word, the glance, or the sign we hoped for never came.

****

Wednesday, October 29, 2008: Ricky and I were nearing the end of our mugs of Sam Adams. Ricky prefers the Cherry Wheat. When available, I usually take advantage of the fuller-bodied Oktoberfest. It was the second time in the space of forty-eight hours that we sipped our beers of choice and did so at the same high-top table, in front of the same television, and at the same sports bar. Oddly enough, this was not an act inspired by superstition. What's more, we committed these acts, spanning forty-eight hours, watching *one* ballgame! How was this possible? Well, you know what they say about the weather in Philly?

Ricky made the trip back to town for the World Series. Late Monday afternoon, we headed straightaway for the dinner table. Mom had the expected prepared. Before, during, and after dinner, Dad exalted the heavens on her behalf. It was all very typical. The actors were keeping to the script; the only deviance was Freddy and Mary's remaining children couldn't spare time for dessert. We hated to eat and run, especially with tiramisu chilling in the refrigerator.

Nevertheless, we dropped our forks and made a beeline for Whistlers Inn, a sports bars/restaurant in New Jersey, that from the roadside looks like an old colonial inn. It mattered not that the first pitch of game five would not get thrown until approximately 8:05; if you didn't arrive at the sports bar of your choosing by 6:30, you could forget about such accommodations as a table and chairs, and forget about barstools. This was the World Series! Such an event doesn't occur in Philly but every twenty-five years or so!

I never did care much for game fives; they always made me more nervous than any other game of a seven-gamer. If your team is enjoying a three to one advantage and happens to lose game five, the pressure shifts right back in your lap. No fan whose team once enjoyed a three to one advantage relishes the prospect of a seventh game. Game sevens are a razor's edge between life and death; they don't merely make fans nervous but have been known to instigate trauma such as hyperventilating.

It was a cold, gray October day—as cold and gray a day as I could remember—not at all what anyone would describe as baseball weather. The conditions became even less favorable in the evening. The first six innings of game five were played through a windblown drizzle. With no sign of letup, umpire Tim Tschida decided to suspend the game. Afterward, he said the windy and rainy conditions threatened to make the game "comical." I hadn't missed a World Series game since 1970, the year the Jim Palmer led Baltimore Orioles were victorious over Johnny Bench's Cincinnati Red, and not in all the years could I recall a suspended game. Worse yet, it rained all day Tuesday, so the game wasn't scheduled to resume until Wednesday night. Despite a three to one advantage through four and a half games, I was gloomy as the weather was ominous. I subscribed to the notion that the weather may have set the stage for a reversal of fortune that would rob us of a World Series upon which we had a stranglehold. Should we go on to lose the suspended game five, we could wind up an umpire's bad call or a bad hop away from a game seven and an epic heartbreak, the likes of which only twentieth-century Red Sox fans could appreciate. *Damn* the rain! Mother Nature doesn't care about the Phils! I could hear Munchk: *God-damnit, Frank! If we lose to the Rays, an expansion team, so help me…*

As it turned out, all my worrying was for naught; the Series never went beyond game five. "Never had a doubt," I later proclaimed. Brad Lidge fired one of his signature sliders past the Rays', Eric Hinske. Whistlers Inn, along with hundreds of other sports bars across the Delaware Valley, erupted in jubilation. We were instantaneously enveloped by a crowd of huggers, leapers, criers, shouters, and fist pumpers—all of them were loud, all of them animated, all of them frothing over with joy. Ricky and I shrank from the crowd, having become observers amid a wild celebration. Victory is gratifying. It can also be a bittersweet affair. We were happy, at least as happy as anyone in the place, and judging from the average age of the crowd we had been through more wars. But for us, a World Series victory, despite only moments beyond the heat of battle, was a time for reflection. We didn't intimate our thoughts that night; the noisy crowd would have drowned us out had we tried. Instead, we sipped, observed, and savored.

The next morning on the way to the airport, we opened up. "Hard to believe that thirty years have gone by," was how I began.

"My God, she would be forty-one," was Ricky's disbelieving reply.

The following October we were right back at Whistlers Inn, sipping the same brews. We finally got what we were robbed of back in 1977, the Phils versus the Yankees. It was a bit slow in coming, but the baseball gods finally put things right. Now it was all up to our beloved Phils to do what Ricky, Munchk, and I believed Schmidt, Carlton, and the rest of our heroes were capable of doing had fate awarded them the opportunity thirty-two years ago. I must admit, October of 2009 would have been a whole lot spicier had our old great-uncles still been with us. No doubt the banter and trash-talk would have been epic, particularly with the Phils in the role of defending champions. If only for a short while, the Series might have infused the Corelli clan with life that for years had been missing. But Uncle Al left us in 2004. A year later, Uncle Nunzio followed. It was sad to see one without the other. They may have cherished their wives, but in a way, they, too, were a marriage. Those two old goats surely socked it to us, though, from 1996 to 2000, when the Yankees won the World Series four out of five years. Despite the Yankees suffering nearly a twenty-year hiatus from being crowned champions of baseball, Uncle Al and Uncle Nunzio hadn't lost their touch, having sharpened their teeth and claws to give us a good working over.

I have no facts upon which to support this theory, but I'm guessing King George's madness had plenty to do with him constantly remind-ed of a specific country's victory in a particular war, which future genera-tions of American students would spend studying. To be repeatedly re-minded of an affair that left a bad taste in your mouth would be enough to drive anyone to madness. Yes, madness. And that was my life from 1996 to 2000: madness. And so this is my cue to shout with fury: "Fuck Derek Jeter!"

The years of 1996 to 2000 notwithstanding, I miss my great-uncles. It sure would have been a blast dragging them out to Whistlers Inn, espe-cially for game one of the Series, which saw Cliff Lee dazzle and befuddle the Yankee lineup for all nine innings. As it turned out, unfortunately, game one, particularly from the Philly perspective, would not be indicative of how the Series would unfold. From a high-top table at Whistlers Inn, while sipping our Sam Adams of choice, Ricky and I watched the Phils get taken apart in what would be the sixth and deciding game of the Series. As the innings passed and hope was fading, I had one reoccurring thought: some-where out there, looking down upon us, were a couple of old great-uncles, only they were looking as youthful and fresh-faced as the day they burgled a pig from an Aramingo Avenue slaughterhouse. Oh, I could just see the two of them—Uncle Al with a smirk and Uncle Nunzio, a twinkle. "Don't feel *too* bad, Frank," is what they would tell me, though their tone would hardly be consoling. "After all, you *are* playing the Yankees."

Above the disappointed sighs and reflective murmurings of a de-flated sports bar, I managed to hear my phone ring. At the other end, from the comfort of his pillow, came the voice of my son. He doesn't have quite the emotional investment as Ricky and me; therefore, his call was not to solicit consolation but to provide some for his poor father and uncle.

"It's all right," I told him. "Better to have made it this far and suffer the disappointment than not to have made it at all." The remark wouldn't accurately describe how I was feeling at that precise moment, but it sounded like the right thing to say to a youngster.

My son and I have had many catches on the front lawn. As far as fathers and sons are concerned, I suppose in that respect we're typical. He's not much of a ballplayer, my son, and this he realizes; but our front lawn catches are time together well spent, which each of us in his own way has come to value. Dropped balls and errant throws are seldom if ever mentioned; for most often our catches are an excuse to have a conversation. Some days, it's the other way around. Either way, I'm glad I was blessed with a son instead of the daughter I had so dearly wished for. Instead of delightful conversations, from which I shall humbly and gratefully confess to having had more learning opportunities than teaching, I might have discovered myself trying to will Munchk to somehow manifest through the flesh and blood of that wished-for ponytailed, boney-kneed progeny. In my life and times, if I have learned one thing, there was only one Munchk; no daughter should ever have to suffer such a comparison.

Tomorrow morning, I'll drive Ricky to the airport. Along the way, we'll touch on our beloved Phils and their prospects for the upcoming season, before plunging into the subject of a girl born with two outs and two strikes.

Baseball and life: The first three innings are childhood; the middle three, adulthood; the last three, old age. Whether it's innings, outs, or strikes, the symmetry is remarkable. It is also tragic. Munchk never made it out of the second inning. That a flame could burn so bright only to be randomly snuffed out is a fate I'll never reconcile; I'll wrestle with it to my grave. As for tonight? When I get home, I'll awaken my son just long enough to tell him I'm glad he's my son. As he drifts back to sleep, I'll remind him that his great-grandfather, great-grandmother, and Aunt Lizzy, along with Uncle Al, Uncle Nunzio, Aunt Theresa, Aunt Dot, Mama Corelli, and poor, old three-legged Max, are all resting peacefully, but from time to time will look down upon us as we waltz through the seasons of our lives.